Carol

Happy 60th

Pin High

– GRAHAM JONES –

Graham x

Based on an original idea by David Croxton

Technical advice: Cold Ashby Golf Club

For Ray Parish

Printed and bound in England by www.printondemand-worldwide.com

www.fast-print.net/store.php

PIN HIGH
Copyright © Graham Jones 2016

A catalogue record for this book is available from the British Library

ISBN 978-178456-371-4

Also available as an e-book:
Mobi ISBN 978-178456-973-0
ePub ISBN 978-178456-972-3

First published 2016 by
Fast-Print Publishing, Peterborough, England.

PIN HIGH

Sudden Death

S he was a little heavier than she used to be and felt the burden of it as she climbed the steep steps to her front door. She would like to be lighter, for him especially. She'd felt his eyes on her abundant waistline more than once. She put the shopping bags down on the top step as she fiddled with her keys. Her eye was drawn to the sticker in the bay window on her right. Vote Green. It was time to take it down. It attracted attention she didn't want and her employers wouldn't approve of it. Anyway, her politics had changed lately. She shared <u>his</u> views now.

She found the right key and then saw it wasn't needed. She pushed the door, light blue, with a large golden 14, and it swung open. She was getting forgetful. Her head was full of other things. She picked up her bags. There was stuff in here he would really like, food he said he'd eaten abroad and in restaurants and she was going to show him how well she could cook. And in return, well perhaps he might stay a little longer each time? He had shown her things she didn't know were possible. And her sex life had arrived with him, too. Around ten years too late, she figured.

She lugged her bags along the hallway to the kitchen and heaved them onto a worktop ready for unpacking and storage, a job she loathed. She had started unpacking before she noticed her visitors. They came silently from the other room, one with a gun, the other with a bag of assorted tools. Neither was smiling.

The hour that followed made her long to die. No matter what they removed or threatened to, she screamed but said nothing. Not a word, no matter what they stuck in her or where. They gagged her, un-gagged her and gagged her again. They abused her foully, abominably, and threatened worse, but still she said nothing. That was how much she loved him.

Eventually they carried her, naked and bleeding, to the bathroom where the water torture began. She would never crack. What would be the point? She knew they weren't going to let her live so this short period of pain was all she had left. There was some relief in feeling the water rush into her lungs as the remorseless hand held her head beneath the surface. The last bubbles of air gurgled upwards. She hadn't let him down.

★

There were times when he preferred a solitary round of golf and now was one of them. That wonderful sky, this green work of art, those cunningly placed trees and the physical release of perfect ball-striking were what he wanted. Things had not gone well at work or at home. He'd intended to produce something life-changing and marriage-saving and found it was life-threatening and marriage-busting instead. He didn't expect to see another Christmas, short of a miracle.

A mind like his wasn't easy to live with. Brilliant clarity of thought, creative, gifted with insights others would struggle to understand in a thousand years, but socially and maritally incompetent and bereft. The pleasures of the former trumped by the latter. The idea wandered into his head that he would happily give it all away, renounce his special talents in return for just a single day of normality. For a single day of normal relations with his wife and the rest of the world. Just to know what it was like to be ordinary.

In all his life he'd had one friend. The rest were hangers-on, acolytes, managers, exploiters or indifferent.

The cause of his present paranoia was the latest product of his genius, simple, powerful and something mankind, were it a sensible species, would celebrate forever. But mankind was a fractious and self promoting species and he was sure what he had discovered would not be used to create new sources of well-being. Not until fortunes had been made and nations exterminated at least. He was using it now, this minute here on the golf course, testing it to find its limits, and his own. There was risk, naturally, but there was always risk. If he was in danger, and he knew he was, it was not from the effects of his invention.

His invention. His was the only brain on the planet that knew what he knew. He had a secret no-one else would ever know. Somewhere in the depths of this remarkable brain, in deepest darkness, synapses had hugged themselves in joyful celebration of a unique connection and he saw for the first time what no other being had seen. And that uniqueness would either keep him very safe or leave him very dead.

Here at least he felt safe for an hour or two. So, he thought, let's put it to use. Trivial use, but fun. He stood alone in the middle of the fourth fairway on his home course. He would never have thought of using it for this purpose but for his wife. Serendipity is a wonderful thing. He wondered if he could make some and bottle it. Concentrate. The shot to the green was about 160 yards and he had a seven iron in his hands. He stood over the ball. C6, he said under his breath. C6 he repeated and felt the automatic movement of his arms and hands as he swung the club head into the back of the ball. It soared liked a beautiful bird high and long. He watched with satisfaction as it landed with a single bounce pin high on the green.

He was absorbed in the shot and the fist that crashed into his jaw and knocked him to the ground took him by surprise. As did the sharp stab of the needle someone plunged into his thigh. His vision blurred and he was aware of being dragged. Time passed. He saw shadows move around him. Then nothing. More time passed and another figure arrived. A tall figure, familiar. He felt himself cradled in someone's arms. Then nothing.

★

The interview room was in shadow. All the windows were shuttered. The only light fell on the man in the chair who couldn't believe what he'd just heard. Code Red? He shifted in his chair. They can't mean it. They've made a terrible mistake. *Think man, think. There must be something you can say to change their minds.* A hand went over his mouth and arms were inserted under his shoulders as he was lifted out of his chair and dragged towards the door. He had time to see a tall man stand up from the shadows at the back of the room and move towards the chair he was involuntarily vacating. *It's him, the bastard,* was almost his last coherent thought, just before the thick absorbent bag was jammed on his head.

He fell silent. There was no point struggling. He had ordered this sort of thing himself, so he knew the routine. None of the cruder stuff would be done until he was out of sight of the room and in the lift. There his skull would be cracked in a single blow from a shiny new hammer, in accordance with tradition. He would lose contact with the material world, be dragged to the company's refuse area, stuffed into a bag and placed on a trolley with similar bags. Then, when it was that trolley's time, the doors of the incinerator, where the temperature reached 2000 degrees Fahrenheit, would open and in he would go with the rest of the rubbish. It was all set out in the company's waste disposal procedures.

Part One: Bad Chemistry

Graham Jones

1 Double Top

'At one level, it is rocket science.' Selwyn Smalling, tall for a Celt, dark unruly hair and glasses, was answering a question from his astonished wife, Anne.

He mumbled an incantation, flexed his arm, squinted along the shaft of his dart and released it at the numbered board hanging on the kitchen door of his large Victorian semi in the south Midlands. Thud. Double-top. He watched his wife, dark hair, blue eyes, gorgeous face and full-bodied, reach up to pull the darts from the board with a quick tug, saw the material of her dress tighten and move upwards and there it was again: a mad priapic surge that left him gasping. He fought it down and took the darts she held out to him. A deep breath and he was steady.

'Once you understand how a dart flies, how it turns through the air and corrects itself horizontally and sinks perpendicularly, if you know the ballistics of the flight and the importance of the speed of release, then with a little bit more info on fuel etc, you could put a rocket on the moon. So aiming a dart is a sort of rocket science. But that's not the way I went about it.'

He saw the incomprehension in his wife's eyes and something else too: a sort of wariness. 'What do you want this time? Pick anything,' he said.

Anne chose something impossible: 'Outer, inner, outer, left to right.'

Selwyn spoke softly to himself once more, took aim and with three quick movements sent the silver tipped missiles spinning to the board. All three landed on the centre rings of the dartboard just as Anne had asked. She retrieved them open-mouthed. Selwyn watched her breasts shake slightly as she pulled the darts from the cork surface. He groaned and saw Anne look at him. That wariness again.

'Wow. So it's true, then. You never miss? Star of the pub team or not, this is something else. You could beat the world like this. Have you thought of that?'

There were things Selwyn wanted to say, but felt it best not to. He was a biochemist because he wanted to help the world, not beat it. Now he was a party trick and a sex addict. What on earth had he done? He looked at his wife. He had made love to her four times in three days, five if you counted the quickie in the car, without a hint of his former difficulties. It wasn't him, of course. It wasn't a new Selwyn. If only. It was this cursed new invention fuelling the passion. That and the fact he loved his wife beyond reason.

'One last time.' Anne said. 'Just to prove it's true once and for all. Get me any three different trebles.' Again the softly-spoken words from Selwyn, then: thud, thud, thud. Treble four, ten and fifteen. Anne kissed him quickly and stepped rapidly back. 'Not now,' she said. 'Not again. It's a bit much.' She took his hand and led him into the lounge. He sat, aching, on the sofa. She sat in the armchair facing him. The sight of her knees, round and dimpled, filled him with a barely tolerable urge to fling himself on her. He noticed her tug at the hem of her skirt.

'Tell me then. It's your pills doing the thing with the darts too? As well as making you randy?'

He nodded. 'Two sides of the same coin: a body control mechanism. Endocannabinoid. Heard of it. No? Well, I'm not surprised. It's a system of receptors that regulate things in the body, like motor or muscle memory. You heard of that?' She had. 'Well that's how it works. That's what I based it all on. The brain can get the body to reproduce movements exactly, over and over again, without conscious thought. I was using the darts as a test exercise because I couldn't go round screwing everyone in the office: 'Sorry, Gladys, would you mind helping me with a bit of research I'm doing. That desk there will do nicely. I'll just pull the blinds down while you remove your knickers, shall I?' He watched Anne laugh and wished she wouldn't. It made her irresistible. 'So I sublimated it all into darts.'

'Who knows about it at work? At Hartmann?'

'Nobody. I haven't said a word to anyone. You are the only one who knows and I wasn't sure about telling you.'

'I think I might have noticed something different. You went from, well, you know what you went from, to an insatiable bull, at me every second hour of the day.'

'How much of a problem is that?'

Anne didn't answer. 'Somebody must know something at work. It must have taken a lot of time and equipment to do this.'

He shook his head. 'You forget how good I am. I should have stayed at the university and gone for the Nobel. Hartmann, God damn their pharmaceutical socks, probably think I'm a quality before quantity man, given how little real output they get from me. Anyway nobody's said anything yet. Knowing how to take it all forward from here is a bit of a problem for me.'

'It's not the only problem you have. And I'm sorry, by the way.'

Selwyn look puzzled. 'For what?'

'If it was me. If I was such a ball-breaker that you left your job with the Nobel prize and everything to earn more with Hartmann. Because you thought that's what I wanted. And for making you so worried about us that you needed to invent something like this. Invent it for us, in bed, I mean. Because you thought that's what I wanted too.'

'It wasn't you.' A lie and she probably knew it. He was a poor liar. She was the reason he'd changed his job and his life. 'So what other problems do I have? You said knowing what to do with it wasn't the only one.'

'I can't go on like this. The sex thing. It's too much. I can tell you want to do it again now, don't you.'

'Dying too. I'll have to lock myself in the loo if we don't. Okay, yes, I did it to make the sex work again for us'

'Well you overcooked it. You've gone from not wanting to at all to wanting it all the time and anywhere.'

'Only when my blood is full of the stuff. But then it is terrible, I admit. It's just supposed to deal with the mechanics and add a bit of desire - to make me <u>want</u> to do it as well as being able to. This massive lust thing is a bit of an unexpected bonus'

'Not a bonus for everybody. Can't you take a half dose, or something?'

'Not how it works. I'm starting on a mark 2. But it'll be a while. Some tricky stuff to get round. But that will make it all more controllable and get rid of side effects like this. I need to set up a lab here though. I can't carry on doing it all at work.' He saw the alarm in Anne's eyes.

'For God's sake don't try anything rash, will you. It wouldn't be worth it.'

He looked across at her and another spasm of undiluted lust crashed through his lower half. 'Can't we? Just a quickie?'

'No!' she said, eyes blazing. 'We bloody well can't. Go and take it out on a golf ball at the driving range or something.' And there it was. Just a simple suggestion that changed everything.

2 *Transferable Skills*

T he drive to the golf club was not a happy one. He liked to think he had the passion of generations of Welsh poets and mystics in his blood and he was as angry as his forefathers would have been at this rejection by his wife.

He drove far too fast for the country road leading to the driving range. He had imagined that solving his bedroom problems would improve things at home and that's why he had developed the blasted drug. Viagra hadn't done it for him. He pounded the steering wheel with his right fist at the injustice of it all. He'd simply been trying to overcome the anxiety he felt in the presence of his naked wife. He'd wanted something to rid him of the curse of self-consciousness and to give him the blind desire that he needed to get his parts ready for action.

And he'd achieved it. His wonder drug had done it for him and now Anne, damn her, is complaining that it is too much. He wants her too much, too often and it lasts too long.

He shook his head to rid it of the bad thoughts and concentrated on the drug's other aspect; the one he had discovered by accident. The muscle memory thing? There is an obvious link between what happens when he uses the stuff for sex and the way it behaves when he throws darts. He should have anticipated something like this. But there is a mystery at the heart of it. It seems to be something he does or says before he releases the dart. And then there is the weird feeling in his arm and hand. Almost as if he isn't the one operating them.

He saw the entrance to the golf club ahead, indicated to turn right and swung his new Volvo onto the drive. He drove past the club house and the main car park, still quite full despite the late hour, and on to the driving range. He got out of the car and felt the cold breeze blowing off the open field of the range and a few drops of rain from the low grey clouds racing by above his head.

For a moment, as the wind chilled him and the bleakness of the spot sank his spirits, he felt like turning back or at least going to the club house for a drink. There was a barmaid in there he rather fancied. Perhaps he could get lucky? He decided against it and hauled his clubs out of the boot, slid a coin or two into the dispenser, put a bucket under the chute at the bottom and pressed the green button. With a clatter, 30 or so golf balls, each one marked with an anti-theft logo, dropped into the basket. There was no-one else in the range so he had his pick of booths. He chose the one at the far end. Half way towards his chosen booth he discovered a nearly full basket of balls left by an earlier resident and he emptied these into his own basket, thinking that would be enough to get rid of the madness still running through his body.

He dropped the first ball onto the mat and looked out across the range. He saw a large featureless field with target markers every fifty yards or so, stretching away to a high fence some three hundred yards from his mat. He swung the club and felt the stiffness in his arms and lower back. Two swings later he was feeling looser and he took aim at a ball. A poor shot rose barely two feet off the ground and settled near the hundred yard marker. A second similar shot followed and it took three or four more before he settled into some sort of rhythm. At last he produced a shot he deemed worthy of his 21 handicap and examined the club. A nine iron, he told himself, 130 yards into the wind. Dead straight. He replayed the shot in his mind, mumbling to himself as he did so: nine iron, stiff breeze, straight, 130. An idea was forming in his head that gave him a quick shot of excitement. He suppressed it because the disappointment would be too great if the idea turned out to be an illusion.

'Nine iron, stiff breeze, straight, 130. Shot A1,' He repeated, unsure what he was doing. Then, with no delay and no practice, but with the shot firmly in his visual imagination, he swung at the ball. He felt his body take over. He was barely aware of the motion he performed. Swish, click! The club face met the ball and it flew high into the breeze, stalled a little as the power of the moving air pushed at it, and fell to earth, eighteen inches from where the first ball landed.

Selwyn gaped, but pushed down the excitement growing in him. He couldn't afford to believe something which wasn't true. He thought about his bedroom success. He would swallow the potion, wait five minutes, feel his anxiety subside and his confidence grow. Then he would imagine his member filling with blood and say the simple word 'up' to himself, to find he was standing, in every sense, full of desire and aching for action. This golf shot stuff must be the same!

Easy, he told himself, one good shot doesn't win a Nobel Prize. He stood over another ball. Nine iron, stiff breeze, straight, 130 yards. Shot A1, he mumbled. Again the strange feeling as his body carried out the order without any planning on his part. Again the ball flew exactly as before and started to stall in the same place. It dropped between the first two, so that they formed a small triangle.

'Shit', he said. Three more tries. Three mumbles followed by a shot. The same result each time. The fourth time he forgot part of the formula, but still ended it with 'Shot A1'. This one went three yards past the earlier shots, but the wind had dropped a little. The next time and the time after that and after that, he simply said 'shot A1' and each time he delivered a virtually identical shot.

He switched clubs and after three attempts managed to connect with a six iron. He visualised the good shot. Six iron, stiff breeze, straight, 160 yards, shot A2. He swung and felt the automatic adjustment of his body as the club dispatched the ball to within several feet of the first shot. 'A2' he said, keeping his mind as clear of images as possible. Again the ball flew exactly as he had hoped and settled within reach of its fellow six iron victims.

Now his excitement was intense and he didn't bother to suppress it. After each good shot, he visualised it, described it and gave it a number. After that, saying the number was enough to produce a carbon copy shot, to within feet, or yards with longer iron shots, of the original. Each time he felt completely confident, without any anxiety or foreboding, and his body took over and repeated, muscle movement by muscle movement, the prototype shot.

He thought he might burst with excitement. As rapidly as he could, he shouted out the numbers and belted the rest of his basket of balls into the growing gloom of the evening, barely aware any more where they were landing. And after each shot he bellowed: Yeeesss; yes, yes, yes, yes, yes.

When all the balls were gone, he stood on the mat, arms raised to the sky, howling with delighted laughter. Cleansed.

3 *Beating Hartmann?*

A s he told Anne, his wonder drug had been made entirely without his employer's blessing. He had not told her the whole truth, however. He suspected that his employers were indeed keeping an eye on him, for whatever reason. So now he needed to get everything associated with the work home to avoid detection. And that was the problem.

Getting yourself, and any possessions, into Hartmann Pharmaceuticals was one thing; getting yourself and those same or any other possessions out again was quite another. Getting a Kalashnikov through Heathrow would be easier. Hartmann dealt in death. Viruses, bio-organisms of unknown and probably forbidden pathology were its stock in trade. Some areas were so restricted the staff entered by secret tunnels and left the same way, never interacting with their colleagues. The insistence on absolute security reached all departments, however; even relatively innocent ones like Selwyn's.

Hartmann had a lot to lose. Selwyn had sat through interminable induction lectures at the start of his life at Hartmann. He'd gone through exercises designed to show how long and expensive a process it was to get from idea to a marketable product. Ten years, on average. Ten years of expensive research salaries, costly raw materials, wasteful blind alleys. He'd seen the slides of how many ideas failed to make it and done the maths. Worse were the pictures of what happened when a product failed. Thalidomide babies weren't the half of it and insurance premiums were through the roof, if they were obtainable at all. So he understood why products in development were tested exhaustively (and illegally on human guinea pigs, too, according to rumours reaching Selwyn's ears) and not a shred of paper, not a single computer file, not a grain of drug that might have handed the prize to a rival was allowed to leave the building.

But it wasn't finished even when a product reached the market, Selwyn learned. For this part some quite scary-looking security men took over Selwyn's induction class. Counterfeiting, widespread and sophisticated, forced the company to extreme measures. It was getting easier by the day and every fake bought by someone was lost profit to Hartmann. Why go red-faced to the doctor confessing embarrassing symptoms when you could get the same drug cheap and fast off the Internet. Except it wasn't the same drug. It might be safe or it might be brick dust. Selwyn was forced to admit that it was all very reasonable for Hartmann to restrict his freedoms in the pursuit of absolute security. He even agreed with his lecturer that Hartmann should chase traffickers and counterfeiters wherever it could at whatever cost to itself and the integrity of human rights legislation. He ended up glad that

Hartmann's Global Security team had a reputation for brawny effectiveness and found it perfectly okay that Hartmann didn't much care how they got their results so long as they got them. This light touch regulation and the high salaries had lured in some of the stars of national security agencies, weary of political correctness and meagre rewards. They were a fearsome bunch. A position in this team was the career pinnacle for spooks and legal thugs, he had worked out. And at the beginning Selwyn was very much in favour. No longer, of course.

As a result, working for Hartmann was no day at the beach. Paranoia and fear characterised the corporate climate. Amongst themselves staff would joke nervously that working for Hartmann got you one of three things: wealthy, famous or dead.

Selwyn started lying awake at nights wondering how he could get everything associated with his secret from his lab at work to his workshop at home. He seemed to have three choices: abandon his work and pray no-one knew about it, hand it over to his bosses and hope for mercy, or smuggle it out, records, products, files, data on both mark 1 and the new mark 2 – everything in fact.

He thought the chances of ending up rich and famous in the first two options were zero. The chances of ending up dead were high, though. If he chose the second option, sharing it with Hartmann, the company would doubtless find very sinister uses for the drug, including military ones, once they found out all its properties. Selwyn would not allow his work to be used in that way. A struggle would ensue and they would win. If they looked like losing, or if they looked like suffering any sort of reputational damage, they would dispose of him, he assumed. He was surprised how calmly he accepted this assumption.

He could not contemplate the first option: dropping the whole project. His drug was simply too wonderful and his pride in it too great to do nothing with it. Number two, sharing with Hartmann, had too many imponderables.

Three months or so after his experience on the driving range he made the decision. Number three. Him against the security system. He gulped.

The Hartmann building was large and modern, part stone, part red brick but mainly glass and steel. Five floors, each edged with a balcony, ran round three sides of a huge atrium. Each balcony, studded with coffee tables, look directly down onto the entrance hall and security area, where the daily drama of entrance and exit took place. Selwyn watched this drama more closely and less obviously than anyone. He noted that outgoing bags were not just searched, but supplied with a coded tag. Staff had to leave in shirt and trousers, or a simple dress, and be body-searched and scanned. Tagged and coded bags, once through the system, had the tag removed again and could be taken outside. Only regulation bags, manufactured for Hartmann and chipped for authenticity could be carried by anyone. Visitors had to check their bags at a security gateway and collect them on the way out. The only exception to this routine was the daily rubbish collection which was taken to a small plant on Hartmann premises and burnt. These bags were collected daily from the offices and taken down by security staff to an inspection area. Here they were searched thoroughly, tagged, sealed and batch counted. If seven bags were batched, seven had to arrive at the incinerator, where they were counted electronically and destroyed.

Selwyn's first task was to get hold of a supply of blank tags - tags without the security code. Since the code was changed on a daily basis, he would have to get into to the IT administration system and identify the code to be used as well as the software that did it. He could then encode his own bags and avoiding the search became the only problem. He felt he knew how to get an un-searched bag, properly tagged, past the guard, with only a slight element of risk. That depended on Julie, a not very pretty member of the security team who had been benefiting from Selwyn's new found sexual confidence, athleticism and stamina, twice a week in the evenings and every Monday morning in her small flat in a Victorian semi which lay handily on Selwyn's route to and from work.

Selwyn regarded these excursions to Julie's flat as a 'duty' he had to perform to secure Julie's trust and benefit his plan. He intended to continue doing his duty even after her services at the security desk had been rendered, however, just so that she would not get suspicious. And perhaps to counteract the attention deficit he felt at home from his wife. In a moment of honesty, Selwyn admitted to himself that his duties with Julie had quite often not felt particularly onerous. Sometimes he found himself quite looking forward to them. Occasionally, when he got the dose wrong, he knocked on her door in a state of some desperation.

He needed help to access the coding system. Getting the IT administrator to his office to fix his computer was simple. He introduced a relatively harmless and undetectable piece of malware through a memory stick into his own office computer and then programmed it to record all new user names and passwords used on the machine. He turned his computer off and when he restarted it the malware did its other trick and refused to recognise the username and password Selwyn used every day. It locked him out.

The technician arrived, entered the company administrator password and log-in details (which the malware duly noted, thank you very much) and had the thing fixed in a trice. It didn't go quite to plan. The technician, no idiot, knew some sort of virus had been introduced externally, whether on purpose or otherwise. There was no other explanation even though his spyware checker had found no evidence of one. Selwyn had to endure a little lecture about using non-standard memory devices and the technician said he felt he should report it. Selwyn slipped him a couple of large notes not to, and, with an appreciative wink, he was gone. Selwyn couldn't believe his luck. To find an employee prepared to deceive Hartmann was unexpected. He'd had no choice but to try the bribe or be reported. Clearly this technician was his own man, working to his own agenda, or in need of a few quid. Selwyn, a confirmed atheist, thanked what ever God had been looking after him and went to work.

Five minutes later, with the technician's administrator login, he was rooting about in the deepest system level of the company's platforms and soon found both the encoding device, complete with a list of codes stretching months into the future, and the software for applying it. The codes were encrypted, but amazingly only at 64 bit level. He would only ever use 256 bit for personal protection. Breaking a 64 bit code was child's play even for the open-sourced 'wireshark' software he was using.

He got the unused tags from Julie's after he noticed that she thought the security tags made nice coasters for her coffee cups, and guessed she had a stash somewhere. Unencoded, they were harmless and no use to any one, so no-one checked what the security staff did with them. He intended simply to ask her for some for use as coasters at home, but one evening at her place, as Julie took a shower, he found a supply of the virgin tags in a kitchen table drawer and helped himself to a few.

Now that he had the wherewithal to code tags for any particular day, the rest was simple. Dangerous still, but simple. He waited for an evening when he knew Julie would be on duty. As the rubbish bags were wheeled through his office on their trolley he slipped an unencoded disc between them and walked with his own coded bag stuffed full of incriminating items to a spot out of camera shot in the lobby. A few seconds later the rubbish bags with his false disc were wheeled through the security gate system and the blank disc sent out an ear-splitting shriek. While the guards' attention was grabbed, he moved past the search area and directly to the gate, ostentatiously offered his bag, tagged and self-coded, to the checking device in the second scanning bay, got clearance, mouthed I'll see you in thirty to Julie, who winked back and waved him through, not caring that, just for this once, she hadn't actually seen the bag being searched, and he was away.

In the hour he spent servicing Julie afterwards, she didn't once refer to his unusual exit, though she did tell him when he asked that she wasn't allowed to say what had triggered the alarm in security bay 1, but since it was him she said it was just some rubbish and a stray disc. A bit of a mystery really, how it had got there. For that, he gave her an extra orgasm and her delighted squeal brought him to a sharper than usual climax, too. But perhaps that was just the adrenaline surge he'd got from the smuggling exercise. Or the extra dose of stuff he'd swallowed to bolster his confidence for it. The stuff was great for that. He always felt he could take on the world with the stuff inside him.

Selwyn, no fool, knew that Julie would have noticed his unusual exit. He was banking that she wouldn't for a moment think he was up to no good, because he could see how enamoured she was and couldn't stop telling him how amazing it was that he desired her so much and demonstrated it so often. He saw it not as sex for the sake of it (though God knows there were times …), but due diligence, and he decided it was a diligence he would maintain for a while. It was indeed his duty.

But there were other eyes than Julie's; eyes which watched CCTV replays of the security incident later, and they did note the odd exit, and the fact that the bag had not been searched. The owners of these eyes decided Mr Selwyn Smalling would merit even closer attention in future. A search of his office revealed nothing and there was nothing untoward in his lab, either. Just a few corrupted files on his hard drive which the technician, perhaps remembering the sizeable sum of cash he'd been slipped and hoping for more, omitted to report. That took some of the pressure off, and just a small but decidedly negative note was left in Selwyn's HR file: 'unaccredited security status', it said. 'Not to be trusted', it meant. Julie's file didn't escape a cryptic asterisk either. 'Schedule re-training', the note said. What that meant would be decided by the head of security later. But, as a precaution, the files on the pair were sent to Global Security who filed them under 'instructions awaited'.

4 Anne puts her foot down

T hree weeks later, on the second Monday of a wet September, around 7 p.m. Selwyn, double-dosed and still horny despite Julie's best efforts, stopped at the driving range on his way home. Already late thanks to Julie, he rang Anne to explain why he would be extra late and tried not to be offended by the indifference, satisfaction almost, in her response. At first Selwyn hit his golf balls unobserved. Within minutes, two occupants of neighbouring booths noticed the excellence of the shots he was producing and came to stand admiringly behind him. Selwyn smiled at his audience and greeted them with a quick nod and a grin. His self-conscious dislike of being observed had evaporated with his new-found abilities. He started to tell them which shot he planned to make – six iron, 160, slight hook- he would say, then mumble 'h4' under his breath and the ball would rise and turn slightly left before falling within inches of the 160 line.

'What's your handicap?' one of the observers asked.

'Just been cut again. Ten now I think.'

'Are you Selwyn, the one we keep hearing about in the clubhouse?'

Selwyn hit one more ball and turned to the two men, resting his weight on the club: 'Yes to the first, don't know about the second.'

'Well, there's all sorts of rumours. People are like that though, aren't they?'

'Rumours? What about.'

'What do you think? How did you go from no-hoper to serial medal winner in weeks.'

Selwyn was cautious. He hadn't heard the rumours. 'Something just sort of clicked, you know. What are people saying then?'

It was the turn of the man who'd spoken to be cautious. He didn't want to speak out of turn. 'Oh, they just wonder. Jealous, mostly, I should think, a bit like me. I can see what the fuss is about though. You hit a ball really well.'

Selwyn thanked them and turned back to the balls. His pride wouldn't let him deliberately mis-hit, but he stopped showing off by describing his shot in advance. Something warned him not to be too good. Eventually, the two went back to their own unsatisfactory effort, leaving Selwyn to ponder what people might really be saying in the clubhouse.

Swinging this damn golf club was no longer enough. The libidinous drive was beginning to leave him no peace. And it was worse at home. He left Julie a more than satisfied woman but he'd barely taken the edge off his own sexual tension. Taking a double dose on the night of the smuggled bag for Dutch courage had worked so well that he now took the same amount most days to enjoy the feeling of invincibility. He was grateful to Julie for keeping the sex supply roughly in line with the demand but dismayed to discover his pleasure ended each time in a soul-numbing post coital sadness. He was beginning to realise that getting the sex out of his system wasn't just a mechanical thing. Like golf, it wasn't a question of any hole would do. Anne was its target. The beast aroused in him by this wonderful, terrifying substance he had produced had a goal in mind. A specific personal objective. Julie calmed the beast a little, but the beast wanted Anne. It wouldn't be still until it had her, how it wanted, as often as it wanted. And the dilemma it caused was dizzying.

He loved Anne. She was stronger than him and her strength scared him at times, even when he relied on it. On the way home, with the risks of deceiving Hartmann worrying him more and more, he reversed his decision to tell her nothing. He needed her support. He would tell her everything. Almost everything. Besides, if Hartmann did come for him and his secrets, they might choose Anne as the route. Or Julie, if they ever found out about her.

It was gone nine when Selwyn eventually let himself in through the front door and found Anne in front of a fire in the living room. She turned the TV off and the lights up a little when he said he wanted to talk.

Her body language as she listened to his story wasn't promising. 'You broke the rules to smuggle stuff out? What the hell is going on in that friggin' Welsh head of yours?' she said.

'Well, they could see I was up to something. They do monitor us, you know, productivity levels and stuff. Mine were dangerously low. In time, someone on my team would have grassed and my office, lab, computers, notes would have been searched. Then it would all belong to Hartmann. I could have let them have it and started from scratch here but I'd be years behind without the data I've smuggled out. Now I can quit Hartmann if I want and no-one will be any the wiser.'

'You're thinking of leaving then?'

'Like the politicians say just before they're sacked, I want to spend more time with my family. You.'

'But what if your family doesn't want you to spend time with it?' She didn't seem to be joking. Her face was dark.

He was shocked. 'You can't mean that, can you?' Her face didn't change. 'Bloody hell, you really mean it. Is it that bad? I mean I knew things weren't great, but I've been working on it. You know I have. Where's this come from? I thought we were okay.'

She shook her head. 'No, we aren't okay. And it's nearly all down to the sex thing. You can't say I haven't warned you. You want it all the time. I dread having you here sometimes because you don't leave me alone, or I find you staring at me and now you tell me you'll be here all day long.'

'It won't be like that. I promise. We'll work it out.'

'We? There's no 'we' in this, Selwyn. It's all you. You'll have to work it out.' One hand was over her face. When she took it away he saw the tears in her eyes. *Christ this is serious.* His insides shrank.

'I just can't keep letting you have me three times a day. I'm not even sure I want three times a week. I could live with every other Saturday. But this is like going back to when we were kids. And we're not kids.'

Selwyn slumped into a chair, defeated. He felt something like anger beginning to grow in his guts. An urge to fight back.

'I can't get it right, can I? Before we were married I was too eager, too. I understood then why you wouldn't go the whole way. There were good reasons, though it nearly killed me. After marriage, it was fantastic for about two weeks. And then not so good and then downright bad. And I'm sorry I couldn't give you kids. That's where it all started, I think. Not enough of a man to give you what you really wanted. Ironic, eh? Then I couldn't start and now I can't stop.' He looked at her, but her face was turned away.

'Where do we go from here? I know what *I* want. What about you?'

She shrugged but didn't reply. After a while she said: 'No idea what I want, really. Just something normal. Other married people seem to have worked it out. What they call the magic has faded but they can still offer each other something, in bed, and out of it. Whatever it is they have, that's what I want. Maybe.'

Selwyn was forcing himself to be calm. Calm was not what he felt. He wanted to explode. He said nothing until he was sure she wouldn't hear the anger in his voice. 'okay. I can see that. And that's what we'll aim for.'

It wasn't at all what Selwyn wanted but he couldn't see any way out.

'Do you mean that? It will mean handing control over to me. If I say go, we go. If I say no, then it has to mean that. And for as long as I want it to it stays as no. Is that doable? Yes?'

Selwyn nodded. 'I promise. You set the pace until this is all over.'

'And you stop taking that bloody stuff, unless it's for a real purpose?'

'You know what that means. Ground zero.'

'Well, if we have to turn the clock right back, so be it. We can at least build from there. We can't go anywhere from here. Agreed?'

'Agreed!'

Anne kissed him. That's a deal then. I'll be back in a minute,' she said. She went upstairs and Selwyn pounded the sofa cushions until he felt a little better. He had never needed a drink quite so much and the scotch he poured himself was as large as any he'd ever had.

Anne returned. She'd removed her make-up and put on her least sexy nightwear. Selwyn felt distinctly more warmth coming from her, despite the pyjamas.

She said, 'while we're on a problem-solving roll, what about the invention? I shouldn't have said what I did. Getting it out of Hartmann was fantastic. God knows how you did that. So, it's in our hands now. What are we going to do with it?'

'What do you think? There are probably some humanitarian things we could do, with a bit more research.'

'Not yet. Later maybe. Monetise it. Exploit it for all it's worth. But try to chemicalise out, or whatever you do, the sex thing. You won't make money turning people into rabid sex fiends.'

'I am not a rabid sex fiend' said Selwyn, stung by the description but not sure it wasn't accurate, given what he'd been up to earlier and what he was still thinking he'd like to do to Anne now. Deal or no deal.

'The trouble is it will attract attention. As soon as word gets out, Hartmann and the rest will be on to it like a shot. They'll want to know who made it. If we get a patent, that'll lead them straight to me. If I don't get a patent, they'll copy it, wipe me out and they'll make the money. It's forcing us to be devious.'

'Okay,' Anne said. 'I think we can do devious. The sex thing the stuff does? Can you tone it down?'

'Not sure. I suppose I can fiddle with it so not all receptors are involved to the same degree. That means the brain will choose where it wants to respond to the drug. Eventually, I'll make different strands for different purposes. We're talking a few years' work though and then mark 2 will make us rich as Croesus.'

'I don't want to wait that long. I'll help you wherever I can, outside the bedroom, but we need to get a move on with this. If I understand what you're saying, you can modify it a bit, but not completely. So there's a risk if we use it unregulated. But we can't go legitimate yet, because if we do we'll have it snatched from us. So if we want to make some money and have some fun we need something where muscle memory is king, money can be made in large dollops and regulation is slack. And we have to take a risk. And soon, before they cotton on.'

Selwyn wasn't sure.

'Why not?' Anne said, 'how many chances is life going to throw our way? Chances as big as this at least? This is it. You make your own opportunities in this world. We just have to do something bold.'

'No. We have to do something smart and decent and be very, very careful. Money isn't everything.'

'Selwyn. Don't give me that. You risked your life to get this stuff out of bloody Hartmann. You didn't do that to save the world.'

'Sad bugger that I am, I think I did.'

'Well, we can do that too. But first, can't we have a bit of fun?' There was a twinkle in her eye that Selwyn spotted. He knew that twinkle! 'A bit of fun? I could be persuaded.'

'Right,' Anne said. 'Let's sleep on it and see what the morning brings.'

5 *Good practice appraisal*

It was early October, almost two weeks later, close to eight in the evening after a cold, windy day. The bedroom curtains were closed and the light from the yellow streetlight offered a little dim illumination. Selwyn was finding it hard work. It was his third attempt today and only the first one had been successfully concluded, for him at least, despite a double dose, a large double dose of his wonder stuff. Everything worked on command, the need was still there, but the enthusiasm and passion were waning.

For this current attempt, he was on top of his wife, who appeared to be doing just enough to meet his requirements, but with no discernible enthusiasm. Typical. Just as he is feeling he can live without it, Anne goes all sacrificial. His encounters earlier in the day had featured Julie in the starring role and she had been much more appreciative than his current partner. In fact, he thought, 'partner' was not the right word for Anne in this mode. 'Recipient' would be closer. He tried to think of something suitably pornographic and for a while an image he was able to recall from his boyhood magazine stash seemed like it would put some water under his boat. It didn't last and he found himself still travelling, but going nowhere.

Instead, his mind wandered past the earlier hour with Julie into his day at work. Today had been his appraisal. Appraisals at Hartmann had never approached the preferred good practice models so beloved of human resource departments. At Hartmann, appraisals were more like interrogations in North Korean death camps. With added spite.

His had consisted of three senior managers, none of whom he saw as qualified to judge the quality or quantity of his contribution to the company, who grilled him about his values and the meaning of loyalty. Selwyn told them what he thought they wanted to hear and they moved on to deal with his standards and productivity which they described as well below the levels set for him at the last appraisal. They demanded an explanation. The only one he had was one he couldn't give them, so he said his evaluation of his work was not coterminous with theirs. The answer seemed to enrage them. They clearly felt their view was not one he could challenge and demanded he reconsider. Since he could hardly say he had been working in thefirm's time on a private project which he'd subsequently smuggled out of the building, having first removed all traces of it, he had no real response. So he said he was sorry. He had been unwell.

And then the bombshell. They asked him about Julie. Thrown off balance he hesitated a little too long and his voice wavered just a little too much as he said 'who is Julie?'

They smirked. They had him now. Intimate relations between staff members, whilst permitted, must be reported to HR. It was contractual. It was in bold letters in the contract he had signed when he took the Hartmann shilling. He had breached that rule, hadn't he?

He denied any knowledge of anything.

They smirked even more hideously. Intimate relations with <u>security</u> staff were not permitted, however. They were expressly forbidden. Why had he not reported his breach and ended it? 'If a thing is forbidden by Hartmann, it can't happen,' he said. 'And if it hasn't happened how could it be reported. Or ended?' Whatever the moral implications of his adultery with Julie, it was clear that the company had him over a breach of contract barrel. If they could prove it. He continued to deny it. They continued to assert it. And eventually a compromise was reached. He would not under any circumstances see Julie again; nor would he engage in sexual or other non-work-related relations with any other female staff members.

'What about the men?' he asked.

Their scorn and fury were silent but cut the air between them. 'Relationships between staff which in the view of management constitute a perversion of normal practice will not be considered consistent with contractual fulfilment and will lead to immediate disciplinary action.' In Selwyn's mind, this paragraph in the contract seemed to contradict several clauses of recent equal opportunities legislation but he felt was in no position to take it further. £250,000 per annum plus bonuses, was not a sum he could easily earn elsewhere. He would suffer the tyranny until his new invention started to bring its own rewards. 'I can see,' the most senior of the three said, 'that you find our regulations somewhat reactionary. It will, of course, have occurred to you that security staff must be at all times objective if they are to function effectively, and that opening yourself to blackmail given the sensitive nature of the work we do, is not to be recommended. And non conventional sexuality, whatever the current legislative framework, still leaves people vulnerable. As does extra-marital activity.'

Selwyn opened his mouth to speak, but closed it again. His only act of rebellion, once the interview concluded and a new set of targets had been imposed, was to call in to see Julie, as usual, on his way home. She too, had clearly been unsettled by events at work and she had a battery of questions for him. He reassured her in the best way he could and soon she was cooing with pleasure. Selwyn was carefully never to let her suspect that his evident enthusiasm for coitus in every conceivable position and in every corner and on every surface available in the house, could be based on anything but desire and, he had hinted, love for her.

He was not, of course, proud of this necessary deception. Sometimes he lay awake wondering how he could live with himself. Then, as the weeks rolled by, he noticed he was developing a tenderness towards Julie which he could see was based on more than just the obvious purpose she served. He was starting to like her. For God's sake, he told himself, that's just one step from loving her. That thought made him an even more vigorous but also more considerate lover. He could see it was having an effect on Julie too. He suspected she was prepared to die for him. Which, though he didn't know it, was just as well, all things considered.

6 *A wife's duty*

Selwyn's mid-coitus review of his day was interrupted when the mobile phone at the side of the bed sprang into life. 'Thank Christ for that', Anne muttered and seized the opportunity to shove Selwyn, still grunting with unfulfilled lust, over to his side of the bed. 'Please listen carefully to the following message ...' the phone was switched off before the vital communication could be delivered. 'Those stupid calls,' Anne said. Selwyn lay gasping on his back; Anne, seized by a rare moment of pity for him, and still trying to keep him in good humour, reached across and with a few brief strokes of a well-practised hand, achieved what several minutes of energetic but one-sided coitus had not. 'Thank you,' said Selwyn. 'At least I felt you meant that.'

Anne didn't respond. Her recent decision to co-operate more in the bedroom had been taken to make Selwyn more receptive to her plan. It was becoming a burden though, and would have to end soon, she thought.

'So why did you marry me, if you don't like me?' Selwyn asked, picking up on a conversation from days ago.

'It's not you I don't like. It's it. Or at least it every time I bend over in the wrong way. You said you were going to stop taking your stuff, yet I still get more sex than a porn star. And it's about as much fun.'

'But you did marry me because you loved me?'

'Not that again. Why else?'

'I don't know.'

'Look,' she said, spotting an opportunity to raise her idea obliquely. 'I was grateful for what you did. Who wouldn't be? Telling the police I was with you all night was a big thing and saved me a lot of trouble. I could never have proved I wasn't part of it if you hadn't lied for me.'

'But that's not why you agreed to marry me?'

'No. It wasn't.'

'So why did you agree?'

'You know why.'

'It might be nice to hear it now and then.'

'So stop trying to bang my brains out and you might hear it more often. What are we going to do with that wretched so-called wonder drug of yours, by the way?'

'Still the same issue: I can't think of a way of using it without attracting the attention of the goons at Hartmann. And if the appraisal session I've just had was an example of their positive and affirmative staff management, I wouldn't want to see them in third degree mode. Listen, just go back to why you married me, or how we got together. That night you were arrested and I lied to get you out, the guy who did that for you must have really been carrying a torch. To do what he did. Beat the other guy up like that'

Anne had been planting seeds for weeks. Fruit at last. 'You mean Jeremy? Jeremy Godwin? 'Jake' he liked to be called. I suppose you must be right.'

'Good for him. The one who attacked you was the one who should have been sent down, not Jeremy. Rape is always bad. Doping somebody first is terrible.'

'He didn't.'

'Didn't what, rape you?'

'No. Dope me. I just got plastered and couldn't stop him. Not even sure I wanted to. But I felt so bad after it, really, really awful and degraded and Jake saw what I was like next day.'

'You never told me that.'

'No. Would you have helped me out like you did if I had?'

'Probably. I was in love, wasn't I. Were you?'

'With you?

'Of course. Not with Jake.'

'But by the time he got sent down I was into you. I did like you by then. I mean I'd seen that you were interested in me and, to be honest, I had started to see that real cool was more than just a haircut and shoe style.'

'So you did love me. And not just because I lied to the police for you?'

'No.'

'NO?' Selwyn's eyes popped.

'No, I didn't then. But I'm sure I did on our wedding day. And still do incidentally. I mean, how could any girl not be in love with a guy who wants to shag her five times a day?'

'So there's hope for me, despite it all?'

'The message is the same as before. Stop killing it now with this sex thing or it will be too late. Stop taking the drug. We had an agreement.'

'Even if it puts me where I was before? Virtually impotent. No desire, at any rate.'

'We've had this conversation. More than once. It would be better than this.'

'For whom?' asked Selwyn.

'Well, it's a clear choice. Find a way. I still want to, now and then, but not all the time. Go to the bathroom more often and sort yourself out. Just don't expect me to be eternally available.'

★

They agreed a truce and watched TV for an hour or so as Selwyn cooked a late supper for them both. After the washing up, Selwyn sat down on the settee next to his wife, who, he thought, got lovelier each year. Selwyn felt he would be devastated if he lost her.

'You know what Jake's up to these days?' Selwyn asked.

'Sort of, but not really. Still golf, I expect. I think he made something of a go of it.'

Selwyn picked up his i-pad. 'You're right. I googled him a couple of days ago.' He called up the website. 'He is still in golf and he did more than make something of a go of it. He turned professional and played in the pro tournaments for a while. Then, it says here, he married his golf with his business studies qualification and started managing other golfers. He has a squad of them now. He looks after them and their interests, in return for a share of their profits from wins and sponsorship, I expect.' Selwyn googled the golfers in Jake's care. Apart from one, he'd never heard of them and couldn't find any wins for any of them except the one he knew.

'What's his name? The one you recognise?' Anne asked.

'Samson Gregory.'

'Never heard of him.'

'He's had a few top ten finishes, which is good in golf and brings in the cash, but he's never won, except a minor thing. I think he plays in most of the tournaments in Europe and South Africa, though. He's got a bit of a name. Something of a character, too.'

'I've still never heard of him.' Anne turned the TV off. 'Where's this heading?' she asked.

'Good question. Jake's team aren't big earners. Taking a team like that round Europe, and beyond, is a bloody expensive business. My bet is that he's struggling.'

'He always did. Not a patch on you. Did you know he envied you back then?'

'He envied me? It was the other way round.'

'Just goes to show then, doesn't it.'

'Goes to show what.'

'Men. Emotionally blind. Emotional morons.'

'So if I'm right,' Selwyn went on, 'he'll need all the help he can get. Did you part friends?'

'I don't know. I never spoke to him when he came out. It was you who told me he was devastated that I'd given him up. I hurt him badly and got him nicked and I didn't fancy the recriminations, so I avoided him. So I can't imagine he'd welcome me with the proverbial open arms.'

'It's worth a try though.'

'What sort of try?'

'Offering him my stuff and all that goes with it. For his golf team. See if we can get a win or two out of them. You never know. It works for me. It might do the same for someone with real talent.'

'You'll never get him to shove untested drugs into his prize assets. He'd be mad to.'

'That's where you come in.' Selwyn looked at her in what he intended to be a meaningful way.

'Take that stupid look of your face. You mean you want me to sleep with him?'

'Bloody hell, of course not. But you could lead him on a bit. Let him think there might be a chance he could get what he missed out on years ago.'

'Who says he missed out? I may have married you but I never promised a virgin bride.'

Selwyn fought back the instinctive jealousy. 'okay, let him think there's more of the same on offer if he plays his cards right. I'll be around anyway, so he'll know it wouldn't be a straightforward offer, and you'll always have a reason to back off if he gets too pushy.'

'Playing with fire with a can of petrol in your hand is a thought that comes to mind.' Anne said.

'He'll bite our hands off when he sees the potential. But we might as well play the hand we've got. And you are the ace.'

'You know you are asking me to do something criminal, don't you?'

'Well that will make us even then, won't it'

7 *Jake*

J ake had started to hate his office. He spent more time there than anywhere
else and couldn't convince himself that it was time well spent. To the left of
the desk he was sitting at, the wall was covered for half its length with
photographs of him and other golfers. They were almost all more famous and
successful than him. The other half was blank. In front of him the picture
window opened onto one of the finest golf courses in Britain, where neither
he nor any member of his team had ever won so much as a brass farthing. To
his right, a door opened up into the office of his secretary, who hadn't been
paid for months and stayed only out of loyalty, he assumed. Next to the door
and beside a stack of small meeting chairs was a large almost empty trophy
cabinet.

On the desk was a picture of himself as a young man, holding a huge
silver cup. He was grinning broadly and being mobbed by an admiring crowd.
He turned it face down on the desk. He could barely remember being that
person. He considered his in-tray: a large pile of bills run up by his
incontinent team members, complaints about the way he looked after them,
demands for this, requests for that. He would dig a long way down the pile
before he found any word of appreciation. Next to the picture was a brown
A5 envelope.

It was marked 'private and confidential' and addressed to Jeremy Godwin,
a first name he disliked and never used.

He picked the envelope up again and realised the name on the envelope
was a clue to the sender. Only one person had refused to call him anything
but 'Jeremy', even though she knew he far preferred 'Jake' and she hadn't
been in his life for over twenty years. So he was both surprised and not
surprised when he opened the envelope and a picture of him and a young
woman in a smiling embrace fell out. He looked at the picture for a moment
before turning it over. *One good turn deserves another. Watch this space.* Nothing
else.

He remembered the young woman well. Of course he did. Anne had
been his first. You always remember even your first kiss, let alone your first
real full-on encounter. He had imagined himself in love. He probably had
been in love. He'd certainly been daft enough to do something really stupid
for her and that had cost him. Eighteen months behind bars that haunted him
still. The cell door locking him in every evening meant he slept to this day
with the door open. He couldn't pass the gym in the nearby hotel without a
trace of nausea at the memory of the harsh routines he'd been subjected to.
He couldn't queue for food and still be in a fit state to eat it when he got to

his seat. There were few things he did that weren't affected by the time he served for helping Anne. He couldn't do it again. Not even for someone like her. But the whole business had taught him a lot about himself. He turned the trophy picture the right way up again.

He moved his gaze from the picture with the cup to the tray of bills and demands. He stood up from his chair and, as always, felt the sharp twinge in his back, a legacy of the injury that finished his career early. Life had been tough and pressured on tour, but it was a life he seemed suited to: rootless, uncommitted to a relationship or family, living off your wits and skills, great camaraderie and fierce competition, foreign climes and wonderful courses. No wonder so many tour pros got depressed when they had to return to civilian life. And he didn't even get his full whack. The sense of injustice worsened the pain in his back. He sat down gingerly and opened the drawer in his desk. Inside was a wooden nameplate. "Jake Godwin. Managing Director". He took it out and set it up on his desk. The picture with the trophy replaced it in the drawer. *Grow up!*

That was easy to say. What was his baseline? He had no proper home life following his divorce and no family. He picked up a list of his employees. 'Deadbeats. Sorry, Samson. Perhaps not you. But the rest are deadbeats.' He looked through the first four items in his in tray. All were bills. He turned to his computer screen and opened the spreadsheet of his accounts. Terrifying. He clicked on the income box which expanded to show the income of his six golfers. Only the one called Samson Gregory had positive figures. The rest were costing him. He clicked 'other income sources'. There were no entries other than a reference to 'sponsors'. He clicked on it and saw a dwindling number of names year on year. At least the income stream was still in the black, just.

He checked his diary, flicking back though the pages, looking for something that would tell him he was an important man with an interesting life, a man of the world. Christ! He hardly ever left his frigging office, let alone the country. He sat very still and came to a decision which made him feel no better. He was going to sell up. It was the only option. There had been offers to buy him out, derisory ones, he felt, though in more honest moments he wasn't sure his business was worth anything at all. The golfers, and the contracts which bound them to him, were the only assets he had. And his spreadsheet told him he was depending on people who couldn't be bothered to get off their backsides.

He looked down at the picture that had fallen from the envelope. A tall confident-seeming young man with his arm round a slim dark-haired girl, very pretty, looked back at him. He couldn't for the life of him remember when it had been taken, or where. And he had no idea who sent it, unless it had been Anne herself. He hadn't heard from her since his 'prison' days. He had no idea where she lived or what she was up to. And therefore no idea why she would send him something like this out of the blue. If it was from her. But who else? And why? Was it an offer?

There was no mirror in his room, but he got up and examined himself in the glass frontage of the almost empty trophy cabinet. He was in good shape, tall, broad-chested, athletic for a golfer. He wasn't conventionally good-looking, perhaps, but he still had hair, a bit tousled and a fairly ordinary brown colour, but hair; his face was friendly, more comforting than handsome, but attractive enough to keep him in admirers, as his secretary would tell you if you asked her. So perhaps Anne was on the loose again and looking through her little black book before trying the dating agencies. Or maybe she'd seen his picture on the one he subscribed to and been reminded of how they'd once been. He was on Facebook, too. She could have come across him there. But to send it like this, instead of posting it online? It was certainly intriguing. Old-fashioned and somehow suggestive, too.

It did occur to him that there was at least one other person in that tale. The boy he'd beaten senseless. What if it was from him and the 'one good turn' phrase was meant ironically? What would that indicate? The boy he'd beaten up had also disappeared from the scene while he was doing his time. He dismissed the idea. He'd checked the guy out years ago. Nothing to worry about there. He cast his mind back. A row at a party had started it. He and Anne had been drinking, he accused her of flirting and she told him to piss off and left. He assumed she had gone home and he left too. There was nothing for him at the party if she wasn't there. There had been a lot of recent rows and he felt he was losing her, but this had been the biggest.

Next day he called at her home and found her distraught. She wouldn't talk to him, shut the door on him. But her friends did more than enough talking and they told him what had happened to her and who had done it. The friends said she wanted revenge and wanted to watch justice being done. So he and two of his mates gave her justice while she watched from a doorway. They beat the rapist, if that's what he was, senseless, working themselves into a genuine fury. Jake was never sure who his anger was really directed at.

What Anne made of it he never found out. Somebody gave her an alibi and she got off scot-free. He got eighteen months in a young offenders' prison for grievous bodily harm, along with his two mates. So the picture could be from the victim, his fellow culprits, or Anne. Or anybody. But Anne was in his mind, now, and he was finding it difficult to move her out again. He wasn't even sure he wanted to. He had risked a lot for her once. He shivered again at the thought of being locked up. He could not see himself taking that sort of risk again.

8   *Human resources*

S amson quite liked the fake grandeur of the massive hotel. Mock Georgian
in design and thickly covered in ivy. Inside, its expensively carpeted
corridors and wood-panelled rooms hinted at an opulent past. A touch he
really enjoyed was the way legends of the game gave these rooms their names:
Nicklaus, Jacklin, Palmer. Would Gregory be next? For Samson, like many
others he supposed, this course was synonymous with the game's great
championship, the Ryder Cup, and in every room photographs of the stars in
tournament action, watched by vast galleries of adoring fans, crowded the
walls. Samson had almost stopped expecting his photograph to be there one
day. A casual visitor, with eyes only for the splendid hotel, the magnificent
courses and state of the art driving range and practice facilities, would easily
overlook the rather plain brick building at the far corner of the overspill car
park, where Samson Gregory, by his own admission the star of the Godwin
team now sat in a small plain office listening to a harangue from the team boss,
Jake Godwin. He could see his colleagues, Jason Bone and Martin Pascal were
suffering just as much as he was. He almost envied the absentee, Ian, who was
competing for a scarcely worthwhile prize, and doing badly, in India.

'Look at these,' Jake was pointing at a pile of papers on the desk before
him. Samson, who had heard it all before, didn't look. Nor did the others.
Samson knew what they were and what they signified. He had heard little else
for the last two seasons from Jake: 'These are just clothes bills, for cleaning and
replacement. You pampered ponces think the sponsors pay for everything.
Well they bloody well don't. I damn well do. Jason.' Samson watched Jason
react. Or rather fail to react. Jason's face was a blank. 'What the hell do you
do with shoes? We get two pairs a year from Footjoy and you go through five
in a month. A month!' Samson knew full well what Jason was doing with the
extra shoes. He'd seen them on sale in the pro shop. It was a piece of
entrepreneurship he fully approved of. He had to, given what he was up to
with shirts.

'It's the new swing.' Jason said. 'Puts a lot of extra weight on the left foot.
Bloody tops keep parting from the soles. Not my fault, blame the shoes.'

Jake turned to Samson. 'Have you seen your shirt bills, Samson? Who the
hell needs that many shirts in a week? There's thirty here in a week when
you're not even playing. What are you doing? Selling 'em?' It was a
throwaway remark that was too near the truth for Samson, who had been
getting an average of fifty pounds a shirt for a signed one. And he just had to
wear it for an hour and be seen in it around the place. How was he to know
the boss would check the paper work personally? The accountant had been

happy with a ten percent slice. Samson was not as sanguine as he appeared. He felt more than a little sorry for Jake who had all the worry and expense of managing this bunch of golfing wasters. He made a mental note to make more of an effort to pay him back for his efforts. He would change his ways, practise more, stop drinking and chasing women. He would. He really would. Next week he definitely would.

'Don't think you're in the clear, Martin.' Jake's anger was directed at a third member of the team. 'There's a hosepipe ban as a result of your laundering habits. Why do you need so many washes. Are you trying to get the skid marks of your bleeding underpants? It can't be sweat marks, because you never break into one. If you lost a bit of weight, we might see a bit of form from you at last. What's your best finish this year? Played twenty-five, missed twenty cuts, placed four times in the forties and last in the other. That's death form that is. One more year's exemption and then it's back to tour school and not even a sniff of earnings. Do you think you are in the right game, son? What did you do with all that potential? Where did you bleeding well put it? Did you bake it in a pie and eat the sodding thing?'

Samson pulled a face at Martin, who studied his nails, apparently oblivious to the onslaught. 'I could blame the management,' he said. 'But I don't. So why is the management so quick to blame me?' He folded his arms around an ample stomach. Samson shook his head. He recognised that as Martin's version of a killer retort. He closed his eyes and waited for Jake's predictable response.

'Because you are the one hitting the damn ball out on the frigging course, you bloody idiot. That's why. Where do you lot think the money comes from for these things, eh? It comes from winnings. And what do we have to do to get winnings? Damn well win now and then. Not much to ask is it? Just a few little top tens, the odd little second or third. God forbid I should ask you to actually win a tournament outright. Every time I send you out it costs me money and there's almost none left. And now there are rumblings from our not-very-generous-in-the-first-place sponsors. They don't want their names plastered all over a bunch of consistent losers. They want to see their caps and jackets worn by players with a winner's smile on their chops. Not on someone on the next plane home because they've missed the bloody cut again. Get a flaming grip, or we'll all be out of a job.'

In case he was asked directly, Samson started to list for himself all the well-worn excuses: bad weather, lousy caddies, sudden and inexplicable scintillating form from their opponents, bad lies, rotten luck and injury. But Samson knew the truth: too much booze, too many parties, a host of distractions and key to it all, far too little practice. Samson saw guilt on his colleagues' faces too. They were as aware of these things as he was. Samson, more than a little depressed by this reminder of how he was squandering his talent, nevertheless wondered whether breaking the habit of easy living would be too hard to achieve. It might be easier to live with the occasional spasm of guilt and regret than make the difficult and painful changes Jake was really asking for. A few good wins and Jake wouldn't give a damn about the cost of extra shoes. A few good wins and Samson wouldn't need to flog thirty shirts a week. And unlike his teammates, he had the talent to get the wins.

The door behind them opened and Jake's secretary, a world-weary, efficient woman in her late fifties, who looked to Samson as if she felt the weight of the office troubles as much as Jake, came in to the small office. 'Your three o'clock's here. Mrs Anne Smalling'

Jake groaned. 'Do I have to? What's she selling?'

'Nothing I know of, but I'm pretty sure you'll want to see this one.'

Jake's eyes lit up. Samson spotted it. Dirty sod, he thought, nevertheless keen to see for himself what the secretary had meant

'Bring her in then. What's her name again.'

'Anne Smalling'

As if on cue, Anne appeared at the door. 'But you'll know me as Anne Grainger, Jake.' She said. The secretary bowed out, closing the door as she went, leaving Anne with four pairs of appraising eyes undressing her as she waited for further instructions.

'Anne, good God! They didn't tell me it was you.' Samson looked from the visitor to his boss and back again. He could see the woman was a stunner, if you liked that sort of well-marshalled corpulence. He did. He could see that Jake did too. The boss was clearly shaken. It was obvious to Samson, even before Jake spoke, that these two had previous. 'Anne! Come in, come in. You are a real sight for sore eyes, and you haven't changed a bit.' Samson reckoned he would have welcomed an old flame like this with a bit more panache and subtlety. Jake had obviously been stunned into cliché. Samson felt sorry for his boss all over again and watched with disapproval as his golfing colleagues ogled Anne unashamedly. 'Filthy bastards,' he muttered.

Samson was impressed at the way Anne, clearly unfazed by this less than subtle male appraisal and approval, let them look their fill and then crossed the room to shake Jake's hand. 'What I need to see you about is a bit confidential,' she said. 'I'm sure these guys are trustworthy but …'

'They are, but they are also just leaving. We've finished our little talk, lads; try to bear in mind what I said. Go and get some useful practice in, hey?'

Without answering, the three trouped out of the door and crossed over the car park towards the hotel bar. Samson turned at the door, caught Anne's eye and smiled. The response he got from Anne was a frosty look and a raised eyebrow. 'Oh God,' Samson said to her, 'don't eat him all at once, will you?' He closed the door behind him, Anne's voluptuous image blocking out the more virtuous thoughts and good intentions that had been forming in his mind.

★

Jake and Anne stood at the window a while, watching them go. Then, when the pleasantries were over, and politeness had been satisfied, Anne sat down and crossed her legs, tantalisingly. She watched with amusement how he managed not to follow the manoeuvre with his eyes. But she saw as the interview went on that he was losing the battle. More than once she found herself talking to a man whose eyes were not on her face, but lowered to her substantially exposed legs. *Nice to see the equipment still works,* she thought.

She didn't take Jake for a fool and was aware that she mustn't overplay her hand. She pulled her skirt down, uncrossed her legs and sat a little more demurely. But only when she was sure the fish had taken a good look at the bait. She was feeling surprisingly comfortable in this role and more than a little surprised at how easily it came to her. *Femme fatale. I've never been one of those before.* Her thoughts were considerably more ambivalent when she felt the tiny shocks of sexual excitement in her tummy. *My God. This is turning me on!* She'd better tone things down a little. There were some signals she didn't want him to pick up. Not just yet, at any rate.

They talked for a while. Their shared past had to be navigated. *This man went to prison for my sake. He beat someone within an inch of his life because I asked him to. He was a wild one then, and so was I.* Anne was keen to remind him of how things had been between them and tried to imply that the way it had ended was something she regretted and would do differently. She could see that Jake was uncertain on this ground. Far too early, he asked her the question she recognised as a gateway to a very different conversation: whether she was happily married. Anne left the question unanswered.

'Look, Jake, I'll come straight to the point. I have something I think you'll be very interested in.' She saw Jake pick up on the double-entendre and reminded herself to be more careful. 'It's something every golfer would give his eye-teeth for. I'm here to talk, in absolute confidence, about a brand-new product. So new it isn't within a mile of coming to market. But it is sensational. This thing will guarantee winners, in the right hands. And 'the right hands' is the reason I came to you, Jake, though I knew it would be hard'. *Christ, there I go again!*

She could see she had hooked him now with the real bait. She would keep the sex lure in reserve if he looked like falling off this hook. She would do her damnedest not to let that happen and was pleased he looked intrigued, and ready to hear more. The next bit was crucial and the bit that made her nervous, even though she rehearsed it a dozen times in her head and with Selwyn. Her mouth was dry and she tried to keep her voice firm, steady and sexy.

'The other thing is, just by way of an early warning, we are going to have to do some work on where it all sits in the framework of the laws of the game. But until we get that sorted we have to assume it could be seen as a breach of the rules. In spirit at least.'

'Is it some form of technology breakthrough. A new club? Because if it is, our sponsors would not …'

'It's sort of technology but not like that. Not hardware. It's probably best to show you it in action and I can do that easily on the driving range. Look, this is so good I could have gone to anybody. I think you know why I came here first. I hadn't forgotten about us. I always followed your career and what you got up to. I don't know if times are good or bad, but this can only help. If you want it to.'

She thought a bit of flattery worth the risk. She saw him look longingly at her legs and hoped she still had his attention for the right reason. She had expected to be feeling more than a little guilt at this stage. After all, here she was, leading this poor guy on, trying to persuade him to take on something that could make his fortune, or ruin him. But she didn't. She loved the sense of power. And Jake was every bit as attractive as she'd expected him to be. She found his eyes on her legs remarkably pleasant; an affirmation of something important to her. She pulled herself back to business.

'And that ambiguity about the rules is the reason I need to be sure of your confidentiality. I've got a legal thing for you to sign. It asks you to agree to keep all of this to yourself.'

'A non-disclosure agreement?'

'That's it. I knew you'd know all about it.' Was pandering to his ego like this just a bit too obvious? He didn't seem to mind.

He nodded his willingness and signed the forms Anne laid before him. Anne had been seriously impressed at Selwyn's ability to produce stuff like this, with a little help from the Internet. 'Clever sod,' she'd told him, on their way to the bedroom.

'Good,' she said once the signing was done, crossing her legs again and watching his eyes drink her in: 'now I expect you have something you want me to satisfy.'

He blinked and was obviously struggling to respond.

'Your curiosity?'

9 *The Pitch*

S elwyn was waiting for them on the range, where he'd been hitting a few balls, as much to try and relax as anything. He saw them coming, picked up the ball on the tee, dropped it in the basket and straightened his tall, lean frame. No introductions were necessary. Selwyn shook hands with Jake as warmly as any man can with the former lover of his wife, and even managed a friendly slap on the shoulder for good measure. This was business after all.

Even at a distance he'd seen that Jake was captivated by Anne. He hoped she'd sold the product as well as she'd clearly sold herself. He worried that his jealousy, instantly aroused, might be a threat to the effectiveness of his product. He told himself to control it, but it continued to burn holes in the lining of his stomach no matter what he tried. He thought this might happen and had taken a triple dose, just to make sure. He felt a bit light-headed and his heart was racing, but that could just be the nerves. This was a pressure situation, after all.

'For God's sake put me out of my misery. What have you got up your sleeves?' Jake looked like a man impatient to be disappointed, Selwyn thought. And perhaps also a man disappointed to find a husband on the scene.

Selwyn couldn't shake his nerves. He'd used the thing under pressure before, in golf competitions at his club. But this was the real thing and he couldn't be sure the product would stand the scrutiny of a professional golfer like Jake. He called on the spirit of his Welsh ancestors for courage and a bit of Celtic fire. It was now or never. He'd risked his neck with Hartmann for this moment. Go, Sel boy! He looked at Anne for inspiration, too, and was rewarded with a smile and a conspiratorial wink.

'Well,' he said. 'A few months ago I was a twenty-two handicapper, now I play off eight, and would be lower if I could fix my putting.'

Jake didn't seem especially impressed. 'Good, I'm thrilled for you. And the way you did it is what you have to show me?'

'Precisely. Name any distance you want me to hit the ball, tell me to draw, fade or slice it. And remember. I was a high handicapper.'

'A hundred yards – straight and high'

Selwyn checked his card, selected the club, peered ahead and muttered the shot number under his breath. He crossed his fingers mentally and addressed the ball. Without a practice swing of any kind he lobbed it to within inches of the 100-yard marker.

'Again' said Jake. Selwyn, starting to grow in confidence, repeated his feat. 'Again.' Five times the trick was performed and Jake's face remained impassive. 'That's world–class' he said, 'but it is only a wedge. Try two hundred, slight fade.'

Selwyn, with an almost causal arrogance born of the certainty now coursing round his bloodstream, checked the chart on the card, took a four iron and repeated his preparations. Whoosh. A swing as perfect as Selwyn was physically capable of propelled the ball in a high fading arc out beyond the 150 marker and two metres short of the 200.

Once more, there was little response from Jake, other than 'Again.'

It took half an hour and two buckets of balls, before Selwyn, almost at the point of exhaustion but exhilarated at passing the test with such honours, got the signal to stop. Jake announced himself satisfied that he was witnessing a real phenomenon. He congratulated Selwyn and said there was no way what he had just witnessed could be coming from anywhere but Selwyn's ability, however it had been acquired. He had examined the clubs, the balls, the grips and found nothing unusual.

Selwyn beamed, as much with boyish pride at this recognition of his talent from a professional player as with relief it was over and satisfaction in the efficacy of his invention. He was a happy man, especially as Anne was smiling at him, too, almost like she'd done in the past.

'Congratulations!' Jake said. 'I have never seen anything like it for accuracy and consistency. I've seen better swings, technically, and balls hit further with the same clubs, but for sheer repeatability, that was world class. It would win tournaments if it could be repeated on the course.'

'It can be. I do it every week in some competition or other. I'm hated at the club. If I turn up, everybody else goes home. Fortunately, I haven't worked as much on my short game, close-in shots round the green, so they can still see the hacker burning deep inside me. No-one, yet, has accused me of anything untoward.'

'And is there?'

'We need to go back inside, I think, for a little chat.'

10 *The soft sell*

'I'm not sure I can tell you exactly what the mechanism is until you've agreed to undergo the test yourself. We can do that as soon as you like.' said Selwyn

'But it is drug-based is it? You have to take a drug to make it work?'

'Look. I am an experienced pharmacologist. I developed this product myself and have taken it myself with only positive effects.' He saw Anne look at him quickly and then away again to smile seductive reassurance at Jake. 'Calling it a drug gives the wrong impression. It is a cross between a form of protein and a form of hormone, a promone I call it, that works with the body's natural mechanism in a very special way to make what you saw possible. But it is just releasing what the body has as a natural capability but which we can't normally access consciously. You know about muscle memory?'

Jake nodded. 'Sort of.'

'Well that's all this is. It gets very technical, but muscle memory is just a standard feature of the brain. A bit like the reflex arc, the bit that lets you pick something up without thinking about it. Muscle memory is what you use when you toss a piece of paper into the waste basket. Or throw a ball. Visualisation, some coaches call it. You see the shot first in your mind's eye and then let your muscles execute it as they've done a thousand times before. It's a completely natural phenomenon. All I've done is harness it, make it completely accessible and reliable. But it's just your body's natural mechanism. It even has a name: the endocannabinoid system.'

'And nobody else knows it exists?'

'Nobody, and so far as I know nobody is within a million miles of developing it independently.'

'So why don't you take it through regular channels? It would make you rich and famous.'

'Because we have some good reasons not to, to do with patents and stuff. This is the best way for now to ensure the product stays with us. But it is perfectly legal. Just not yet above board, if you see what I mean.'

'All sounds a bit too weird for me.'

'Try the thing and I guarantee you'll be convinced. And if you don't trust me, ask Anne whether she knows of any laws that have been broken.' Jake looked at Anne.

'He's right,' she said. 'You could say that there has been some unconventional behaviour and not everything Selwyn has done has been best practice, but the only thing he has stolen is a little time from his employers and I know of not a single law that has been transgressed.'

'No transgressions, eh? Some posh language around. Usually means people are trying to pull the wool over your eyes.'

'We aren't. When you've tried it and you're in, we'll be absolutely open with you. But if you want to stop now, we have a list of other options to try. All in golf, though we know it works in other sports too. Some of your rivals will be very interested.'

Selwyn could sense that Jake was keen, but not wanting to show it. He was probably thinking a bit of reluctance on his part might lower the price. Selwyn wasn't worried about that. He was worried where the keenness came from. Was it the product or was it Anne, whose legs were crossed and whose skirt was way too short for Selwyn's comfort? He followed the line of Jake's gaze and saw it move from Anne's knees up her legs to the hem of her skirt, dangerously close to what Selwyn considered his preserve. The acid jealously returned, but to Selwyn's surprise, it lost out to the spurt of lust he felt looking at his own wife, for God's sake. Triple doses did have side-effects after all.

'okay, okay.' Jake said. 'But it is still a drug and there is drug testing in golf. Started in 2008. No convictions yet, so far as I know, but one of my team was subject to a random test last year. UK Anti-Doping the outfit's called and they have inspectors; just a small team but inspectors are inspectors. They also have Doping Control Officers and Chaperones. You wouldn't believe what the chaperones have to do. They have to lock themselves in the cubicle with you, the golfer being tested, that is, and as you have a leak they have to ensure the whole area surrounding the penis is visible so they can observe the stream of urine going into the container and verify that it is coming from the end of your dick and nowhere else. You have to stand there with your pants flapping round your ankles and your shirt pulled up and tucked in. Sounds jolly doesn't it.' He looked at Anne who flashed him an ambiguous eye signal. 'Anyway, that's the system. We could probably get round it if we had to, but it is there.'

Selwyn wasn't alarmed by this turn in the conversation. He was well prepared and asked the questions just so Jake would hear the answers better. 'Do they test blood or just urine?'

'Just urine'

'No problem then. If we ever need ways round it there will be lots of them, from bribery, to substitution or even delay. But there's no need. This thing leaves no trace in urine and is gone in measurable quantities even from the blood within hours of ingestion. On top of that, it mimics perfectly normal hormones, such as testosterone and you would have to launch a specific search to find it.'

'okay, so no problem with drugs testers. Bit of a joke anyway. If you ask me it's all a waste of time and money because no steroid known to man could make you hit a golf ball better. Or so I thought till I watched you. What about side-effects?'

'Look, we'll probably have to go through all this again with your team, if you chose to use it. I absolutely guarantee that you can take it without any problem and then you can make your own mind up. How soon do you want to give it a go?'

'Tomorrow.'

'Tomorrow? I can't do tomorrow. Can you get here Anne?'

Anne could, and the arrangement was made. Up till now it had been Selwyn's plan to get Anne on her own with Jake. Now he wasn't so sure. Jake was a good-looking man and Selwyn knew chemistry at work when he saw it.

11 *Calling the shots*

Next morning, a bright, frosty November Tuesday, Anne and Selwyn rose early, breakfasted and showered, the first together the second separately, at Anne's insistence. Selwyn had been much less insistent since she'd brought the problem into the open, but she was taking no chances. She left the bathroom, naked but for a small towel held protectively across her abdomen, and turned away quickly when she saw Selwyn, stark naked in the bedroom doorway, looking at her, just in case the last traces of the chemical left him lust-wracked and incapable of pacifying it by himself. She did look quickly back to see whether or not the sight of her ample but firm rear end had produced an effect on Selwyn. Nothing visible, at least, which was good news of a sort. It meant, given his behaviour at other times, that his male functions were now almost entirely dependent on the blasted substance; and that could not be healthy. She looked away again so that Selwyn wouldn't get the wrong idea and disappeared into what was her bedroom these days. It wasn't good that she felt about him like she did. But she couldn't imagine anyone but a raging nymphomaniac (which she was convinced were male inventions, not real women) would cope with Selwyn's urges.

They made him gross in her eyes. At the peak of his need his attentions were selfish, bestial almost and certainly very unappealing. She had reached the point where she would rather have no physical contact with him than provoke another bout of frantic thrusting and grunting. But that brought other problems. She was still a woman with needs. She hadn't lost interest in sex per se. Just sex with her husband. She didn't consider herself a hard or bitter woman. She understood the problems Selwyn had faced earlier in their marriage and that he had tried to overcome them for her benefit. She felt sorry for him and for herself too. But life had to go on and if her marriage did go under, she was determined it would not take her with it. There was work to do and money to be made. For that, at least, Selwyn deserved her gratitude and, despite all the current reservations about him, her admiration.

She heard him go down to the kitchen where the remains of their breakfast still littered the table and work surface. A carton of orange juice, box of porridge, milk, banana skins (not an omen for the day ahead she hoped), yogurt pots and cold toast covered most of the table still. She heard him clearing them away and the sound of running water suggested he was cleaning the sink. This was unlike Selwyn. Immaculate at work, he was a slob at home. She guessed he was doing this because he wanted everything to be good when Anne came down. She had pretended to be displeased that he was not able to come with her and he had thought her anger real. She told him he was sending her into the lion's den while he swanned off on some work jaunt.

He'd protested, to little avail, that it was an unavoidable commitment and missing it would require an awful lot of explanation. Anne could tell he was lying. She could read him easily. She suspected something awful had happened at Hartmann but he hadn't said anything to her. She knew something was amiss with Selwyn and that he was keeping something from her. Years ago she would have grilled him expertly until she was sure she'd arrived at the truth. In her view, all men were womanisers, Selwyn no different from the rest, and there was usually a woman, or some guilty secret involving a woman at the heart of all their pathetic attempts at deceit.

These days, from her perspective in a separate bedroom, she could hardly care less if he was screwing a posse of alley cats, so long as he left her alone.

She put Selwyn from her mind, hoping he would clear away downstairs so completely that she could make a quick getaway. Her immediate problem was what to wear for the encounter with Jake in Birmingham. She had not been unaffected by the way he looked at her yesterday, and remembered how close they'd been as teenagers. He had been her first. She suspected, from what she recalled of his fumbling at the time, that she had also been his. The way he looked at her offered plenty of evidence that embers had started glowing again and she felt ruthless enough to use it. In any case, it offered the prospect of some human and enjoyable encounters for her, too. And that was a danger. Whatever her own desires, capitulating too quickly would not be a good idea, it seemed to her.

She chose something with trousers and a high collar, in black to complement rather than set off her complexion and dark hair. She wanted to look elegant, professional and just sufficiently alluring, without any over-the-top sexiness. She could play the tart as well as the next woman, but not today. A future treat for him, perhaps, if he did as he was told.

By eight she was ready to leave and so was Selwyn. They discussed cars and she took the Volvo. She felt it suited her mood and choice of persona better than the Golf, which Selwyn would take.

Before they set off, her for Birmingham, him for Reading, she let Selwyn run her one more time through her lines. She knew she was word-perfect but wanted him to know it too. She understood the nature of the 'promone' and what it did. She understood the mechanisms that made it work and how they had to be recorded to make the system efficient. Most of all, she was absolutely briefed, though she hadn't needed telling on this score, about the need for confidentiality. It was vital, Selwyn had said over and over, that as few people as possible were involved at this and any future stage. If Jake needed help with the learning curve the system demanded, it would be provided by Selwyn now and for the foreseeable future.

A quick peck on the cheek, the kisser Selwyn, the kissed Anne, and they set off.

12 Chemistry

Ten miles north of her home, Anne took the slip road onto the M5 and joined the slow-moving traffic towards Birmingham. She was, she noted, excited. She felt this was a new chapter opening in her life. Whether it was the prospect of finally finding a market for the promone or whether it was simply the old 'Boy Meets Girl' story, she couldn't tell. Probably a mixture, she thought; and with that thought came the realisation, explicit in her own mind for the first time, that she did want Jake to make a move, make a pass at her, for its own sake and not just as an encouragement to participate in the project.

★

Selwyn's gloom deepened with each mile southwards down the M40. He turned off early to take the country route, hoping the pleasanter drive would lift his spirits. He had been genuinely scared by the tone and contents of the appraisal and in the days and weeks following it had become convinced that he was under surveillance, and Julie with him. He needed to warn her, soon, without scaring her and then he needed to dump her, as gently as it was possible to dump someone who had fallen in love with you. And he was convinced Julie had done that. She as much as said so on his last visit, just as she climaxed for the third time. He tried to sum up what he felt for her but couldn't, because the drug was responsible for most of it. On the rare occasions he had seen her with none of the chemical in his blood, he had been unimpressed. Too much weight, too little dress-sense and rather untidy hair. When the love potion, as he thought of it, was racing round his blood and setting his heart beating fast and raising his member at the very thought of coitus, she was more than attractive enough and, naked, a fulfilling partner for a man with a desperate need to bury himself into a woman's softness or lose his mind.

So much for the physical. In other aspects, he thought, Julie was everything Anne wasn't, or was no longer willing to be. Kind, considerate, emotionally intelligent by instinct, and in love with him. But for her own good he would have to dump her. He pulled over in a lay-by to wipe away the unexpected tears.

★

Anne turned the Volvo onto the wide drive of the famous club and headed to the overspill car park. She saw Jake at his office window and felt his eyes on her as she got out of the car. She hoped he was disappointed that she was wearing trousers and hoped the tight top she had chosen would offer him compensations.

The weary-looking secretary greeted her with a show of politeness and ceremony but little warmth, ushering Anne into the office and offering coffee, which Anne declined with a sisterly smile.

Jake seemed a little nervous. She could see the uncertainty in his eyes and wondered if she had made the right choice of partner after all. 'How much does she know about why I'm here?' Anne said with a nod in the direction of the secretary's office.

'Zilch. You're not even in the diary. Anyway, I'd trust Mary with my life.'

'Don't.' She said. 'Not her, not anybody. Keep everything on a strictly 'needs to know basis' for now. You can trust me. I won't let you down.'

★

At roughly the same moment Anne was tutoring Jake on the need for confidentiality, Selwyn arrived at the reception desk of a large and ugly commercial building on an industrial estate just off the M4, near Reading. He told the receptionist he had an appointment with Mitchell Walker and a uniformed man at the desk consulted a list and buzzed through to an office somewhere in the bowels of the building. Selwyn took the seat they offered him and waited, pretending to read the in-house magazine as he did so.

'New lines on cancer research at Merricole' was the headline. 'New products being developed on our Reading site are expected to complete preliminary trials shortly. Hopes are high that the new lines will make a significant contribution to the treatment of several major cancers.'

As well as a major contribution to Merricole coffers, of course.

He looked up to see a beaming figure striding towards him, hand outstretched. Mitchell shook his hand and then, to Selwyn's surprise, hugged him. 'Is it business or pleasure, or something else brings you here. Takes a lot to get a Hartmann guy on Merricole territory, usually.'

'All of the above and then some. It's been a long time. Too long.' Selwyn wasn't entirely clear why he'd rung Mitchell to suggest they meet. The burden of his secret had bothered him for a while and he had felt the need to share it with another professional. Mitchell had seemed the obvious person on that score: an old friend in the same line of work. If anything happened to him he wanted Anne to have the support of another biochemist: one he trusted; one who didn't work for Hartmann. Again, Mitchell was the only guy to fit the bill: a biochemist, an old pal from university and employed by Hartmann's major rival, Merricole.

'Far too long,' Mitchell agreed, 'so let's get out of here and go somewhere more congenial. You don't want to have to go through security. It would be the full works for you. You know you triggered the Hartmann intruder alert as soon as you walked in, don't you?'

Selwyn said he wouldn't be surprised if they had one. And if they hadn't they should definitely get one.

'Do you ever get back to the University? Back to Aston, or even Birmingham at all? Jesus, we had some fun there, didn't we, as well as doing loads of good stuff, I mean. Well, you did most of that, you clever sod; I just rode around on your very fast-moving coat tails. Exciting times.'

Selwyn liked Mitchell's candour and ebullience. Mitchell had been something of a hedonist in Birmingham and had regularly taken the more reserved Selwyn out of himself and broadened his social life considerably. He was pleased too by Mitchell's accolade, because he knew it was true and he knew Mitchell meant it. He had been at the forefront of academic research and now he wished he'd never left it.

They drove back across the M4 towards Reading. They crossed the Thames and arrived at a largish house, with a grand lawn which ran down to the river banks. 'My humble abode. In this country at least. Got one in France and a great one, just far enough North of Benidorm, in Spain. Merricole salaries aren't that far behind Hartmann.'

Selwyn was impressed. Mitchell was clearly earning much more than he did. 'What the hell do you do for Merricole that brings this sort of dough in?'

'Ah,' said Mitchell, 'If I told you that, I would have to lock you in my very damp cellar and lose the key.'

13 Secrets

S amson Gregory, lean, well-dressed and more troubled than he appeared, had also spotted the arrival of the dark-haired lady from yesterday. Her car passed the bunker where Samson had spent the last two hours playing the same shot, over and over again until he was sure he would be able to repeat it under tournament pressure. He strolled over to a spot which gave him a view of the car park. She was dressed in a more muted style than the last time, he noticed, and wondered if it was deliberate.

He was disappointed because he had liked what he had seen of her. But even today, there was plenty to look at. Way older than him, but probably what he needed to steady his rocking ship. Mentally, he added her to his list and then took her off again. That sort of stuff had to change, too. Everything had to change. He had to focus on his game.

He was good enough and still young enough, twenty-nine, to keep playing on the tour for another fifteen, even twenty, years - if he looked after himself - and he intended to make sure he achieved the recognition his talent deserved. A first really big win would be a start; one win would restore his confidence and his bank balance. And it wouldn't hurt his chances of finding a woman who wasn't just a groupie out for whatever she could get, either. So he was out practising his bunker play, because the playing statistics he got from Jake showed that to be an area where he was weaker than average.

Everything had to change. But principally, he did. He had to start winning. There was more than a little bluster and show in the way Samson conducted himself and let himself be represented. Inwardly, he craved something more than he had. Watching the woman go into the office he took his wallet from his rear pocket and checked the business card he'd put there yesterday. Anne Smalling, Company Director, it said, above an email address and a mobile number. He slipped it back in the wallet pocket and took out his own card. Just his name and twitter account. Nothing here about 'PGA champion' or 'Open Winner 2012'. Because he hadn't damn well won them. Well that was about to change. A photograph caught his eye, of his mother. The poignancy of that single photograph took a while to sink in. Where was the photograph of the wife he loved so much, of his children, of the places they'd so enjoyed together? There weren't any because he didn't have any. The empty pockets were a rebuke and a warning. Things were going to change. He watched a hawk high above his head circle, cruising effortlessly on rising currents of air. In awe, he saw the vertiginous dive into the field and felt sad when the bird climbed again, its beak empty, the prize missed.

He went back to his bunker play and stopped only when Jake came out of the office and asked Samson to help him clear the range and then to close it and keep it closed for the remainder of the morning. Samson was understandably curious but he got nothing out of Jake. So, as part of the drive to change himself, he did as he was told and closed the range to any prying eyes, except his own.

Clearing the range was a simple matter. Customers already there could finish but not refill their baskets. Arriving customers had to be turned away with a polite explanation and a token for a complimentary session. The ball dispensing machine was shut down as an extra precaution and 'closed' signs were brought out of storage and erected. Samson worked without enthusiasm but without demur. His task over, he made straight for the office where he expected to be able to chat up the dark-haired woman from yesterday, if only to find out what was going on. But before he could get there, she came out of the office, speaking into her mobile phone and walked towards him, in the direction of the range. Still speaking into the phone, she passed him without acknowledgement, as if she didn't see him. Samson smiled to himself. He'd seen that trick before. He knew it meant she fancied him.

14 *Cloak and dagger*

S elwyn was sitting on Mitchell's sofa, looking down the lawn to the river, when the phone rang. The screen told him it was Anne. 'Hi,' he said to her and 'Excuse me, I have to take this,' to Mitchell, who nodded his understanding and went out to put the kettle on again.

'What's up?'

'Nothing. It's all going fine. Just he wants ten grand up front, in cash and no questions asked, before he'll even do the trial. And I agreed. '

'Bloody hell. Let me think. Okay. Tell him he can have that, but he needs to pay it back out of the first £100k he makes from his team, once the experiment is running. If he won't sign for that, there's no deal.'

'That's clever. He'll go for that. I take it you can get the ten grand?'

'Get his details and I'll transfer it straight over. Course I can get ten grand. Text his stuff across. I need the sort code and the account number. Name of the account would help but not strictly needed.'

'okay. Got to go.'

Ten minutes later, in front of a patient and curious Mitchell, Selwyn transferred £10,000 from his savings into his current account and across to Jake's bank.

Jake watched it arrive on his i-Pad and nodded to Anne.

'A pity you went that route. I thought the other offer was a more interesting one.' Jake, given licence by their past, hadn't been able to hold back.

'I don't think that was really an option. I'm a respectable married woman.' Her expression suggested otherwise.

He asked her what came next and she handed him a small bottle with colourless liquid in it. 'Is it thirty minutes since the first dose?'

He looked at his watch. 'thirty-two,' he said.

'Well, this is the active ingredient. Like I said, the first was a protective fluid and a catalyst. This will work in five minutes. You've had your money. Now take your medicine.'

He downed it in one. 'Delicious', he said, pulling a face as if at a bitter taste in his mouth. 'What next?'

★

Selwyn and Mitchell faced each other across the living room. 'You're kidding, Sel, you've got to be.'

Selwyn assured him he wasn't.

'Well, why are you telling me? Why me specifically and no-one else?'

'Who else would believe me? You know what our industry is like. When I say I am being watched and under suspicion, you know it's true and what the consequences could be if someone decides I'm guilty of espionage, or whatever they'd call it.'

'You'd be sacked without trimmings, in my company.'

'This is Hartmann. Nobody just gets sacked. I'd be disgraced and prosecuted at best.'

'And you can't tell me what you did, or even if you did anything at all?'

'I did enough to arouse their suspicion. But I haven't done anything to harm their interests, or anything I signed up not to do, apart from a bit of tomfoolery and a minor infringement of some of the dafter rules. You know what they're like. And that's God's own truth.'

'So what is it you expect of me?'

'Mainly what you're doing now, Mitch. Listening. That's been a help on its own. Look, I've put down all the details in a letter and lodged it with my solicitor. It wouldn't be safe to leave it with Anne and besides there are things in there I don't want her to know - ever. The letter will tell you what you need to know. You'll be able to pick it up, you'll need good ID, at this address, immediately anything happens to me. Anything bad and unexpected I mean. I am sure nothing will, but you never know. Actually, I'm not sure of that at all. Sorry for all this cloak and dagger stuff, but apart from being in the trade, you were my best friend, are still I hope, and I know you won't let me down. There won't be much you can do for me, but there is another name in the letter, a woman. Not Anne. If anything bad has happened to me she needs to know very quickly and be helped. Because whoever does it to me will have her name on a list, too. She doesn't know anything, but they won't believe that. Do you think you can do all this.'

Mitchell looked flabbergasted. 'I can't believe any of this.'

'But will you do it?' He held out the note with the address of the solicitor and a password.

Mitchell took the paper. 'I hope to God this is all nonsense, but of course I'll help.'

'There's one more thing. In the papers are details of something I was working on. You know enough about how my mind works to be able to piece it all together. It's mine, not Hartmann's and I bequeath it to you. I can't tell you what it does but it is potentially very powerful. Developed by you or Mellicore it could be a power for good. Hartmann would use it for killing. There is a mark 2 version, which I think is even better and much safer, but still in embryo. I haven't put any details of that in the papers. Anne will know where to look, but I don't have it in a state where it would make sense to anyone. If the worst does happen, Anne will contact you and help you find the mark 2 documents. All in all, I guess it's two years away from a finished product. Maybe three if I am not involved.'

'What does it do, this wonder stuff'

'You'd never believe it if I told you, which I can't, in case this is all nonsense and I survive. But my real sin is that I've used it myself and I am using it for real with human guinea pigs.'

'What on earth possessed you to do that? That's taking crazy risks?'

'Greed. And desperation for someone who doesn't really give a hoot about me.'

'Anne?'

Selwyn nodded and Mitchell looked suitably sorry.

'And, Mitchell, there's another reason. A bigger one. This thing is my baby and it's beautiful. I want to see it walk and talk. And I want to be admired for it.'

15 Jake's hot shots

Jake was warming up by hitting a few golf balls. Anne stood out of his view admiring the smooth athletic way he could still swing a club. She could feel the warmth of attraction running through her. But she was undoubtedly conflicted. What it would do to Selwyn was a real dilemma. Denying him what he most wanted whilst giving it to someone else was about as much damage as a wife could do and for a while, quite disgusted with herself for being so weak, she resolved to be good. Then Jake would do something particularly appealing and her knees would turn to water. There were times she would not have been able to resist an advance from him, but fortunately perhaps, they were not times when he made one. *Cheating at sport is not immoral, it's just sound business, but cheating this badly on your husband is. Get a grip on yourself. Bloody hell, woman. It's just a crush. Grow up for God's sake.*

Then the real work started and she found relief in focusing on that. Each time he told her he was happy with a shot she gave it a name and number and made him say it as he visualised the shot. Eventually, she had a page full of notations and names, relating to different clubs, distances and ball flights, draws and fades.

Then she asked Jake to name a shot he wanted to play and gave him an example. 'Say, 180 yards, slight draw, no wind.'

'okay, let's take that one.'

She looked on the chart she had made while they were practising and found the shot note. B6 was the name.

'okay, seven iron. Stand over the ball, clear your mind, say 'B6' and then play the shot.'

Jake did as he was told and the ball lifted and turned slightly left before landing 181 yards away.

'Do it again. Say B6 and hit the ball with the seven iron'

He did it four times and the balls came to rest, after identical journeys, within inches of each other. Anne was delighted it was working so well. She filled with pride at what her husband had done. After the fourth shot, face flushed with excitement, he threw the club in the air, grabbed Anne and kissed her full on the mouth. She didn't stop him and Selwyn and his achievements were swept from her mind. After a second or two he broke away. 'Sorry, don't know what came over me. Just I was so excited and you look so damn nice...' He reached for her again but she pushed him away. Sanity had returned to her as soon as she'd been released. She knew what was happening, had expected it, but couldn't give the game away to Jake. She was suddenly sure of one thing though. *If I'm going to be seduced it won't be by another artificially randy sex fiend.*

'More shots,' she commanded, 'Until you are absolutely convinced.'

Half an hour later and Anne had convinced Jake that what he had taken was restoring his golfing prowess. 'This is way better than I've managed for years,' he said. She could tell from the looks he was giving her, as well as from his over-enthusiastic lunge and kiss, that it wasn't just his golfing skills that were being revived. He could hardly keep his hands to himself, and she was finding it difficult to continue a resistance she didn't really want to put up. *Not while it's Selwyn's stuff talking. If I'm going to do it I want it real and honest or not at all. If I'm going to do it.*

'Listen Anne, that stuff is terrific. And so are you. It's everything you said and more and I will buy into whatever you think we should do with it. How do we sell it to the guys?'

Anne, pleased at the outcome as well as by her resistance, said she would help with that and they agreed she should be in charge of breaking the news to the team.

Then Anne found herself swept up again.

Jake went on: 'I should never have let you go in the first place. I wouldn't have, if you'd waited for me. But I can't bear what this is doing to me now. I haven't wanted anyone so much for years. I feel I could make love all night.'

Here we go again, thought Anne, and despite her recent resolve, visions of a lunchtime tryst on his office desk while his secretary was elsewhere drifted into her head. She came to her senses just in time.

'Whooah, stud,' she said. 'That's not included in the price. I still have a husband and I'm not part of the deal. I can't do this. Not now.'

'But you aren't ruling it out completely?' Jake's wild eyes were pleading.

'I think it's time for a lunch break, don't you? We could catch up with that nice Mr Gregory I saw earlier. Sound him out a bit.'

'Samson? Nice? Listen, be careful with that guy. He's a hound. Know what I mean? But if you offer him an easy way back to the top, he'll probably snatch your hand off.

16 Samson takes a hit

T he hotel bar was nearly empty and Anne and Jake had no trouble finding a table. Nor was there any trouble finding Samson, who was more than ready to join them for lunch. He was curious to know what was going on, but not so stupid as to ask too directly or too early. That something big was in the air he had no doubt. He had asked Jake's secretary, but she was obviously as ignorant as he was, and more than a little disgruntled at being seen to be ignorant. Samson could see she resented the dent in her reputation as the expert in all matters Jake. It would all come out in due course, he was sure.

So Samson, his interest piqued, sat and listened and watched with growing impatience. In vain. Jake and Anne chatted about the past, about old schoolmates, avoided the topic that forced them apart years ago, and avoided the topic that had brought them together again. Until, that is, Anne said to Jake that Samson would have to know at some point, so wasn't this a good time to fill him in, test the water and enlist his help in broaching the subject with the others?

'What subject?' Samson just managed to ask, his mouth full of steak.

Samson saw Jake get tacit agreement from Anne. Then he told Samson he had tested a new wonder substance, a performance enhancer, that he had found amazing. Samson could feel the scepticism growing as chewed on his steak and listened. This didn't sound too good to him. He knew he was the best of the bunch, a potential world-beater he'd concluded after an especially good practice session, and now he was starting to put the work in, too. Really grafting. His desire had come back. He was not going to waste his talent any longer. He was going to surprise everyone with what he achieved. Everyone but himself. And now this stuff. Jake's description sounded fanciful and Samson wondered if he'd been on the wine all morning. But if it were true, if it did what Jake said, then it sounded like a leveller, and that would make his superior skill and new-found industry redundant. Samson was disturbed deeply by what he was hearing. He told himself to stay cool, chewed some more and listened.

'Every ball I hit went just where I wanted it, every time. I could hit it two hundred yards and drop it on a sixpence.'

'I can do that without any 'substance'.' Samson said.

'No, Samson, you can't. You just think you can. That's part of your problem.'

'On the practice range, I meant. It's different out on the course, I agree.'

Anne told him that her husband had tried it on the course, in competition, and he found it worked as well on the course as in practice.

'He's an amateur, though. Tougher for Pro's.'

'Isn't the difference between practice and proper play the same for everyone?' Anne asked and Samson just shrugged and stuck a toothpick between his teeth. He was thinking hard. The more he heard, the less he liked it.

'There is only one way to test it though, isn't there?' said Anne. Samson ignored her.

'So, let me get this right. Provided I have hit a shot before, and provided I have visualised and named it and provided I have the stuff in my veins, I can repeat any shot under any conditions perfectly every time, because you have got access to my muscle memory?' Samson allowed his scepticism to show.

'More or less,' said Anne. 'Except you are the one with the access, not me.'

'But,' Samson continued, unable to hold back his concerns any longer, 'if all our team took it and we all played perfectly, wouldn't we all win everything in a dead heat, every time? And how would that look?'

Anne explained, a touch condescendingly in Samson's view, that the drug didn't eliminate skill differences between players. Good ball strikers would hit the ball better with the drug than poor ball strikers using it. The skill gap would remain, even though they would all get much better. So there wouldn't be dead heats. In any case, putting didn't show the same improvement as other shots, presumably because each green was different, and the general ups and downs of courses would still leave an element of chance. There was also no reason why every member of the team should take it at every tournament, and they could all leave off it at some events.

'We mustn't get too greedy,' she said.

Samson was still not convinced. It was a lot to believe. But he noted how quickly the talk had got round to winning tournaments and that certainly got his attention. These people, whoever they were, must be serious. Jake clearly wasn't drunk and there must be something in it for him to be bringing it to Samson like this. 'So we all make a lot more money?'

Anne smiled. 'A lot more.'

'And although this might seem a bit premature, how much of what we win do you guys take?'

'We want sixty percent of all your winnings and sixty percent of all sponsorship, image rights, branding, etc, etc. Sixty percent of everything.'

'Jesus. That's a huge share of the cake. That must be too much by about twice.' Samson was kicking himself for being such a lousy negotiator. He felt that by moving onto the details of financial management he had conceded the principal of the thing and lost the chance to hold out for a better deal. He was a golfer, not a politician and he rarely regretted it. 'What makes you think we'll fall for that?'

'Well, for one, you won't have to worry about a thing. We take care of everything else. All travel and accommodation costs, food, clothes, equipment, caddies, everything. What you get is pure bunce. And we expect the company to make 10 million in year one. Forty percent of 10 million is four million. How much did you earn this year?'

Despite himself, Samson felt the excitement. *Stuff the money, let me get my hands on a trophy.* He calmed himself. 'Okay. What we earned was nothing like that. But this is a big risk we're taking. How do we know it's safe?'

'Safe? Well, my husband is the inventor and has been taking the stuff himself for some time with no ill effects. Obviously this is all very confidential and there have been no official trials. We will become your agents on tour and we will take care of all medical requirements. You will be carefully and intensively monitored and any unusual symptom or signs will be dealt with very quickly. At our expense.'

'But if this gets out we're finished. There's testing on tour now. This would finish our careers. I can't see the lads being up for this.'

Jake shifted around in his chair when Samson talked about the risk and getting caught. Samson had rarely seen him looking so uneasy and it didn't help Samson warm to this stuff Anne was pushing so hard.

'I guarantee they will when they've tried it,' Anne said. 'We can handle the dope testing. That really is not a problem. Firstly, this is not a banned substance. It is a natural product. Second, they test only urine, not blood. This stuff doesn't show in urine. But you will need to be discreet. That's why we, my company, will handle all press and publicity matters. We know what we're doing.'

Samson was still unhappy. Part of him wanted a bigger cut and was playing hard to get. He knew why they'd come to him first. They needed him on board. He was the team leader. If he said okay, the others would follow, and it needed the whole team. He had rarely felt so uncertain. *Jesus, I'm having an attack of the moral vapours. Not like me. What the hell do I do now?* When Jake got a call and went back to the office to meet someone, Samson was left alone with Anne. To him she looked like a woman weighing up her options. What would she do to get him on board? Would she go that far?' *Stop it you lecherous sod. You've put all that behind you, even if she is as tasty as you've seen for a while. Remember those legs? And take a gander at that bosom. A man could have a lot of fun with those. Stop it, you sleazy, sexist, horny devil. Stay focused.*

'There is one side effect.' Anne was not looking in his eyes as she said this, he noticed.

'And that is?'

'The stuff turns you into a super stud. You can do it as often as you like, within reason and what's more, get the dose right and it makes you <u>want</u> to do it all night, too.

His eyes widened: 'You mean it's a sort of Viagra with benefits?'

'Indeed. Much better than Viagra.'

'How do you know?'

'I am a happy woman again. My husband takes regular doses. He can't keep his hands off me.'

'I'm surprised he needs to take anything to feel like that.'

'okay. So how about we give it a trial run?' Anne said, her face all innocence.

He wasn't expecting the offer this quickly and was lost for a response. *Bloody hell. You've cracked it Samson, my son.*

'On the range I mean, you idiot.' Samson smiled at her cleverness and found himself won over.

'Okay. I'll give it a try. To be honest, I'm not all that interested in the side effect business. What I mean is, I don't really need it. I'll see what it does on the range and then we can have a word with the lads. I think it's got to be all of us or none of us, don't you?

Anne agreed. 'But will you keep that side effect a secret between you, me and the bedpost?'

He said he would and she patted his hand.

Samson was still wondering to himself how all this would square with his new attitude and approach to the game. If the stuff worked like she said then it would just complement his new regime. It would still be him doing it. This was just a little assist to get him properly underway. Once he was established he'd go clean completely. This stuff was just a helping hand. He didn't need it really and certainly not long term. This was the chance to get going again. He'd take the stuff until he got his first win. Once he'd got that, he'd stop. He talked himself into it as best he could.

Jake returned and Samson suggested that he should round up all available golfers for a meeting in his office later that afternoon. 'Not too fast for you Anne?' He took her shrug for assent and they set off for the range.

★

The team had assembled in Jake's office. Only Ian was still absent abroad. Jake sat behind his desk as always. The team ranged themselves in a semi-circle in front and Anne tacked herself on to the end. Samson stood by the empty trophy cabinet.

Jake called the team to order.

'Samson has some news he wants to give you. So listen up and ask any questions afterwards.'

Samson knew that he could be a skilful manipulator of the truth and of men, if the occasion demanded it. He saw this as such an occasion and if he was going to sell the stuff he might as well sell it big. He took the team through a colourful account, cobbled together from Jake's description and his own trial, of his recent experience with what he called 'the performance agent'. He made it sound like a glucose drink. He told them how it had improved the consistency and accuracy of even a giant of the game like him. He painted a picture of championship wins and untold millions. He played down the dangers and built up the benefits and safeguards. He was, he discovered, a born salesman. He finished by pointing at the empty cabinet. 'I want to see this full. Every shelf with shining silverware and our names in rolls of honour all over Europe.' It was in the bag and he winked at Anne.

'Right. Any questions.' There were two. 'Does it taste nasty?' and when that was answered in the negative, the final question was: 'Can we give it a go now?

Anne led the way to the range.

Samson, feeling more than a little deflated as the adrenalin drained away, sat on a low bench, legs outstretched, arms folded and watched his teammates. Their yells of surprise and whoops of satisfaction told him what he needed to know. His own success with the potion hadn't been a fluke. He could see that Anne had been telling the truth about it being a winning formula. He closed his eyes and tried to imagine himself as world number 1, lifting a major trophy. Where was the joy, the sheer delight he should have felt? Winning like this wouldn't really be winning, would it? Half an hour later, as his fellow golfers set out for the bar in an elated mood, laughing and slapping each other on the back, Samson made sure the range was open to the public again and then went back to his bunker practice, trying to shift the dark fog that had settled on his soul.

17 *Hartmann investigates*

The room in Hartmann Pharmaceuticals Ltd was gloomy. The blinds were three-quarters shut and the lights were all off. Three men sat round a table. One was clearly in the chair. This man, old, lean, his white hair perfectly groomed, spoke now with an American accent. 'Item three: alleged security breach. Don, what's the latest on this?'

The man addressed as Don, corpulent, sweating slightly, mid-fifties, looked in the notebook in front of him. 'We have him under surveillance and no question he's acting weird. We aren't sure he took anything out, though. Not yet.'

'Of course he took something out!' the old man snapped. 'What on earth would be the point otherwise?'

'Well, his bag wasn't searched, but it did have a tag and went through security. We haven't seen inside it, of course, but nothing appears to be missing from the building.' Don was sweating a little more.

'So he has a tag on his bag that security haven't put there. So who did?'

'Well,' said Don, 'I guess he must have done.'

'And just for fun, you think. He did it just for fun. Risked his career for an empty bag?'

'I guess not. But we have no proof.'

'Proof? What's proof? Since when did we need that stuff? He puts a tag on his bag, creates a diversion and walks out with it. That's proof. He's a senior analyst on £250,000 a year and he risks it for an empty bag. You nuts? Who's helping him? Anybody?'

Don Rawson shook his head. 'The surveillance shows that he has visited the security staff member Julie on a number of occasions in the last two weeks.'

'How many, what's 'a number'?'

'Four.'

'So they're having an affair. He's screwing her.'

'Again, there's no proof sir. We have no cameras in the house and they never go out as a couple so we can't observe their behaviour together.'

'So what's he doing? Meals on wheels? He's showing her pictures of his family? Of course he's tupping her, what else?

'There is one more thing sir. He paid a visit to Merricole early this week. Met someone there and left the building with them.'

'Who? Who did he meet?'

'We don't know sir. The camera angle was bad, but it was a man about the same age.'

'Camera angle? We have cameras in Merricole?'

'Not exactly sir. We're patched into their system. There's a slight delay but we see what they see. We've had it for six months. We can't identify the guy he met, but reception didn't bat an eyelid when he walked out. Badged up and all. He did a great job avoiding the cameras.

'And I suppose that isn't proof that Smalling is betraying us?'

'Looks pretty bad for him sir, but it would depend who he met and we don't know.'

'So,' said the old man, 'he took something out of the building, he's humping the security staff and meeting our rivals behind our backs. That does it for me. What code status do we have now? '

'Second stage, sir, Orange.'

The third man, his face in shadow spoke softly: 'Go to Code Red.'

Don was shaken. 'Red sir? That's Red? We have no hard evidence sir. We can't go to Red on that basis.'

The third man spoke again. 'Is that your considered opinion, Rawson, or just noise coming out of your unpleasant little mouth?'

Don looked terrified. 'Just noise sir.'

'Good. Then Code Red it is. And now the woman, what's her name?' The man moved his face from the shadows to reach for a pen on the table. He was young and good-looking, with ice-cold eyes.

'Julie Maidstone, sir. I interviewed her a few days ago. It was her annual appraisal so there was no reason for her to think she was being singled out or under any sort of suspicion.'

'And how was she?'

'Terrified, sir. She could hardly speak at first. I did the routine appraisal stuff and she calmed down a bit. When I raised the security incident she fell apart again. Obviously she knows she has done wrong and I suspended her for a month. If she comes back, which I doubt, there will have to be re-training.'

'I don't think she will be returning. Did she admit to an affair? Did she know why Smalling smuggled his bag out?'

'She admitted to a friendship and I could only press her so far on the affair. She said he came round to talk about things his wife wouldn't be interested in. Apparently they listen to music together. She swears he never laid a finger on her.'

'And you believed her?' This was the old chairman.

'No. I'm sure there is a lot more to it. So yes, I'm pretty sure he is sleeping with her, sir, yes, and it isn't because of her looks.'

'Anything else?'

'She did know, obviously, that he had taken his case out uninspected and used her for that purpose. She didn't seem to hold it against him though. She hadn't asked him what was in the bag, she said. The only thing she said of any note at all was about golf.'

'Golf? The game?'

'Yes sir. She said he had become obsessed with it in recent weeks. He talked of little else. When he talked of leaving the company, which he increasingly did, it was always in the context of golf; professional golf, she said. He even missed one of his regular appointments with her because he was going to see a group of pro-golfers, here in the Midlands somewhere, she believes.' Rawson stopped.

'And that's it?' the chairman again. Rawson nodded.

'Clearly guilty of several major breaches of company security and policy to the point where she has endangered the company's interests and possibly, very possibly, lives.'

Rawson was about to say something in Julie's defence when the younger man leant forward again and turned his eyes on him. Rawson sat back defeated.

'Code Red. Alert all agents, Rawson. With immediate effect.'

Rawson got up and left the room. As he approached his office, two burly men stopped him entering. They escorted him downstairs, out of the building and into a car. Two hours later his office was emptied of all contents except the desk and chair.

★

'But I'm scared stiff. I'm sure I'm being watched. From across the road. Just a feeling I have. And I keep thinking I'm being followed. What are we going to do?'

He knew that her fears were not baseless. It was perfectly possible that Hartmann was watching her. And him. God. Merricole. What if they'd seen him go to Merricole? Maybe the car switch with Anne had fooled them, if they were watching. Nevertheless he tried to reassure her.

'I can see why you might be scared. They know I got some bags out without a search and they've put two and two together. They think you helped. But they can't have proof of that because it isn't true. You didn't help me. They haven't got a stick of evidence against either of us, How can they build a case on nothing? So the worst they can do is sack us. And I'll take care of you; you know that.'

'But what did you take out? And why?'

'Just a personal item. Something I'd been doing for me, but in their time and with some of their stuff. But it was just for me. Just a new sort of painkiller, that's all.'

Selwyn could see that this was a poor explanation. To take the risk he did he must have wanted to shift a headache pretty badly. It had to be something immensely valuable. But Julie was by now head over heels in love with him and ready to believe up was down if he told her it was.

He wrapped her in his arms and held her against his chest, till she stopped crying.

'We will keep on seeing each other, won't we? You won't stop just because of this, will you? Will you?'

'Of course not. How could I stop seeing you after all this and all the good times we have together?'

'They are good, aren't they? You like them as much as I do, don't you? You must do or you couldn't keep doing it like you do. It's amazing.'

'Of course I do.' He was lying. The last few times he had been able to perform his duty physically, just, but the emotional side had gone. He just did not want to any more, with her at any rate, and finishing the job, from his point of view, had been getting harder. Even doubling and then tripling the dose had no effect.

'You know I do. It's obvious. I think you're lovely and I'm not going to stop seeing you. But there is a 'but', I'm afraid.'

He could feel Julie's eyes on him, but it had to be said.

'We have to give it a little rest. We need to stay apart for a little while. Just a little while. And it would be better if you were to use your work suspension to go away. I'll give you enough to keep you in comfort for a month or so. And then you can contact me and we'll take it from there.'

'Why, though, if there's nothing to worry about?'

'Because of the fact that we're seeing each other; they've found out that much and if they find out how much we're seeing each other and what we get up to, it's bound to make them think something is going on.' It was the best he could do on the spur of the moment. He had deeper fears for her than he wanted to say.

There were tears again before Julie agreed. 'Can we do it once more before you leave, and I promise I'll go away tomorrow, or the day after?'

Selwyn nearly sighed at the thought, but he didn't and he complied with her very reasonable request as best he could.

18 *Christopher Stamp*

Mitchell Walker had a phone he rarely used. He gave its number only to one or two people. People he wanted to be able to reach him at all times. It was housed where he worked and the enhanced signal beamed to every other device he owned. If he didn't answer, and it would have to be a very special set of circumstances that caused this omission, the responsibility was with his work people to answer and deal with the emergency. Because it was nearly always an emergency when that particular number was called. He had given it to Selwyn after their meeting two months ago, so real had been the fear that Mitchell had seen in his eyes.

Just a day or so later, on an early November morning, a red sun coloured the Thames but left the frosty lawn still sparkling white; Mitchell had just finished breakfast in the conservatory of his Thames-side house when that phone rang. The man on the other end introduced himself as Christopher Stamp and said he was acting on instructions from a close friend of Mr Walker, Selwyn Smalling, and that he had some urgent and important business to conduct. He asked for a password which Mitchell gave him without having to search for it. Stamp said he would very much appreciate it if Mr Walker could call at his office at his very earliest convenience and bring some solid ID with him, a passport and a driving licence would suffice. This morning would be appreciated.

So this was the solicitor Selwyn had told him about. He knew why the call was being made, of course. He knew there was no point asking his next question, and he wouldn't get an answer, but he said it because it was the most natural thing in the world to say: 'Has anything happened to my very good friend?'

'I understand your anxiety, but I am afraid I can tell you no more until we are face to face and I have seen your valid identification.'

Mitchell was in Stamp's office in Redditch as soon as he could organise transport to take him there. His office consented to a fast car and driver. 'Has it got clever plates? I don't want the police thinking they can stop me just because the driver's doing a bit more than their law allows. Oh good. Registered to? Okay. Still alive? No? Good. I'd sooner stiffs than prisoners.'

Mitchell was used to convenience in work-related matters, telephones, cars, houses, apartments, passports, money, weapons, information, travel, VIP lounges, hassle-free airport transfers were all standard perks. In return, the demands were high. In the ten years since he had worked with Selwyn at the university, Mitchell had demonstrated to the people who recruited him that he was worth every penny. But he made sure that the people who recruited him and others who thought they had secured his services from time to time, didn't know as much about him as they thought they knew. And that fact certainly applied to Selwyn Smalling.

Mitchell took in Stamp's office at a glance. Old school solicitor's lair. Solid desk with imposing tomes that were probably never opened. Heavy soundproofed door; sturdy but comfortable chairs; an antique glass-fronted bookcase and heavy plain blue curtains framing a window onto the street below. On one wall a photograph of a young and pretty HM the Queen looked across at a portrait of Winston Churchill in bulldog pose. Mitchell, who had been shown straight in to Mr Stamp's office, produced his ID, which Stamp photocopied and filed, shook hands and sat down.

Mitchell had the man sized up in no time. Shrewd, tough, seen-it-all-before mind lurking behind benign upper-middle class features and persona. A man designed to be underestimated. A man used to milking the misfortune of others without troubling his conscience.

'I hope I am not the first to bring this particular item of bad news?' Stamp's voice was firm but respectful and devoid of all accent.

'You are, but since Selwyn explained the circumstances under which this meeting would take place, I assumed there was some bad news. How bad?'

'You really do not know? That surprises me.' Mitchell wondered why he was surprised. What did he know?

'I am afraid Selwyn Smalling is dead.' Mitchell's face was deadpan. Stamp went on: 'I can see you are not overly distressed by the news. That is perhaps as it should be. My instructions were clear in any case. In the event of the arrest of Mr Smalling, I was to wait to see what the outcome was before acting in this matter and was to take further instructions if at all possible. If he failed to call for more than two days and if I could not subsequently contact him personally on a number he left me, I was also to act. In the event of his death, which happened yesterday evening, I was to act as soon as I learned of it. Fortunately, he had left a note with my number on it, in his wallet, asking that I be informed. The police found it and called me, just before I called you. They will undoubtedly pester me further.'

'The police are involved? So not a natural death. Aren't you finding all this a bit strange? Didn't you think Mr Smalling's request very odd? Were you not tempted to tell the police? In fact, don't you have a duty to do so now?'

'Not a natural death? All death is natural, Mr Walker. All death has an agent, a cause. But I know what you mean. His body was discovered in a bunker on a golf course. More than that the police would not tell me. Could not tell me, quite probably.

As for your second very pertinent question. My duty is to my client, dead or alive. I cannot exceed his wishes unless I am expressly ordered to by a judge, who would issue such an order only on grounds of national security or another matter of great general importance. Until that order arrives I will do exactly what my client paid me to do, no more and no less. I am not at liberty to help the police with their enquiries. I will leave that decision to you.'

Mitchell Walker knew this was not true. Stamp would tell the police everything the minute they asked. That couldn't be allowed.

Stamp handed him the package. It didn't look pristine. 'Has this been opened?'

'Not by me. It was not in perfect condition when I received it. If you mean am I aware of its contents, then no, I have no idea.'

Something about Stamp was not quite right. Mitchell was sure he was lying, or keeping something back at least. Stamp might warrant a second visit if anything started to go awry.

He signed for its receipt and left. Sitting in his car outside the office, Mitchell saw Stamp at the upstairs window and wondered how he would take what would happen next. A visit from one of Mitchell's less scrupulous associates. It would shake some of Stamp's established beliefs about England and the rule of law to the core. Mitchell hoped Stamp would have the sense not to get himself hurt, or worse. He opened the package quickly as if anxious to see what it contained. He read rapidly and with a sadness that surprised him a little, gave his instructions to the driver. '14, Pershore Road, Bridgenorth. There's no hurry.'

The door was painted a light shade of blue with the number 14 in large gold digits. There were a few steps with a handrail up to the door and bay windows on each side. 'Mid-Victorian', Walker muttered for no apparent reason. Nerves, probably. A faded sticker, 'Vote Green' was still in the window, above the one telling callers the occupants didn't buy anything at the door. Mitchell tried the handle gently, found it locked and went back to his car. He said something to the driver, who got on the car phone to call the office. Mitchell reached in the glove compartment and took out a device. He walked nonchalantly back up the steps, placed the thing over the lock, turned the door handle, pushed and disappeared silently inside.

Ten minutes later, calm and impassive, he came out again, closed the door carefully behind him, locked it with his device and got into the car, next to the driver. He seemed to be focused entirely on the steps and the car door, but he didn't fail to notice that a man walking a dog took a photograph of the car number plate as they drove away. The Hartman surveillance unit, he thought. Not part of his operation but not a threat.

'Good luck with that, mate,' he said under his breath, and his driver looked across at him, wondering what he'd said. Walker made another telephone call. 'No, nothing. Signs of something though. I'd say somebody got there before us. There was a Hartmann-type goon outside the house, so it could be a case of left hand and right hand. Yeah, I know, bloody amazing. No limit to bureaucratic cock-ups is there? Fine. I think so too. The wife's the one we need. I'm on to it. Seeds are sown.'

The man with the dog sent off the number plate photograph. The results showed the car was registered to James Cotter, a property developer in Bromsgrove. And what was left of him had been scattered ten years ago at a local beauty spot by a grieving wife.

19 Bury one get one free

F ive days later, on a suitably gloomy November morning a small group, including Anne and Mitchell Walker gathered at an old church in the village where Selwyn had lived, to lay him to rest. An autopsy had been performed and the date for an inquest set.

Anne had been surprised at how few condolence cards she had received from Selwyn's friends. It made her very sad to think he had so few. Chief amongst them in terms of its elegance and the suitability of its sentiments had been one from Mitchell. Anne had found it very moving and she determined to invite Mitchell to the funeral. Searching for a way to contact him, she found Mitchell's special number amongst Selwyn's effects and called it. He had picked up, unsure what to expect and found himself talking to Anne, whom he'd known through Selwyn, and not much liked, despite her charms. She wanted him at the funeral, because he was Selwyn's best friend still and almost no-one else had been invited, at Selwyn's request. He was happy to attend and he gave her his more regular number. 'That one you used is mostly for work,' he said, when he and Anne were alone in the single car following the hearse from undertakers to the church for the ceremony.

He offered his condolences and said she must call him if she thought he could help in any way. She thanked him and said she might well need his services. He asked about the autopsy results, which he already knew by heart, and she gave a vague reply. It seems he had a sudden and massive heart attack, she said, and that there had been an uncontrollable surge of adrenalin that had overwhelmed him. The inquest would say more, she hoped, but it looked more or less like natural causes. No one was suspecting foul play.

'I am,' he thought. But he said nothing.

'He told me he'd bumped into you a few weeks ago,' she said, 'when he went to Merricole. What was the meeting about?'

Mitchell shrugged. 'Just boring work. Joint ventures, information sharing, that sort of thing. He wanted me to join him in a private venture he was working on.' Mitchell was dangling a hook.

'Really? Well he was very keen to get to your meeting. Left me a bit in the lurch to attend it. I hope it was worth it.'

Mitchell was silent. She went on: 'Do you still do research, at Merricole? You still active in the labs?'

Mitchell shook his head. 'No. I wasn't much use to them. Never really good enough. Not like your genius husband was. He still rated me enough to ask me on board for his project though.' Still no reaction from Anne. He could wait. Give it time to sink in. 'So they moved me into other areas that suited my talents better. I ended up where I am now, in what we have to call product safeguarding services. PSS. Only one vowel short of the truth if you ask me. But it pays well, once you get well up the ladder.'

'It's a pity you and Selwyn drifted apart. He really liked you. He could have done with some stability and a good friend or two in the last years. He hasn't had an easy time and those bastards at Hartmann, and I mean it when I call them that, never really appreciated what they had in him.'

'They appreciated him to the tune of £250,000 a year plus bonuses, allegedly.'

'Which he never got. The bonuses I mean. In fact, at the last appraisal they actually fined him for underachieving against target. That's why he did what he did to them, I think.'

'What did he do?' Mitchell knew full well what he'd done. The beans Selwyn had started to spill at the meeting on the Thames had been poured out fully in the letter with the package. But Anne told him something new.

'Threaten to leave. He told them he was going to go. He said he had had an offer from Merricole. Did he?'

'Possible, but I wouldn't know about it. I'm more about firing than hiring. It didn't come up in the chat we had while he was at Merricole. He was talking about private work, with my help, but in addition to Hartmann, I thought.' Still no bite.

Anne put her hand on his arm and thanked him for coming. She knew he didn't really like her and, tall and obviously strong though he was, he wasn't her type either. Something not quite right about his eyes. She liked his calm, though. He seemed, what would be the word, steadfast. Yes, she thought, he seems steadfast. And he was a biochemist. And, it seems, Selwyn had trusted him and wanted to work with him.

A little later than scheduled, the two funeral cars arrived at the church. The coffin was taken from the hearse and the few mourners followed it up the aisle to a bench at the front of the chapel. After a mercifully brief ceremony - Selwyn's will had asked for no tributes as well as few mourners - the body was borne out to the grave, dug fresh that morning and still covered with a green astro turf sheet. The coffin, followed by the mourners, made its slow way down the central path toward the designated plot at the far end, next to a laurel bush.

The undertaker in charge of the ceremony went ahead and waited by the grave. When the coffin approached, carried by four of his employees, he bent down and pulled back the flap of Astroturf covering the mouth of the grave. He looked down into the pit and recoiled in horror, suppressing the shout of disgust and disbelief that rose in him. The mourners saw the look of horror on his face and stopped in their tracks. All but Mitchell, who raced around the coffin, looked in the grave and turned to indicate that no-one else should approach.

Down below, its head completely severed from the body and placed as if carefully by its side, was the corpse of a woman in a white shroud stained with deep patches of red. Her eyes were open and looking straight at Mitchell. *Well this is a neat touch,* he thought and wondered whose idea it had been and quite whom it was designed to impress. Him? Strewn across her bosom was a form of necklace chain with a round object. Mitchell knew it was a security tag. He knew from his visit to Julie's that she used them as coasters. He saw too that there was a red cross drawn on her forehead. He thought it best to say nothing about these two oddities. That's for the police to work out, he thought. He'd been expecting some sort of comeback ever since he'd paid her a visit and found he'd been beaten to it, by another branch of Hartmann probably, and this was presumably it. *You have to hand it to Hartmann. They know how to look after their own.*

Part 2 Villamoura

20 *Home alone*

The aftermath of the funeral had been horrible. Selwyn's body was taken back to the undertakers. Julie's body was removed and examined forensically. That there was foul play in her case was not in question and, of course, that fact cast doubt on the cause of Selwyn's sudden death. Another autopsy was ordered and this time the findings were less clear. The pathologist's report suggested that the adrenalin could have been externally administered and there did seem to be an excessive amount of a testosterone-like substance, possibly testosterone itself, the pathologist couldn't be sure, in the body. Selwyn's heart attack could have been induced by the person or persons responsible for Julie's death, since there was clearly a reason for placing Julie in Selwyn's grave, though no-one knew what it was.

Anne's sadness was not helped by the treatment the whole affair got from the press. She felt soiled by tabloid speculation about the alleged affair between the woman in the grave and the man who'd so nearly joined her there. The red-tops had a field day. They had no details of the affair, so they invented them, stitched together from interviews with neighbours, gossip from Hartmann workers and the odd phone hack. They published pictures of the two, side by side, as if they were together in the photograph.

She read the sickening, hypocritical press releases from Hartmann, lauding Selwyn and praising Julie, both loyal dedicated workers, according to Hartmann's PR statements. She wondered about suing them when extracts from glowing appraisal reports were printed. *Blatant lies.* She even got so far as ringing the family solicitor, Christopher Stamp and would have taken it further had he not strongly discouraged her. Not like him to miss out on an earner she thought. He sounded rather strange, too. As if he couldn't wait for the call to end. She called back two days later, but he was on extended leave, his office said. Anne found this unsettling, as if the ground was shifting beneath her. *Stamp on leave? Extended leave? That isn't like him. Dry old sticks who live for work don't just suddenly go off on leave. Maybe he's ill? But he didn't sound ill. He sounded scared!* Anne's conclusion did nothing to dispel the feeling that something was terribly wrong.

Anne stopped buying papers. Soon she had to stop watching the news. Now there were pictures of her, too. *Where the hell had they come from?* She recognised some as from an old photo album. She rushed upstairs and reached onto the top shelf of a wardrobe where the old albums were kept. There they were still. Had she or Selwyn put them online? She was sure they hadn't. Some of them were really quite private and some were beach shots she found very embarrassing. The media clearly thought otherwise and this part of her torment lasted some time.

At the inquest on Selwyn, because no-one had established any form of link beyond friendship between him and Julie, despite the sordid rumours and insinuations of the press, the coroner thought that on balance Selwyn's death was naturally caused, brought about by an accidental overdose of energy-related substances he was taking to boost his golfing performance.

The coroner also noted that the pathologist had been puzzled by the red dye marks, apparently indelible, across his forearms, in the shape, roughly, of a triangle. He thought these were unrelated to the cause of death. A red cross-like mark had been found on Julie's severed head. But the substance was very different, a sort of mud mixed with blood, her blood, and it could have been the result of the rough way the body had been handled generally. Even the police could see no connection between the two phenomena, despite the speculation, ranging from erudite to highly fanciful in the national press. More pictures of Anne, very fetching in black, continued to appear on a daily basis in the red-tops, one of which had got hold of those pictures of her in beach mode and dug up the story of her supposedly colourful youth to spice the story up and keep it running. Anne was mortified. The pictures were all from the one album. *How the hell had they got their dirty little hands on them?*

Only after the coroner's verdict, not to everyone's satisfaction, could Selwyn be buried and Anne was left to sort out her views and feelings as best she could. And gradually, things quietened down. By Christmas she moved from the front page to the inside stories as the press lost interest along with the police. Mitchell, who rang regularly to see she was all right, told her that somebody had a word with the chief constable and apparently orders gradually trickled down to the entire force. Even the more enthusiastic coppers got the message that this was not something to waste any more time on. She was grateful for that small mercy and never got round to asking Mitchell how he knew.

At home, alone, night after night and day after day, unable to face going to work and granted extended compassionate leave from her part-time job in a local college, Anne roamed the house as if to mimic the restlessness of her mind. To her surprise, she grieved for Selwyn. Her surprise came from the conviction that, whatever she'd said to Selwyn, she had never really loved him. Two whole days she wept, almost continuously, until a calm overtook her and she dried her eyes. Then she missed him, dreadfully. His wit, his insights, his inability to hold any view other than passionately, his sheer physical presence about the place. Other things tormented her: the empty bedroom, all the clothes in the wardrobe, his study and workshop full of the last things he was working on and the letters and articles he had written and sent, or written and discarded, to newspapers and magazines. Loved or not, he had been a huge part of her life, had shaped her thoughts and opinions, had helped her with college work and taken care of so much of the detailed and messy administration of her daily life. He was, she realised now, irreplaceable, in every way but one. She thought about their sex life. It had never been good. Either he couldn't get it up, or he couldn't keep it down. No middle way had ever been found. That's why she couldn't believe he had been 'seeing' Julie, a woman far less attractive than herself. Which Selwyn would she have appealed to? Not the sexless one and not the sexed-up one either.

And lastly, she came to the core of what she missed about him. He had loved her. As a person, as a wife and as a woman he had loved her and in doing so, had validated her. He had made her feel like the real deal and, given her starting point, given where she was when he rescued her, that was something she would love him for. Now that he was dead she could love him. She hoped he would know.

After a week or so she was able to think about her future. Before the death she had been on the brink of an affair with Jake. With the stuff in his veins, but unaware that was the cause, Jake had pursued her relentlessly and occasionally recklessly. She hadn't been planning on holding out much longer, but had wanted to make sure she extracted the maximum benefit from her capitulation. Now, since the death, understandably, Jake had kept his distance. He must have known she was deeply affected. It would have been obvious even to a man less sensitive than she gave Jake credit for that the horror of the whole business and the way the press had handled it meant that she would have no emotional room inside for anything else. So she wasn't surprised when he sent his condolences, didn't attend the second attempt at a funeral for Selwyn, offered his support but stayed away from her. And for a while she was glad of it.

But the day came when she felt it was time to get on with things. She rang Jake and invited him over to see her, making it very plain that she just wanted to talk about the work he had been doing with Selwyn and how it could now be taken forward. She sensed he was nervous, unsure how he should speak to her, so she told him: 'Don't treat me with kid gloves. There are no taboo subjects, but just remember I can't start up where we left off, because I'm not in that place any more. If and when I am, you'll be the first to know and if you've gone off the idea by then, so be it. I'll take the risk.'

He was round to see her next day, an unseasonably warm early January day: 'You've been through a hell of a time, Anne, it's great to see you looking so upbeat. That first funeral was the worst thing ever. At least they didn't try to use the same grave for the second one.'

'Well, they couldn't bury him in a crime scene, could they? Anyway, how are you? Still taking the tablets?'

'No. Stopped that when Selwyn went. In case there was a link, you know. In case it was the stuff. That got Selwyn, I mean. The boys are still going though. We've been very busy in your absence and I think we are about ready for the first big test.'

'There wasn't a link between the potion and his death, Jake. I think he was killed.' Jake was visibly shocked. 'By somebody wanting to make it look like he'd overdone it on uppers or something. It wasn't natural causes or self-induced. I just have this feeling about it. You know, when I came back from the funeral, the first one, I am convinced someone had been in the house. Just one or two things weren't quite where they should be and I'm sure I hadn't put them there. Selwyn's study and workroom were always a mess so they could have had a merry old root in there and I wouldn't know. But I think I know when somebody has been in my knickers drawer.'

'Like you said. You were just back from the funeral. You can't have been at your best. You could be imagining it.'

'True. But it would explain how all those photographs got out. So the feeling persists and is one of the reasons I think his death wasn't an accident either. Poor Selwyn'

'Connected with his 'promone' discovery, you think?' Jake's concern was audible. Anne, with the future of her project in mind, thought it best to defuse the tension.

'Nah. No-one knew about it. His firm accused him of a breach of security, though no-one's asked me about that and the company did their best to show respect for him, but a simple breach of security can't be enough for anyone to do this. You're right. I'm overwrought and imagining things. But if the stuff was in any way responsible for his death, you know like a freak bad reaction to it, then it could only be because he was overusing it, taking massive doses to keep improving. I think we have quite a bit to learn about the stuff yet. We need to treat it with a bit of respect, but there's nothing to say it isn't okay in reasonable doses. Worth the risk for fame and fortune, anyway.'

'We still want to give it a go, the boys and me. How about you? We need your say so.'

'No point stopping now, is there?' she said. 'It's Selwyn's baby; the only one he ever had and I'd like to see it through for him. It's a bit like he's still alive while we are following this through. I'm glad you're still up for it. Nobody reporting any ill-effects?'

'Side effects, you mean? No-one's said anything to me. It doesn't work so well on the driving part of the game, though it helps keep things long and straight and it's no use at all with putting, because the slopes and shapes of the greens means you're never repeating a shot exactly. Same problem with a few other specialist shots. Fantastic for the rest, though.'

' And you're not worried, given we can't be absolutely sure about Selwyn, not to mention the suspicion we'll come under from the authorities and the press, that It could be a little hairy, here and there.'

'Of course I'm worried. I've been inside and it isn't a day at the beach. I've always said I will never do anything ever again that could put me back inside.'

'But you've just said you want to carry on with the promone. Giving it to the boys.'

'I know, and I meant it.'

'But there is a remote chance that we could end up in trouble as a result. Why are you doing that? I could find another team.'

'Why am I doing it? Why did I do what I did last time I got done?'

'And is it the same reason this time?' Anne's voice was low.

'I think you know the answer to that. But there are no strings attached. I'll play along for the ride whatever happens to us'

'Well, it will be a very interesting ride.'

'And since I've raised the other matter,' Jake said, 'It did seem to me that something was happening between us before, before...all this.' He was speaking very gently. There were tears in her eyes. She nodded for him to go on. He waited while she wiped her eyes. 'Not surprisingly though, all this has knocked us both back a bit and maybe knocked everything on the head for good.' He put his hand on hers and spoke more gently still. 'But I am here for you, for whatever you need me for and whenever you feel the time is right, if you ever do, I am ready to pick up from where we left off. And if that time never comes .., so be it. You'll still have a good friend.' Anne wondered if he was sincere. She hoped he was even if only for his own sake. Hypocrites end up hating themselves eventually.

'Thanks,' she said, crying again and then smiling, 'that's good to know. At the moment all those parts of me are just dead. No response at all. I can't be sure if they'll ever come back. It was such a blow. And then the business at the funeral ...'

'I never mentioned I got an envelope with a photograph of me and you, did I? Was it from you?'

'No,' she said. 'Selwyn's idea. He was trying to soften you up. I told him it was a daft idea. I said it wouldn't work.'

'It did work. I'm not totally sure why, myself. But the photograph sort of said something about me, about who I was and what I was here for. Crazy, I know. But bloody Selwyn nailed my colours to your mast even before you walked into my office.'

She didn't reply and they sat a while in silence. The hum of the fridge from the kitchen emphasised how quiet it was. He broke the silence as softly as he could: 'Okay. Stop me if you don't want to hear any business stuff.' She motioned for him to carry on again. 'Right, then. Here's the deal. The boys have been practising like mad. No caddies or anyone else involved. They have their charts more or less complete and can use the drug and the codes without attracting attention and with incredible results. Samson looks like a world beater. If I could just get him to stop chasing skirt I'd be happier. He's like a wild man at the moment. No woman under fifty is safe near him, and I'm not sure about the older ones either. He seems remorseful one minute, says he's going to turn over a new leaf, then the next he's squiring some new thing round town.'

'Well so long as he keeps his mouth shut when his flies are open, we should be okay. Remind him what happened to Woods after the press got its teeth into his bed-hopping. So, that's good, then; when are we go?'

'Okay, we thought Portugal next month in a place called Villamoura. It's the Portuguese Masters' Championship. Big, but not mega. Ideal for our first. One snag, though, is the supply of the stuff. We're nearly out. How much have you got?'

She had very little, but something told her not to reveal it. 'Shouldn't be a problem. I'm sure we'll get back into the manufacturing process before long.'

'We?'

'Sorry. I was still thinking me and Selwyn. I mean, I will. I have his notes; in a secure place, don't worry. If this place was searched during the funeral they won't have found anything related to our project.'

'So where do you manufacture it?'

'Let's keep things on a need to know basis for now, shall we?'

'Fine by me. Listen. Why don't you come to Villamoura with us? You'll love the place and it'll do you good. You don't have to work do you?'

'That's a great idea, if I won't be in the way. It'll be so good to have a break. A bit of warmth and sun are just what the doctor ordered. And work isn't a problem for the next six months at least. They've been very good.'

She knew what Jake hoped would happen once he got her away from the baleful influence of the house and the memories, and could hardly begrudge him his hopes. She was hoping for a similar renewal herself. 'Great,' he said, opening the door to leave. 'Don't forget the supply issue.'

As soon as he had left she picked up her phone, called up the contacts list and selected a number.

'Hi,' a voice said. 'You've reached the voicemail of Mitchell Walker. Sorry I can't... ' the automated message was interrupted by a real time voice. ' Hello, Mitchell here, sorry about that. Couldn't get to my phone in time. Who is it?'

'Mitchell, it's Anne. You know you said if there was anything I wanted, anything at all and you could help, you would?'

Mitchell confirmed his intention to serve her in whatever capacity she might desire.

'Well, I have something in your line of work I'd like to talk to you about, but not on the phone.'

'My line of work?' Mitchell said.

'The one we talked about before, at the funeral. Biochemistry. Do you want to come over for dinner one evening?'

21 Phillip Henshaw

Portugal, Phil Henshaw decided, was not meant for the winter, not by nature, design or inclination. On a January day like this one, under dark cloud with regular rain and a temperature of 16 degrees, the landscape looked dreary and defeated. The faces of the visiting golfers betrayed their disappointment at the lack of blue skies and warmth. Phil's few Portuguese friends loved it though. A few weeks when they could use the whole of the day, didn't have to shutter their houses against the heat, forgot what the flies could do to your food and slept in peace in cool and airy bedrooms.

Phil didn't mind. It was great to be back in Villamoura whatever the weather. He stopped his car on the hill above the course. Looking down he could see the eighteenth fairway where, years earlier, he'd had just about the best day of his life. He pulled an old newspaper from the briefcase on the back seat. It was yellowed and stiff with age but the memories it called up in Phil were fresh as yesterday. He'd been king for a day here. He'd won it, lost it and won it again. Life dealt some odd hands. Of all places to start a new career it had to be Villamoura. His mood was upbeat. He'd won here before. He was damn well going to make a success of it again. He laughed at himself. *You self-important prat. It's just a job. Get on with it.*

He drove his car to the entrance and parked self-consciously in the spot freshly marked out as 'reserved: P. Henshaw. Chief Executive (Euro tour)'. He walked to the rails on the edge of the course, closed his eyes and bowed his head. Villamoura. That magic win. At what point in his life does a man recognise how much he has changed, grown, become almost a different person? Usually when he meets an old colleague or friend who hasn't made that trip and who shrinks before his eyes. The old self found things exotic and scary that the new man finds commonplace and routine. Villamoura had been a key moment on the path that had taken him from small town, small-minded golfer to whatever he was that made him worthy of filling this new post. The sort of man he once was had struggled with the cosmopolitan challenges of tour golf. He had found himself intimidated by it all. Alone on tour and unable to make an impact he'd given in to too many of the temptations of a travelling man. *Oh God, what a shit I was. A prize prat who thought he was the bees' knees when I'd got drink inside me or a woman in my bed.*

His wife had helped him at first, boosted his confidence. *Thank you Helen, I wonder if you know you saved my life.* But then came the rows, over money, over his constant travelling, over almost everything. Soon his wife was the biggest of his worries. So he avoided calling her. *Have you forgiven me Helen? I am so sorry for what I did, but I couldn't see it was my fault. I just thought you didn't* know what I was going through. It never occurred to me that the truth was just the opposite.*

There were times, sitting in terrible hotels, hungry and wondering how he was going to pay his caddy, when he thought his wife was right. He should give it up. But then he'd go out, the sun would be shining, the crowd would get behind him, he'd find himself out with some local favourite or international star and for few hours, all would be right with the world and he knew who he was again and what he wanted to become. *Yup, there were good times. Maybe more than I know. I'm not always sure I'm remembering it right, because when it was good it was very good and when it was bad I was usually drunk.*

He limped on for a few years, waiting for the time he would turn the corner and make it into the elite. His wife left him, took the house and the kids. He didn't stop loving them, he loved them still, but he loved golf more. *It's true, Helen, I still do in my way. I still care for you all. I hope you know that.* And, strangely, with his wife gone, his game got better. He started climbing leader boards that had scared the pants off him only month before. He was beating big names regularly, making money, sending good wages home, ringing his now ex-wife with more confidence and hearing in her voice what she would never say, he suspected: that she was sorry for doubting him. *That was my arrogance Helen. I just assumed you'd come to your senses when I should have been making all the moves. When I did, it was too late. You'd gone for good. My fault. Mea maxima culpa.* And then Villamoura. His high point. The making of him and very nearly the undoing of him too.

Villamoura. For three days he blitzed the course. Sixty-six, sixty-six and sixty-nine put him 5 shots ahead of the Spanish favourite at the end of the third day. *Jesus, that felt so good. I felt so good. I couldn't believe how I was striking the ball. And I was sober.* He handled the TV interviews with aplomb and hoped his ex-wife was watching. He didn't want her back. *Of course I did. I just thought I could snap my fingers and you'd come. What a stupid idiot.* But he did want her respect.

But golf championships are four day events and the evening before the final round tests a golfer's mettle like nothing else. Phil tried to keep out of everyone's way, ducking the press interviews, avoiding the bars, but there were people everywhere. Some wanted to offer advice, some to get it. Some had business plans to show him. Others just wanted an autograph and a photograph. And then there were women. *Oh my God, the women.* It seemed they were everywhere and they were nearly all good-looking and obviously keen to share the company of a soon-to-be famous, soon-to-be rich golfer. One in particular stopped him in his tracks. She was a dark-haired, dark-skinned woman with a figure he couldn't keep his eyes off. *I don't think I've ever felt what I felt when I saw her. It was like dissolving with lust.* He saw from her smile that his interest hadn't gone unnoticed. She came across to him and introduced herself:

'Hi. I'm Sofia. I saw you play today.' Her large dark eyes looked straight into his. Her hand was on his shoulder. Phil was melting. 'But tonight I think you need to relax. All that courage deserves a drink and you can buy one for me, too.' Her English was perfect and her voice soft and full of promises. Phil looked into her eyes. *Bottomless; deep as my life.* It was the only place he dared look, but it didn't stop him being aware of the rest of her, now very close to him.

He had fallen for this sort of treatment before and from less attractive sources than this. One more wouldn't hurt, would it?

His mobile phone rang. Just in time. He flipped it open and pulled out the antenna. It was his ex-wife, wanting to congratulate him, or talk money, or the boys. He made his excuses to Sofia. *I can still feel now how my heart was beating. I was cursing you Helen, even as you were saving me, I was cursing you.*

'Hi. You being a good boy and getting plenty of rest? I saw your interviews, by the way. You looked great, honestly, I don't know, sort of in control. And modest, bloody hell were you modest. Don't be too much like that tomorrow or you'll not win. Get out there telling yourself you're the best there is and stick it to them. We'll all be watching. Your dad's coming over to watch with the kids. What you up to now?'

'Not a lot.' Phil's blood was starting to move round his body at a more normal rate. Lust was giving way to a leaden common sense. *I've never wanted to be good less in my life. It was as tough as anything I've ever done. But I did it. I went to bed alone.* 'I'll just take a few course plans, tomorrow's positions and stuff, to bed, maybe watch a video of some of today's play and try to get some sleep. That might be the hard bit.'

They talked for a few minutes more. He knew he still loved her and God, did he owe her! He wondered vaguely whether there was a prospect of a reunion and whether he even wanted it. *I'm not sure that's how it was. I think it was like I said earlier.* He wanted the kids. *That's certainly true.* He missed them like mad. She wished him well and said the kids were wild with excitement. He closed his phone and thought for a minute of returning to the bar to see if the lady with the heart-stopping curves was still there. He stood still with clenched fists for a full minute before turning away and heading for his own room. *Well I tried.*

Just after midnight he fell asleep. Five minutes later he woke up as the villa door downstairs closed softly and he heard footsteps mounting the stairs. Only his manager and agent had keys, and probably, he then realised, half the staff of the golf course. He was more curious than afraid and he switched on the bedroom table light just as the door of his room opened. *You'd think I'd be scared, but I guess I knew what was happening. I'm not sure I wasn't hoping it was her. Was I? Bloody memory!*

The two women put their fingers to their lips and walked over to his bed. He would have said something, but one of the women was the dark-haired one with the shattering figure. She reached her hand behind her back, tugged the zip and let the red dress fall to her ankles. He had not been wrong about the figure and he felt himself respond, powerfully, despite all the warning bells beginning to ring. The second woman, smaller, slightly heavier but with beautiful red lips and flashing eyes removed her dress too and Phil could not but admire the underwear.

They moved to the bed and Phil, in his last message from planet common sense, signalled that they should stop. 'Ladies. I don't do this sort of thing.' He was about to lie that he was a married man, but he realised firstly that they wouldn't care and secondly, that his erection was winning the battle with his conscience and he didn't much care either.

The one he really fancied sat down on the edge of the bed, pushed the duvet cover back and looked down to where his real intentions were undisguised. She took hold of him softly, applied gentle pressure and moved her hand deliciously up and down. *No memory problems now. Can you blame me? This was the best and worst moment of my life to that point. Is that true? Only in a sense, probably. The best sensual moment, and the worst moral one.* Phil was aware, dimly, that the other woman had moved round behind him and entered the fray. A hot shock of lust filled his lower gut and he reached out to the one he could still see. She moved compliantly into position beside and beneath him whilst the one behind him pressed her breasts into his back and did something unspeakably nice with her hands.

Phil was beyond thought. *I can't vouch for a single thing from here on. Whether it was the booze or the other, I don't know.* As with his golf, his body took over and his mind stayed well out of it. Things happened to him that he had not experienced before, even remotely. It occurred to him that these two were no ordinary golf groupies. He was even more certain when the one he fancied ever so slightly less, slid a condom over his second, or possible third, erection and guided him to the one place in the universe he really wanted to be at that moment. The thought that these ladies had been sent by someone other than a well-wisher, died in his conscious mind at the point of entry and he fell into a deep well of pleasure that lasted for a long, long time. *I'm ashamed now. I don't think I was then, was I? I'm not sure I should be ashamed now, but I just am. Why analyse it further? Helen, I am so sorry. If I ever get the chance to make it up to you I will, whatever it takes.*

It was four-o-clock when they left. The stock of alcohol in the fridge and cupboard had disappeared, largely into Phil.

When they had gone, he slept at last, not deeply nor dreamlessly as he had hoped and imagined, but fitfully with increasing panics about the day ahead.

At seven, his manager popped his head round the door, took in the general dishevelment of the place and the empty bottles, knew at once what had happened, shook his head and said. 'Breakfast in half an hour, then range, then interviews. Get your arse in gear, Henshaw. England expects and so does your bank manager.'

What followed was the worst and the best day of Phil's life. *I suppose that's even more true of the day than the night. I can't let one bloody night define me though. And I don't think I have. It's just a pity, Helen, that you haven't been part of it. Take care, love. Kiss the kids for me. Or are they too big for that now? Say hi, then, and tell them their Dad loves them to bits.*

22 *Marilyn Duclos*

P hil turned from the railing at the sound of his name. 'Mr Henshaw?' Phil admitted it. 'I'm really pleased to meet you at last.' The woman addressing Phil, with just a hint of a French accent, was tall, with handsome suntanned features and shoulder length hair. Phil liked her instantly. She had a radiant smile, directed straight at him on full power. 'My name is Marilyn. Marilyn Duclos. I head the admin team?' The upward inflexion, not normally a favourite with Phil, seemed fine to him in this context. He made a note to forgive it in his daughter next time. 'There are four of us, all female I'm afraid.' Phil saw no reason for fear. She indicated a direction she wished him to go and they walked side by side out of the car park.

'Miss Duclos. I have seen your name at the bottom of some very elegantly written letters.' She accepted the compliment with just the slightest of nods and a quick glance sideways at him. 'And I can tell you too that your team's reputation goes before it.'

'Really? In a good way I hope.'

'In the very best of ways. My predecessor and all the tournament directors tell me that your team is the one absolutely indispensable element in this whole tour organisation. Without your team, nothing would get done.'

'That is very flattering, Mr Henshaw ...'

'Phil, please. I prefer informality.'

'Very flattering. Would you like to meet the team? They are at their busiest at the moment with the tournament just a few days away, as you will appreciate. But they will of course not forgive me if I did not introduce you to them, Mr Henshaw.'

'Phil.' He said.

She nodded her apologies. 'That may be a fault of ours. We are sometimes a little formal and reserved. But four women, three young women and me, we need to be able to keep a distance from all the footloose young men, caddies, players, technicians and so on, who approach us sometimes in ways their wives and girlfriends would not approve. We have need of formality at times, until the rules are understood.'

Phil smiled. He had heard about these women. He knew that they were formidable. He knew, too, from his predecessor, that they were not nuns. 'Of course, ' he said, 'perfectly understandable.'

'I hear you won this tournament Mr Henshaw (he gave up) some years ago. That must have been some day for you.'

'More than ten years ago. I was lucky.'

'I looked up in the records. You were not lucky. You had three excellent rounds and were 5 shots ahead on the last day. You would have been unlucky had you not won.'

'Well, I had a bad night's sleep, was feeling pretty off on the tee and was back to level before I knew it. And I was playing with the local hero, who then went one shot up with the crowd cheering him to the rafters.'

But I know you won, so how did you get it back?

'That's where the luck comes in. There was a tremendous thunderstorm and we were off the course for three and a half hours or thereabouts. I slept through it all and came out fresh as a daisy. My opponent made a bad error on the last hole and put his ball in the water. You know the last hole here? Very dangerous and he took a risk he didn't need to.'

'And you, Mr. Henshaw, didn't take a risk?'

'No. I played too cautiously.' He saw her amused look. 'Not something I was always known for. Is that why you're smiling?' She smiled some more and nodded, ' but my bogey was better than his double so we went to a play-off. By that time, it was too dark to continue. I had a great night's sleep and we came back the next day. His supporters had gone and I could tell he was beaten, just from the look in his eyes.'

'What sort of look was it?' she said.

'Well, not to put too fine a point on it, he looked as if he'd spent the night with some very active ladies. And perhaps he had.'

He looked to see if Miss Duclos was shocked. He needn't have worried. The radiant smile had returned.

'You see how history gets it wrong,' she said. 'I heard exactly the same story about day four. Except you were the one looking shagged out, Mr Henshaw.'

'Phil.' One last try.

'Phil.'

23 *Brief encounters*

C ristina had been woken by a phone call at three-thirty to be told there was a staffing emergency, and had been at work behind the coffee bar in the main transit hall of Faro airport since five.

She spotted her supervisor across the hall. He was heading in her direction. Oh God. More groping. She wiped her brow with a hand towel and prepared herself to repel boarders. This one was no worse than the rest. More persistent maybe.

'Hi Cristina. Why you look like that?' He was Moroccan. Almost nobody here was Portuguese and Cristina resented the expectation, from customers and staff, that she should be a polyglot for 10 euros an hour.

'A double shift might be one reason. Lecherous German customers might be another. And that dim-wit', she pointed to her only assistant on the stand, a young man of Lebanese origin, 'is definitely number three. If he ever gets anything right first time he ruins it by getting the next thing doubly wrong. It's crazy. You should fire him and get me some real help. And hire a few people who turn up for their shift more than half the time, too.'

'Ah Cristina. You lovely when you are angry. You lovely when not. You just lovely.'

By now his arms were round her waist and he manoeuvred her into the small private space behind the bar. The was just room for them and a broom cupboard. His hands were making free with her. 'You give me kiss and I see what I can do. You give me more than kiss and I will definitely do it.' His breath smelled of stale onions.

'Okay, if you promise. It will have to be quick. Einstein out there won't last long on his own.' She saw him grin. She had him now, 'But not here. In the cupboard.' She opened the door and felt the trapped heat on her face. She stepped back a little and with a quick kiss on his cheek she pointed inside. He squeezed her breasts as he passed her and went into the hot dark cupboard.

'Not enough room in here for ...'

Instead of following him in, she shut the door and turned the key. The light switch was on the outside and she made sure it was off. There was no seat in the cupboard and barely room to sit down. She heard his knocks on the door. Gentle at first and then louder. Then furious. Out front though, as Cristina knew from previous experience, the noise was lost in the general hub-hub of Tannoy announcements, the echoing din of a thousand people in a big vaulted hall, and the hiss and gurgle of the coffee machine. He was safe where he was for a couple of hours. And if he passed out, or worse, well so much the better. None of the others had died. And if it cost her the job, so be it.

She was glad Faro was not the biggest airport, because the work was bad enough as it was. For a while she ran between the bar and the tables, serving, making coffee, shouting at the dim-wit, taking money, putting croissants in the microwave and smiling, always smiling, no matter what she felt. A German tourist put his hand on her bottom. If she'd been wearing a skirt instead of trousers it would have been worse. Cristina reacted and dropped a half full glass of orange juice on his nicely pressed trousers. She was proud of the way practice made it look so natural the German actually apologised for startling her. She gave him some paper towels and went off to get the croissant and jam he'd ordered. She picked a stale one from yesterday's leftovers and spat in the small tub of jam. Her smile as she set the dish down before him was angelic. Two hours later, she released her sweating, exhausted, chastened captive.

In a brief lull, about eight, she saw a young man, quite tall and extremely good-looking, tanned even in February, not always a good sign, but well-dressed in white trousers and a blue linen shirt, leave the arrivals hall and head toward her. He carried a single leather bag, slung casually over his shoulder. As he got nearer, he caught her eye and came to the bar.

'Buenos Dias,' he said in Spanish, 'Habla Ingles?'

She thought for a second. Why couldn't the damned English be bothered to learn a language or two? She decided this one was worth a bit of trouble, though.

'No Senhor. Pero hablo Espanol.'

'Ah. Soy Ingles. Hablo solo un poco Espanol. Tiene un cafe para mi?'

'Cafe con leche?'

'Perfetto, grazias'

They looked at each approvingly for a while. She smiled encouragement at him.

'Quieres cenar con migo esta noche?' He was trying to ask her out for dinner.

She laughed and decided to wait a little longer to see what the limits of his Spanish were. He had reached them, almost.

'Cenar? Con usted? No es posible para mi tener la cenar con un ombre que no se'

She thought he looked a little disappointed, so she said:

'Pero donde? En que restaurante? A que hora? It could be interesting to get to know you.'

She knew that would make him laugh. 'So you do speak English. Look, here's my number. I'm staying at the Villamoura golf resort. Call me anytime tonight. Maybe we can eat about ten, or earlier if you want.'

'Are you playing golf this week?' He nodded.

'Are you famous?

'Soon will be,' he said. She looked at the name on the card he handed her.

'What a strange name. Samson Gregory. Samson. Are you strong?'

'Sometimes, but just now I'm weak at the knees. You are very pretty.'

'I know. Too pretty for you. But if I get no better offer, perhaps I give you a ring.'

She finished making his coffee, set it down in front of him and watched as he downed it in one.

'Best offer in town. Just wait till Sunday. You'll be fighting through crowds to get what you can have for free tonight. So long as your name isn't Delilah.'

'Cristina', she confessed.

She saw him look away and followed his gaze down the hall of the airport. A man, nowhere near as attractive as the one in front of her, and this time obviously English, was hurrying towards the arrivals hall.

She felt Samson grab her hand and raise it to his lips. A gallant Englishman? she thought, in no particular language. She heard him say he would see her later.

Cristina watched him go and thought he probably would.

★

Samson set his face into what he hoped was an expression of disapproval. His caddy, Larry Topham, had clearly had a bad morning and Samson's duty, as he saw it, was to make it worse. Caddies had to know their place. Give them an inch and they'd be ruling you. Too many of them already thought they won the tournaments, with the golfers little more than stunt men. Topham was about to learn his place.

'Where the hell have you been? I've been hanging around here for bloody hours. What's going on?'

'Sorry boss, I completely forgot you weren't coming to the course by taxi and I hadn't got the hire car. Frank's caddy was using it and we only have one between the two of us. No excuse, no excuse. Still, from what I could see you were making good use of your time. Good-looking chick. Miles better than some of the monkeys you've been running around with. You pulled?'

'None of your sodding business and what do you mean 'monkeys'?'

'Well, you know. There's been a lot going on on that front lately and I suppose the barrel gets close to empty at times. The bottom has to be scraped. And not all the scrapings were as tasty as that young girl at the coffee bar.'

Samson was horrified. Not only was his caddy wresting the initiative from him, he was doing it in an almost humiliating way. Samson decided he had better give the managerial reins a sharp tug.

'Christ Larry; you're not paid, and paid a bloody fortune I have to say, to document my love life. You're paid to make sure I win this bloody tournament. So what have you been up to?'

Larry ran through his list: he'd got the kit and the clubs across to Villamoura, checked the villa, sorted the early administration, made sure everything would be okay for Samson, booked a couple of practice rounds, one a really tasty one with a couple of Ryder cup veterans and seen Samson draw an extremely rich partner in the pro-am.

'Not bad for a man with a hangover,' Samson conceded, 'good caddy party last night was it? You sounded rough when I rang earlier. You know, the call where I asked you to pick me up? Were you still in bed?'

Larry said nothing.

'You look a bloody disgrace, Topham. Here's me doing my best to look like the sponsors want me to look out on the course and waddling up behind me is a belly with a bag strapped to it and a bright red face gasping for air. Pull yourself together. This is a sport. We're supposed to be role models.'

They boarded the small hire car Larry had begged off a mate and drove out of the airport onto the motorway for the short trip to the golf resort. Samson knew it well and it was one of his favourites, luxurious and full of high and low-life distractions. The bars, restaurants, and general facilities were all five-star. As was the local brothel. Larry promised that Samson's rented villa was one of the best on the course. When he talked about the tournament admin staff, the four women who really made it all tick, Larry was just doing what his boss expected of him. Two were possible, one a highly probable, but their boss, Mme Duclos, untouchable, according to Larry's account. Samson listened and wondered if he could be bothered with any of them. He found himself wanting to make the Friday cut more than almost anything else. Still being in the tournament for the final two weekend days had become the most important thing to him. Or suddenly, the second most important thing. The first was whether the coffee bar girl would call as promised. How had that suddenly become a priority?

Samson was half asleep next to Larry as he ran through the arrangements he'd made: a practice round at two this afternoon, Monday, with Martin and Sergio (and Larry confirmed he meant the Martin and Sergio; which woke Samson up a bit and made him whistle in appreciation), another round on Tuesday morning, no partner yet signed up, and then the sponsor's day pro-am competition on Wednesday when he'd drawn the only billionaire in the field as his partner, the sponsoring body's owner and chief executive. Larry assured his boss that a brand new car, delivered in any country he chose, would be the least he could expect if he guided the big man to victory in that.

What Larry had described had made an impression on Samson, who was now sitting up, thinking hard. Five minutes later the little hire car pulled up in the car park of the golf resort.

Larry went round to Samson's side of the car and opened the door for him. Still deep in thought, Samson got slowly out of the car and stretched the last of the tiredness out of his body. 'Larry,' he said, with an unexpected rush of affection and goodwill for his hard-working caddy, 'you and me, we're damn well going to win this one.'

'Yes, boss. If you say so.'

★

By the side of the media tents and huts, and the rows of terrapins and temporary offices that housed all the administrative and executive officials of the European Tour circus, a huge trailer had been parked. Inside, five or six staff had a small office and an adjoining workshop. The Ping guy sat chatting to the Callaway guy. Samson stopped, out of sight, just outside the door to this trailer. He listened with a smile on his face to the two men extolling the virtues of their respective brand. '450 yard drives with our new ball and driver. You'll need fairways longer than airport runways.' 'Sure. 400 yards off line and into trouble. We just go for straightness; leave length to the golfer'

Samson, tall, lean and looking fitter than for years, mounted the steps to the trailer entrance and stepped inside. He had a problem club to be fixed. He could see they recognised him and they greeted him warmly enough.

Samson was looking for the first of the two and the man identified the problem straight away when Samson offered him the club. They went outside and Jeff, that was his name, carried out some measurements, put the club inside a laser machine and read some results off a computer, before putting the club gently and well protected into a vice and hitting it forcefully with a hammer. Then it was back to the laser and the measurements and the treatment was pronounced a success. 'There you go,' said Jeff, 'Patient fully recovered.'

Samson smiled and shook his hand.

'How long you been with us Samson?' Samson told him.

'Are you going to win for us this time?' Samson told him he was good and ready and at 66-1 a bloody good bet.

The engineer looked interested. They shook hands and the man went into the trailer to rejoin his pal. Samson waited outside the door.

'Think he's got a chance?' the Callaway man asked.

'If he doesn't get too pissed and keeps away from the women, he's definitely got a chance. He says he's good and ready.'

'He may be ready. He'll never be good. Not using your stuff anyway.'

'66-1, though. I'm going to have piece of that.'

Samson heard the unintended advice and slipped away, with a little bit more determination added to his growing inner conviction. This was his tournament. He felt ready to be good, too.

★

At two that afternoon, two seasoned professionals, one a major championship winner and both of them Ryder Cup warriors were waiting on the first tee, ready for a practice round. Their caddies were chatting nearby. The course, rolled out over sixty immaculate acres, was in magnificent condition. Everywhere was sparkle. Emerald, silver and white. Exotic foliage embellished the rolling green vistas; the white villas, for members or visitors, were pristine. Opulence, luxury, nature tailored to perfection and a sky that was faultlessly blue. It was only February but the temperature was twenty-two degrees. The light breeze was warm and scented.

Everything was in place. Only Samson was missing.

The golfers checked their watches. Martin called to his caddy. 'We'll lose the slot if we don't get off soon. You sure we are waiting for a third? His voiced betrayed his Teutonic origins only slightly.

'Deffo.' He consulted his sheet. 'Sammy Gregory. Never knowingly prompt.'

Sergio groaned. 'We might as well get started. He'll have his leg over a barmaid somewhere. I don't know how he gets away with it. If I did it, after one go, I'd have a paternity suit slapped on my ass and a posse of divorce lawyers waiting for me in the scorer's tent. Come on Samson; where the hell are you?'

As if in response a golf buggy careered over the hill and stopped abruptly next to the tee. Apologies were given and accepted and the golfers shook hands. Samson drew his ball out of the caddy's hat and went to drive first. The others watched him. Samson, elastic and balanced, knew he had a swing others envied. Even these two would be taking notes. And this time he was going to turn his talent into results. He was going to show the world who was boss. He aced it.

'Ball' said Martin. 'Great ball. You been putting some work in?'

'What him?' said Martin's caddy, nudging his friend Larry, 'Work's a four-letter word'

They set off, the three golfers ahead of the three caddies. After four holes Martin's caddy confessed his astonishment to Larry. 'If your guy gets his putter going and if he can take this form into the tournament, you're on for a top ten.' Samson didn't let up. He burned the course up as if to impose his will on it. It was a tour-de-force and Samson convinced himself that the promone stuff had almost nothing to do with it.

After the full eighteen holes, Samson swaggered off the course aware of the impression he had just made on two of the tournament favourites. Larry told him later that word had got round and there wasn't a caddy in the tournament who hadn't seen 66-1 as the way to an easier life.

★

At seven precisely, Samson's phone rang. A broad grin split his handsome features. 'Great. That would be delightful. Where can we find you?'

Cristina's call convinced him this was going to be his event. He sent Larry, busy polishing shoes and clubs and waiting for the laundry to finish, to collect the young lady who, if he examined his feelings more closely than he was wont to, had struck a chord that resonated with greater sweetness than he had ever heard.

24 *Uneasy lies the head ...*

P hil was enjoying a rare moment of time to himself. It had been hard work to get it. All the crap no-one else wanted dropped on his desk. The pressure Phil had anticipated had arrived threefold. Free for now and wanting to clear his head, he wandered through the tents and the offices and onto the fringes of the course, soaking up the atmosphere. It was still only a practice day, Tuesday, but there were already sizeable crowds following the leading players as they rehearsed for the bigger days ahead. He leaned on the rails round the practice putting green and watched one of the world's most famous screen faces practising for the pro-am tomorrow. Pretty good golfer too, Phil noticed. He admired the smoothness of the actor's action as he stroked the ball into the hole, time after time. Smooth bastard in every way, then.

He looked in at the physiotherapy trailer and booked himself a free massage for later. Getting back on the golf range after a long lay-off had come at the price of a bad back. Useful stress management though. Belt your aggression out on the golf ball and keep calm at other times.

The guy who booked him in asked for some credentials and when Phil produced a card: PGA, Tournament Chief Executive, he noticed the masseur become more respectful and he liked that. Phil noted that his appointment placed him between two major winners and thought that was good enough for him. This job was no more than he deserved. He'd done his time, he thought. He'd paid for his sins, done right by his wife and children, made himself honest and self-respecting again, kicked the booze, worked bloody hard in the service of the game and this was his reward. He was determined to make the most of it. *There's a price to pay for leadership, so make sure you don't miss out on the rewards.*

He wandered slowly towards the driving range and saw Samson Gregory coming towards him, with a very pretty young woman; a local probably. They were clearly getting on very well and Samson's eyes were bright as he looked at her. Phil had known Samson years ago, had in fact taught him as an apprentice. He was just about to hold out his hand and utter some sort of greeting, when the couple hurried past, not even glancing in his direction and with no hint of recognition from Samson. *No change there then; still self-obsessed and chasing skirt.*

Phil turned to see who they had been so eager to greet and saw a man he recognised from his early playing days as Jeremy 'Jake' Godwin, and a strikingly proportioned good-looking woman in dark clothes and red shoes. *Wow. Jake's doing well if he's got a piece of that.* He was pleased to see an old friend like Jake. They hadn't spoken for ages! He saw Samson introduce the young woman to the other two and watched the four of them walk away, laughing, towards the villas.

Phil saw two young boys run up to Samson waving autograph books and pens. Samson smiled, spoke to them while Cristina translated, wrote in their books and patted them on the head. Phil was surprised. The Samson Gregory he had known was an arrogant little tyke, immensely gifted but who thought the world owed him a major championship and that he could get one without too much effort. And what Phil read of his career antics since then hadn't changed his view. So what was going on with Samson? And what a pretty girl! Out of my league, he thought. But who isn't these days? *Maybe Marilyn would give it a go with her boss? A bit of a risk for her, and for me. Worth taking though.*

★

He stopped outside the equipment manufacturer's trailer, watching with amusement the strange mixture of hi-tech measuring and aligning and old fashioned blacksmithing. The day had warmed up considerably and the sky, a routinely cloudless blue, promised much for the week ahead to Sunday. There was the pro-am tomorrow, and he'd already seen the quality of celebrity that had attracted, and then four days of competition. On a day like this it would be easy to forget the crushing nature of some of the problems facing him. He'd been reading the memoirs of a recent prime minister. *God, those guys have it tough. Even tougher than me.* On his first day in office Downing Street staff had taken him to one side and told him things that terrified him. Dangers, threats, horrifying events, things on the horizon that could spell the end of humanity. And all were burdens he would have to carry alone and in silence. Avoiding the end of the world was his responsibility and a burden he couldn't share. *Well, I know a bit about that.*

Phil didn't fool himself his problems were as important, but there were memos in his in-tray about matters which he would have to call right or lose his job and risk wrecking the tour as a whole. *And stuff I can't broadcast or delegate.* This walkabout was having the effect he hoped it would have. He felt the strong pulse of the tournament and the beating heart of enterprise and competition as a welcome counterblast to the horrors of his in-tray and his spirits lifted by the minute. *Yup, this is good, this is worth fighting for.*

He walked a yard or two to where he could see the course and took it all in. God, what he wouldn't give to have it all to do again and how differently he would do it. He remembered the total joy of winning this tournament. Not even the lack of a real crowd or the unusual circumstances had been able to take even the slightest edge off it. It had been orgasmic in its intensity. Hence the flatness later, he supposed. Yesterday, he had seen his picture and name in the hall of fame, which had made him swell with pride. Any regret at how it had proved unrepeatable and how his career had petered out, far too early, in slow decline and injury was forgotten as he replayed his triumph. *Nothing remotely as good in ten years since. But not all bad, either, or I wouldn't have landed this job. No mean achievement that, either. Give yourself a pat on the back, Phillip.*

Now here he stood again. The course was in even better nick than back then. He summoned it all up again: the weather, the crowds, the cheering, the whole mix of super-charged testosterone-packed competition overlaid on a picture perfect resort, full of happy punters, spending their money with more abandon than they should, cheering their heroes, content to be herded like sheep behind ropes, falling silent when the stewards raised their markers and trying, stealthily, to take pictures of the stars, using banned cameras and phones, wondering what it must be like actually to be one of the professionals, needing nerves of steel to maintain knife-edged precision with disaster waiting, potentially, at every turn and shot. *Bloody hard, I can tell you. When you lose you're gutted and even when you win, you're hollowed out from the stress and pressure of it. The nerves you get are unbelievable. You wonder how you can stand and hold a club, never mind hit a ball. But you're a pro, so you don't show it, you hold it in. And that makes it worse.*

And he had been one of those heroes, wielding his golf club and conjuring magic shots from the depths of his experience and courage, fighting down the crippling nerves and executing the most delicate of hand and eye co-ordinated shots when your whole body felt out of all control and, at times, your very sanity was tested. How could anyone be asked to make a four-foot putt that was worth half a million euros? That had been him and he would give anything, absolutely anything, to travel back in time and be given the chance again. Knowing, of course, what he knew now. *Ah yes. Always the key that. The chance to avoid the mistakes and cash in on missed opportunities. I know it's not just golfers who feel that, but pro golf does focus it more than most things. A million euro putt missed is a lasting wound. I should know.*

He felt a hand on his shoulder. It was Jake, a smiling Anne by his side. Jake was reading his thoughts: 'I don't need to give a penny for them. It's written all over your face. We all feel the same. Every time those ex-pros at the TV station get in the commentary box, they tell me, the first five minutes they are full of envy for the guys whose turn it is now. But look at you. Top of the tree, looking down on the likes of us still struggling to get something out of the game. Congratulations, Phil. Couldn't happen to a nicer guy.'

'Jake. I <u>thought</u> it was you I saw earlier, with Samson. I was hoping we'd bump into each other. Great to see you again. God, have we got some catching up to do! Why don't you stop by the office when you get a chance. I've some great scotch in there.'

Jake was all smiles as he introduced Anne, without really spelling out their relationship, Phil noticed. *Hmm, I wonder.*

'You'll be welcome, too, of course, Anne. How do you take your scotch?' Phil was struck by her statuesque proportions and envied Jake his luck, if these two were an item. The contrast with his own lonely and isolated state wasn't one he wanted to dwell on. *Don't go there, sunshine. She's out of your league. Not got Marilyn's class, though.*

'Neat, though a gin and tonic would go down better. Can I add my congratulations to Jake's. I'm not sure I'd want the job, but I'm glad the tour is in such good hands.' Phil was getting used to sycophants and a world where your enemies present themselves as your best friend. Who could you trust? That's why he needed a partner, a female partner. As a friend as much as a lover. But as a lover as much as a friend.

They chatted on, reminiscing as they walked and found themselves back beside the practice green. 'See the big guy putting?' said Phil, 'The one with the nose? That's Stefan Greiff. Worth more than the entire British economy. He's our sponsor and if he doesn't win the pro-am tomorrow, I shall be very disappointed. He's paired with one of your guys, Samson. Bit of luck that, for Samson, unless the caddy managed to fix it somehow, which wouldn't surprise me. Who is his caddy.?'

'Larry Topham.'

'Definitely wouldn't surprise me in that case. Larry knows his way around,' Phil said. He pointed discreetly out onto the practice green. 'See the guy talking to the other one in a green shirt? The tall, thin one? ' *This might shock 'em a bit, but no harm getting the word round.*

Jake said he did.

'Know who he is?'

Jake said he didn't.

'He's the senior doping inspector. I only found out they'd be here yesterday. We found him a spot in the pro-am too. We'll have him tested if he wins.'

'I didn't know they had them in golf,' Anne said. 'Do they come to every tournament then?'

'No, they don't. One in four if you're unlucky. They've never had even a sniff of a positive on this tour. Only two in the States and they were exonerated on appeal. It's a farce, but we have to do it. They don't bother us much. They just check out the winner, and a random sample of others. Anyway, keep it to yourselves, but there are rumours flying around about why they're here for this one. They're starting as they mean to go on.' *So put that in your pipe and send out the smoke signals.*

'What rumours,' Jake asked. Phil looked at him carefully. He'd gone a little pale around the cheeks he thought. *What's up with Jake? Have I touched a nerve? Jake's as straight as they come. If he's up to no good, God help us.*

'Oh nothing specific. You know what this game's like about cheating. Paranoid. But apparently the satellite TV team claims it has a story it's going to break. Just needs a bit more evidence and they think they'll get it here. The inspectors are the sponsor's way of countering it. Shows the power of the man. The sponsor with the glorious conk. He insisted we bring them in. Doesn't want his brand tarnished.'

'So it's rumours about drugs, then is it?' This was Anne. Phil looked at her, too. She seemed much more composed than Jake, whose hands were clenched together far too tightly, Phil noticed. *This isn't looking good. I'll get Matt onto this couple.*

'Something and nothing I expect. It's about getting an unfair advantage in one way or another. The TV staff won't say what they've got. There are hints that someone has got a new technology in play, God knows what, that gives them a few extra yards, or a bit more precision, or whatever. But yeah, there are hints about performance-enhancers, too. Like I say, something and nothing. The sponsor's just taking precautions. Makes him look concerned. You all right, Jake?'

Jake clearly wasn't all right. His face had lost all colour and he was clearly struggling for composure. *Oh my. I really have struck home. What the hell is this all about? His squeeze obviously knows nothing about it. Cool as ice, she is.*

'He's been like this for a couple of days,' Anne said. 'We nearly didn't come. I told him he should stay at home, Samson could have handled matters. But he wanted to come for my sake and this is the result. I think it's a bit of food poisoning. He feels better for a while after he's thrown up. And that's clearly what he's about to do now. I'd better get him back to his room; I don't want him spoiling your nice shoes!'

'His' room. Not 'our' room, Phil noted, though everything else about them suggested itemhood. They shook hands quickly and Anne led Jake away to his presumed assignation with a toilet bowl. Phil, wondering what had really caused it, but not wanting to delay their departure, wished him a speedy recovery and went in the opposite direction. He was heading for the tent where he would find the admin team: three young ladies and Marilyn Duclos. *Well that was an interesting encounter. Definitely one for Matt to follow up.*

★

A few hours later, Phil opened the door of his sumptuous rented villa to a wary-looking Marilyn with two brown-paper shopping bags in her arms. 'I hope you meant it,' she said, 'now that I've got this lot.' *Jesus, that French accent is a turn-on.*

'Come in, of course I did. Here, give me those.' He took the bags and set them down on a polished granite surface in the large modern kitchen area to the rear of his lounge. 'Why would you think I didn't?'

'Oh, I know you meant the invitation and I meant it when I said I'd cook if you laid on the booze. It was the bit about no strings attached I wondered about. It doesn't look good coming round to your place, does it?' *No strings attached doesn't mean anything in this game, though, does it. The strings have a habit of appearing from nowhere.*

'We could hardly go round to yours. You said it was a hovel. I've done something about that by the way. You can move in tomorrow. Next door, not here.' *Come on Phil, boy. You're fooling no-one, throwing your weight about like that. Think no-one will notice? All the tongues will be wagging. Next door? You've got to be kidding.*

She made an impressed face. 'I'm not really impressed, though,' she said. 'We should have had decent accommodation in the first place. Any one of us works harder than your pathetic tournament directors - why do you need three of them, by the way? - and they get palaces while we get cupboards. If I was a feminist I might think it was something to do with the fact that we are women and the directors are always, always, bloody men.'

'Things could be changing on both those fronts. But don't give me grief about the bloody directors. There's only Matt here for this one. There's always four of you every time.'

'Just teasing, probably. I've brought stuff for a nice casserole and a fattening dessert. You okay with that?'

He was. *Does she think I need feeding up? It's not a mother I want. Not just a mother, at any rate.*

She set about unpacking and looking through the cupboards for the things she needed. He opened a bottle of wine. 'This place is well-stocked,' she said, 'as well as being massive and posh.' She swept her arm out in a gesture meant to indicate the grandeur and opulence of her surroundings. 'Aren't I a lucky girl.'

'I think I'm the lucky boy.' *Oops! Too much?*

She looked at him. He saw the caution in her eyes.

'How so?' she said.

'Having someone cook for me.' *Rescued. Thank you, brain.*

'Is that all you meant? We have an agreement, remember.'

'No. It isn't all I meant. I think the agreement was that we could talk a bit more informally here and it wouldn't matter if we drank a bit more wine than is good for us. I need to pick your brains about how things work on the ground here and what to look out for. Who to butter up and where the bear traps are. Just that sort of thing, really. I think I've sort of sussed it, but it would be nice to have it confirmed.'

'That's not a problem. Anything else?'

You bet. 'Well. There are things I might want to unload. Some worrying things that it would help me to talk through with a sympathetic and discreet listener. But she would have to be very, very discreet.'

'That's not a problem either. So, really, you want a friend?'

'For now,' he said.

'For now. And for later?'

'That would be for the friend to decide.'

She was quiet for a while, chopping meat and washing vegetables.

'I don't want to sound arrogant or anything. Getting an invitation like this usually means one thing. You want a friend, but a friend with benefits would be even better. I don't want to disappoint you, but that's not me. I don't do casual, and I doubt I can ever do serious again either. I think a friend is all it can ever be. I'm sorry if that's a dampener.'

It was, but he was too proud to admit it. She was a fine woman and he knew what his hopes, if not intentions, had been when he made this invitation. But he had said no strings and he would honour it. He wouldn't say it about future invitations, though. You never knew with women.

'No, that's fine. You can tell me why you feel that way if you like. Meanwhile, this bottle needs some serious attention.'

He thought her smile, though a little sad, was one of the most attractive he'd ever seen. *And I don't believe a word of that earlier denial. She's here for a reason and it isn't to make a new pal.*

25 *The pro am*

S amson usually woke early, after a sober night at least. On this particular Wednesday, it was six o clock. No need to check the weather. It would be a repeat of yesterday and the day before. He looked around the bedroom of his rented villa with approval. Not large, but very nicely appointed with a great en-suite. Samson was going to copy it at home, when he'd made a bit of money. His thoughts came into focus. He had three things to ponder. The first was sleeping in bed beside him; Cristina, after only two nights together, was already more than he'd bargained for. The second concerned the substance he'd been taking, the wonderful effect on his golf and the unreal one on his performance in bed. Just when he'd wanted to be tender with Cristina, take it slow and loving, his body had forced him to go at it like a demented rabbit. He wasn't sure whether Cristina was impressed, scared or just brought up to serve the needs of her men folk without demur. He'd done it with her (to her?) three times in half an hour last night, with precious little regard for what she might be getting out of it.

His final issue was today's mini-tournament, the pro-am and his incredible luck in drawing the sponsor himself. Given who he was, winning the pro-am for him could almost be more lucrative than winning the tournament. And winning both would make him a superstar as well as super rich. He had won before, though no-one remembered and it barely counted even with him: the Madeira Islands Open where the prize money reflected the paucity of the entrants – all journeymen professionals, none of them names most fans would recognise. His win hadn't featured in any of the papers, to his disappointment though not surprise. So that's why it hardly counted as a win. That apart, joint fifth was the best he'd managed. So winning here would be life-changing. Utterly. And the pro-am would be a good start. Should he slip his sponsor-partner some of the juice, he wondered?

So, in order of importance to him, Samson dealt with his issues. Cristina first. Something about her had appealed right away. It wasn't just her looks, though he loved her face and the wonderful large brown eyes, or the fact she had no idea who he was. It was the whole package, really, character, charm, looks and that extraordinary confidence and openness; her complete self-possession. He loved the way other men looked at her, and the way she seemed unaware of it.

He knew what he was like with women. Almost anyone would do, especially in the past couple of months. There had been times when he disgusted himself with some of the slappers he'd ended up with. He shut from his mind some of his less appealing bed mates and turned his thoughts back to

Cristina. Because of all that tacky stuff, he felt he didn't deserve her, but the notion of letting her go, let alone sending her packing as he usually did after a couple of nights, wasn't on. This was an interesting new journey for him and he wanted to see where it ended. He wondered if he was in love and concluded that it might be the start of something like that. He reached under the bed clothes and felt her warm round backside. The effect on him was immediate. 'Not just love, then,' he said, heading for the shower.

As the cool water hit him and the potency subsided, he thought about the second issue. However he framed and justified it, he was about to cheat in a professional golf tournament where cheating was not just frowned upon, it was despised. Golfers accused of cheating quickly found themselves ostracised. Just the accusation was enough, it didn't have to be proved. So, he told himself, weighing his options, he could stop the experiment with the substance, keep the respect of his fellow golfers, win sod all and end up desperate for a slot in tournaments like the one at Madeira, but at least keep what little self-respect he still had: the poor but honest option.

The other route was to take the promone stuff, risk his health and reputation, win as often as was wise and end up living in luxury for the rest of his life, possibly with Cristina and their kids. Kids, he thought, where did that come from?

The two choices were stark. No risk, poverty and the death of all ambition; or high risk with possibly unimaginable riches. And my chicks for free, he nearly added before remembering his still sleeping new experience in the bedroom. He had no idea how he would handle winning if it wasn't down to skill. How would he live with himself as a cheat? He tried to dismiss it as something to be dealt with. Pushed under the rug and dealt with. Like he'd been doing for weeks. It would only matter if others found out. So discovery by others, not self-loathing was the risk he ended up weighing against fame and fortune.

Samson rarely hesitated long over a problem. Give him a choice and he made a rapid decision. And having made it, carried it through as resolutely as he could. It was what made him a good golfer; and it could have made him a great one with more temperamental steadiness. Even now it didn't occur to him that there was a third choice: work harder, live cleanly and let his talent take him where it would.

He didn't debate things for long and as he turned his face up into the shower jet to let the cold water finish the job of waking him fully for the day ahead, he had already decided. And it would start with the pro-am this afternoon.

And that brought him to his third issue. Another easy decision. There was no way he could let Stefan, his golf partner in the pro-am this afternoon, use the potion. There just wasn't time to coach him and the risk of discovery would be too great. He could hear Anne's warnings in his head. He didn't doubt that Stefan would cheat if he could - you don't get to be a billionaire without a bit of that, after all - but he wouldn't keep it to himself. So, no dope for Stefan. Samson would have to turn on all his own skill, with a little help from his friend in the bottle, and do what he could for Stefan.

He slid back into bed, disturbing Cristina as he did so. He wrapped his arms round her and pressed himself into her back. Again, his response was instant and this time there was no resisting it. Cristina wiggled her backside against his hardening member and turned to face him. He slid down the bed and buried his face in her breasts. 'Again?' she murmured, sleepily. 'Really?' He slid further down and she said nothing more. For a while, both of them were incapable of speech.

★

Two hours later, after a hearty breakfast delivered to the villa, and with Cristina watching from the sidelines, Samson was on the putting green, working on the only aspect of his game where he wasn't supremely confident. The juice helped with most things, but not much with putting. For that, you needed to read a green, judge the pace, and pick a line. Unique judgements almost every time. It wasn't Samson's special strength. Like all pros he was unbelievably good at it, but others were even better and his lazy streak meant he hadn't put in the hours and hours needed to refine his touch. As a putter he was only superhuman. He needed to be divine, and today, with the lovely eyes of Cristina firmly on him, he felt he could be. Ball after ball rolled into the hole and after a solid hour's practice he felt ready.

Cristina called something to him and pointed left. He looked where she pointed and saw his partner coming onto the green, with his hand outstretched. Stefan Greiff was a bear of a man, with, a little bizarrely for a German perhaps, a tam o'shanter perched at a jaunty angle on his blond locks. His nose, bulbous and pitted, and his laughing eyes, were the first things you saw in him and the ones you never forgot. Only in anger did that beam of humour ever leave his eye. And he did angry really well, sometimes as a management tactic and sometimes genuinely so. And seeing him genuinely angry was another thing few folk ever forgot. With him was a man dressed like a caddy, carrying the golf bag like a caddy, but with the demeanour of a man not used to a subordinate role. *Whoa. An extra from a Tarentino film.*

'Guten Morgen, Herr Gregory. Deutsch, Englisch? Wie Sie wollen.'

'I think it had better be English. I can do a bit of Spanish, if you like, but I hear your English is excellent. And it's Samson, by the way.'

'Stefan,' he said beaming, 'and I have many flatterers. 'Excellent' is too strong, but we'll manage. This by the way,' he indicated his caddy 'is Bradley Manning.' Bradley's eyes brushed past Samson by way of acknowledgement and then resumed their restless observation of Stefan's immediate environment. Samson felt he was meant to be impressed by a man who turned up for golf practice with a bodyguard. *Some days I've turned up with barely a body.*

'Now, how do we going to do today?' Stefan asked.

'We are going to win, I expect. Your flatterers also tell me you can play a bit.'

'I don't know what exactly 'play a bit' means, but I have 8 for handicap. Bloody good for a chap with no time to play, not true?'

'Bloody good, as you say. What would you like me to do today, to help you. You know the format?'

'Fourball, better ball. Forward tee for amateurs, God be thanks. Help on the green, please. Bradley here is bloody good at many things, but not so good as a caddy. So you do his job. Lines for the putting, slopes and all that. Maybe shot choice when I ask. Not much point trying to coach me unless you see something very bad, very wrong. Then tell me.

The main thing is I talk to Bradley this morning and when I tell him who my partner is he makes a face like this.' Stefan demonstrated by pulling a face that would have been impossible for Bradley to do. 'He says you are in fantastic form and that we could win. He told me to put money on you for the big tournament and I did. You know what your numbers are? Sixty-six to one! Or they were until my bet. If you win, I get nearly seven million euros.' He watched Samson's evident discomfort and laughed.

'You put a hundred thousand euros on me winning?' *He's got to be kidding. And I'm worried about being legal.*

'Only a joke. As sponsor I am not allowed to gamble on the tournament.'

Thank God for that,' Samson said.

'So I asked my son to do it for me. He is nearly as rich as I am and he put 200,000 on you. On the nose, I think you say. '

Samson did the sums. 'Well then,' he said, 'if I win, he'll earn about 12 times more than I get.'

'If you win, Herr Gregory, you'll get more than the prize money. I am looking for new players to sponsor my company – not just about food, drink and cars as you know, we have many leisure resorts, own half of Ireland and have a huge medicine factory there and on the Rhine in Switzerland and Merricole, in England – and I will pay well.' His hand, paw almost, was on Samson's shoulder as he said this. You going to win, yes? Like Bradley says? He thinks you have some tricks up your shirt.'

No pressure, then, Samson thought, wondering what was meant by the 'tricks up your shirt' remark. Did these guys know something? 'I'll do my very best, Stefan,' he said.

'And if you and me win this pro-am I will also be a very grateful partner. I hope your other partner is as grateful as I can be.' He inclined his head in Cristina's direction. 'She is very nice. You have others here, or is it love?' he saw Samson hesitate, which told him all he needed to know. 'Oh I know; not my business; trouble with a nose like mine is it sticks out into everything. She is lovely. Look after her or I might steal her from you.' And he slapped Samson on the back, just a touch too heavily.

Samson's caddy Larry arrived and Samson introduced him to Bradley, who stopped his vigil only long enough to shake Larry's hand and say 'pleased to meet you' in a way that indicated exactly the opposite. Samson saw Larry's mouth open to say something in return and then close again when he realised Bradley's attention had moved elsewhere.

At one-thirty precisely, the starter on the first tee announced Samson and Stefan's match. Their playing partners in the fourball were a tall thin man with a very expensive-looking set of clubs, brand new, Samson thought, and an up and coming young star from the far east, already with a tour win under his belt and a predicted glittering future ahead of him. Somebody, probably the youngster, had excited enough interest to draw a sizeable crowd, who applauded politely as each name was announced.

Samson checked his pulse; slow and steady, a sign the promone was at maximum efficiency. First on the tee, he felt invincible and sent a straight drive hurtling toward the perfect spot on the fairway.

'Ball' he heard Stefan say as the applause died away. Then the steward's markers went up, silence was imposed and Stefan addressed his ball, thirty yards ahead of the pro tee. For a big man, and an amateur, his swing was more than adequate and his power was immense. His two hundred and seventy yard drive took him within twenty yards of Samson's ball. Samson, followed by his caddy, caught him up and congratulated him. 'Great shot, Mr Greff'. The bear turned its head: 'Stefan, please. Call me Stefan. Better for both of us.'

This was the first real test of the late Selwyn Smalling's potion. Not quite a tournament proper, but, Samson told himself, with enough damn pressure to be as good as one. More in some ways. Stefan had seen to that. Samson had a strong sense that his mettle was being tested, and he responded to that sort of challenge as he always did: do or die panache. Whatever else was missing in Samson's sporting character, it wasn't competitive fire. He was a scrapper. But now the potion worked its magic. The young star from the far east wilted in face of Samson's unremitting accuracy with his irons, and seemed on the point of giving up completely when one or two of Samson's long putts dropped as well.

The reverse happened to Stefan. He was inspired by Samson's magnificence and responded with his best round for years. By the end, as they stood on the green of the difficult eighteenth, with a just completed birdie and net birdie on their cards, they had annihilated their immediate opponents and were pretty confident of an overall win. Stefan was in a hugely expansive mood. The world around the green was his friend and he shook hands with spectators, caddies, officials and his bodyguards more or less indiscriminately, slapping even the women on the back.

'Samson Gregory, you are better than Woods, better than Niklaus. You are unbeatable. How the hell you do that? You were never more than 3 metres from the pin. How the hell you do that? Go on tell me. I keep the secret. I never see anything like it.' Behind the bonhomie was a deadly earnest. His eyes betrayed him.

Samson noticed it, laughed and hid his nervousness well. *Jesus, I'd better tone it down tomorrow. This guy's onto me. Was it really just luck of the draw that got me this match?*

'No tricks, just blindingly good form. Happens to everybody once or twice in their career. Generally lasts a few months and then goes. Henrik Stenson; Luke Donald. Couldn't lose if they tried for a season, and then it went again. You have to make the most of it while it's there I guess.'

'Sure, sure', said Stefan, looking unconvinced. They went into the scorer's tent, checked the scores against the markers' card and signed for their own. The scorer whistled softly when he saw the cards. 'That'll take some beating'.

'Wasn't all me by any means,' said Samson. 'The sponsor here was absolutely unbelievable. He was better ball on six of the holes and just as good on a few more.'

Stefan was beaming. They didn't have to wait long to discover that, amazingly, the sponsor's boss and owner had won the sponsor's shield, for only the second time in the history of the tour. Stefan's broad beam broadened some more.

Later, on his second bottle of champagne, he said to a stone cold sober Samson. 'You win the big one, Sammy. You win the big one and then we'll talk.' Samson noticed that the grin had disappeared. *Sugar. I'm playing with the big boys here. Make or break time, Sammy.*

26 First of the big ones

'Stop it!'

'Stop what?

'Stop pulling that worried face every times he hits a great shot.'

Anne was right. He was a bag of nerves. The conversation with Phil Henshaw had started it and just about everything that had happened afterwards confirmed it. He was certain this was going to go wrong and he would be back behind bars. There was an excitement in the crowd around him and Anne that he'd never felt before. Nearly half the people on the course for the pro-am were trying to catch a glimpse of Samson and Jake had been jostled and pushed to one side more than enough. A surprising number of the people pushing were women. Samson's attractions were clearly not confined to the superb mechanics of his swing and the cut of his immaculate clothes.

Jake was alert to anything that suggested people were starting to think there was more than met the eye in Samson's immaculate golf. Another terrific shot soared to within inches of the pin. 'Stunning,' said a woman in the crowd just in front of him. 'I don't know what he's on, but if he ever bottles it ...' Jake nearly choked and Anne dug him in the ribs.

'Jesus, Jake. Man up. What the hell's the matter with you?'

Jake shook his head. He had rarely felt less secure. There were spies everywhere he looked. That guy over there with the camera. He was sure he'd seen him before back at the base in England, filming team practice. Why was that woman in a red coat making notes? Who were all these people calling on their phones? A hand fell hard on Jake's shoulder and he leapt guiltily. 'Sorry mate; can we sneak through to get to the ropes. My kids can't see anything back here.' Jake moved away sharply. English? What were English people doing here? Were they policemen?

The air around him was polluted with secret messages from all the phones he saw people using. Any single one could be fatal. *Why on earth had he got involved in all this?*

'Money!' said Anne. For a moment he thought she'd read his mind. 'There's money in my purse and I left it in my bag on the back of the chair.'

'Which chair?'

'On the balcony. At our table up in hospitality. Christ, there's a ton of euros in it. I'd better get back quick. Coming?'

With a last hunted look round the crowd, Jake followed Anne up to the hospitality area balcony.

'Shit. It's gone.' Anne stood by their table, her hand over her mouth. She searched under the table and Jake asked people nearby if they'd seen anything. No-one could help.

Jake put his arm round her. 'It could have been handed in. You sure you left it here?' Anne nodded. 'There's a lost property downstairs. You stay here and I'll go ask.'

Jake had no luck. Nothing had been handed in. He tried the admin ladies who were sympathetic, but hadn't had any messages about a lost bag. The minor calamity had taken his mind off the potentially greater one he feared would soon engulf him. But what he found on his return didn't help his equilibrium. At the table with Anne was a man he didn't recognise. *Trouble without a doubt. But what sort of trouble?* On the table between them was a half empty bottle of wine, three glasses, and Anne's bag.

'You got it. How?'

'Jake, this is Mitchell Walker. I don't know where to start. He saw me leave my bag and took charge of it. And he's Selwyn's replacement. In the lab, that is.'

Mitchell stood up and offered his hand. Jake took it but didn't like the look of him. He looked like competition. Serious competition.

'Selwyn's replacement. How come? What do you mean, Selwyn's replacement.'

'Mitchell's an old friend and colleague of Selwyn. They were great friends once but sort of lost touch, right, Mitchell?'

Mitchell nodded.

'And what brings you back on the scene now? Did you know he was here Anne?'

Mitchell deferred to Anne. 'Okay,' said Anne, 'No I didn't know he was here. But I'm glad he was or I'd be minus a fair bit of cash. He saw us go down on the course and was waiting for us to come back, to introduce himself to you and that's when he saw my bag. Anyway, think back to when you asked me for a further supply of promone. I confess I was keen to keep you on board. What would you have said if I said I had none.'

Jake shook his head and shrugged. It crossed his mind to tell her he would have been relieved. But it wouldn't have been true. His nervousness was more recent, connected with the reality of cheating in an actual event.

'Well, I couldn't make it. I needed someone else for that but didn't want to worry you. So I sussed Mitchell out, thought he was sound, then I let him in on it and he used the formula to make some more. It isn't just something you can make in the kitchen. It needs his skills and equipment. And now we have a regular supply. Sadly, Mitchell tells me it is volatile. It goes off in a matter of days. So it can't be stockpiled. And that means he'll be a necessary evil (sorry Mitchell, you know what I mean) for a while.'

'And why are you over here, Mitchell? Why do you need to be at the tournament.' Jake's paranoia prompted the perfectly reasonable question.

'See him?' Mitchell said, pointing to the tall thin man leaving the green to go to the scorer's tent.

'The doping guy? Yes, We know about him.'

'They don't visit often. Why do you think he's here? And how do you think he got into that particular fourball?

Jake's fears weren't being allayed. Mitchell went on. 'My company works with the inspectors. To tell the truth, we have the contract. UK Doping outsources the work to us. Which means I have access to UK Doping emails, perfectly legitimately. As soon as Anne let me know what was going on, I saw the danger straight away. I've read every one of that guy's emails and he's here at the request of the tournament director himself, a very worried man called Phillip Henshaw, though he's pretending otherwise. You know Phil? Good. I was with him this morning.'

'You were with him this morning? How did you manage that?'

'Well not me, so much as my alter ego. I'm not officially here, but Professor Niall Millican of University College Birmingham is. I could see from the emails that Henshaw was troubled: he knew something was up, had caught all sorts of corrupt scents in the wind, so I wrote to him too, as Millican, and planted a few more suspicions in his mind. He is now convinced that there are some newly invented technologies being put to wicked use. Range finders and stuff. Oh, and if you come across any of the tournament directors, (there's one called Matt Prosser) be very careful. They're Phillip's eyes on the ground, specially briefed to look for any funny stuff. It's not the most foolproof of strategies, this Millican thing, but even if they stop believing it nothing will be lost so long as they don't connect Millican to me and then me to you. So mum's the word, eh?'

'Way too fast for me. What's going on Anne?' Jake's earlier fears were now crystallising round this man.

'I am sorry Jake. You must be able to see I needed a confidential manufacturer. As soon as I told Mitchell, he saw the obvious flaw we all did. He thought oh-oh, drugs tests, at first, like we did. And when he saw that Henshaw was sticking his nose in, Mitchell hatched this plan to put him off the track. He's using Henshaw's suspicion to lead him in completely the wrong direction. And we know Phil so we can reinforce the misdirection.'

'But,' Jake said, 'that sounds a bit flaky. How long is that going to work for? And why draw attention to it, to the possibility of cheating, I mean?' *Christ, I'm in the hands of amateurs and madmen. They can't believe Henshaw won't see through that.*

'You're right,' Anne said, appearing to read his mind again. *I wish she would stop doing that.* 'He will cotton on eventually. But this isn't a long term thing anyway. It's a case of a quick killing, maybe even just the one season and then onto the next thing. Or a couple of seasons off and then another go. We just need them to stay away for long enough and trust to their good sense, too.'

'What do you mean, good sense?' Jake wasn't reassured.

'Well, how far is it in Henshaw's interests to expose this sort of thing in a sport he oversees? Look at football with FIFA and athletics with the IAAF or the Olympics with the IOC? Do their chiefs look like they're enjoying themselves? Henshaw will do anything before he goes public on this. Anything. That's what we're counting on.' Anne sounded very sure of herself.

That doesn't square with the Phil I know. Fearless Phil, the caddies called him. He'd take on any shot if there was half a chance of winning. And it had cost him a few titles, too. And the inspectors? Would they show 'good sense' too?

'And I thought this would be simple,' he said.

Mitchell intervened: 'You just manage your golfers and it will be. Leave the rest to Anne and me. I'm sure Anne will keep you up to date.' Anne put her hand on Jake's. 'Don't worry, Jake. Just keep the lads in order for us. Not too much greed. And keep that Cristina close to Samson. She's good for him.'

'Who's Cristina?' asked Mitchell.

★

As they lay in bed that night, with the big day before them, Cristina was full of questions and Samson was delighted at her interest and keen to explain as much as he could. 'I need to try it,' she said. 'To understand, I have to do it. I need to get a stick, club, sorry, and a ball and go onto the grass to try it. Then I know what is difficult and what is not.'

'Plenty of places on the tour where you can try that on the days before the tournament.'

'Ah, but you leave on Sunday, maybe you say even Friday. That is my last chance at learning from a professional.'

Now there's a statement with a question in it, if ever there was. He smiled at her

'You wouldn't come with me even if I asked you. I bet your father would have a fit.'

'Have a fit?'

'Go mad. Be angry.'

'I deal with my father. If I want to do something, I do it and tell my family later.'

'Do they know you're here?'

'Yes.'

'And with me. Overnight with me?'

She looked at him and then away again. 'No. They think I got transferred to work here. For the tournament. And my boss at work think I am ill. He wants to sack me anyway, for locking him in cupboard.'

'Okay then,' he said, 'we have two questions. First, if I asked, would you come round on tour with me?' He stopped her answer by placing his hand gently on her mouth, 'and secondly should we not go to meet your parents to tell them we are an item?'

His hand stayed on her mouth as her eyes widened and tears formed. He took his hand away and she fell round his neck. 'Two days, nearly three,' she said, 'and you want to meet my mother and father?' *Whoops!*

'Steady,' he said. 'This is not a marriage proposal. Just a partnership agreement. And initially, for one season only.'

She was on top of him now, kissing him with real passion and moving rhythmically above him, with alarming consequences for a man who had done his duty twice already and who needed his strength for the morning. He swung her on to her back, admired the lovely curves of her body and the soft glow from her skin, then rushed to the shower for a drenching. She followed him in, turned the tap to warm and reached for the shower gel. Later, he said: 'If I win on Sunday, we'll go to see your family on Monday and fly to England in the afternoon.'

She hugged him and kissed him and he fell into a profound and profoundly happy sleep.

27 *On the tee*

A stiff early morning wind flapped the brightly coloured flags as the sun levered itself up over the horizon ready for another full day's work across the golf course. The large gates guarding the road into the resort were pushed slowly open by two stewards and the first of the crowd rushed in, anxious to commandeer their favourite position. Some raced to tees one and ten, the starting tees, where they could marvel at the power and accuracy of the driving. Others mooched around the tents and offices, where they were allowed, hoping to catch a glimpse of their favourite star and get an autograph, ostensibly for the kids at home.

The catering tents served their first customers, the toilets got their first users too, as did the fringe shows, the merchants, the manufacturers, the tourist board and the resort marketers. The crowd grew steadily as the time for the first starters approached.

The media trailers showed signs of life. New cables were added to the old ones and lines, connections and power cables traced confused patterns round the power vehicles, the director's control trailer, interview areas, lights and microphones. In the commentary box, set high and to the side of the club house, two or three of the satellite company commentators took their seats. Others, trailed by sound engineers and camera crews, set out for their starting vantage points. In a studio in England, the show had already started, with interviews, analysis of form and clips from the previous year as a warm up. In the press section, weary looking men, fresh from their beds and a hard breakfast, blinked into the low light of the morning and wished the day was over. The cat house they'd discovered last night was one of the best on tour and they were looking forward to further patronage tonight. The golf was an unwelcome intrusion into their licensed debauchery.

The practice green was full, as was the range. Golfers chatted to each other or to their coaches, some trying to iron out a basic swing fault, others desperate to find something, some new swing trick they could take with them out onto the course. Yet others simply steeled themselves for the first tee shot and tried to get in the zone, the mental state that was needed to carry a man through eighteen holes of successful competitive golf at the highest level.

The crowd collected round every vantage point the range offered, pointing out the golfers to their neighbours. The weather was set fair and shorts and coloured tops and sun hats were everywhere.

Something in the air infected everyone. A crowd picks up a mood and becomes a living thing in its own right, shouting, groaning, cheering as one. Now, there was excited chatter, laughter, occasional rhythmic hand-clapping and here and there, for no clear reason, a cheer would go up. Small groups would suddenly break into a trot and then a run, as if chased by predators or heading for a water hole after a thirsty day on the plains.

Expectation filled the veins of spectator and competitor alike. And in a glass case in the clubhouse a huge silver trophy awaited the winner, along with a cheque for a million euros.

★

Phil, answering a last minute emergency call for a replacement starter and glad of something practical to do, arrived at the tenth tee at 6.50, ready to start the first three-ball from his tee at 7. He stood behind a white dais, checked his schedule and blew into the microphone to make sure it was on. *Here we go. First tournament of the Henshaw era. First of a glorious new golfing epoch, if I don't cock it up.* He watched the golfers arrive and saw how edgy they were and how they coped in different ways. He remembered his own state of near panic at times at the start of an event like this and how he had hummed nursery rhymes to himself, silently of course, to get some sort of grip on his emotions. *I used to think the lads in the trenches in 1914 couldn't have felt worse. I was wrong, of course, but not by much, I bet. Look at these poor sods. Terrified.* He watched the tournament favourite, generally deemed an affable, pleasant sort, arrive at the tee. His eyes were hard and his gaze fixed. He said not a word to anyone. His focus was the club, the ball, and the narrow strip of fairway ahead of him. His caddy said something. It sounded like, 'aim for the tower, slight draw, full swing.' The golfer barely nodded. Phil went through with his announcement and the player acknowledged the cheers of the crowd without breaking his practice routine. Then he placed the tee peg in the ground, a ball on top of it, and almost before the crowd had time to realise that this was the real thing, there was a crack of the club and the ball sped off exactly as the caddy had ordered, straight for a distant tower and turning gently to the left. Wild applause from the crowd and the player relaxed visibly. 'Nice to see you Phil, thanks for the intro.'

And so it went on for the next couple of hours, a new group every 15 minutes, until Phil saw Samson arrive at the tee. *This should be interesting.* Everyone knew Samson and his reputation had been enhanced by his spectacular performance in the pro-am. He went through his routine and Phil introduced him. Samson was much more relaxed, it seemed, than that first player and many later ones had been. He acknowledged the crowd and shook hands with caddies and officials alike. Phil looked in his eyes. There was something there he couldn't quite describe, something beyond focus and determination; Phil thought it looked like a sort of rapture as if Samson was in a state of religious intoxication. *Bloody hell. There's definitely something different there. Can't just be the new girlfriend.* What Phil was seeing was the look of a man supremely confident that he was about to achieve his destiny. *Always was a cocky sod. Let's hope he stuffs it.*

Samson's drive was hit with such sweetness and power that the crowd forgot to cheer. Mouths agape, they watched it fly down the fairway and as if on rails, turn left at the right moment and settle out of sight in the middle of the dog leg facing the green. *That is just not humanly possible. One in a million, that shot.* A wedge, and a smooth one at that, would get him to the green for his first birdie of the day. Eventually the crowd woke up to what they had just witnessed and the cheer was deafening and prolonged. The guys in the commentary box heard it and craned their necks to see what had happened. A control room voice in their earpiece told them and the pictures of Samson's electric start were soon beamed around the world. Every bookie in the universe shortened his odds at that moment.

Phil watched Samson saunter off after his caddy and thought he had never seen a drive like that in his entire life. *I said a new era. I didn't mean a new bent one, though.* It was fully three hundred and sixty yards, yet hit with pinpoint accuracy and still able to turn at the right point as if laser guided. 'Absolutely unbelievable.' Phil thought. You could do a drive like that one time in a thousand on the driving range, but to produce it off the starting tee in a tour match was impossible. Yet he had seen it. Phil's own suspicion, independent of the worries planted by anyone else, began with that shot. By the time he saw the score card at the end of the day he was a confirmed sceptic. Something was going on, Phil was sure. And Samson was at the heart of it.

★

Cristina followed Samson round the course, sometimes standing within touching distance. The cameras had picked her up and the TV director was making sure she appeared in as many shots as possible, whoever she was. By the fourth hole, the cameras were firmly focused on Samson and his partners. He was four under par after four holes and heading for the record books. Cristina didn't know she was becoming a star across Europe. Her eyes were on Samson. With each hole and each shot, she understood a little more. But there was not a lot to understand. Samson's play was a purely visual treat. Balls soared to within inches of the hole with astonishing consistency. Not even the greatest golfers had played like this. The commentary box was split between those who thought this was a near perfect performance and those who thought it <u>was</u> perfect. They soon ran out of superlatives. The director barking in their ears only semi-jokingly banned the use of 'amazing', 'stupendous' and 'incredible', with or without preceding adverbs and sent up a copy of an English thesaurus to the commentary box.

Anne and Jake, also out on foot on the course, were a little less overwhelmed. This was too much. Samson was in overdrive. They had seen him do this in practice before, or at least Jake had, and knew that he could easily keep it up till the end. They got close enough to the caddy, Larry Topham, at one point to give him a note to pass to Samson. 'Cool it, we've discussed this, remember', the note said, and Larry, who read it of course, wondered what it meant as he passed it to his boss.

The string of birdies ended with an eagle at the first par five, and only after that did Samson fall in with his manager's wishes.

Jake checked their course map against the starting times and worked out where their other protégés would be. They soon found an easier way of finding them. The leader boards around the course had four names at the top, showing how many under par the players were and which hole they were currently playing. To Jake's horror, all four leading positions were being held by his team. Jake flashed his playing pass at an official, grabbed a buggy from the vehicle park, promised to return it in ten minutes, urged Anne to get in and set off to deliver the same message to the other three that Samson had received.

They returned the buggy and watched the leader board. None of the four improved their score to par from that point, but it hardly mattered. Samson had been ten under when he got the message, Martin and Ian six under and Jason five under. They finished the round still at the top of the leader board and Samson had equalled the course record.

There would be a clamour for post-round interviews, Jake knew, and he had to get to the golfers before the media did. He waited by the last hole and ordered each one to get to the scorer's tent and leave by the rear exit and not to give any interviews unless he was with them. With any luck, he would get in front of the microphones first.

As each of the players left the scorer's tent, by the rear door as agreed, Anne bundled them into the back of a van, borrowed from the official vehicle park again, and drove them away. They would have to appear before the microphone, that was contractual, but she would deliver them over to the satellite company only when Jake had done his bit. She smuggled them into her villa put the four under oath not to move until she called them, turned on the TV, told them to watch the interview and learn, and went to watch Jake in front of the cameras.

There was bedlam in the media area. Everyone wanted a piece of Jake's golfers and Jake was having trouble explaining that they would appear, in due course, once they had interviewed him. No-one wanted to interview him, they explained, everyone all across Europe was gagging to hear from the golfers. Jake, when at last they let him speak, pointed out that contractually he had the right to speak for his golfers and appear on their behalf. If they wanted him to bring his players in, there would be a special fee, but first he wanted to have his say and hear what the boys were going to face.

'You mean you want to get the story straight?' said the woman interviewer.

'There is no story. That's the point. Now, let me go up first and I guarantee you'll get your pound of flesh, and not a drop of blood, later.'

So the cameras rolled with Jake facing a hostile interviewer. 'Jeremy Godwin, the four leading players are all from your stable. How do you explain that, given their rankings.'

'Not a lot to explain, Madelaine, that's golf. Unpredictable as ever. If it's the same tomorrow, I'll be delighted, of course, but very surprised.'

'Jeremy, Jake, come on, there's got to be a reason. What did you do? Feed these guys an extra weetabix?'

'Well we do treat them well and what's changed in recent months, and we have not competed for nearly three months before this, is the iron discipline we've managed to instill and the endless hours of work these guys have put in. If it's down to anything, it's got to be down to that. Look, a guy like Samson, you saw it today, unbelievably talented. He's always been one of Europe's best prospects and no-one has a touch round the greens like he does, but now he has allied that with the sort of discipline it was hard to get him to accept before. And he's the leader. The boys would follow him anywhere. They idolise him. He teaches them, they copy his hard work and the progress we've made has been unbelievable. There is no substitute for talent, and these guys have that in abundance. But you need perspiration as well as inspiration and Samson has shown us the way.'

'That's great, Jake, but some folk are going to find it hard to believe that the leopard has changed its spots, aren't they?'

'Well Madelaine, seeing is believing. And we are not talking about leopards, are we? We are talking real live human beings who can develop, change, have insights, get converted on the road to St Andrews, which is where Samson's heading, by the way. Don't you think so Madelaine? People can change? People deserve credit when they take the straight and narrow path? These boys have worked damned hard in the last few months and this is the first chance they've had to show the world the fruits of it all.'

Jake winked at Anne, the sign that she was to bring the boys in. When they appeared there was bedlam. Flashbulbs popped, cameras were hoisted aloft, seasoned journalists found themselves elbowed out by young paparazzi desperate for a photograph.

Somehow the four managed to get on the platform, arms around each other's shoulder, to confront Madelaine. Jake, watching from the sidelines, knew that Samson and Madelaine had form together. He was surprised, almost, that Samson didn't wink at her. Samson had told him, years ago, that they'd had a fling and that he'd managed to open a few doors for her, as he put it. Even in that atmosphere Jake could see how the electricity crackled between the two of them.

'First of all boys, congratulations on four fantastic rounds of golf. Samson, if I can start with you. 10 under par and a course record. Where'd that come from?'

'Madelaine, it's no surprise to us really. We've always known we had it in us. You always know when you've got it in you, Madelaine, don't you think, but somehow getting it to the point where it all explodes just needs that extra something. I'm sure you've been there too. For us, we have Jake to thank. He opened our eyes to what we needed to do and you know Madelaine, once you've done it once, and it's felt so right, you just want to keep doing it again and again, you know. You just want to get that feeling again, over and over. So we started doing it right and Jake got us working to keep it right. We've had three months of hard work, and with each one of us Jake has found something special. You know what it's like Madelaine when somebody does something special for you, really touches a nerve. It may feel odd at first, but then you think oh my God, yes; I've been waiting all my life for someone to show me that. And then you can't stop. Does that make any sense Madelaine?'

It was as well the camera was not on Madelaine. A deep red flush had come over her face and her eyes had widened. There were other changes too, that she was even less proud of and that the camera could not have detected.

Eventually she remembered where she was and what she had to do. 'There are bound to be some who ask awkward questions, though, aren't there, Jason?'

Jason clearly hadn't a clue what the last few exchanges had been all about, but Samson was impressed at the way he dealt with the flummoxed woman. 'Hey Madelaine, thanks for your congratulations. We haven't always had the best of press, you know; we've had some knocking copy, including some knocking copy from your outfit, Madelaine, so it's nice to see you giving us a bit of credit for a change when we do our country proud and put Britain top of the leader board. What was your question, again?' Madelaine moved to Ian.

'I was wondering how you felt out there when you saw what was happening. Your team ahead of all those famous names, Ian?'

Things were back on track. A question about how he felt. Samson, alert for any errors from his team mates, could almost hear the media training kick in. 'I don't think I have the words to describe it. It was amazing, totally amazing. To see some of the names up there and us in front of them, I don't think I can tell you what that feels like really.'

And from there cliché followed platitude and was topped by banality. The interview was over. Jake reappeared and promised a full press conference at the end of the tournament, when, he said, not if, one of his team had triumphed.

There was, however, a post-mortem in Jake's villa. Anne was present, sitting at the front next to Jake, who looked shattered. He had seen his crime come close to discovery. He knew they were on to something, these journalists and he felt the shades of the prison house drawing round him again. He was furious with his players:

'There has to be a strategy. We all have to agree it, again, and this time bloody well stick to it. You can't go breaking records willy-nilly, out of nowhere and all at the same time.' *Not without giving me a bleeding heart attack.*

'Boss.' It was Ian. 'It's damned hard. When you've been where we have been, ignored, never on TV, alone on the course as the crowds follow the other lot, barely covering our costs but playing with millionaires with their own helicopters. That's hard. So when you get the chance, it sort of goes to your head and you just want to go for it. The first cheer did it for me. Then I got a crowd round me, first time ever at something like this, and then this bird with big knockers and tight shorts blows me a kiss. Hell. I'm only human.'

Jake glared at him, red-eyed with fury. 'You think that's an excuse for getting us all sent down, do you, you stupid idiot?' Ian recoiled. But the lessons had been learned. They knew now, first-hand, what would happen if they didn't stick to the strategic plan. Patience was needed. If it wasn't their turn this week, next week it would be.

Anne, to Jake's dismay, stood up and applauded them. 'I thought you were magnificent. I will be proud to make you all millionaires, too. My husband would have been proud, too. But, boys, for God's sake be careful. There are some very nasty people out there. Now, stay out of the bars, where those people and the press will be lurking and get a good night's sleep.'

And they all did as they were told. Except Martin, who drank whisky all night in bed with a girl he picked up at the roadside outside the resort.

28 *Millican's theory*

M artin woke exactly an hour after he'd gone to sleep. The girl who had kept him company for most of the night was standing at the foot of the bed, going through his trouser pockets. 'You won't find anything in there.' He tried to say, but managed only a croak. His mouth parts felt glued together and he had a raging thirst.

At the sound of his croak and the sight of movement in the bed, the girl picked up her things and fled, taking with her what she hoped was the thing she had been sent to find, all the pills and creams from his overnight bag, drawers and cupboards. Going through his pockets had been an afterthought, an almost reflex reaction after all her years in the profession.

Martin, as yet unaware of his loss, noted the time, groaned and went to the bathroom, where he put his mouth under the tap and, despite warnings to the contrary, imbibed copious amounts of the water that poured from it. His next move was to get the painkillers to do a job of work on his stabbing headache. He was no stranger to hangovers, but this was a Lulu. He couldn't believe it was just the whisky. He looked everywhere for his favourite analgesics but found nothing. He searched his drawers and cupboards and noticed that all his medicines and creams had vanished. The girl, of course, but why? Without the distracting fog and pain of his hangover he would have hit on it earlier. He rushed to the wardrobe and his clothes bag. He pushed aside the clean golf clothes and found the extra compartment. The small bottles, unmarked and full of clear liquid, were still there.

He rang reception and got some painkillers. He took four and then, having examined the box and concluded that the adult safe dose was around eight a day, another two, hoping his Portuguese translation was accurate.

When the pain had subsided a little and the sickness in his stomach with it, he wondered what he should do. There could be only one explanation for the disappearance of all his pills, creams and potions. So should he tell Jake, or should he keep it to himself? Telling Jake would be to admit what had gone on last night and while Jake would not be shocked, he would be angry that his express orders had been disobeyed and Martin knew his place in the team was far from secure. He had cost Jake much more than he earned and now that he had a chance to repay his debt he was putting it all at risk by his antics.

Anyway, it was probably not as serious as it looked; probably just one of the other teams guessing that some sort of performance enhancer was behind yesterday's success and wanting a bit of it for themselves. Well they would spend a fortune analysing iron tablets, vitamins, glycosomate and pain creams only to find that's just what they were. So there was no harm in keeping stumm.

Martin was not brave and more than a little selfish. 'Least said soonest mended' had been drummed into him by a mother who believed in education by aphorism and had left him with a battery of sayings and old wives' tales for every occasion. She hadn't, however, equipped him with one that would prevent him yielding to a penchant for hookers, a predilection that had caused him to fiddle his expenses for years, in the absence of more legitimately available income from the tour.

The thought of breakfast caused him to heave. Should he take the stuff, today, he wondered. He'd been ordered to drop back down the field, so why bother with the drug? Martin had noticed that it didn't just improve his performance on the course. At first he thought his new potency was an effect of the better fitness regime that Jake had insisted on as they practised with the drug, but then he noticed a fall in capability if he stopped taking it for a day or two. In fact, once he stopped it, the effect was reversed and he lost all sexual interest and function at the end of a week's break from golf and the drug. So he had taken it every day since, sometimes twice and once three times and had the time of his life. He was a regular in certain Midlands' nightspots and had developed a reputation with the hookers he favoured as the John who always got more than his money's worth. Some of them had started to avoid him, despite his being a safe source of money. Safe, certainly, but hard-earned, they told themselves.

So now, feeling like death, but aware that young and fit as he was, he would be fine by lunchtime, he opened the first promone bottle and thirty minutes later, the second.

After the second he told his stomach to give him a break, and it did. Impressed, he asked his headache to go away, and it complied. That was not something he had noticed before, but this was a new supply. Perhaps it was new and improved. Exhilarated and fully fit, he went off to the early morning team meeting, feeling invincible.

★

Phil passed the villa as the young golfer was leaving. He recognised him as Martin Pascal, one of Jake's team, and remembered starting him yesterday. He noticed the sheen of youth and good health the man exuded, despite the extra weight he carried, and felt a pang of envy. They greeted each other and the younger man vaulted the low wall around his villa and almost skipped away towards the clubhouse.

Phil's went into the functional space that was his office. Nothing personal had been allowed to dilute the sense that this was a place for work and nothing else. There was no drinks cabinet, no pictures on the wall, no trophy collection or, on the solitary desk, no executive toys. There was no picture of Phil's ex-wife (of course) or children. Phil checked his watch. Matt Prosser, his tournament director, opened the door and apologised for being late.

Phil beckoned him in, looked down the corridor outside his office and closed the door.

'Bit cloak and dagger, Phil. What's going on?'

'Yeah, sorry about that. I wanted to fill you in before our visitor gets here. I'll keep my voice down; these walls must be very thin. The guy you are about to meet is not who he says he is. He may well be what he says he is, but he definitely isn't who. He claims to be a professor of Physics but doesn't say from which University. I haven't been able to find him on Google so far. He doesn't know we're on to him, though.'

'So why are you giving him air time?'

'He comes highly recommended and has some great references. Ones I can't ignore. And, whoever he is, he has some interesting things to say. I'd already agreed to meet him and read some of his theories before I checked him out. The fact he's a phony doesn't invalidate his story. And I can't work out why he would be here telling me what he's telling me unless he genuinely believes it. Lastly, he might be false, but his referees aren't. One of them I simply dare not approach. It isn't a man whose word you question if you want to keep your job. The other two, when I contacted them, said they knew about the reasons for his visit and that he was keeping his real identity secret. They knew exactly who he was but couldn't tell me. What mattered was whether he talked sense or not. Now, one of those two was a peer of the realm and the other a very famous Nobel prize winner. And, as I said, they confirmed their references for this man who says he's Millican.'

'And you are sure the ones you were talking to were real people?'

'As sure as it's possible to be. They sounded real enough. Genuine, I mean. I could check the telephone numbers, I suppose. But it seems a bit over the top to go that far for someone just offering advice.'

'So what are you thinking now?'

'I'm thinking he's probably MI6. I challenged him on the phone about his identity. I told him straight out I didn't believe he was who he said he was and he asked me to contact his referees. I told him I had and he simply said 'well then; there you are.' Strangely, it all adds to his credibility rather than the other way round. He gave me permission to tell you all this, but we both have to sign the Official Secrets Act and tell no-one else. Here's your copy. You have to do it now, before he will talk to us. If you don't he will simply vanish he says and 'do it the hard way. ' Don't worry. Signing the OSA is no big deal.'

Matt signed and handed the document back to Phil, who witnessed it. 'Do what the hard way?'

Phil shrugged.

★

Everyone, Anne, Jake and the three golfers, Samson, Jason and Ian, was present in Jake's villa when Martin arrived for the meeting. There were still two hours before the first of their tee times and, putting apart, practice was hardly needed.

'Okay, here's the strategy. First of all we want all of you to make the cut, whatever that turns out to be. We'll keep you informed. At the moment we predict a score of one over par will stay in. We have Samson down as the winner. Martin can come fourth, but the other two, Jason and Ian, listen up, have got to come nowhere. You two have got to underperform really well today. We've practised how to do that. If anything goes wrong with Samson's game, we need Martin to take over at the top and if Martin looks like he's not coping, Ian can cover him. Jason is backstop for all of you so keep your eyes on the leader board and watch out for messages passed from me or Anne. We don't want to have to pass them through caddies. They may have hearts of gold or they may not; just don't trust them. We think one of them is paying too much attention to what's going on already, asking too many questions. Don't think your bagmen are always on your side. They have access to all your stuff and are not beyond taking a bribe or two. And given what we know this place is famous for - he meant the cat house and the avenue of whores outside the centre - watch out for honey-traps.'

Martin's head was in his hands.

'Have you all got that? Obviously because of the need to cover, it is important you keep up to speed so make sure you all keep nicely topped up. Any questions?'

Martin had a question. 'Is there enough of the drug to keep us going. I mean we know that the inventor passed away some time ago, and we were rationed a bit at one point. Are we okay now?'

Jake turned to Anne for a response: 'Yes,' she said, 'all systems are go on the supply front. We get a completely new batch every week and any effects you report on your performance sheets are sent off to the manufacturer for analysis.'

'Who does the quality control?' Martin was feeling unusually bold.

'That's down to me. I take full responsibility for the source of the product and am confident of its integrity. You may think that an odd word to choose, but I mean it in both senses. I can vouch for its provenance, if you like, and also think that we are simply enhancing a natural bodily capability. This product would be no use if you were not already brilliant golfers. So, the formulation and ingredients are identical in each batch, yes.' Jake noticed Anne's fingers were crossed behind her back.

Martin had no more questions. Samson wanted to know how many he should win by and it was agreed that he should go as low as he could for today, day two, play his best, in other words, and assess it then on a daily basis. They were learning as they went along, Jake said, and this was the first four-day competition test. It might be important to build a big cushion, in case there was a scoring collapse later. And Villamoura on a windy day could be a real test. A really strong wind could introduce an element of chance that only a good lead could counter.

So, keep taking the tablets was the message. And Martin didn't mention that someone else had taken his.

★

Phil brought his visitor into the room. 'Professor Millican, this is Matt Prosser. Matt, Niall Millican.'

Matt's scepticism found immediate expression: 'You should have tried Mulligan. More appropriate, perhaps, for the sport.' Phil shot Matt a look. Less aggression, it said.

'No, Millican is my real name; has been for some years. On my passport and all. And I am a physicist. Been that for years, too. The only thing I can't reveal is my employment background.' He spoke with a soft Irish accent. Galway perhaps?

'We can guess, given what we have just signed.' Matt said. He didn't appear to have understood the signal from Phil.

'As you say, you can guess. I doubt you'll guess right, though, or right enough for it to matter. In any case, I won't be here long. I have a job to do and then I'll reincarnate somewhere else.'

'But still as Niall Millican? Not as Doctor Who?' Matt again. Phil was despairing and tried another look. *Christ, Matt, call the dog off.*

'Well, perhaps I do understand your resistance. But it would be better if you had an open mind.'

'okay. Are you wearing a wig, by the way, or is that red stuff real.' The third look had clearly not gone home either. *What part of 'shut the hell up' does Matt not get. Does he want us all killed?*

'It is real hair. The spectacles are necessary for my sight, and this light beard is also not an attempt at disguise. I have no need of disguise. You don't know me in any case. And after today, you will never see me again.'

Matt gestured his willingness to continue. *Big of you Matt. Now leave it to me.*

Phil took over. 'You know and Matt certainly does that I have been trying to get to the truth about the accusations flying around the tour. A scandal would damage the tour enormously. We would possibly never recover. My information that there was some substance to the rumours came from a trusted source and when you contacted me, Niall, I felt it would be useful to meet you.' He looked across to Matt. 'Matt, Niall was aware, from his undisclosed and undisclosable sources, that I had been alerted to a possible scam and what he had to offer was information on how it might work. How it might be operated. As I say, and as he knows, I checked him out and his referees insisted I take him seriously.

So, I had my suspicions well before Niall contacted me. But what I saw on the tee yesterday worried me enormously.

One of the competitors, a talented golfer by any definition, hit a tee shot which, in my view, was well nigh impossible, even granted the improvements in equipment and ball manufacture since my day. My first and lasting thought was that the ball was being controlled in some way; guided, steered, whatever you want to call it and the blow from the club, after a beautiful swing admittedly, was supernaturally hard. In my view you can hit them long or you can shape them, but you cannot do both more than one time in a thousand. This was a one in a thousand shot off the first tee in a tour championship. Impossible. That shot was, somehow, technologically aided, in some way.'

'You're right.' Millican intervened. 'You know obviously what I mean by Drone technology. Amazon is going to use it to deliver your books, because it is cheap and reliable. But at the cutting edge of a related technology, at the edge where small particles of matter are converted to energy and back again, the latest thing is to add speed and power to drone-like guidance systems. And it is worryingly inexpensive now the research is over. Almost anyone can use it. My, shall we call them 'employers', were using it, though of course we had not thought of golf balls. We were doing things with it that would win us the next Afghanistan type war in days. Our enemies were in for a surprise. Until the idea was stolen and the trail led to your friends on the course. The four young men who did very well yesterday.'

Matt seemed stunned. 'Are you serious? You have this amazing technology that could be put to great humanitarian use and make a fortune and someone steals it to make golf balls behave better? That's absurd.'

'An absurd waste, I agree, from our point of view. But actually ingenious. The thief knew what he had stolen, but had no interest in making bullets, shells and superfast drones. He stole it to prevent that, perhaps. But how better to make money than by using it in the highest paid sport of all. If you put all the prize money and sponsorship money together for the two major tours in Europe and America you have more than a hundred million pounds, but that is peanuts against what can be won by a betting syndicate. Especially one that knows it can't lose.'

'okay,' Matt said, 'tell me again how it works.'

'$E=mc^2$. You are familiar with that? Einstein's famous equation, so simple yet at the basis of all there is. That there is anything at all, anywhere in the universe, that there is even a universe, is down to the truth of this little equation. Matter is energy and energy is matter. They are different forms of the same thing. It is possible to convert matter to energy and back again to matter. All that is needed is an impact, a big bang, if you like. A golf ball with the right properties, struck at the right speed with the right sort of club, will convert enough of its mass to energy and back again to produce the effect you saw. Add a guidance system to that and you have made possible what you saw yesterday. And at the heart of this is a British invention called graphene. You've heard of that? Good, well the next stage of development from that super thin but super conductive and massively strong material, is what I'm talking about. A sort of liquid, malleable, transformative graphene, whose particles come in and out of existence according to certain factors. It is brilliant, but like Einstein's theory, unfortunately brilliantly simple, once you have the tools.'

'And the guidance systems?'

'Already there for the drones and for driverless cars, come to think of it. You need a very detailed photographic map of the course and then the right computer programme. After that a small system of transmitting beacons, really quite small things can be set to take the ball where you want it, depending on how hard and high you hit it. Google drove its driverless test car millions of miles without a software or hardware induced accident.'

Matt was speechless. 'It certainly explains what I saw yesterday; and on more than one occasion. Can it be done from anywhere on the course, with any club?'

'So far as I am aware, the possibilities are limitless. You can do the guiding from a laptop.'

'And what do you expect us to do with this information?'

'Prove I am right and stop the cheats before they ruin the game.'

'Who are their backers? They can't be doing this alone.'

'That is tricky. I think you need to look to your illustrious sponsor for some help there. He does after all manufacture quite a lot of things which need propelling.'

'I agree somebody big has to be behind this, but it can't be him,' said Phil.

'Why not. He seems the obvious one to me,' said Millican

'Because he is the one who got me worried about all this in the first place. He's the one who got wind of some major attempt to beat the system. He thinks it is something substance related, though he doesn't rule out technology. But he is the one who insisted on doping inspectors and who has recruited a caddy to spy on his golfing boss.'

'Has he indeed. Which caddy I wonder would that be, now?'

Phil told him. 'Larry Topham. Samson Gregory's bagman.'

'That,' said Millican, almost forgetting his accent for a moment, 'is extremely interesting. Extremely interesting. But of course, if your sponsor were using the technology it would be in his interests, would it not, to stress the substance angle. It keeps you away from the real cause. It wouldn't surprise me if he supplied the inspectors as well as insisting on them just to keep you pointing in completely the wrong direction.'

Phil nodded thoughtfully and shook his hand as he left. Oddly enough, Millican's performance appeared to have left Matt less convinced about the technological explanation than when he started. It was all too Star Wars for him, he said.

And if Phil had looked out of his window a little later that morning, he would have seen a small boy running around in a red wig, with large clear glass spectacles and a beard he'd found dumped in a bin near an ice-cream stall. But he didn't.

29 *The disloyal bagman*

O n Wednesday as the pro-am finished, Larry, still hardly able to believe what he had seen from his boss, watched open mouthed as the only billionaire he had ever met ran in circles round the edge of the green shaking hands with everyone he could find. He was a picture of joy unconfined. Then it was Larry's turn. The big bear of a man came up to him with outstretched arms and clasped him in a hug. 'Well done Mr Caddy, he shouted. Then he whispered directly into Larry's ear. 'Make sure we talk before I leave the reception. It will be in your interest. There is a down payment in your bag. Just the start. Be sure you talk.'

When Larry was left alone to put things away and clean up before he got to the players' reception, he checked the bag and found the brown envelope. Inside were 500 euros. No note. Nothing else. Larry finished his tasks as quickly as he could, changed out of his caddy overalls and went to the reception. He saw the German as soon as he entered. It was hard to miss him anywhere, but here he was on the stage about to make an announcement.

Stefan made a speech more about his company than the golf and more about his own win than anything else. People laughed, but they felt they had to. Some of the jokes, the ones aimed at governments and politicians, were applauded.

He finished and worked the room for a little while, finding his way to Larry eventually. In the noisy room, with chatter in many languages at the same time, there was no danger the conversation would be overheard. It was in any case brief. Stefan simply hadn't believed what he'd seen from Sampson was natural. He wanted information. How was it done? And if it was done by substances, he wanted them. The smile had gone from his face. He asked Larry to go back to his locker and look in the bag again. If he was happy and prepared to help he could keep what he found there. If he did a good job he could count on much more. And the job was to steal anything relevant and get it to Stefan. Larry nodded. He was sure he would be able to help. Stefan turned away without a word or a handshake. The smile was back on his face. Larry looked round and saw Cristina with Samson. Samson was talking animatedly. But Cristina was looking straight at Larry.

Now, two days later, on the Friday, day two of the competition proper, and while Sampson was having a back massage before a scheduled team meeting, Larry saw his chance to earn a better living that he made from caddying. His boss had been better behaved, of late, but that didn't compensate for all the insults, slights and impositions he had received from that source over the years. So this, Larry argued, was about economics, not loyalty, and if the bastard was cheating, well then it served him right. And if not, no harm done.

He let himself into Samson's villa, using his duplicate key card. He had every right to be there and a thousand reasons, ready if needed, for being there just then. Samson was getting treatment for his back and Larry had fixed the appointment. He had not forgotten Cristina, but he knew she swam at this time each morning and had watched her go to the pool. He had seen her watching him talking to Stefan and knew he had to be careful. She was no fool and had every reason to protect Samson's interests.

Inside the villa he moved swiftly from room to room checking every possible hiding place. In the bedroom he saw a bag he knew belonged to Samson and opened it with one swipe of the zip. Inside he found what he was looking for. Two small glass jars with the clear liquid he'd seen Samson taking. Larry had just the one jar with him. He wasn't expecting two containers and couldn't risk mixing samples in his single jar. Another risk. He zipped the bag up, left and locked the villa, hurried to his locker room and took out the spare jar he'd put in his locker. He emptied a little from the jars he'd stolen into his own jars and took the originals back to the villa. Five minutes later he was out and walking nonchalantly back to the locker room. He didn't see Cristina watching him and couldn't know she had seen his entire operation.

★

'I didn't take anything, honest boss. Nothing.'

'Yes you damn well did. You were seen. You had the two bottles in your hand.'

'But I put them back. I got scared at what I'd done and put them back.'

'But there's some gone from each bottle; where's that?'

'I took it for myself boss. I had heard all the talk. The caddies don't talk of nothing else. We all know there's something going on, and then I saw Martin having a nip and I saw where he got it from and where he put it and reckoned you was all doing the same. And I saw what it did to you; and I heard you talking about the other thing, the stud thing, with Ian. You didn't know I was there. I put two and two together and went looking for it. Thought I'd have a go tonight.'

'Where is it now?'

'Inside me.'

'How much did you swallow?'

'Just a bit from each bottle'

'Together?'

Larry nodded and tried to look scared. 'Shouldn't I have done that?'

'Don't know. We were told half an hour apart. But it shouldn't make any difference. Listen, if you're lying I'll kill you. Or more than likely somebody else will. If that stuff's not inside you or you tell anyone else about it, or give it to anyone you're as good as dead. Got it? What were you talking to Stefan about the other day? At the reception?'

'Stefan. What's he got to do with anything? We wasn't talking about nothing. He just said thanks and what a great boss I had and if he ever needed a caddy he knew where to come.'

'This had all better be the truth.'

'It is. On my life it is.'

★

'It's all getting a bit messy.' Anne was getting ready to go out to watch the team perform on the second day. She was talking through the open bedroom door to Mitchell, who was sitting on her sofa in the living room.

'First we have the four tops scenario, all four places on the leader board for our team, then we have Larry telling Sampson he knows what's going on. And that's just what I know about. What else could there be? Oh yes, that question at the meeting earlier. About the batches and the variable quality. Where did that come from?'

'Possibly from the fact that each batch is a bit different and certainly the stuff I make can't be the same as Selwyn made.'

'Now you tell me. 'Not the same' is not 'variable quality'. Why on earth can't it be the same?'

'For a start Selwyn was a bloody Nobel Prize winner in the making. He understood the ins and outs of what he was doing. I don't. I follow his instruction as best I can, but he left things out of the instructions because he knew them and assumed everybody else would. So I have to sort of guess some of the stuff and because I don't really understand the process, which is part biological, part chemical and part physics, with a bit of maths and magic thrown in, I can't be sure each batch is the same. In fact, I can be pretty sure they're all different, but they should all work fine, nonetheless. Have you heard of the Endocannabinoid system?' Anne shook her head. 'Vaguely. Is it a factor here?'

'It certainly is. The Endocannabinoid system is a system of receptors in the brain. Selwyn was a bloody expert and he knew how to switch them on and off. The only man in the world who did.'

'What do they do, these endo thingy receptors?'

'They regulate pain, mood and appetite. Include sexual appetite I'm told. They also provide a pathway to muscle memory for the main part of Selwyn's stuff. He understood it and I don't. So I have to experiment my way through to the solution.'

'You mean you don't really know what you are doing. You could do real damage to these guys?'

'Very unlikely, but theoretically possible. I guess the proof of this pudding, like most puddings … But I have got detailed notes on each batch. So if we get a super one, or a rogue one, I can reproduce it or eliminate it.'

'Jesus. I wish you hadn't told me. I don't know I can live with that.'

'Oh come on. It's not as if it's going to kill anyone. There's nothing in it that can do that. And every effect is under conscious control, more or less, once you know it's there, isn't it? I mean if you feel randy and know what's making you randy, you can go and take a cold shower. You don't have to find a convent and rape all the nuns.'

'But,' he went on, 'it would be much better if we had the mark 2 Selwyn was on about. That sounded something of a major breakthrough so the effects could be separated out.'

'I keep telling you Mitchell, he may have told you that; he never said anything to me.'

'But he said you would know precisely where it would be, the mark 2 stuff. He said it would be a year or two in development, but would be infinitely superior to mark 1'

'So you keep saying. He was a damn sight more forthcoming to you than to me, then. When did he tell you all this? At that meeting you had? You sure there's nothing I don't know about? Because I sure know nothing about a mark 2, notes or anything.'

She wasn't sure Mitchell believed her but was pretty confident he couldn't have any definite proof that she knew of an improved version. *He's damn well not going to get his hands on that. That's for later development, and I'm keeping it in my hands, thank you very much Mr Walker.* Perhaps Selwyn did say something, but Mitchell can't know it's true. It's not as if he has it in black and white. *So I'll just keep saying I've never heard of it until I'm blue in the face.* It was Larry she was worried about. He knew too much. How on earth were they going to keep him quiet?

'okay. So we press on with mark 1 and keep our fingers crossed,' Mitchell said. *Good boy!*

★

Samson was relieved to get back on the course and he was sure that applied to his three colleagues, too. They had an early afternoon start and Samson, unlike the others, he imagined, had warmed up properly. He was confident of repeating what he had done yesterday. This time he planned to be just as spectacular on the holes he'd had to rein himself in on yesterday. Another course record was in his mind.

He set off confidently, playing with the same partners as yesterday, this time from the first rather than tenth tee. From the start it was clear to the spectators that another special day was in prospect and before long, the crowd around Samson was enormous and the noise following each wonderful shot deafening. By the time he got to the tenth tee to start his back nine, he was five under and had reached the holes he had slaughtered yesterday. A three iron down the middle and a second shot across the corner should have given Samson an easy birdie but he pulled his third shot into a greenside bunker and had to get up and down for five.

Still, there were no bogies on his card for either of the two days and he had no intention of putting one there.

Martin was not having a good day. For a few holes, everything was as he expected. Control was perfect and the codes, read from his own chart, not the caddy's, worked fine. Then he felt a switch turn off inside him and no matter what he did, he couldn't turn it back on again. His legs felt heavy and his arms too light. He could not focus properly. He was down to his own native skill now, and with the night he'd spent, the scotch he'd drunk and the lack of sleep, native talent wasn't enough. He featured just once on TV, getting a triple bogey seven and then they and the crowds deserted him for richer pickings. His round of eighty was in some ways better than he deserved. It would mean he would miss the cut and play no further part in the championship.

Ian and Jason got home without mishap, both over par for this round but well within the cut. For Samson, though, the glory continued; he walked up to the final hole, the infamous eighteenth, needing a birdie for a second course record equalling round in a row.

He was aware of the cameras on him, thought of the millions of pairs of eyes they represented, and basked in the presence of such enormous numbers following his progress in real time. He took it all in. The sunshine was glorious and the air warm and scented on the early evening breeze. The crowd, lightly dressed and in raucous mood cheered his every step to the green. He was a new hero, sprung fully-formed from nowhere to show them a different way of playing the game they loved. They had seen magic and worshipped the magician. He had shown them delicacy and they had admired his touch; he had shown them power and they had swooned. Now he was about to show them how to putt. He was aware, though they were not, that his putting was not part of the act. This was him and his skill against the trickery of the green. The putt was long and treacherous. Uphill first and then downhill and turning to the right to the hole some forty feet away. He had put it so far away to add to the occasion. If it went in he could name his price with the people around the green. He struck it firmly and it reached the crest where it seemed to stop. The crowd groaned. Slowly, and it had in reality never actually stopped, it rolled again gathering pace downhill and turning in towards the hole. The crowd was screaming for it to turn more and keep rolling, when on the very edge, a blade of grass width from the cup it stopped. Samson looked after it with his putter pointing at the hole, willing the ball to fall. It didn't. He started to move and the ball toppled gently into the hole. The crowd exploded with delight. They mobbed him, despite the best efforts of the stewards, on the green and for Samson, it was a moment he would remember for the rest of his life as the happiest he had ever been.

Fifteen minutes later he was less happy. He and Martin had been selected for random testing by the doping team and he was standing in a cubicle, his trousers round his ankles and his shirt held aloft while a 'chaperone', an old man of eighty or so, peered steadfastly at his penis which point blank refused to operate under those circumstances. Until Samson remembered to visualise it and the golden stream poured obediently forth.

30 Bye-Bye bagman

On the Saturday morning, at around 11 a.m., a red BMW sports model pulled up in front of the farm building in a remote rural area ten miles from the Villamoura course. The farmer had been well paid to ask no questions and warned what would happen if he did, or if he opened his mouth at all. Inside the building, gloomy and evil-smelling, a man had just endured his darkest and most painful hours. He lay on a bed of metal rollers, the surface of an ancient cattle-grid, chained and totally defeated, caught in a terrible despair and weeping with hopelessness and pain. The two-pronged pitchfork that had blinded him had hovered for what seemed like minutes in front of his terrified gaze before it was plunged into his eye sockets. The gag which stifled his bestial screams was covered in the blood from his eyes and from the broken nose he had suffered in the earlier beating as he'd been dragged from the car and into the building. There was no part of him that didn't want to die and get this over with, except the small, dwindlingly small, part of him that was desperate to live.

The BMW door opened and Stefan Greiff's caddy, now smartly dressed with a straw trilby and sunglasses, got out. He was met by two other men, casually dressed and sweating from the heat inside the building they had just left. They handed the BMW driver, whom they knew simply as Bradley, a mobile phone.

'This is his,' one of them said, with a gesture towards the building. The driver switched it on, grunted with mild surprise when he got a signal, and noticed, over the screenplay photograph of Larry on the green of some golf course or other, that there were seven missed calls. He turned it off and slipped it in his pocket.

'I take it he gave us what we wanted?'

'No bother at all. Hardly worth the effort. He would have told us anything at all, if we'd asked. But we had a bit of fun with him first. Turns out he was a bit fond of his toes. Wanted to keep 'em a bit longer. He was even more fond of his dick, so we let him keep that, for what it'll be worth without his balls.' They didn't mention the blinding, which they'd done just for their own amusement.

If the man with the sunglasses felt anything at all on hearing this, he didn't show it. 'So we've got the stuff he nicked? He didn't give it to anyone else?'

The two men handed over two small jars and a thick wad of currency. 'This is it all right. No question.' Bradley took the bottles and handed the notes back to the men. 'Bonus,' he said.

'What about him?' One of the men indicated the shed.

'This whole heap of shit is Code Red. You know what Code Red means?' The men didn't. 'It means his future is all in the past. See to him and then get rid, properly. Clean up well and the body disappears. Completely. Shove it in a bag and bury it deep in the middle of nowhere. There's plenty of that round here.'

'Sure.' And with that Bradley got back into his car and with no word or gesture of farewell, drove away. The other two watched him go and then turned back towards the shed, where an unconscious Larry twitched in response to nightmare visions that were about to come true.

A mile down the track, Bradley opened the window of his car and tossed out the jars the men had got from Larry's golf bag. For Larry he felt a moment's remorse. But someone had to take the wider view, see the bigger picture. That's what he was paid for. Still, an innocent life is an innocent life and Larry hadn't done much wrong. *He should have stayed loyal. There's a lesson there for us all.*

★

Samson and Jake were in urgent conversation. It was an hour to tee-off and there was still no sign or trace of Larry. His mobile was now dead, his room, shared with another caddy, had revealed nothing and none of his usual associates had seen him at all that morning. His room-mate said there had been an early phone call, about 4 a.m., the guy thought. Larry had got up to answer it and gone outside so as not to disturb his friend. When the room-mate woke up again, it was 7.30 and no sign of Larry. His clean caddying overalls were still in the room, but other day wear had gone. So it looked like Larry had got dressed at some point, but the room-mate didn't know when. And in answer to a question from Jake, the caddy didn't think Larry had been completely his self recently. Something had been bothering him for a day or two, but he didn't know what.

The final thing the room-mate volunteered was that Larry always slept with his wallet and passport under his pillow, apparently a legacy of a theft he'd suffered years ago. The guy had looked for these and they had gone and weren't in the room safe either. So Larry had got dressed and gone out with his wallet and passport, sometime between four a.m. and seven-thirty.

'What about the car? Does he still have the hire car?' The other caddy produced the keys. 'We share it and there's just this set of keys. It's still parked round the back.' Jake knew that Larry claimed the whole vehicle on his expenses and suspected this other caddy did the same. He reckoned, though, that this was not the time to raise it as an issue.

'Well, not a lot more we can do. We are off in an hour. Where do we get a caddy from?'

'I think I'm looking at one,' said Samson, looking at Jake.

'You want me to traipse round with a bag in this heat?'

'If you want me to win this prize money. What other choice do we have?'

★

At nine-o-clock on that same Saturday morning, two figures, one tall and upright, one old and slightly bent, entered Phil's office, where the secretary was expecting them. They were shown a seat, offered coffee, which they declined and after five minutes were shown into the august presence of the chief executive of the European Tour.

The men shook hands and introduced themselves as the lead visiting inspector from the European doping unit and the chaperone who had so diligently performed his duty in the presence of a urinating and slightly amused Samson and an embarrassed and worried Martin. On an impulse he wasn't able to stifle, Phil wanted to wash his hands after he'd shaken those of the two men in his office. He contented himself with taking a tissue from the box before him and discreetly using it to wipe his palms.

The two men offered identification and Phil peered at the cards and letters they held before him, his hands clasped behind his back. Once he had nodded his approval the inspector placed a box on the table between them and Phil sat back in his chair as they opened it. Inside were two sealed containers, each holding a small amount of pale yellow fluid, and two envelopes. The inspector, whose voice still carried the flat vowels of his Lancastrian upbringing, explained the process.

'Yesterday, on the advice of the tour team and in accordance with the testing regulations, we selected two competitors to undergo random sampling. We cleared our decision with the tour committee and chose the leading player, as is standard practice, and a player whose results had varied from a previous performance by a margin that was outside the normal. The two players are those named on the envelopes.'

Phil leaned forward to read the names of Samson and Martin and sat back again.

'The samples were taken under the supervision of the chaperone, this gentleman on my left, who is content to answer any questions you may have about his role. The urine samples were passed into receptacles and poured from them by the donors themselves into sealed vials with an identity tag and not touched by the chaperone until the seals were in place. They were then taken to a storage unit, and with the identities anonymised, carefully stored and eventually analysed by the team we have on site. Often samples are sent away, but not on this occasion, where we are fortunate to have a portable laboratory.'

Phil made a note to ask a question later about expense. Some of this seemed a touch over the top.

'The results of the analysis are in those envelopes and are known only to the analysts, who do not know the identities of the donors, of course. Would you care to open the envelopes and read the results?' *Here we go. Bit of a crunch time, this. But if Millican's right, this'll be clear.*

Phil indicated he was content for the inspector to complete that part of the process and the envelopes were opened using a silver letter opener from Phil's desk.

The inspector read out the formal introductory lines of the first report, on Samson. He read the name of the analyst, the procedure used and the date of the analysis. Finally, he read the signed assertion of the analyst that he was satisfied the process was properly conducted and that the results reflected an accurate state of the contents of the urine. The inspector read the line under 'Key Findings': higher than average levels of testosterone, consistent with the age of the donor and the circumstances of the donation. No further unusual ratios or volumes.'

'So it would seem that we can put Mr Gregory's mind to rest immediately.'

He opened the second envelope, sliding the silver blade along the crease of the envelope in a way that made Phil wince.

'Key Findings. Substantial traces of alcohol at a level indicating that the donor would have started the competition with levels which would have adversely affected his performance. Testosterone levels significantly depressed, possibly by the alcohol. No other significant ratios or volumes.'

'Well, less reassuring news for our second contributor. He started the round in a state which would have him banned from driving, but which would not have helped his golf. I recommend a warning and a retest at future venues, since he missed the cut in this one.'

Phil assured the inspector he would tell the golfers concerned immediately. The inspector said they would all receive copies of the reports in the next few days and held out his hand. If he noticed any hesitation in Phil's response, his expression didn't betray it and the handshake was firm, if very brief. As soon as they left, Phil went to the bathroom and washed his hands for a full three minutes. Later he checked with his PA Marilyn how the testing was being paid for. She said it wasn't a tour based expense and she didn't know who was meeting the bills. That worried Phil. *You get what you pay for in this world.*

★

Stefan's villa overlooking the eighteenth hole was sumptuous, but still less opulent than his own mansion home and the places he was used to. He had nonetheless decided to stay and see the end of the contest. His interest was personal. Two things, possibly three, were behind his decision. One was a near certainty, soon to be confirmed he hoped, that someone had found a way of cheating and he wanted a part of it. A big part. Probably all of it, if that could be managed. Secondly, he wanted Samson Gregory to be the leading name behind his push to expand golf in Germany. Stefan saw his native land as vastly underexploited in golfing terms, and ripe for a major commercial investment that would serve as his legacy. A grateful nation would remember him forever as the father of German golf. And the third, he was not sure why, concerned the dark-haired girl in Samson's villa. Stefan had seen that the air between her and Samson was sticky with the promise of later pleasure. He could see them deliberately postponing the time they would be alone together so they could enjoy it all the more and meantime, the space between them spat and crackled with lust. He wanted some of that again. An oversupply of available women had spoiled his appetite, but the dark-haired, dark-eyed girl was something else and he had started to itch, just a little, and meant to scratch it.

Meanwhile there was business to attend to. Larry the caddy had done his work and been appropriately rewarded for it, Stefan hoped. Bradley had brought in the liquid late that afternoon and it was currently being investigated in the portable and very well equipped laboratory Stefan had arranged on site. And Larry, Stefan had been assured, would not open his mouth about any of it.

Someone knocked at the door and came in. 'They're here,' was all he said. Stefan nodded and two men were ushered into the room and given seats on the sofa opposite Stefan's favourite armchair. A coffee table with two picture books of German golf courses and a bowl of fruit squatted between them.

Stefan, rather unnecessarily, introduced himself and invited the other two to do the same. The tall one spoke first. Stefan noted the flat vowels and wondered which part of the UK they represented. Not Scotland, he thought, but somewhere harsh and northern. At first the accent made the speaker difficult to understand for Stefan, whose English had been learned in America and from American films and TV, but gradually, after he had asked the speaker to slow down, it all came into focus and the words made sense to him in their own right. He stopped having to translate them in his head and relaxed. For a few minutes, as part of this linguistic acclimatisation, and partly because he was genuinely interested, he talked to the two men about their backgrounds and how they had come to work for him and what they thought of the experience.

He asked the shorter, slightly bent older gentleman how old he was and then asked why he still felt the need to work at eighty. The man had no answer beyond a need for an income and a sense of still being useful, even if it was only helping people pee into bottles. He explained there were many other aspects to the work and that he had started in the pharma arm of Stefan's empire. He was clearly not overawed by the great man's presence. When Stefan commented on that, admiringly, the chaperone said that at eighty you don't give much of a damn any more about any of the stuff the world thinks is important.

Stefan admired him even more, but was slightly disturbed that his loyalty would not therefore be automatic and unquestionable. The man, as if reading his thoughts, said, in German, 'Don't worry. You can rely on me. I am not a problem for you.'

Stefan was impressed. An Englishman who spoke good German. A rare beast. He nodded his approval and turned to the inspector. He asked if everything had gone well and whether their authenticity had been questioned. The inspector assured him it had not. They were from the same stable as the official team, after all, so who, other than the tour directors would question their presence. It was sometimes useful that the left hand was not in even remote communication with the right.

Stefan smiled. Who would ever think that a team of inspectors, with impeccable paperwork and practised procedures was anything other than the real deal? And besides, in the event of questions asked, he had a good enough paper trail back to doping HQ asking for support at this venue. All faked, of course, but very well faked indeed. And as a last resort, bribery always worked. Always. It was just a matter of the sum being big enough, or the threat real and believable enough.

'okay,' he said, 'so how are the results?

'Well, as you instructed, we reported clear findings apart from a little booze to management, as we were instructed to, and they are happy that all is well. The samples were then thoroughly analysed and the results are in. They were difficult to believe so we are having them redone. Unless anything emerges from that then we can say categorically that Samson Gregory is not using illegal substances to boost his performance. They are doing a final check, as I said, but they were pretty clear that there was nothing in the urine. They would need a blood sample to be absolutely sure, but the analysts are sure that anything producing the effects reported to them would show in urine, and it didn't.'

Stefan asked about the samples. The older man confirmed that the samples had to be genuine. He had supervised the process and seen the samples emerge for the tip of the urethra. There was no way the players could have influenced the sample.

Stefan agreed, thanked them and they left with instructions to do further tests on the ultimate winner and one other from Jake's team. Stefan repeated his orders that tour officials were to be told only that the results were clear, whatever the truth. The real findings were for his eyes only. The two men bowed and left.

Stefan sat back in the ample armchair. Sometimes his life wearied him. Who could he trust? Who could he really get close to? He saw fear and respect in everyone's eyes. If he walked into a room the atmosphere changed immediately. If he sat in on a meeting no-one said what they really thought. They said what he wanted to hear. He had no friends he could be sure of. Women were often out to trap him, 'friends' sold stories to the press. Emails and texts had to be guarded and cautious, at all times. And the compensations? Power, ease, wealth, luxury. In the end you didn't notice them, or you feared their loss more than you enjoyed their possession. He needed someone close he could confide in, but doubted the possibility of finding someone to share his opulent prison for reasons other than a fear of leaving.

This current matter was an example of sorts. His instincts made him sure that something big was happening. Some of the golf he had seen was outside the reach of anyone relying on human skill alone. There had to be aids of some sort, chemical or technological, he wasn't sure which, but his money was on chemical. And he was throwing enormous resources at uncovering it. The entire inspection team at this tournament was in his pay; he had bought the labs and the equipment and his sponsorship of the tournament itself was so extraordinarily generous that it guaranteed no awkward questions would be asked. But in the end, the one thing he could not guarantee was the truth. That depended on individuals, and they always had their own agenda. There were some whose souls you could buy. But they were false by definition. The really useful ones always remained free agents, outside his control.

Five minutes after the inspector and the chaperone had left, another visitor, Bradley, brought news of the liquid that Larry had stolen. Stefan asked Bradley questions about its provenance and Bradley was able to assure him that this was the very same liquid that Larry had taken from Samson. He had gone with Larry to the locker room, he said, lying fluently and undetectably, and been handed it personally. Since then, it had been in his possession the whole of the time up to the moment he had handed it to the analysts.

Stefan looked at Bradley, one of his most recent recruits, personally headhunted following glowing references from an impeccable source and immediately promoted to his chief security field officer, following the unexpected demise of his predecessor. Bradley had put his life on the line for Stefan's cause once already, had perhaps even killed for him and Stefan had little choice but to trust him. Still, he was very new and a little caution was needed. No-one was ever really impeccable. 'And the results?' He sat forward as if in anticipation but his tone suggested he wasn't expecting revelations.

'Negative. The liquid is chiefly water with a small quantity of two or three other substances, vitamins, stuff to ease joint pain, but nothing that would produce any effect on the body and nothing that was in any of the urine samples.'

Scheisse. Stefan slumped back in his chair, lost in thought again.

31 A virtual life

Jake's phone vibrated twice in the pocket of his caddy's overalls. Reluctant to interrupt the final preparations for round three, but unable to resist its insistent buzz, he pulled it from his pocket and looked at the screen. It was a text from Larry. He showed the screen to Samson. 'From Larry!'

'What's he say?'

Jake looked at the screen. 'Can't read the thing without my bloody glasses. Here.' He handed the phone to Samson. Samson took a minute to absorb the message. 'He says he's sorry. He feels he let us down and has gone home. He's packing the tour in and concentrating on his family.'

'Didn't know he had one.'

'No. Me neither. I think he had a mother still; but I didn't know about family. I didn't treat him well, did I? Took no interest in the bloody sod, unless he fell down on the job. Then I'd bollock him.'

'Well, he's getting his own back now.'

At that point, Samson's phone chirped. 'Text' he said. He reached for the phone and examined the screen. 'This is from Larry, too.' He read it and nodded. 'Same message more or less. Bit odd that. Friendlier than I'd have expected, in the circumstances. I'll text him back.'

Samson frowned with concentration as his thumb raced over the keyboard. 'Understand. Sorry for it all. Look after yourself and if you change your mind, let me know.'

Within minutes Samson was reading the message from Larry's phone thanking him for the concern, but that he wouldn't be changing his mind and his plane was leaving shortly. The text wished him luck in the tournament and Larry's phone signed off for the last time.

Last minute checks were made on equipment and then Samson, with Jake as his caddy, strode onto the first tee to a tremendous reception.

32 *Three's company*

B radley sat in his car, the red BMW, reading the message from Samson on Larry's phone. *They fell for it. But why wouldn't they? That'll buy me some time if I need it.* He smiled and texted a reply before slipping the phone back into his pocket and giving all his attention to the larger electronic device on the seat next to him. He reached over to get it. The screen told him the car was five kilometres away and slowing down. It made a left turn and stopped. Bradley waited for ten minutes and then set off for the location the tracker in the target car had identified. The terrain was scrubby, hilly and very remote. The road was little more than a track and very dusty. He drove slowly to keep the dust level down. He knew there was no need to hurry. He didn't see a car, dwelling or human being the length of his journey. Eventually he stopped the BMW, took a gun from the glove compartment and fitted a silencer. Silently, he moved up and around the contours of a small hill and took cover behind a barely adequate clump of grimy bushes. Just fifty or so yards ahead of him he could see two men digging in the hard soil. Clouds of dust rose in the still, hot air. Next to where they were digging was a large bag of the sort that golfers use to take their golf gear on board a plane. The men were sweating and cursing loudly. One of the men was Polish and Bradley smiled in recognition of the man's native language profanities and obscenities. *It's a shame; but no great loss to humanity. Think of the greater good.*

He waited until the digging was near completion, then, when both men had their backs to him, he approached rapidly and shot one of them in the back of the head from close range. The other turned quickly and barely had time to register surprise at the identity of his assailant before he too lay crumpled on the floor. Bradley stripped off the clothes splattered with the first man's brains and the second man's face. Wearing just his boxer shorts, he threw his clothes into the hole. He searched inside the jacket pocket of the larger of the two men, the one missing a face, and removed a thick wad of banknotes. 'Bonus,' he said. Sweating from the effort, he dragged and rolled the bodies into the deep hole they had dug and manoeuvred the heavy golf bag on top of them. He took the car the three had arrived in and returned to his own car. He dressed quickly in a spare polo shirt, slacks and sandals. He swapped the electronic gear out of the BMW into the other car and drove the beamer, stolen a couple of days earlier and fitted with false plates, back to the grave and parked it near the hole. He took Larry's phone out of his pocket and was about to toss it on top of the bodies when he changed his mind and put it back in his pocket. *Might still come in handy.* From the BMW boot he took a can of petrol, a rag and some matches. He enjoyed the gurgle of the petrol as it left the container and splashed down onto the three bodies. He used the last of the petrol to soak the rag and tossed the can into the hole with the bodies. He drove the beamer over the grave and got out. He found a long broken branch from a nearby tree, lit the petrol-soaked rag and dropped it near the car. From a safe distance he used the long branch to push the burning rag into the hole beneath the BMW.

The flame was powerful from the start and Bradley had to shield his face and turn away quickly. From a safe distance he assured himself that all was burning satisfactorily and he returned to the car the men had arrived in, the one he knew was safely anonymous, and drove away, happy at a job well done. He hadn't really expected the two men who'd killed Larry to give him away, even if they had been caught, but you couldn't be too careful. They were murderous thugs in any case and the world was well rid of them. He hadn't liked what they'd done to Larry. It was unnecessary. Plus you never knew who worked for whom. He was certain they wouldn't grass him up now. He thought of an example he had once heard, as a student at Oxford, from his philosophy tutor. He was quoting Bertrand Russell on the dangers of assuming things on the basis of past experience. Russell said that chickens in the farmyard assumed the farmer's wife had their best interests at heart because each and every day for as long as they could remember she had brought them something delicious to eat. So they trusted her and ran towards her as she approached with the bucket of seed corn. Then one day she slit their throats. And I've never trusted a farmer's wife since, he thought and laughed at his own joke. Pity the two men hadn't read as much philosophy as he had. And now they were dead and he was alive. *Just another benefit of a good education.*

33 Jake's disappointment

J ake couldn't help admiring Samson as he stood over the ball. He could see the power waiting to be unleashed. What wouldn't he give to be able to do what Samson could do, with or without chemical help. He knew Samson had talent in abundance, perhaps more than any he had ever seen. What he lacked was belief and discipline. And perhaps the belief was the most important thing. Samson had once told him that the reason he didn't want to train was that it would rob him of excuses for failure. *Can you believe that? How many of us do that? Put up with a level of unhappiness rather than risk doing something to change it, in case it makes you more unhappy? Do I?* But now, Jake could see the belief in Samson's every gesture. He wondered how much was down to the drug and how much to Cristina.

He watched Samson's drive soar down the fairway, as near perfect a shot as was possible, and set off after it with the bag. He caught Anne's eye in the crowd and smiled at her. Last night she had finally given way. Last night, the woman he'd been dreaming of for the last few months, had slid naked into his bed and offered whatever he wanted. And he bloody well hadn't been able to do a thing. He had not known frustration like it. In the end he had admitted defeat and Anne, he imagined, was quietly chuckling to herself. Well, part of the problem, of course, was that since he had stopped taking the Selwyn treatment, things hadn't been quite the same. Some of the drive had gone and he guessed there was a link with the stuff, even before Anne confirmed it. So he'd expected a drop in the urge but he hadn't expected the mechanics to fail as well. *Confidence, eh? What had he been saying about Samson?* Still, he would make up for it tonight. He was resisting the temptation to take some of the stuff. *No way. It'll be as nature intended or not at all.* He looked at Anne again. Her eyes were on Samson, though, and no wonder.

Samson was playing golf as it had never been played. It was faultless. Jake was pleased to note that Samson was following instructions and hitting some shots deliberately away from the hole, picking the wrong club, giving himself the wrong shot number, whatever was needed to fall short of absolute perfection. And still, after the first nine holes, he was five under par after three birdies and an eagle. The crowd was rapturous. *Not too much, Sammy boy. Let people see you're human now and then. I'm not going to prison because you can't stop showing off.*

After the tenth, Anne pressed a note into his hand: Jason was playing out of his skin again and was back in fourth, but Ian had suffered the same apparent malaise as Martin and couldn't get going. He had been ill after the fifth hole and now, after finishing with seven over par, was pale and gasping for breath in the medical unit. Apparently the inspectors were sniffing around again, too.

Jake was horrified by the note and worried again not just about the immediate problem with Ian but about the wisdom of the whole business. He would never have entered into this sort of thing on his own. It was Anne, damn her. For the second time in his life he was risking everything for that woman. That's what had turned him into a frustrated flaccid wreck last night. He wanted her too much. He'd been desperate to perform. And this damn venture was all for her. One minute he'd be all for it, geeing up the team, making sure they were obeying the 'rules', checking for adverse signs. And the next he'd be a wreck, venting his loose bowels in a villa bathroom, jumping at shadows. What depressed him most was knowing the die was cast. Turning back was not an option. Either his number would come up or it wouldn't. Come up. He was getting obsessed with things not coming up.

Jake, sick at heart and hating himself, turned his attention back to Samson, who rarely needed anything from his caddy. Everything was done according to the chart that Samson had put together so carefully in the preceding months. Just occasionally, more for the sake of the cameras than anything, Samson would confer with his caddy, and he came over for a chat now. 'What's up? Ian's right off the leader board. Everything okay?'

Jake tried to be reassuring and hated himself all over again for the lie he was about to tell. If any part of his fears were not selfish, it was knowing he was putting lives at risk: 'Just following orders, I think. Jason's still doing well so we don't want too many questions asked.' Jake saw that Samson was not fully convinced and wasn't surprised. Anxiety must have been written all over his face.

'Eight iron. This is shot 12a, b1, c2, d1.' Jake just caught the words from Samson and recognised them as the card's code for 180 yards, slight headwind, high draw.' But d1 was something he'd not heard before. He had to assume Samson knew what he was doing.

Samson struck the ball exquisitely. The TV commentators were ecstatic about the wonderful crunch as the club met ball first, then turf. Samson watched it arc up and inward towards the pin. Jake wondered how long it would be before Samson got bored by this level of perfection. He clearly hadn't reached that point yet. Jake suspected Samson was feeding off the crowd's reaction to his shots and he watched him closely for signs of anything untoward. All he saw was apparent delight at the adulation he was receiving. Jake saw him look and catch the eye of a pretty face in the crowd while the ball was still in flight. Jake had seen him do this before: when the ball dropped near or even in the hole, as he knew it most probably would, Samson would look back at the pretty face as if to say 'that one was for you.' It worked every time. This ball landed and hopped forward, checked and rolled straight into the hole. (Jake wondered if D1 meant go for the hole) In the middle of the raucous clamour, Samson turned back to the pretty face which was looking calmly back at him, full of intent. He smiled at its owner and winked. She smiled back, but Jake noticed that nothing else passed between them. The Cristina effect, Jake decided. At the end of the round, Samson led by nine shots. *Well he can't lose from that position.*

34 *Haven't we met somewhere before?*

On the tenth hole, watching Samson make yet another birdie, Anne was joined by Mitchell, virtually unrecognisable in large dark glasses and a baseball cap. She wasn't surprised when he raised the subject of the promone again. She'd made her worries clear enough last time.

'It's all perfectly safe, you know Anne. It's being made to the highest standards, you needn't worry on that score.'

'By whom?' Anne asked. 'I don't see you doing much work on it.'

'I have access to a private lab,' he told her, 'and some of the best equipment money can buy. As well as good staff'

'From Merricole?'

'From my employers, yes. I'm allowed a small team for private work, but they only make the components, not the finished product so there's no reason for them to suspect anything. I am no Selwyn, but I'm getting better and I'm within a hair's width of understanding everything about it, process and product.'

'That hair's width is the bit that worries me. That means what we're getting is variable. I can see that from some of the reactions we're getting. Martin tells me it cured his stomach and head, for God's sake. All he had to do was tell it to. And I can see from Cristina's face that the priapic effect is still in full swing in Samson. And now Ian's in some sort of difficulty; is that down to the promone as well?'

'Probably not, but you're right. That 'hair's width' is an unacceptable level of variation. It isn't dangerous though, because, as I keep repeating, the ingredients themselves aren't dangerous. They're all there in the human body in the first place. Though we actually take most of it from chimps and lately we've started synthesising some. And I will get it completely right. Of course, if we ever get the mark 2 Selwyn told me about, we'll be sure to have the problem cracked.'

'Chimps? Bloody hell, Mitchell. Chimps?'

'They share 99% plus of our DNA. Exactly the same stuff as in humans but with chimps it doesn't matter if the donors die, so we can take huge doses from an individual donor.'

'It sounds like our golfers are bloody guinea pigs for your experiments. We'll make it this way and see what that does to them and then make another batch and see what that does.'

'Absolutely not,' he said, a little too quickly and emphatically for Anne's liking. 'Don't let crazy thoughts like that stop you giving us feedback. We really need to know what each batch does for the golfers.'

Anne didn't really want to hear any more. It was beginning to raise too many questions.

'So is there any news on the mark 2 front? That is what we really need to make this thing secure.' Mitchell asked.

Anne looked at him. 'Well, I don't know what we do about that. I'll have another search when we get home, but, like I said, he may have told you to ask me and then died before he could tell me!'

'Perhaps if we look for it together, that might help?' Anne wondered if that was a proposition. She hoped not. She still found something about Mitchell creepy. And besides, she was trying to find a way back to Jake. The previous night had been a disaster. He had been just like Selwyn before the change. Crippled by performance-angst. Why did she do that to men? Selwyn, in a fit of frustration, had once called her a ball-breaker. Perhaps the poor man had been right.

Over Mitchell's shoulder she saw Phil Henshaw approaching, with someone she didn't recognise and he was with them before she could alert Mitchell.

'Hi. Sorry to bother you. Hello again Anne. Can I introduce you to Matt Prosser, one of the tournament directors.' Matt looked at Anne and she knew immediately that there was no point trying her charm on this one. His eyes showed not a flicker of interest. 'I'm very pleased to meet you.' Matt said. 'you're a long way from home. Are you a big fan of golf are does something else bring you out here?' Anne had no immediate answer. 'Whatever the reason,' Matt went on, 'it's our gain and I hope you have a wonderful time. I'm sure we'll run into each other again and I'll ask how you're getting on.' Matt's words sounded like a threat to Anne, who still didn't know quite what to say.

Anne felt Mitchell nudge her foot and remembered what he'd said about Matt Prosser. 'He is Phil's eyes' Mitchell had said. She had to be careful of him. She found her voice. 'I'll look forward to that Matt. I'll store up all the questions I have and fire them all at you when we do bump into each other. I warn you, they'll be pretty basic. I'm just learning what this game's all about.'

Matt said something inconsequential in reply but she hardly heard it because she could see Phil looking hard at Mitchell and was alarmed when he said: 'Haven't we met somewhere? Sorry to be so corny. I can't place you but I am sure we've met.'

Mitchell's response was calm. 'I was just going to say the same thing about you. Such a familiar face, but I can't think where we've met. What about TV. Have I seen you on the box, somewhere?'

'Possible. I used to play this game a bit. I even won a big event or two, including this one.'

'That'll be it,' said Mitchell, 'You're in the Hall of Fame. I saw your photo earlier. Phil Henshaw. Should have been a world beater and nobody knows quite why you dropped out of sight. Good to see you back in the big time, anyway. And really big time. Chief Executive. What does that involve exactly, in a golf tournament?'

Anne turned her eyes on him as an encouragement to be open. 'Oh just this and that. If the crap gets too big to flush, they send for me. Just generally keep an eye on things. Spot trouble before it becomes real trouble. Matt here helps me sort the problems on the ground when my instincts prove right.'

'Wowl,' said Anne, trying to look impressed. 'what brings you over to talk to the likes of us small fry. Are you working now? I mean at this minute, talking to us. Is there anything we can help you with?'

'Oh, no. I just saw you on my way to the caddy area for a beer and thought I'd say hello. It was Mitchell here who caught my eye.' He saw too late that this was not very gallant. 'And then I saw that he was with the charming lady I'd met with Jake and seen around the players' enclosure several times. A very welcome addition.'

Anne, less than impressed by Phil's lame, belated gallantry, nonetheless encouraged him with another smile 'It has been nice to meet you again, Phil. Don't let us make you late for wherever you were heading. The caddy area, was it? Do you know some of the caddies then? I suppose you must do, from years back.'

'I do, yes. But it's good to keep in touch with the workforce. Caddies keep this show on the road. Every golfer would have a bad back but for them. And they know all the current gossip.'

'What's doing the rounds this year?' She could see Phil grow wary, as if he knew this was more than a casual chat. She felt Mitchell's foot touch hers again. A warning to drop the interrogation, no doubt.

'Oh nothing much. Technical stuff, mostly. Some of the guys just take it a bit far with the equipment and the gadgets, that's all. Just that sort of thing.'

'You're not kidding,' said Mitchell, 'some of these guys, the players I mean, look as if they're using radar. I mean they're on a different planet altogether. They've got to be getting help from somewhere. I mean, you were good, but were you ever that good?'

'No, I couldn't compete now. These guys are fitter, they train harder and practise more and, yeah, there are new technologies around, though hardly radar, I hope. Are you sure we haven't met?'

Mitchell grinned and shrugged. 'Don't think so, but nice to meet you now. Don't let us keep you from the caddies and that beer you were talking about. Let us know if you discover there are robots playing out there, won't you?'

'Not much of a threat.' Mitchell said when he'd gone. 'Didn't even recognise his old professor when he saw him again. Still, I'd be interested to know what those caddies are saying. You fancy sounding him out Anne? I mean when that other guy, Matt, isn't around? He'd be putty in your hands if you got him alone.'

The 'putty in her hands' made her think of last night's sad business with Jake. She would make it up to him tonight. And with Jake in her bed, what Mitchell was suggesting was simply not going to happen. A Mata Hari role wasn't one she fancied. And nor was Phil. *Handsome enough, but a bit cheesy.* 'Speaking of threats; I think Cristina knows Samson is on something. She's been asking all sorts of weird questions about diets and vitamins and what golfers do to keep their nerve. I'm sure she knows something's not right.'

Mitchell looked worried but said nothing at first. 'She'll be all right as long as she's with Samson. If anything goes wrong with that, we may have to buy her off, I suppose.'

'Or somebody'll bump her off,' said Anne, 'like they did to Selwyn.' Mitchell's face was all concerned sympathy.

35 *Anne and Jake*

Anne waited until she had seen Samson finish the round and then went to check on Ian in the medical tent. Thankfully, he was sitting up and looking better. The talk was of food poisoning and she did what she could to encourage the thought. When the doctor left the room she asked Ian what he had done and he confessed that he had doubled the dose and taken an extra one again this morning. He'd done it, apparently, because he'd felt the effect waning on the previous day and had struggled through the final holes using, as he put it, old technology. He meant he'd fallen back on his own, rather streaky, talent. Anne told him to keep to the proper dose in future and asked him if there had been other side effects. He shook his head. He'd heard, of course, that some of the guys, some of the time, had felt incredible effects, but he hadn't had that. What he had discovered, however, was that his memory as a whole, not just his muscle memory, had improved. He had discovered it by accident and then started to work on it. Ian was a reader. He loved the classics and as Anne listened, he started to recite David Copperfield. *Good God, it's amazing. He's word perfect. What the bloody hell is Mitchell up to with that stuff.* She let him run for five minutes or so and still he hadn't come to the end of what he had memorised.

'And I won't,' he said, 'not for another three novels. And that's just Dickens. If you want it dirty, I've got Fanny Hill and Fifty Shades tucked away up there, too.'

Anne smiled, a little nervously and asked if he'd told anyone else. Only his family, he said, and they were thinking of ways he could make it pay. 'Course, they don't know it's a drug doing it.' *Well that's one consolation. But it won't be long before they find out. We've got to stop this soon and let it all die down before I do anything with Selwyn's improved formula.*

'Well, keep it that way till we've banked a bit more cash, hey?' said Anne. 'And we start that job tomorrow.' Ian nodded his agreement.

Anne patted him on the back wished him a speedy recovery and went back to her rented villa. She wanted to sit down and think through the implications, but found Jake on her doorstep and invited him in.

'Look, about last night,' he began once they were inside, but she silenced him with an upturned palm and a shake of the head.

'There are much more important issues to think about than the state of your member', she said and gave it a playful rub. 'We'll deal with that matter a little later, if we can, one way or the other.' Her hand was still cupped provocatively around his parts and she could feel the effect she was having.

'My,' she said, 'this is a change. What brought this on?' Jake grabbed her round the waist and pulled her to him.

Jake knew it would work this time. He kissed her gently on her neck and lips and told her he loved her.

'Well, you probably think you do.'

'No. I know I do. If I think anything, I think I probably always have, over all these years. But I know, absolutely know, that I love you now.'

Anne put her hands round his face and kissed him back. Then she moved closer and guided his hand between her legs. 'That's it,' she said a moment later, 'just there, oh God yes.' *Oh, that's much nicer. No more smash and grab, wham bam, thank you, ma'am. Go for it Jake.* She enjoyed Jake's gentle attentions and lay quietly smiling in his arms when he at last got it right for her. And then she got it right for him. *There you go; I can't see what all the fuss was about.*

It was peaceful, relaxed and loving; Jake got up and took a bottle of champagne from the fridge. He opened it expertly and filled two glasses. 'To us,' he said. The glasses clinked. 'And to our two joint ventures, love and lolly,' Anne added. *Love and lolly, but not necessarily in that order.*

Before the bottle was empty and despite Jake's obvious relief and pleasure that things had gone well between them, Anne could see he was not free of darker thoughts. She gave him a penny for them. 'Same old theme. It's my damned conscience. I can't get over the fact that we could be poisoning those lads for our own benefit. You told me what Mitchell said about the quality and production control and I haven't been able to shake the thought of what would happen if a really bad lot got through. Look at us just now. It wouldn't have been like that if I'd given in to the temptation to down a dose of the stuff. I'd have been like a wild thing. And look at Ian today, and the others earlier. We don't know what this can do. We should stop now and forget we ever started. We don't need all this for a life together do we? God Anne, suppose we kill one of them. Or they overdose because they're trying too hard to win? And, you know, at another level, I can't take the cheating. It goes right against the grain with me. It does with nearly any golfer. Samson surprises me. That he uses it, I mean.'

Anne didn't share his worries. *What the hell, these are grown men. They can make their own minds up. Nothing in life is fair or sporting, even in sport, for heaven's sake. It's all bloody anarchy, all of it, life. You take what you can get away with and hurt as few as you can. But there's no God and no eternal retribution, just somebody else's rules, made up for their benefit. So why play to them when you can make your own?*

'You're post-coital and had too much champagne, is all. You've had the stuffing knocked out of you even more than I have. Get your hormones back in gear and it'll all look fine again. I'd say an hour, tops, should do it.' She didn't believe what she was saying even as she said it. Not in Jake's case. She knew it ran deeper. Things generally did with him.

Jake shook his head. 'No, I've been worried about this from the beginning. At the very least we should tell the guys the whole truth, everything we know about the drug, and let them decide. At the moment we could be murdering them.'

Anne was alarmed. Appeasing Jake's conscience would be a long term project. For now she had to keep him going and keep him silent. She used the best weapon she had. 'How much do you want me? Want to be with me, I mean?'

'A lot,' he said.

'Well, being with me means manning up and keeping your mouth shut. Got it?'

Jake looked unhappy, but he nodded. 'Got it'.

36 Stefan and Bradley

Bradley knocked on the door and went in. Stefan was standing by the window of his rented villa, watching the last of the golfers through binoculars. By his side was something Bradley recognised as a wireless signal jammer. He'd used one himself recently on a job. You point it at a transmitter, mobile phone, router, whatever, and the signal suffers so much interference it as good as dies. He had stopped a police car from calling in to base during a job in Sweden and that had bought him enough time to get away and leave the cop to his fate. He hadn't checked the details, but the cop would never draw his pension, he was confident of that. And very unhappy about it, too. The cop had done no-one any harm. But he had to think of the bigger picture. There was always a bigger picture when your conscience started playing up. There had been a lot of big pictures for him of late.

Stefan turned to him and smiled. 'My partner in the pro-am is still strong. He is making the others look like amateurs. And yet he has no assistance according to your samples and the inspectors. At least they say he has no assistance of a chemical nature. We do not know if there might be something else. Just to be sure, though, I should like to speak to Larry, was that his name? He might have picked up something else. Maybe the other caddies too. Do you think you could speak with them Bradley?'

'Well sure, but not Larry. He's no longer with us.'

'What do you mean?'

'He took your money and some more from me and departed for Blighty.'

'Blighty? What's Blighty?'

Bradley switched to German where his grasp of nuance and argot was greater, much greater, than Stefan's in English. 'He'd had enough of his boss, not the easiest man to work with and when he saw that Samson was under suspicion he decided to pack up and go. Didn't want to get caught up in any scandal. He was absolutely convinced, wrongly as we know, that there was something in the bottle he stole for us and that Samson Gregory is cheating.'

'Was he? And did you tell him that the bottle turned out to be vitamin flavoured water? Not even glucose?'

'I didn't get a chance, Stefan. The first I knew about his leaving was in a text from his phone, thanking us for the money and hoping we teach the 'bastard' (he said this word in English) a proper lesson. He did say something else. He said Samson had stopped asking him for precise distances and the usual stuff caddies provide. That's another reason he left. He felt he was just a glorified porter (two more words in English, when the precise German equivalent eluded him).' I think he was implying Samson had some device or other.'

'And is it possible that there could have been something of that nature?'

'Well, Larry (careful with the tenses, thought Bradley) is sure there is something going on. And he feels the other caddies are uneasy, too. Opinion is split between chemical enhancement and techno-trickery (a very long single German word served him well here), but, on balance, the caddies think it must be technology, because they think anything else would be too great a risk with the inspectors around.'

'Well, if the inspectors did blood as well as piss, they might be right.'

'But, Stefan, anything powerful enough to help golfers as much as you think Samson's being helped would have to leave a trace in every body fluid. The inspectors would have got it. What's that little pharma company you own in the UK? You could ask them.'

'Merricole. Stupid English name for a stupid English company. Getting stuffed by its rivals. But I have already asked them (Bradley knew; he'd seen the email thread) and they agree with you.'

'So it looks like technology. Where does that take us?'

'To the Euro tour boss. He is a very worried man and he has his sources of information on the ground. Fix me a meeting for tomorrow, Bradley. Let's see what he knows now.'

Bradley was about to leave when Stefan called him back. 'Bradley. I know there is something with the golfers. Whatever it is I want to own it. I must have it. You must do whatever it takes, whatever you need to do, to get it for me. From now on that has to be a number one. You understand? Absolute number one. It is why I am paying you. Is there a problem for you?'

Bradley gave him the assurance he wanted. But of course there was a problem. One employer was paying him to get his hands on the secret and others were paying him to prevent it. Even for a man of Bradley's talents, that presented a considerable challenge.

★

Late that same evening, Phil was working late on last minute arrangements for the final day when his telephone rang. 'Hi Matt, no go ahead it's fine. I'm still sorting a few things for tomorrow.'

'You have a meeting fixed with Stefan Greiff. I'm calling to say I won't make it. Food poisoning. I just won't be able to get there. But I need you to do three things for me and they are very very important. Will you promise?'

God, there's something wrong here. This isn't like Matt.

'Sure. If they're within my power. Are you okay? Is everything all right, I mean apart from the obvious. Where are you? In your villa?'

'I'm fine. And no, I'm with a friend. These are the three things and don't ask for an explanation. Just say yes you'll do it, or not. But make it a yes. First, you are right about Mitchell Walker being Millican and there is a hell of a lot more, but it is absolutely imperative you say nothing about it to anyone until you hear from me again. Especially at the meeting tomorrow. Promise?'

'Of course.'

'Second, at the meeting with Stefan you keep quiet about your concerns over performance boosters and stick with the line on technology. Promise, yes or no?'

'Yes.'

'Third, if you need any help while I'm not around, you'll contact Bradley Manning before anyone else and follow his advice. He's a friend. A really good friend. I'll text you his private number. Promise? Bradley first? Yes?'

'Not a problem. Is there anything I can do for you, you know, on the sickness front? Or anything else?'

'No. Got to go. Urgent need. Keep your promises, Phil, please. I can't tell you how much it matters that you do.' And the phone went dead. Ten minutes later a phone number arrived by text. Bradley's private number, obviously.

Phil paced his office. *What the hell was that all about? He can't tell me how important it all is? Why the hell not? He sounded odd, but then, he did have the runs and other stuff probably. Why did he want me to lie at the meeting? What did he know? Should I keep my promise? Well yes, I sort of have to, for fear of cocking things up. But that means I have to lie to the sponsor, just about the biggest backer in golf. And lies have short legs. What happens when the sponsor finds out I lied. Jesus Matt, this is a fine mess you've got me in. And Bradley? A good friend? What's that judgement based on I wonder?* Marilyn! Marilyn!

Marilyn came through from the outer room. 'You rang, boss?'

'What do we know about Bradley Manning?'

'You mean Herr Greiff's assistant? Well, not a lot except he's coming here with Herr Greiff tomorrow, for the meeting.'

'You fancy a drink at my place, in about half an hour, when I'm done here?'

'Still no strings?'

'Not the merest thread.'

Hey, did I imagine that? For a split second she looked disappointed.

'Okay, then. Thirty minutes it is.'

37 A Matt-free meeting

P hil's office was not large so he could see some advantages in Matt's
absence from the meeting. Stefan and Bradley were already present, and
the atmosphere in the room was hot and claustrophobic. A fan in the top
corner of the room turned and whirred uselessly. It was Sunday in February
and only nine in the morning. Phil opened the window, but closed it again
when he saw that there were lots of people milling around outside. He didn't
want the conversation overheard.

'I am sorry Matt Prosser can't be with us. He would have a lot to add to
today.'

'Who's Matt Prosser?' asked Stefan. Phil told him. 'Is he the guy you told
me about, Bradley?' Bradley said something quietly in German and Stefan
turned back to Phil. 'Apparently he is very poorly. Bad seafood last night. He
rang Bradley this morning.'

'And me last night,' Phil said. Bradley had more information. He said he'd
been with Matt last evening, planning for this meeting, and Matt had agreed
to ring Bradley again early this morning with some extra information. He'd
made the call but been too ill to say much. He asked Bradley to let Phil know,
and he was (just a slight miss of a beat) keeping that promise. Phil looked
sharply at Bradley, but his face was expressionless.

'We may be better off without Matt. Keep things amongst friends,' Stefan
said.

Phil said nothing. The sponsor is always right. Stefan went on: 'What do
you think is going on out there? In the golf games, I mean. There are some
unbelievable rounds being played and I had the benefit of playing in one
when I won the pro-am. Is there cheating? You will not have forgotten how
much money I have put into this tournament and this tour and any suggestion
that all is not good will have very bad effects on my companies and, Phillip, I
can assure you, very bad effects on your tour and your personal prospects.'

Phil wasn't surprised that the sponsor was applying pressure. Only that he
was applying it this early and full on from the start. Stefan really must be
alarmed, or want something very badly indeed. *Well, I can stand up to a bully
like Stefan.*

'That's why we need Matt. He has been doing the watching and the
talking and he promised me he would be here to give you his findings. I
know he was investigating the possibility of performance enhancers but
couldn't come up with anything.'

'No surprise. It's not true. I have had the results from the inspectors, my
inspectors in case you didn't know, and other samples obtained from key

players by certain caddies in my pay have been analysed. And they are all clean. The outstanding players are not using performance enhancing drugs.' *He has caddies in his pay? Do I believe that or am I being conned here? And the mobile lab does unofficial testing for him? This is a sponsor too far. When this is all sorted, I'll take it higher.*

Bradley seemed to spot Phil's consternation. 'To put your mind at rest, Philip, Matt and I have spoken a lot in the last day or so. He's doing for you what I do for Stefan, so we decided to work together. We were sharing a beer last night, talking about this meeting and what's going on. We came to the conclusion that it's all nonsense. We know there are no drugs, because we have done the rounds with caddies and they laugh at the idea. If that was happening they would know, and they don't. But the trouble with an alternative theory, technology, is that it all seems to rest on the word of a scientist no-one can lay their hands on.'

'But who happens to be a highly respected physicist. I know that for a fact.' Phil said.

'No,' said Bradley, 'You know for a fact that there is a respected scientist called Millican and you have seen references for him. What you don't know, is if the references and the man you met are a match.'

'You mean Millican could be phony and real?'

'If you like. My bet is that the real Millican never set off. Something will have persuaded him to stay at home. Anyway that's the conclusion Matt and I came to last night. Definitely no chemicals and very unlikely that there is a technology solution. It would be just too complex.'

'Not if you listen to Millican.'

'Listen to who? Millican/schmillican. Bring him here and let's test him,' said Bradley.

Without Matt, or Millican, Phil had nothing but anecdote to offer. 'There's nothing more I can say. What were you hoping for?'

'I was hoping you had an answer. But you don't. You say this Matt has an answer, but he is not here. You quote a scientist, but can't verify his credentials (Bradley had taught him that phrase. Stefan delivered it with pride and an ounce of threat.) I wish I had a job where I was paid so much for knowing so little. I hope you are not going to be a big disappointment to your sponsor, Mr Henshaw. That would not be a comfortable position for you. I need you to … (he paused and Bradley whispered something in his ear) … get your arse in gear. And soon. I look forward to you telling me the answer to my problem; how is this all being done?'

Stefan closed the meeting and said: 'I have great faith in Bradley here. He is a good man in all sorts of ways and never makes a mistake. Even here he could be right. But I think he might be jumping too quick. The technology is possible and I would love to have it for my company. Make my cars go even faster and with no drivers. Superb. If there is something I will find it and keep it. It must not be spread around. That's what sponsor money buys me. So we need to make sure there is absolutely no noise about this anywhere. No press. No police. Nothing. Got it?'

Phil said it was hardly in his interests, or the tournament's interests for him to spread wild speculation about the reasons for the superb golf they been privileged to watch.

38 Phil is turned

Matt's phone call and subsequent absence from the meeting had worried Phil as well as putting him at a disadvantage. Why was there no further message from him? He dialled his mobile, but it was switched off. He left a message and told the girls in the office to send Matt to him the minute he showed up. Then he decided to find Millican, if he could.

Around noon, an hour or so after the Greiff meeting, just as Phil was at his most busy and needing Matt urgently, he got a text from him. The text simply said that Matt was in trouble and was in hiding. He asked Phil to meet him in an out of the way location, a few miles outside Villamoura. There were some sketchy directions and that was it. Remember Bradley, Matt texted. Phil rang Bradley, who seemed surprised, but not shocked. 'What should I do? What if it isn't Matt?' Bradley urged him to go but to be careful, asking who else it could possibly be?

'Oh. One thing Phil. Turn your phone off. You can't be tracked then. Just in case Matt really is in hiding from someone.'

Marilyn, with instructions to hold the fort, got him a staff car from the pound and Phil sped off on the road away from Faro into the deserted coastal stretches to the east. After 7 kilometres he saw the sign for the bridge Matt had described in the text and turned right. Now the road became a track again and clouds of dust rose behind the wheels of the car. Phil stopped in the appointed lay by and got out. He was alone. There was no sign of either car or person. No animals were grazed in these marshy salty stretches and there was not so much as a derelict hut to suggest any human activity. Phil found the isolation unnerving in the circumstances. He turned to look over the rail of the bridge and down into the valley below. *That water looks deep. I wouldn't want miss this bend in the dark and end up in there.* Apart from the lapping of the water and a gentle sighing of the wind in the marsh grass, there was silence. Phil waited, sweating slightly from the heat and apprehension. *Something smells about all this. These things don't happen in real life. Matt wouldn't put me in this position without good reason, though. If it was Matt.* Ten minutes went by. Nothing. Twenty minutes later Phil was about to switch his phone on and ring Bradley, when a car swung round the bend and slid to a halt on the bridge.

The driver, wearing a hood that made it difficult to see his face, got out of the car and walked with rapid aggressive strides towards the rail where Phil was standing. As he got close, he threw the hood back. 'It's you,' said Phil, 'What the hell are you doing here?'

Mitchell smiled. 'I came to kill you. I thought I'd send you and your car over the edge with you spinning and screaming inside.' He pulled a large knife from a sheath across his chest. 'This is how I'll persuade you to get in.'

Phil was brave enough, but bravery can get you in trouble in a situation like this, unless you know what you're doing. And Phil hadn't had the training needed to handle it. He looked at Mitchell and decided that, in a straight fight, he could take him nine times out of ten. Only nine out of ten, because anyone could get a lucky blow in now and then. But the knife reversed the odds completely. Phil wasn't scared of Mitchell. It was the knife that terrified him. He decided to appear too scared to speak. Mitchell smiled again.

'I was sure you'd be pleased to see me; a fellow countryman out here in the wilds. Something safe and comforting in a very alien environment. But something tells me you're not. Something also tells me I'm not quite what, or who you were expecting. Who were you expecting, Phillip?'

'Matt Prosser,' Phil croaked as if just finding his voice. As soon as he'd said it, he knew he should have dissembled. But his brain and his mouth weren't co-operating quite as he would have liked.

'Now there's the problem, right there,' said Mitchell. 'You spoke too soon. I just asked and out it popped. Far too talkative. That's what I am here to put a stop too. Too much loose talk, to all sorts of worrying people, about chemicals, and performance and technology and fake professors and all of that nonsense. Now, what would you prefer, death or a deal?'

'Deal.'

'Good, because don't forget, we are a very resourceful bunch and we also know where your ex-wife and family live and, you know, living with the knowledge that you have caused harm to come to loved ones is sometimes worse than a quick death. Not that I am promising it will be quick.'

Phil nodded, his eyes wide with apparent fear. And now he really was finding it hard to speak because the air in his lungs refused to behave as it had always done. There was a band of tightening pain round his chest. Breathing was something he could manage only by focusing his whole attention on it. It wasn't fear doing this to him. It was rage. A boiling anger had taken him over. He squeaked with what Mitchell assumed was fear and Mitchell looked at him with disgust.

'For God's sake, calm down and pull yourself together. We're going to do a deal remember?' Phil looked at him sideways through wide eyes. He didn't believe this man was going to let him go. And somewhere down inside where he was still functioning as a sentient creature, very deep inside, beyond the almost insane urge to launch himself at Mitchell and the equally powerful instinct not to risk it, he was wondering exactly who Mitchell was.

As if he read his mind, Mitchell said: 'You must be wondering who I am to be able to do these things to you. To bring you as close to death as you've ever been, and believe me, friend, you are still very close to a very unpleasant death. Who am I to offer you a deal to save your pathetic skin?' In the distance, perhaps a kilometre away towards Faro, a car could be heard, heading in their direction.

'Ah, the cavalry, I hear you think. Don't get your hopes up. Turn and look over the rail when I tell you.' The car got nearer and then appeared on the bend. The driver barely gave them a look as he sped round the corner, across the bridge and away the other side. 'You see how he went round the bend? That's because he knows he is the only car on this road today. He would have been amazed to see us here, but people in these parts have learned not to be curious.'

'What's the deal?' Phil was recovering. He had used the minute or two to collect some sort of thought process and had realised that this man would have killed him straight away if that had been the only option. Phil was going to appear ready to promise anything. What he would actually do could be worked out later.

'Simple. You work for me. You do exactly as I tell you, you report to me on a daily basis and you keep your mouth shut when it comes to any independent thought. You tell people only what I tell you to tell them and you keep your nose out of anything else. And above all, I want no more talk of performance enhancers linked to the Jake Godwin team. None! Clear?'

'And who are you? Who do you work for?'

'Oh, now aren't those big questions. Not anyone you need to be ashamed of, but people you need to be very afraid of, in your situation at the moment. No more questions.'

'Bradley knows I'm here; and why. He knows about Larry too, Says he's is not back in England, but round here somewhere.'

'Does he now Phil? Well I don't see Larry or Bradley here, do you? It's you and me, Phil. And as for Bradley? I wouldn't look for too much help from that quarter. He's Stefan's man. If it suits Stefan it will suit Bradley and Stefan won't give a toss about you.'

'Well tell me who you are and it might help me. I'd sooner know I was working for the good guys, not the bad guys. Are you British Agents?'

'And would you class them as the good or the bad guys, Phil? Because 'good' is a relative term, and when the enemy is very wicked indeed, then their enemy is good by default. But we have the power in this game, Phil. The Force is with us and that makes us the good guys. Automatically. It makes us the side you want to be on. But if it helps your conscience, then I suppose you could call us the good guys. What we want to achieve is in the interests of most ordinary folk, I would say. So rest easy and do as you're damn well told.'

'And Larry? Where's Larry. And Matt?'

'Well, Phil. I am afraid there was no deal to be done with Larry.' He let that sink in. 'And Matt? Well, he is our guest for as long as this takes. He did a deal pretty quickly and is depending on you for his future well being. He's hoping, no he's praying you won't let him down. Now, that's the end of question time. You do as I say or your ex-wife and more importantly your children will have some very unpleasant visitors. And they will be the bad guys. And then they'll turn their attention to Matt. And you will be dessert.' With that, he made a gesture with his thumb that Phil should go.

Phil, relieved beyond measure but still angry, stumbled to his car. The keys were in the ignition. He drove away watching Mitchell in his rear view mirror. He was using his mobile. *I'd give my eye teeth for the number he's calling.* Phil started to run through his options but couldn't get past the threats. With Matt in danger they appeared few. If the threat to his family was real, he had none.

39 *Samson agonises*

S amson woke from a deep and contented sleep. He opened his eyes, saw Cristina next to him and was flooded with a sense of happiness. He could not remember it ever being like this before. Usually he woke with a sinking feeling, akin to despair, at what lay before him (not to mention beside him), making sense of an empty life with a wasted talent. Now he had Cristina. He could not help but be an attentive (if at times, he knew, extremely demanding) lover, and he was showing her a world of glamour, fame and wealth that she could not have dreamed of. It was impossible to think it would last and he wondered if she might just be taking him for what she could get. But it didn't feel that way. And if it was, she was playing the part of a woman in love very well. Samson got up without disturbing her. This was his big day. The final round and he had a handsome lead. He was playing so well that even Cristina, whose knowledge of golf was still very recent, had told him that he was a class above the others, even above some of the very big names.

There were only two very small clouds on his horizon. The first was Stefan. He did not know why he was a danger, but he didn't trust him. Why had he been talking to Larry (as Cristina had reported) and what had happened to Larry since? But secondly, he suspected that Stefan wanted Cristina. Whenever they were close, in the players' hospitality area, for example, he would seek her out and his hands were always on her shoulders and arms or he stroked her cheek, almost like a lover. But his eyes were the worst. Samson could see the longing in them, dangerous in a man that powerful, he knew instinctively. Dangerous if he got what he wanted and worse if he didn't.

His second concern was a novel one for him. It was a troubled conscience. The way he was winning was wrong and he was beginning to hate it. He looked at the bottle in his hand and emptied the contents down his throat. He turned to leave the bathroom and saw her watching him. Naked, brown and entrancingly lovely, she had slipped out of bed and into the bathroom doorway, just in time to see Samson empty the first bottle. No point stopping now. He unscrewed the top of another, which he drained, too. She asked him what was in the bottle, but he only smiled in return and seized her round the waist, his hands exploring the wonderful contours of her backside.

'Not now,' she said, 'after you win. You keep your power for the golf. You need all of it today. And I give you something special nice if you win.'

'When I win.'

'How you so certain. Is difficult, Jake says, to win from the leading position. The others take risks to chase. And they know the score they have to get. You don't.' She patted him on the front of his shorts and then squeezed what she found there. 'Oh dear. What a pity to waste such a hard boy. But he will be happy later. I promise. But how can you be so sure you win today?'

'You've seen me play. You know what I can do.'

'But every golfer has bad day. Every person. Why not you today?'

'Because,' he said, 'I have a little secret that no-one else knows.'

'In that bottle?'

'In that bottle.'

'Is that what Larry stole?'

'You are smart as well as incredibly beautiful.' He reached for her again but she danced away. 'Yes, I guess that is what Larry took.'

'What does it do, this stuff? It must be dangerous.'

'No, not for me, not for anybody who is careful. I dropped down to a half the dose weeks ago without any problems. It lets me hit the ball like a ball should be hit and the same every time. It's complicated to explain, but I'll tell you all about it when I win. Just for once, just to make doubly sure, I've taken the full dose again. This is a new batch, very pure Anne says. I threw away the stuff Larry brought back, just in case.'

'But all stuff like this can be dangerous. And then there are the rules. This must be against the rules.'

'Well, why should it be? It isn't on a list of banned substances, it doesn't make me stronger and it's only any good if you practise with it like mad, in a very disciplined way, and have the talent to start with.'

He didn't think he'd convinced her. Cristina, still naked and delicious, put her hand on his arm. 'We need to talk about this. It is not good. It is against the rules, I am sure. I don't like you to win this way and I think it will harm you in the end, one way or the other. You must promise me we talk later, about this and about Stefan.'

'What about Stefan?'

'He molests me. He wants to take me from you. And I am frightened that if I do not let him he is a powerful man who can do bad things for you.'

'He molests you?'

'With his hands and with his eyes. You've seen him. I know you watch him. I know what he wants me to do and he is used to having his way.'

'And are you going to let him?' Samson was still not sure that Cristina was as committed to him as he was beginning to feel to her.

'Do you want me to let him? He would make us very rich'

'No, of course not. But he hasn't asked you yet, has he?'

'Yes,' said Cristina, 'he has. I got a note from his office. He asked me to visit him on his yacht when the tournament is over, and to have dinner there tonight, after you have left. He thinks final day and you will be on plane home. He doesn't know you are staying and what we are planning to do. His yacht is the one you say you like out there in the harbour.'

'You're joking. That thing is Stefan's? Bloody hell. What a bastard. What did you tell him?'

'What do you think I told him. He is very rich, very powerful. He can break people like me and even people like you.'

'You said yes? You said you'd go?'

'I said nothing, not yes or no. I wanted to hear what you think I should say.'

'Cristina; you are a free woman. I have no claim. You have to do what you want. But if you ask me, I think we should string him along for a while. You can sit on his table tonight, but take me as your partner. And tomorrow, we meet your parents before I fly home.'

He saw that his response was not quite what Cristina wanted, but didn't know why. She was quiet for a while.

'We talk about these things later, yes? These are very important things, Samson.' She turned and put on a golfing jumper which fell to a level that Samson could hardly bear to look at. 'okay,' he said. 'Tonight we talk. Afterwards.'

40 Catch me if you can

S amson, on the first tee with a nine shot lead and one round to go, had every reason to think he was about to win his first real tour title and become the Portuguese Masters champion. He was not nervous, but he was horny. He could not rid himself of the sight of Cristina in the bedroom this morning and the drug now coursing through his veins at full dosage, a new batch brought in by Mitchell, was having an unusually powerful impact on his libido. He needed to clear his mind and concentrate on the task ahead. *Anyway, a nine shot lead. I can defend that with one arm. Even in this wind. No problem. Should have got myself sorted beforehand though. Still, nine shots. Just keep the thing in play. No big numbers. Let the chasers do the pushing and the panicking. Gently does it.*

The starter, a well known figure on the tour, dapper and with a pronounced Scottish accent, announced the match number and tee time. The pairing was the final one of the day and was expected to yield the eventual winner, who would crown the day's events by clinching victory on the final green with the final shot of the tournament. Not until the last putt dropped could a score be verified and a winner declared. Samson's partner was a young Frenchman, beginning to make a name for himself, but who had also never won a significant tournament. Two groups ahead, Jason had already started his round and was going well, with orders not to do better than fourth position.

Samson's plan was to go round in par. Nothing flashy, just the standard score. To catch him, the young Frenchman would need to score nine under par, an almost impossible task. Samson could probably have managed a par score unaided, but the potion was a helpful safety net and took away his nerves. And nerves could reduce even the best of golfers to a faltering wreck. For the first seven holes the plan worked. Samson consulted his chart diligently, choose the club according to the list, repeated the mantra to himself and hit shots of such perfection, the crowd would gasp in amazement before releasing their astonishment in a yell of delight when the ball bounced safely on the green and rolled towards the hole. Three times Samson forgot to make the adjustments for a less than perfect shots and had to miss easy putts for a birdie. The commentators remarked on his poor putting performance and wondered if another course record would have been possible had his putter been hotter. They showed his technique in slow motion and detected that he was pushing the ball a little to the right and possibly standing up too quickly after each strike. Only one of them suspected that the misses were deliberate.

And then, after seven holes it all changed. Something happened to Samson's vision: he saw everything with pin sharp clarity but without any depth. All before him was a flat canvass without perspective and then the perspective would try to assert itself, but like in some medieval religious painting, get it all wrong so that distant objects were far too close. *What's going on? Where's the bloody pin? Is that bunker near the green or ten yards short? Shit. This is terrible.* At first this affected only the putting, and Samson three putted the eighth, ninth and tenth. On the tenth, where he wasn't sure if the hole was three feet or thirteen feet away, he struck the ball too hard and only a lucky bounce as the ball cannoned into the back of the hole saved him from something far worse. Two birdies and a par on the same holes brought his opponent to within four shots, no longer mission impossible.

Worse was to come. Jake, still caddying, asked Samson what was up and Samson told him. Jake was therefore trying to read the putts for Samson. On the eleventh hole this worked and the three putting stopped. But another birdie from the young Frenchman brought him to within three shots. After that blow, Samson was afflicted by a far worse plague. Firstly, he felt his strength drain away whenever he repeated the distance code and second, try as he might, he could not bring himself to hit the ball. He stood over his second shot on the twelfth hole, waggled his club head, stared at the ball, waggled the club head again, stood up, walked away, read the chart again, said the magic incantation again, stood over the ball and repeated the whole performance. When he stood up a second time, he saw Anne, watching from the crowd following the match, bite her hand with anxiety. Clearly something was very wrong. He saw her trying to catch Jake's eye, but Jake's face had a panicked look and he seemed to Samson to be completely out of it. To Anne's right he noticed the tall doping inspector and the chaperone watching him with professional interest.

He could see the crowd was agog as if they too sensed something big was afoot. *Jackals. They just want to see a gladiator come a cropper. They don't care how long this takes so long as they can give the thumbs down and watch me buy one. This is a better spectacle than any golf shot. Bastards.* He could imagine what the commentators would be making of it. They would be awash with theories and learned insights, but couldn't possibly know the truth. They would be blaming nerves and the debilitating fear of failure, but would never guess what Samson was enduring. The problem with his vision had entered a new phase and what Samson now saw was completely bewildering.

Samson and Jake were in a huddle, pretending to consult a yardage chart. 'I just can't damn well do it. My mind, or my body, or both, won't get into the groove to let me swing. I try to start and my head just fills with the most lurid sexual images and I get an erection. I can't even see the ball. I just see, well you can imagine what I see. It's like a porn site I can't switch off. I've got to have some relief. Now. Or I'll never clear my head.'

'What sort of relief?'

You know what sort. You've taken the stuff yourself.'

'You mean sex?'

Samson nodded.

Jake raised the obvious objection to that course of action.

'Then I'll have to withdraw!'

A referee, Hamish, drove over to them to investigate the slow play. 'He has violent stomach cramps and a splitting headache, Hamish,' said Jake as Hamish, immaculate in freshly pressed shirt and shorts, drove up in his pristine and newly polished buggy. 'We need a 15 minute medical break to get him to the loo, get some medical attention and have him fit to resume. The alternative is that he shits himself here on the course, in front of all these people. We need to borrow your buggy.' *Well done Jake. I thought you'd lost it. I owe you one.*

Hamish pronounced himself appalled at the vision conjured up by Jake. He looked at Samson who was bending over, his eyes firmly closed, clearly trying to contain himself. 'okay take the buggy. 20 minutes max, or I disqualify him.'

41 Slapper

S amson left Hamish to make the announcements over his walkie-talkie
and, as the TV commentators debated the legality of the decision and any
precedents they could remember, he hobbled into the buggy, and sat doubled
up as Jake drove through the crowd, collecting Anne as he did so, and headed
for the players' hospitality unit.

'What's up?' asked Anne, unsurprisingly.

'It's that bloody potion.' Samson said, 'I took a full dose, twice the usual
amount for me, and can't see what I'm doing for lust.'

'For lust?'

'I'm helpless with lust, sexual desire if you want and it won't get better
unless I get laid pretty damn quick.'

Anne, who was possibly the only woman on earth with reason to believe
this apparent absurdity, asked Jake what he intended to do. Jake took the
buggy to a spot behind the hospitality venue where they couldn't be seen, he
hoped.

'Get him laid and get him back on the course.'

'But what if we can't find Cristina?'

'Who's talking about Cristina.' Samson said. Just about anyone will do. I'd
shag Jake if he had the equipment.'

'You want me to do it, don't you?' Anne said.

'You got a better suggestion?' Samson croaked.

'And Jake. You'd let me?'

Jake shook his head. 'Of course not. I was thinking of Cristina, too.'
Samson wasn't sure she believed Jake and when he saw the anger flare in her
eyes, he was sure of it. Poor Jake, always piggy in the middle.

Samson intervened from the back of the buggy: 'A hand-job would do.'

Anne turned round and slapped him hard across the face. 'That's the only
hand job you're getting from me.' He sat up and she did it again. 'Apart from
that one.' Samson shook his head and looked round. 'That's done it,' he said,
getting down from the buggy and taking a few practice swings. 'That feels
more or less normal again. I can see straight, at least. The shock of the slaps
must have done it. Pity that. Not the cure I was hoping for. I bet I could've
talked you into it Anne.'

If the first two slaps effected only a partial cure, the third one brought
about a full recovery. Samson was helped up from the floor, just in time to see
Anne, wild-eyed with fury, walk away, a picture of outraged womanhood.

They drove back to where Hamish was waiting. 'Fifteen minutes. Good.
Is he fit to continue?' Samson assured him all was well and that he'd taken

nothing worse than paracetamol and a dump. Hamish, victim of a mild compulsive disorder, took a handkerchief out of his pocket and wiped the seat where Samson had been sitting. He dropped the cloth into the rear storage compartment of the buggy. He held his walkie-talkie to his ear, spoke briefly to someone and signalled that play could continue.

Samson stood over the ball he had been unable to hit a few minutes earlier, feeling ninety percent sure everything was all right. He said the code under his breath once more for good measure. He felt the sting of Anne's palm on the side of his face and his mind cleared. He swung the club and made a faultless connection. Game on again. From that point, the young Frenchman played almost as brilliantly as Samson, but to no avail. They approached the final green with Samson four shots to the good and both balls sitting in the middle of the green. Samson, some think deliberately, three putted after the Frenchman holed out for a three. Samson won by two shots. His first ever tour victory and prize money of close to a million euros. *Take that, world. Screw you, commentators. This is for you Cristina.* Jason ran onto the green and hugged him. 'Brilliant. Fantastic. I came fourth, by the way. But you were terrific.' Samson thanked him and looked round for Cristina. He saw her. She was on a balcony overlooking the green and standing next to her, his arm round her shoulder, was Stefan.

42 *Some explaining to do*

Phil, still shaken by his ordeal at the bridge and back on the course just in time, was first up before the cameras after Samson's win. That's what you expect as a chief executive he thought. Nearly murdered in the morning, crucified in the afternoon and with any luck, slaughtered in the evening with Marilyn. *God, can I share any of this mess with her?* His anger at Mitchell's threat against his family was subsiding. He had managed to get through to his ex-wife and, without alarming her, told her to watch for anything unusual and to call the police if she was worried about anything. She had been reassuringly normal. He put to the back of his mind that he was now Mitchell Walker's creature. *Whoever the hell he is.*

Samson would be next up before the cameras, after the card checking formalities and the presentation of the trophy. Looking down from the platform, with Bradley in his eye line, Phil smiled at the interviewer, trying to look more confident than he was.

'Phil, great tournament?' the interviewer shoved the large furry microphone closer to Phil, to indicate an answer was required. 'Is that a question?' the interviewer nodded encouragingly. 'Well yes, it was a great tournament and a worthy winner who gave us a bit of a fright along the way.'

'What was your take on that. What happened to Samson on the eighth.'

'Well as I understand it, Madelaine, and it's a bit delicate, Samson was trying to fight off stomach cramps, get to the end of the hole and make a dash to the loo. When the referee arrived he made a decision that play could be discontinued due to sudden illness and Samson was taken to a relief station.'

'You mean they got him to a loo.'

'Exactly that. And before you ask me what caused the problem, I can only say that the authorities are looking into the possible cause, but Samson himself thinks it was raw eggs in a hollandaise this morning, made worse by the stress of losing those early holes.'

A few more straightforward questions followed and Phil batted them easily aside, insisting that it had been a great tournament even though the eventual winner had led from the start. The standard of golf alone, he said, justified calling the tournament a special one. Then the interviewer took a different tack.

'Phil, we are delighted to have you with us, as a former winner here, but for the benefit of the public, can you tell us a bit more about your official role.'

'Sure. My title is Chief Executive. I oversee just about everything connected with the different tournaments across Europe and elsewhere. Asia, South Africa.

'So you don't organise any one in particular?'

'I have a roving brief covering all the tournaments.'

'And you have oversight of security and anti-corruption matters. Would that be a fair description?'

'Well, it might be if there were any suggestion of corruption to be detected, but there isn't. Of course, there are anti-doping inspectors, if that's what you mean and I do have oversight of the inspectors' on-the-ground operations. It's all pretty low-key in golf, of course. No one has ever been detected using anything on this tour.'

'So you are saying there are no drugs in this sport?'

'I'm saying there's no known drug that can make a man, or a woman, Madelaine, hit a ball further or better, so why would anyone take anything other than aspirin or a cough medicine? Drugs just aren't an issue in golf.'

'So will Samson be tested today?'

'If there are inspectors on site, as there are today, the winner and one other is routinely tested.'

'So who is the other. We hear it's Samson's stablemate, Jason, who got the fourth spot and a tidy prize pot.'

'It may well be. But that would be a random selection and, while I don't want to prejudge what is a very thorough process, there is in my view no chance of any abuse being uncovered, for the reasons I've given.' *Don't lose your temper or you lose the argument and give this cheap little interview a weight it doesn't deserve.*

'okay Phil, we'll go with that for now. Very clear what your views are on cheating by medication. What about other forms of cheating?'

Bloody hell. What is going on here? What does this lot know? There's nothing going on you idiot woman, nothing at all. Turn your guns on football and athletics. This sodding sport pays your wages, so wise up, woman. Calm, now. Steady. 'Madelaine, I don't want to take any shine off this tournament by talking about things that don't happen. Golf is a sport where the golfers regulate themselves and are scrupulously honest about it. And your cameras are on everything. Any slight deviation from the rules or the highest standards of course etiquette is pounced on by viewers and emailed straight to your lot, who use it to spice up the broadcast, of course, and we understand that.'

'Phil, we have seen some fantastic golf in the last few days, mainly from the Godwin stable, and we have seen some strange events, too. Occasionally we have seen shots that, under the circumstances, should not be possible.'

'That's pro golf for you.'

'Are you aware that there are theories circulating that some of it was achieved by unfair means? Not drugs but devices.' *DEVICES?*

'Devices?'

'Yes, technology, Guidance systems and high level stuff we simple hacks don't understand.'

Prove it or shut up. 'And is there any evidence of all this? I mean it sounds like science fiction to me. You cannot be seriously asking me to comment on completely invented fantasy.' *Watch it Phil, you're losing your cool. Hold it in. Think ice.*

'Well, we have a statement from a highly respected physicist who says there are ways it could be done and that he's talked to you about them.'

'Madelaine. I know who you mean. I hope you checked your sources because we investigated that man and he turned out to be as genuine as a seven pound note. He blagged his way into our offices and fed us a cock and bull story based on no evidence at all. As a matter of routine we checked him out, and his science, and the one was as fake as the other. There is no known way that any current technology could be used as an aid. It is simply impossible. If you have fallen for it, Madelaine, you are likely to make yourself and your organisation a laughing stock.' *Hope that comes out okay. Sincere enough.*

'So you reject it out of hand?' *Course I do, you silly cow. Haven't I just said so?*

'Absolutely impossible. I reject it totally.'

'Thanks Phil, can I just ask you one more thing?' Phil, feeling pleased with himself, agreed. *Phew. Out of the woods. Get me a drink somebody.*

'Since we've been talking about spectacular striking, what are your comments on these pictures picked up by our aerial cameras this afternoon?' And on a big screen over his head, Phil watched Anne slap Samson three times and storm away in magnificent style.

43 To the victor the spoils

S amson had a new caddy but he simply couldn't get rid of the old one. Larry seemed to have become addicted to texting. He sent them to Samson, to Jake, even to Cristina. Each one made it clear that he was sorry to have let them down and he realised his mistake, now. In some he was in England, in a new flat in the Midlands. In others he was abroad. He offered news and comments on events and always replied politely but blandly to anyone who bothered to contact him. His spelling had improved remarkably, but Samson put that down to phone technology.

Eventually, Samson got the message that Larry had a new job caddying in South Africa and was flying out that day. He would be signing off now, he said, but hoped to meet them all again someday, on a golf course. He wished them all well and told them not to worry about him.

Samson was beginning to feel some remorse for his unthinking treatment of Larry. In fact, Samson was feeling remorseful on many fronts and had been in serious mode ever since his win. Perhaps a period of sober reflection was to be expected after the adrenalin of the victory. A low after a terrific high. Except there had been no victory high. Instead, he was surprised to find himself depressed by the manner of its achievement. He thought he had confronted that issue and made a sensible choice. But the plain fact was that he was unhappy at having won under false pretences and was within an ace of deciding never to do it again.

Samson loved golf. He thought of the early death of his mother and the terrible way his father had reacted to it. No wonder he'd turned out wild. Only golf had saved him. What would he have become if he'd stayed out on the streets? Golf had given him status and recognition and a sort of home. And then he had betrayed it. First by being such an arrogant sod and squandering his talent and now, much much worse, by threatening its reputation. He was a cheat and currently a very unhappy one.

He was sitting on the sofa in the villa he was now paying for out of his own pocket (he should have been on the plane home) with Cristina's head on his lap. The issue of Stefan's arm around Cristina's shoulder had been resolved in five minutes when Cristina explained she had misunderstood Samson's instructions to 'string him along.'

'I was stranging him' she said. And Samson had believed her, corrected her grammar and made love on the strength of what was left of the promone in his system. Even that's a sort of cheating, he told himself. How long he wondered before Cristina got tired of it and decided Stefan was the better bet. He could see she had a choice now, between the insecure future he was offering and the virtually royal opulence Stefan could give her. When he asked, as delicately as he could, she reassured him. But then she would, wouldn't she?

And Samson had to admit that Stefan's yacht, where they'd surprised Stefan by turning up for dinner as a couple, had been truly magnificent. The sort of thing Samson could never aspire to. Three tiers, sixty-eight or so metres and 30,000,000 euro. And the food had been absolutely sumptuous. Sampson could hardly blame Cristina if her head was turned when his own was positively swivelling. He hoped the fact it was him and not Stefan who had promised to meet her parents the next day counted with Cristina. That and the fact that he was better looking than a bear with a huge nose.

Whatever Stefan thought of the stunt they'd pulled by turning up as a couple, he was a charming and sophisticated host. Towards the end of the evening, he made Samson an offer he could hardly refuse. 'Now that we know from inspectors that the spectacular golf was down to your talent and nothing else, I am happy to say that I have an offer for you. I want you to say goodbye to your management team and join me. Golf means very much to me. It is my only real recreation and I am a little sad that it is not so popular in my fatherland as it should be. There are some good German golfers but they have no status at home. They are not what I think you call 'cool'. You Samson are very cool. You are the coolest. You would be a fantastic figurehead for my plans. You could name your own salary, within reason. What you say? You interested? If you are, I will tell you my conditions. Ah, I see you are surprised I have conditions. But all my offers come with strings. I never make them unconditional.'

Samson was very interested. He had no ties, contractual or emotional, to the Godwin team that couldn't be severed. He asked a few questions, more for form's sake than any genuine need to know. He wondered for a second whether Cristina was one of Stefan's conditions, but no-one would stoop that low, he told himself. So finally he said he would consider it. Seriously consider it. If the conditions weren't too onerous.

'Good,' Stefan said. 'Then here they are. It will be very good if you do well at Wentworth. A win would be fantastic, but I know in golf, there is too much luck to demand that. But a top five place would be great. And the second condition is that you must win one major championship, Masters, PGA, US open or the Open at St Andrews in the next year. You must be a Major winner. What do you say now?'

Steep, but Samson was still interested. After all, winning championships was what he was in golf to do, wasn't it? And now, of course, there was every reason to think he could do it. Stefan clearly thought so.

Samson left with Cristina hanging on his arm. He wondered if she had received a renewed offer too. She was a little subdued, which led him to think she had.

Whatever the cause, Samson felt a heaviness in his heart. Here he was, sitting on his sofa in his plush villa, the head of the world's most beautiful woman on his lap, a multi-million-pound deal in his back pocket and a significant trophy and cheque on the table beside him. What right did he have to be anything but ecstatic?

He met the parents, a pleasant affair with Cristina doing her interpreting role charmingly and erratically. He flew back to England, with an excited Cristina in tow. He couldn't stop her talking about his offer from Stefan and the more she talked the less sure he was of Stefan's motives. This was no way to prepare for a big tournament.

★

Anne had instructed Jake in what to say in TV interviews about the infamous slaps. Mortified and ashamed though she was at this intrusion into her privacy she recognised that it was simply too interesting an event to leave unexplained and that only an explanation that was interesting in its own right would kill off the curiosity behind all the You Tube hits. In the end, she had to do the talking herself. No-one wanted to see Jake. The tabloids were interested only in Anne and, she felt, only in certain parts of her. *I'd get my tits out straight away if I thought that would satisfy them. But that would just feed the beast red meat and they'd be back for even more.*

On camera and in print she acknowledged that the slaps had been part of a domestic and private dispute. She conceded that she and Jake were an item and that Samson had said something completely out of order about her partner and about her own trustworthiness. Exactly what had been said she declined to say and vowed never to reveal it. But once the tabloids understood that even quite large amounts of money could not get her to change her mind they began to get really nasty. The broadsheets came to her defence and started talking about harassment. They printed racy pictures of her too, she noticed. *Bloody hypocrites.* Anne found the constant intrusion, the rummaging in her rubbish bins, the attempted hacking of her telephone and the telephoto lenses appalling. She may have hated it, but she understood the motives behind it all only too well. There were papers to be sold and for a brief moment, she was selling them. She might well have capitulated if the sums offered had been just a little bit more obscene. She was after all, she told Jake weeks later when the fuss had died a little, in it to win it and she laughed at the sight of Jake's shocked face. 'Anyway, I might as well have told them the truth because what they invented was far worse. I'll spit on every copy of the Sun I see for the rest of my life.' *That picture. Me all over the front page and the banner headline: Slapper!*

Eventually, Anne's horror at the constant depiction of a vastly distorted version of her life and character gave way to a period of intense dissatisfaction with her real ones and, for some reason she couldn't quite get to the bottom of, a return of deep grief for Selwyn. And then it was over. Anne was, above all, a pragmatist. Life, she said to herself, just has to be lived as you find it, not as you'd like it to be. After a few million more hits, the pictures disappeared from YouTube and the satellite TV company never showed them again. The most persistent of the tabloids tried to do a deal with her: they'd drop the story and their digging into her life generally in return for a few candid shots of her. She was tempted until she discovered what sort of 'candid' they had in mind. That sort of underwear was for her bedroom only. Even that refusal was futile. Countless photo-shopped glamour shots, her own head, some other body, peppered the Internet and Anne, outraged at first, then flattered, eventually learned to see them as part of life as it is and not as she'd like it.

The problem that remained for Anne with Jake was no longer sexual; that was all very satisfactory for both parties; nor was it historical, since both had reconciled themselves to the distant past and even Selwyn, after the recent flare up of mourning, was a fading memory for Anne; the problem was moral. She could not persuade Jake that the drug issue would ever stop being a threat to them all, especially since Mitchell was delivering ever less reliable products. It was a bad dose that led to Samson's hallucinations (and that's what a doctor said they had been) at Villamoura, and the same bad stuff had caused Martin Pascal (the golfing pro they always sent to the most distant tournaments) to get involved in a knife fight over a girl in a Hong Kong bar. His wounds had healed but keeping the story under wraps was an ongoing struggle.

But when Anne asked Jake what his objections really were, he told her he couldn't get round the fact that it was plain wrong. Cheating was anti-golf and he saw himself as the worst kind of traitor. A mercenary one. Anne never understood that sort of moral scruple. She saw sport as an entertainment for boys and men who found it difficult to grow up. Sport was fundamentally too trivial a thing to throw up a moral issue of any depth. Why was golf any more or less important than tiddlywinks? And who in their right mind worried about how their tiddles got winked? *In football, the richest clubs buy up the best players, assemble the strongest teams and win title after title. How is that not cheating?*

On the other front, the chances and consequences of discovery, Anne was still sanguine. She was sure the product would be stabilised and it was even now much more often harmless and effective than disruptive. Besides, there had been two more wins, one each for Jason and Ian, and a second place for Martin, along with top ten finishes for each of them in all four tournaments since Villamoura, with a huge boost to the earnings of Jake's company. She knew these immense amounts of cash, the effect on his business, the fame and the sudden rush of sponsorship would go a long way to easing Jake's conscience. It would not be forever, she told him, 'just a year or two and we'll really be in clover.' Anne's work on Jake extended of course to the most private areas of his life. She suspected he was already at the point where he couldn't contemplate taking his team out of the deal if the consequence was losing her. And she made sure he knew it would be with as much regularity as she thought good for him.

Part 3 Wentworth

44 *Bradley's holiday*

Bradley Manning, his current incarnation, closed the door behind him on his way out of the final meeting of the three-day briefing-cum-assessment exercise. The grin on his face could not have been wider as he punched the air with his fist. He skipped down the steps of the impressively large building on the south bank of the Thames two and three at a time, as if to convince himself of the agility he'd just demonstrated to his employers, even at the advanced age of 37. Not only had the briefing gone well and his mandate for the 'golf' project been renewed and extended, but he'd passed the 'fitness to operate' test with flying colours and annihilated much younger men in the general aptitude test, where thinking power counted much more than anything else. He'd got new strategic targets, too. Or not so much new as retreaded. It meant Phil Henshaw and co. would be seeing a lot more of him. Mark 2 promone was the prize. 'Major national importance' they'd called it. 'Mustn't fall into the wrong hands', by which they meant only into their hands. The very substantial salary increase mattered less to Bradley than the confidence his bosses had expressed in his being the right man, the only man, they trusted to do the job.

It had earned him two weeks off. From this employer at least. Stefan was himself on long-term leave and wouldn't need him for a while. Whether he would get free of Mitchell and his needs was less sure, and he certainly didn't want to jeopardise that relationship right now. That one was brewing up nicely and Bradley could see how it would play nicely into his long-term goals. And those of his paymasters. Or one of them, at least. Mitchell shouldn't need to trouble him for the next week or so though. Bradley was pretty sure he had left everything under control and up-to-date. Mitchell had all he needed to keep Phil Henshaw under his 'guidance'. And Bradley's freshly-renewed mandate gave him the means to keep it that way. Phil would now be getting regular updates on the movements of his children and their mother. How welcome those updates would be was not Bradley's concern. He had sympathy for Phil, of course, but there was always the bigger picture, Bradley consoled himself. The needs of the many at the expense of a little suffering for the very few. Phil was one of the few at the moment. Bradley would go so far to protect him, but no farther. If the balloon went up, Phil was on his own.

He did have a few regrets about this whole affair. There were bits he hadn't fully explained to his bosses. Bits where he'd been beaten to the prize. Selwyn had been one. Right from the moment he'd received the tip-off from the IT technician in Hartmann, who turned out to be a useful plant in all sorts

of ways, that Selwyn had bribed him and was up to something, Bradley knew
he was probably onto something big. But what? He made it his business to get
to know Selwyn. He'd turned up as a member at the golf club, got talking to
him on the range and in due course, invited him to a round and a pint. So
he'd seen the spectacular improvements in his game. He should have guessed
earlier that there was a connection between Selwyn's funny business with
Hartmann and the golf, but it was a pretty big leap of imagination and he
regretted not making it earlier.

And Selwyn hadn't been exactly forthcoming. Bradley had tapped his
phone, broken into his house, and that of his mistress, all to no avail. It was
the little bug in Selwyn's bedroom that had revealed the truth. The bug and
the camera. He had photographs of Anne that the tabloids would give their
eye teeth for, but they were now all secured in the building he'd just left, in a
file marked 'for my eyes only'. You never knew when they might come in
handy.

It was Selwyn's wire-tapped discussions with his wife and the subsequent
connections with the Godwin team that had put Bradley on the right track.
He had more or less reached a full understanding of what was at stake when
an alert from base warned him Selwyn had been outed. Hartmann had finally
decided Selwyn was too big a risk and too 'independent'. He would have to
go. The IT guy had seen Selwyn's file with a huge red sticker on it and then
come under suspicion himself as the only way Selwyn could have breached
the security tag. The IT man was now elsewhere, with a different name,
where he would still be of use to Bradley.

On the one hand, Bradley blamed himself for what happened next. He'd
taken a day off to go home and see his mother. It was her sixtieth birthday
and they hadn't seen each other for months. On the other hand, Bradley
didn't think he'd done much wrong. Okay it was an office rule that you
didn't ever procrastinate on stuff as important as this, but what can be more
important to a guy than his mother's significant birthday? The reception he
got from his delighted mother convinced him he was right. Selwyn's death
suggested he wasn't. If he'd gone looking for Selwyn a day earlier, who
knows how things would have turned out?

Selwyn had been alive when he found him out on the golf course where
the tracking device said he would be. Still breathing, just, but incapable of
speech and with a weird look, pleading almost, in his eyes. Whatever had
happened to him had not happened that long ago. Bradley looked round but
saw only a couple of golfers on a distant hole. Bradley concentrated on
comforting the terrified Selwyn, who died on him two minutes later. Bradley
was sad, but professional. He searched his pockets, took out his wallet, saw the
card with Stamp's name and number, memorised them both when he saw the
message saying 'please contact in case of emergency' and slipped it back in the
wallet after some hesitation. He didn't want to be found there, or seen. He
took a quick photograph of the strange red marks on the body and left Selwyn

for some innocent golfer to find. But the Stamp number and the message on the rear of the card told him what he had to do next.

Bradley determined from that moment to make no more mistakes. He was not sentimental but he hated waste. And Selwyn's death was a waste. What he had in his head could have earned millions from a grateful nation. Bradley had listened in to Selwyn's rationale for going it alone and incognito, namely to avoid a Hartmann induced death, and this is where it had got him. So Bradley wanted to make up for his mistake. Nothing could bring Selwyn back, but a grateful nation might still benefit from his invention.

He'd gone straight to Stamp, imposed his very considerable authority somewhat rudely on a reluctant Christopher and read the letter in the package. He was very interested in the mark 2 it mentioned. That was the prize. That would make up for losing Selwyn. He gave the package back to Stamp with a few terse instructions which Stamp understood completely and left, making sure Stamp saw the gun beneath his coat. Then he went to a Victorian semi in Redditch. He climbed the few steps to the window with the 'Vote Green' sticker and found the door open. Julie was in the bath, but not looking at all well. He noticed and photographed the red daubs on the white shroud she was wearing, said a prayer for her and stepped back out onto the landing. A rapid search of the house revealed nothing. Not even a note from Selwyn. On his way out, he picked up her laptop, just in case, left through the front door as if taking the computer away for repair and locked the door behind him.

He requisitioned a disguise kit and a dog and for the next few days sat in a car or patrolled the street outside her house, waiting for the inevitable to happen. He saw the collection team arrive in a small removal van and wondered who they belonged to. Hartmann internal trash, he felt sure. An hour later they left again, Julie's body doubtless inside some of the furniture they took as part of their cover. Later the same day he saw Mitchell arrive and leave and photographed his number plate. He didn't expect much from that and wasn't surprised when the owner turned out to be dead. He recognised Mitchell though. He'd come across his work before. *Could be a very useful idiot.*

45 On home soil

T he caravan upped sticks in Portugal and moved on. For Phil this meant a break from tournaments and a return to Wentworth, his office, golf's headquarters in England and the venue for the next big contest. He couldn't wait. It would make keeping in touch with Helen and the children that much easier. Besides, Wentworth was paradise and Phil's office was a complete contrast to the hot and cramped conditions they had endured in makeshift accommodation in Portugal. The building itself, home to English golf, oozed tradition and style. The white castellated clubhouse was a sporting icon and Phil could perhaps be forgiven his pride in having the premier office in it. He forgave himself, anyway, as he assumed did Marilyn, who, apparently naturally and seamlessly, had transformed herself into his personal assistant.

The setting was magnificent and from the window of his office Phil was able to survey his kingdom and bless his luck in inheriting it. This, Phil told himself and anyone else who would listen, is what almost all golf courses aspire to be. Few ever get there, he said, and if there is one that surpasses it, it will have some pretty knackered grounds-men and green-keepers. He was pleased that Marilyn still smiled every time he said it.

The office itself was large and furnished in a modern style, grey woodwork, steel and glass cabinets and a red carpet. Phil's desk, as befits a chief executive of his stature, had not a scrap of paper on it. Two clever executive toys and a large flat-screened computer were the only things on its surface and Phil knew that Marilyn worked hard to keep it that way.

He was in love with Marilyn. He didn't know when he'd first come to this conclusion, but there was no doubt in his mind. She was telepathic where he was concerned, he felt. He was unable to hide his moods from her and the longer they were together the more radar-like she became in anticipating his wishes. He loved her elegance too; something he assumed she got from her French mother. He could see she was not conventionally beautiful, but her grace and the care she took with her appearance made up for that. In any case it wasn't a deficiency in his eyes. He found her face handsome and wonderfully expressive. But it was the smile that did it. Whatever Phil was feeling, the smile would make him happy. It was as if her face had been designed around the smile and every part of it got involved. Her eyes narrowed and glistened, her delightful nose wrinkled splendidly and her red mouth widened and curved in the most natural bow he could imagine. He wanted that smile in his life for good. He wanted to own it and be able to tell the world: 'See this smile? I'm responsible for that.'

There were sadly for him few signs that his feelings were returned. She was content to socialise with him, alone or in company. Their conversation was immensely relaxed and even intimate. Certainly he had no secrets from her (apart from the one, he thought). But he couldn't make the breakthrough. Once or twice he'd thought she was ready to be kissed, but always, she managed to extricate herself skilfully. It was driving him mad. It was as well his normally active libido was well below par. The threat to his loved ones was to blame for that.

He could tell she knew what he wanted from her. He hardly kept it secret when they were alone and on a couple of occasions she had been forced to tell him in direct language that she was not in a position to have a relationship. Infuriatingly she would not tell him what the block was. She asked for his patience, just about the only thing he didn't want to give her.

'Phil,' she said one day in their third or fourth week back from Portugal. 'You're not happy, are you? You have not been happy for some time. Are you going to tell me or do we just go on pretending everything is fine?' She was sitting on the arm of a long grey sofa that Phil had often imagined sharing with her, horizontally. Her legs dangled and swung. He noticed they were still brown from the Portuguese sun. 'And before you say it, I am not trying to start a conversation about us. So what's up?'

'Well, there's the general pressure of the job. But we've talked about that.'

'We've talked about how you feel like the Mayor in 'Jaws'. You have to keep the show on the road despite what's going on under water.'

'I know I said that, and it is true in a way, but it trivialises it. We're losing the battle in Europe. We keep beating the Americans in the Ryder Cup but all that does is show the punters how many of our stars we've lost to the American tour. I'm struggling to name one of the Ryder Cup team who doesn't play in the States with the odd condescending trip across the Atlantic to play Dubai, or somewhere. We're losing audiences at live tournaments, sponsors on a weekly basis and the TV franchise is talking about reducing transmission time and cutting the budget. Lose them and it's curtains. So, I reckon we are one big scandal from a total disaster. And avoiding that scandal by any means possible is what my job has become. That and sucking up to the broadcasters.'

'Are you sure you aren't exaggerating it a bit?'

'Hardly at all. I'm underestimating the problem if anything. What I shouldn't do though is see it all as a defensive issue. There are offensive moves I could make too. But for that I need a bit more confidence than I have at the moment. It's a bit lonely this job. There is no-one I can really share things with.'

'Not even me?'

Phil was tempted. 'No, not even you. Not as things stand, at any rate - and that isn't a move, by the way.'

'What about Matt? Why did he suddenly disappear off the scene? He looked like a potential running mate.'

'I wish I knew.'

'You must know. Someone in a job like that doesn't just run away, skedaddle without trace. Have you had a word with anybody? Like the police, or his family?'

'Matt has no family. This sort of job and families rarely mix. And as for the police ...'

'As for the police what?' she asked.

Phil thought for a moment. He looked at Marilyn and couldn't help himself.

'Can I trust you?'

'You know you can.'

'Trust you with my life?'

'Seriously? What's the matter? What's going on?'

Phil unburdened himself. He told her everything that had happened and the currents moving below the surface.

'How often do you get the photographs of your family?'

'Every day. From different places. Shopping, going to school, cinema, out to friends. Somebody obviously has them under surveillance the whole time.'

'Well,' she said. 'Now that I know what's troubling you, I can start sharing the worry. You fancy a platonic hug?'

'I think a platonic hug would add to my troubles,' he said.

'Well, let's start there and see where we end, shall we?'

★

One day later, the atmosphere in Phil's office was chilly. Stefan was in town. A visit from Stefan was rarely a day at the beach and this one was no exception. It was plain that something was eating him. Something big. It was equally plain that he wanted answers and was used to getting them.

Phil had been on the receiving end of an harangue from Stefan (whose private plane was waiting to whisk him back across to Germany as soon as he'd finished slicing Phil) about the state of the game and the need to keep the press in control if the tour wanted to keep sponsors like him. Phil felt his position was hopeless. He wanted to be able to talk about the measures being introduced to keep an eye on the Jake Godwin team and to tackle the corruption at the heart of the game. Except there weren't any measures. He wanted to say how sure he was that performance enhancement was behind it all, but he didn't dare. Mitchell would kill his family if he did and anybody could be in Mitchell's pay, or be paying him. And Matt had sworn him to silence, too.

'People will not believe it,' Stefan was saying, 'if that *verdammte* team keeps winning like this. Two more wins in South Africa and a second place in Asia. They will never believe it is natural causes. And if they doubt the honesty of the tour, they will doubt the honesty of the sponsor. The dirt will rub off on my cars and no-one likes a dirty car.'

Phil looked at Bradley who stared back with a silent reminder that he was to toe the agreed line. Phil would have ignored he stare, and his promise to Matt, at that point under most circumstances. But for all his personal bravery and for all the reasons he could see for being open and honest with Stefan, he was completely silenced by the threats to his ex-wife and kids. He recognised his debt to Helen and loved his children to bits. He didn't doubt for a second that the threat to their life was real. The pictures he had received of his wife and children only this morning were on his mind. With a heavy heart he did what Bradley wanted and followed the script.

'Well,' Phil said, 'at the risk of boring everyone, we have gone as far down the chemical route as we can. We have tested the winning golfers and others to destruction and there is nothing. Privately, just between us, the Jake Godwin stable has been blood tested and apart from a slightly raised testosterone level on a couple of occasions, not in any case unusual in young men under stress and in an excited state, there was nothing. And we used your people at Merricole to do the tests Stefan, so you will be able to verify that what I am saying is true.' Stefan said he had been shown the reports.

Phil went on: 'So we agree, there are no drugs involved. We also agree that something very unusual is happening and that there is something 'mechanical' about the way these golfers are playing. Through contacts in the Home Office I tracked down the real Professor Millican. He does work for our government and is highly regarded. We have flawless references for him.'

'He's the reason I'm here. You couldn't produce him last time. Is he here this time?' asked Stefan.

'No. We have him on conference facilities. Do you want to talk to him?'

Stefan agreed and Phil switched on the screen nearby. The internet connection snapped in and a very different-looking Professor Millican appeared before them. Phil thought he saw Bradley smile, then stifle it.

'Good morning' said Mitchell/Millican, with a polished English accent. ' I can see some of you thinking how different I appear this time. And you are right. I am not the same man you met before. I apologise that it was necessary to send an emissary to meet you in Portugal. My public appearances are currently much constrained and travelling abroad is impossible. For health reasons, shall we say.' He was introduced to Stefan and Bradley. Millican went on: 'The man you met was well briefed, however, and would have given you a correct view of my work.'

Stefan had the first question. 'I have heard how you explain these tricks with the golf balls and I understand the theory. My own people do not know how this is done, but they agree it can be done. They have two questions. You, or your alter ego, told Phil Henshaw that the propulsion and guidance was possible with the right club and the right ball. Why can we not tell by examining the clubs and the balls used whether they are the ones that produce this effect?'

'A very intelligent question. My lab has reproduced this effect with a standard, though very expensive club of the type many golfers, including Godwin's team use. So any solid driver will work. As for the ball, the graphene coating is liquid and it does not survive the blow in any measurable quantity. What the golfer needs is a way of introducing this liquid, and it needs just a tiny amount, onto the ball, anywhere on its surface since it then grips and adheres. It is easily done in an undetectable manner. A complicit caddy would be the ideal mechanism. There will be some post-match residue, but only very expensive lab equipment would detect it and it evaporates completely, or rather assumes other energy or matter forms, within minutes.'

'That all sounds very convenient for someone trying to fool us, professor. Are you? Trying to fool us?' This was Bradley.

Millican shrugged. 'I work with this technology every day. It is amazing. Whoever stole it clearly now has the capacity to manufacture it, but what else they have in mind, we do not know. You believe what you will, but hear this: if we can recover it from its current unlawful possessors, Herr Greiff, Stefan if I may, we will be looking for a responsible partner to help us take the implementation forward. But it is up to you whether you choose to believe in it or not. If not, of course you go no further. If you believe me, there are ways we can work together to find the wretch or wretches. You know, for a while I believed it might be you who took it. Get it back and you get development rights. You would become more powerful than governments.'

'I already am,' said Stefan.

'I mean than all the governments put together. They would fall over to do your bidding.'

Phil wondered how soon it would occur to Stefan that he was being given shadows to chase so he would stop looking for substance. He could not imagine that this piece of theatre would fool him for long. But perhaps it wasn't meant to. 'So how will we be able to prove that it is happening? And how can we stop it in the meantime.' This was Phil, still reading from the script. Bradley had told him to ask a few questions and look convinced.

'We are developing jammers which stop all communications between ball and direction finders, but since they are also new technology it will take time and they are not ready yet.'

Phil asked another question: 'The science sounds genuine enough and the energy/matter interface is very interesting, but when a ball receives a signal to change direction it needs internal propulsion systems. An engine in a golf ball?'

'You have not fully understood what goes on. A part, a very small part, of the golf ball is no longer matter, so long as the ball is in flight. It is energy. And more, it is intelligent energy. It follows code and once a signal is received it moves its energy to change direction towards the signal. And the signal is so tiny, we need special jammers, as I said not yet ready, to find and stop them.'

'This gets worse,' said Stefan. 'Intelligent energy? Tiny signals? Little green men to operate it all?'

'Well, a little green keeper, anyway. One rogue groundsman could install all that's needed in an hour, given a buggy and no interruption.'

'And why, assuming you are working for Her Majesty's Government, do you not have your men on the ground trying to check all this out and put a stop to it.'

'There are two assumptions there, and who knows if either is correct. But, Stefan,' Millican continued, ' as I say, the skin will not be off my nose if I am telling the truth. It will be off yours.'

Stefan clearly did not like reference to noses. 'My nose tells me that this smells,' he said. Millican shrugged. 'If that is all, Stefan, I have an appointment.'

Stefan waved at him as if he were an irritating wasp and Millican disappeared from screen.

Phil was standing by the window. He looked down and watched a man in a hoodie, with a gait very like Mitchell's, saunter across the yard from the media centre down towards the car park. Headlights flashed a signal, a car door opened, the hooded figure stepped inside and the car roared away. Phil, who'd been obliged to set this exercise up, did not believe it could have deceived Stefan. Mitchell was skating on thin ice he thought. *I hope to God it cracks when he's on it.*

'Why are they trying to get it back?' Stefan wanted to know. 'They have the materials and processes already. They have the technology and science. And if others are already using it, the cat has already jumped out of the poke, has it not? It is no more a secret.'

Good point, thought Phil: 'They want to punish and deter, I expect. What good does catching any criminal do? On top of that, there will be uses the thieves don't yet know about. If it was now developed further and used by the owner, the thieves would get the benefit, too. The price would shoot up and the buyers would come running. Perhaps more dangerous buyers?'

'Kuhscheisse.' Stefan was clearly not impressed.

★

Phil poured a scotch for himself and a gin and tonic for Marilyn.

'So you don't think Stefan bought it?'

'Definitely not.'

'And what do you think he'll do.'

Phil shook his head and said nothing. Eventually he said: 'Last week you told me you weren't in a position, I can't remember exactly what you said, 'to enter a relationship' was it? What made you change your mind? Given, you know, the 'non-platonic hug'. Quite a few of them in fact. And very nice too. What did you mean?'

'I have a husband.' Phil shrugged as if to say so what?

'You never said, and I didn't ask because I knew. You do have personnel records. It's not exactly unheard of for married women to ..., well, you know.'

'We are divorcing, or rather I am divorcing him.' He wants to do it in France and I want a London divorce.'

'Because English law tends to favour women?'

'Exactly. And under French law if I am known to be in another relationship I can more or less kiss everything good-bye. But that's not all. He's a tour pro, my soon-to-be ex. A veteran now, but a two-time tour winner. You will know him. And it won't look good if he starts saying the chief executive nicked his wife.'

'I don't know of a tour pro called Duclos.'

'That's because Duclos is my maiden name, not his surname. He's doesn't play the big tournaments these days, but you'd certainly know him. You've played with him more than once, and he was at Villamoura when you won.'

'Not Andre?'

'Andre. I can't believe you didn't know, despite the secrecy.'

'Well, I didn't. His name wasn't in your file. Perhaps I didn't want to know.'

'Anyway, I never said 'no' to you, just 'patience'. I still do, but perhaps a bit less of it now and then. You think?'

He thought.

'Well, well,' Phil said. 'Another fine mess you've landed me in.'

46 Inspectors screened

S amson came into the tournament at Wentworth feeling for the first time in his life that he had been aptly named and determined to give the pygmies a thrashing. He loved the course and blitzed the field on day one and day two. Only England could produce a Wentworth, he thought. As beautiful and treacherous as Albion herself. Long narrow fairways turn just at the wrong moment; beautiful trees catch balls and fling them carelessly onto unplayable lies; bunkers lie in wait for even perfect shots and little rills and rivers tinkle menacingly in your ear. It is a true test for champions and Samson reduced it to the level of a benign municipal course designed by amateurs for amateurs. Two sixty-fives left him six ahead of the nearest rival, a man with a reputation so feared in golf that many a competitor has wilted just to learn that this man was chasing him. Samson saw the leader board and shrugged. He knew that, right now, he was the best player in Europe and maybe even the world.

He sat watching TV with Cristina in his hotel room after the second day and saw an item on his performance. He watched himself swing the club and saw how the camera lingered on his face. Then there was a piece to camera from Madelaine. She spoke about the sudden and rapid improvement in form of one or two golfers from the same stable. They had gone from no wins to being unable to lose and now here was another, Samson, winner at Villamoura, streaking ahead again. Was it a coincidence, she speculated, a wicked twinkle in her eye, that the doping inspectors, so long conspicuous by their absence, were now everywhere you went? She turned to the man by her side, a lean man with a face like a hawk and distinct twinkle in his eye. This was rare indeed: an inspector eager for publicity? Samson saw what was going on straightaway. *There's a man on a promise from Madelaine if ever I saw one. Well good luck with that, mate.*

Samson's interest grew as the man wittered on. He told the camera how inspections had been turned up full volume because there had been suspicion at the highest level that all was not well. Some people, he said, thought there was some sort of technological explanation, better clubs, better balls, better range finders, or even something more complicated. But, he continued, suddenly anxious to communicate what he had earlier sought to conceal, that sort of technology would apply across the board and bring about a general improvement. This amelioration (he hadn't been able to resist a show of superiority in his broadcast) was confined to a few and the explanation had to be different. Of course it could be just talent, sheer hard work, good coaching, and he hoped it was. But if it was something more sinister, he hoped he could find and eliminate it.

Samson was sure he was right about the inspector's motives for breaking cover as spectacularly as this. 'You know what I think, Tina. I think that that miserable old bastard is on a promise from the lovely Madelaine if he spills the beans and gives the broadcasters a real story. That's the talk with the caddies and it looks like they're right.' Cristina laughed. 'That would be an interesting pair to see together,' she said. 'Would he have to give a sample first?' 'No. But I bet she has.'

On screen Madelaine asked the inspector if he was saying the improvement he described could be drug-induced. He said he didn't know, but if there was evidence for it, he was determined to find it. Samson was sitting on the edge of his seat. Madelaine produced a list of the players in the Godwin stable, read out the names and asked the lean inspector if they had been subject to more than usual attention by his team. The inspector said he was sadly unable to confirm or deny that, but to Samson's intense annoyance, he said it in a way that clearly confirmed it. Lastly, Madelaine asked about any weaknesses in the testing system that could be exploited and the inspector gave her a long list, from illness to delays due to other commitments to sponsors etc. But the biggest, he said, was the absence of blood testing, something he hoped to rectify in the near future. Samson was screaming at the screen: 'They've had more blood out of me than Dracula gets from seven frigging virgins,' he yelled.

Madelaine thanked the inspector and then to Samson's utter amazement, stroked his hand briefly in clear camera shot. Samson saw the lean inspector beam. *Christ, it's true. The bastard's cracked it with Madelaine. She'll bloody eat him alive.*

Cristina turned the TV off after the broadcast. 'They know. They are going to get you. You have to stop.' Samson told her not to worry. They weren't ever going to get him on that sort of thing. He could guarantee it. Samson asked her to trust him. He knew what he was doing. There was no danger at all, now, he said. Absolutely none.

He saw the tears in her eyes and knew that he loved her. He hoped she loved him as much. They went to bed and for once, after a few kisses, Samson fell fast asleep and slept deeply and dreamlessly, as if he were a man with nothing on his mind. And nothing untoward in his body.

47 *Martin's last message*

M artin Pascal called the waiter over and ordered a gin fizz. 'Plenty of
gin, mate. Understand? Mucho gin?' The gin arrived and Martin
signed against his room number, throwing a large tip onto the tray. The
waiter bowed and withdrew. Martin liked that.

*A bit of deference after all the shit I've swallowed over the years. It's my frigging
due and about time too. No surprise is it that I ended up where I did, bottom of Jake's
shit heap? Look where they sent me, all the crap tournaments nobody else wanted. No
wonder I was never motivated. You can't hit a ball properly when you've spent the
night in the car and have to borrow a local as your caddy.*

*Bloody Jake accusing me of wasting my expenses because I didn't always have
enough left over to pay my bills. How did they think I was going to spend my off time
when that's all there was on offer? Course I was going to go to bars and stuff. Stands to
reason. No surprise I lost a bit of money here and there. And bloody caddies want too
much money anyway. And the prices hotels charge! Bloody mini bars. Freaking
extortion, nothing short of. But I did my bit. It's not my fault I was bottom of Jake's
rankings. It was the crap they made me do. Shit resorts and shit accommodation. They
wouldn't do it, would they. Send Martin. He'll do it. No bloody wonder I couldn't
climb the rankings. All right now though, eh? Good times rolling in eh? Couple of top
tens myself, too. Doing my bit.*

*Yeah, all right, some of it is down to the promone stuff. I mean, a bit of it was at
first, definitely. But it's no bloody good up here in this Swiss mountain palaver. Or
Austrian. Wherever the hell we are. Air's too thin. You have to take twice, three times
as much to get half the effect, that's what I think anyway. So that's what I do. Not
good for the figure though, too much of it. Look at these bloody man boobs. Where the
hell did they come from? Tell you what, though. On the course, all the good results
lately, a lot of that was down to me and some extra work and a bit of belief, you know,
I mean it was me doing the improving not the frigging promone or whatever the sodding
hell it is. But the promone is definitely good for in the sack, can't deny it. I can stay up
half the night dancing and playing and drinking and stuff and still get it up when I need
to. Twice, three times if I had to. And still make an early tee time. Bloody fantastic it is
for the old rumpy. But the golf? Nah, that's down to me, mate. It's me doin' all that.
And I'm damn well going to spend my share of the mazoolah. Bring it on.*

He summoned the waiter from the bar on the opposite side of the lobby
by pointing exaggeratedly at his empty glass. A minute or so later he watched
the man collect his drink from the bar, walk past the huge picture window
framing a classic alpine scene, mount the carpeted steps to Martin's mezzanine
area and place the drink carefully on the table. Martin tipped him again, just
to get the bow. As the waiter made his way back across the floor he was

stopped by a tall man who had entered the hotel just seconds earlier. The tall man whispered something in his ear. 'No more for the drunk on the mezzanine. I'll have a scotch and ice.' The waiter nodded and the tall man whipped Martin's extravagant tip off the tray and put it in his pocket. 'And don't take any more of his money either or I'll have to tell your probation officer.' The waiter bowed, smiled and went to get the scotch.

'Ah if it isn't the faithful Gavin. Welcome, welcome. Have a drink?' Martin didn't much like his caddy, but anybody was better than his own company sometimes.

'Already taken care of.' Gavin took in their surroundings with small appreciative nods. His eyes stopped for fully a minute on the large window framing a deep valley backed by brown, grey and green peaks, capped with a ring of snow even this late in spring. 'You happy with the accommodation this trip, Martin? Scenery good enough for you? Air bracing enough? Not too many cowbells and food that swells you up? Locals friendly? Mini bar well stocked? Austrian chicks putting out okay?'

'You having a laugh? Remember what we used to put up with? Or I did. You wouldn't come on the really rough ones. Jesus, no wonder I didn't win. Hiring locals as bagmen. Sleeping in shit chalets. Not anymore, eh? Worth celebrating, all this is, you think. And that's what tonight is. Celebrating. Not here though. I mean this is nice, yeah, but it's half way up a friggin' mountain and as dead as my auntie's fanny. Deader. The bright lights of the valley are calling. I'll show this town a good time.'

'We're on at twelve tomorrow.'

'So?'

'Just saying. We'll need an early range, so...'

'So if it gets too late I won't go to bed, because two hours' sleep is worse than none. You're carrying the friggin' bag. I'm just walking and swinging. And screw the range. I'm not on Jake's list for this one. Don't have to come anywhere, he says, best if I miss the jolly old cut, even.'

Gavin knew what he meant. Martin's beans had been spilt weeks ago. Gavin knew the full story.

'So why bother showing up at all. Save the expense and stay at home?'

'Because as well as being crap sometimes we've got to be seen to be crap. You know why.'

'Well, if you <u>are</u> going to town, maybe I should drive you or get a cab.'

'You drive? Why? I'm not pissed.'

'Well the roads. It's a bit icy and the bends are a bit tight some of 'em. Need a bit of caution.'

'I could drive you under the table. You want to come?'

Gavin shook his head. The waiter arrived with the scotch and left untipped. 'You know this is Samson's week at Wentworth? Him and a couple of the other lads?'

'He'll bloody skin 'em. Samson's in the form of his life. Yeah, go Samson. Bring us some more lovely notes. He's my bloody hero, Samson is. Swing nearly as good as mine. Kill 'em Samson.'

'How many of those have you had.' Gavin indicated the gin.

'The first, this is.'

Gavin sighed, knocked back the scotch and walked away without a word. Martin watched him go, and a heavy feeling began to grow in his guts.

His phone buzzed and he was surprised to see the the name on the text notification. Larry Topham, it said, and the number tallied.

Larry was after a job according to the message. *Why didn't the silly bugger ring?* He wanted Martin to advertise his availability in the players' hospitality suite. How was Martin anyway? 'Fine,' thumbed Martin, adeptly enough. ' Because,' texted Larry, 'I've heard that the stuff is affecting nearly all the others one way or the other.'

Martin's thumb went into overdrive again. 'You know about that stuff?' 'Course I do,' came back from Larry. 'That's why I got the push. Only Samson's not affected' keyed Larry. 'Funny that'.

Martin thought for a while then tapped again: ' he's probably on mark 2.'

'Mark 2? Whassat?'

'Not sure I know myself but we're all waiting for it. It's what stops us telling 'em where to stick their stuff. And the money, of course. Anne's old man, before he snuffed it, is supposed to have been working on a mark 2. That's the word, anyway. You know what? Got drunk last night and the night before come to think. Had a great time and told the girl I could go all night if I had some of the stuff back at my place. So she came back and we both had some. I was still doing it to her while she was asleep. Not really, but I could of. So God knows what mark 2's like. You know when it cured everything for me? You know, like just tell your headache to go away and it does? That could have been it. Mark 2.'

'I hope you didn't tell her, this girl, about the stuff, did you? What it does apart from get you hard?'

'Might have done. Too pissed to remember. Told plenty of others though. Nearly all the girls. Most don't understand, or don't care. Not into golf. Just like the money.'

'Where are you staying? Might come over to watch.'

'You dirty bugger, Larry.'

'The golf!!!.'

Martin sent his last ever text. It had his hotel name and postcode.

48 Bad news day

S amson had rarely felt better. He was out last today with the feared rival from South Africa. He had slept well, resisted Cristina still naked and musty with sleep, showered, breakfasted and practised. Now, announced on the first tee by the same lugubrious Scot as always, he was ready to give his rival the game of his life. It didn't quite turn out like that. Despite feeling so good, Samson couldn't quite get his game together. He consulted the charts, most of which he now knew by heart in any case, spoke the incantations more from habit than anything and let his body do the rest. But it didn't quite want to. It was fractions out and those fractions meant bunkers rather than greens, trees rather than fairways. Samson was frustrated. *I knew this would happen to me eventually. Just keep calm, keep playing your shots and hang on to some sort of decent score. Don't let the big man get away.* At the end of the day, he wasn't back in the pack, but he had lost the lead and was two behind the South African, who despite his reputation as a fierce warrior, or because he had learned to be generous in victory, commiserated with Samson and reminded him there was always tomorrow. Samson promised to hold him to that, because it looked like they would be partnered again.

He left the course, remained upbeat through the customary media interviews, checked and signed his card, thanked his caddy and went home to Cristina, who kissed him, said never mind and took him out for something to eat. They had just finished and Samson was laughing at something Cristina had said in fractured but endearing English, when Anne and Jake appeared at the restaurant door, clearly looking for someone. There were grave looks on their faces; Samson, waving to catch their attention, was instantly anxious. Whatever they were going to tell him could not possibly be good. Nor was it.

'We've just heard some bad news about Martin,' Jake said. 'Apparently he had a car accident this morning. Went right off at a bend on an alpine road in Austria. Took half a barrier with him. Would have been quick we think. His caddy went to identify him and it is definitely Martin. It was a miracle the caddy wasn't with him. Funny thing is that Martin was on the way to the police station when it happened. The caddy says someone had daubed his car with red paint the night before. He reported it to the car hire firm and they asked him to drop it in via the police station. The caddy was going to do it, and Martin was going to let him but at the last minute Martin decided to go himself. Snap decision for no real reason. His caddy said he'd not been himself for days. Strange moods, heavy drinking sessions and crap golf. Not that there's anything strange about the last bit.'

'Christ. Poor Martin. Bloody hell. That's a bummer. Poor sod. It was an accident though. Definitely?'

'What else? And it was one waiting to happen according to Gavin.'

Samson sat for a while in silence, head bowed. Cristina reached across to take his hand. He smiled a sad smile at her.

'So what we suggest, Samson, is that you get out on the course tomorrow and win it for him.'

'I'll do my best.'

He could see Anne scrutinising him. 'Love is good for you Samson. I haven't seen you looking so good for ages. You look really healthy and fit. You should knock spots off the old Boer tomorrow. Don't take too much of the stuff, though. Just in case. A bit variable sometimes.' She smiled at Cristina and left. Samson asked Jake to join them and ordered him a beer.

'What was all that about, Jake. 'A bit variable sometimes'?'

'Oh nothing. She's a mother hen really.' Samson remembered the sting of her slap across his face. *Some bloody mother hen.*

'Come on Jake, she must have meant something.'

Jake was tired of carrying the burden alone. 'Well only that Mitchell is no Selwyn and we can't be absolutely sure of the consistency of each batch. It will be better when he finds out how to make a more durable formula. Nothing dangerous in it though. We've been through all that, haven't we? What Anne meant was take it in moderation like you said you were doing. Half doses; quarter doses even and not every day.'

'But you've been letting Jason and Ian and Martin loose with it. You know what they're like with stuff like that. You can't give a kid a tube of Smarties and say only eat the one. Jesus, Jake, that's criminal. Who knows what really killed Martin.'

Jake had no answer. He could only repeat that mark 2 would sort it all out. Selwyn had laid the foundations for it but the trouble was, only Anne knew where the formula or whatever was and she wasn't letting on. She didn't trust Mitchell enough as a chemist to let him loose with it. She wouldn't even admit it existed to him, Jake. 'And I shouldn't be damn well telling you, either.'

'You're not telling me something we don't all more or less know already. We all thought she was working on it. Instead, she's letting us possibly kill ourselves with the unreliable stuff and when we're gone she'll find some other suckers for the next stage. You have to stop her doing that Jake. And get the others off that drug. Don't just warn them, damn well stop them.'

'And stop the money too?' Jake asked. 'How do you think they'll take that?'

'Can't spend it when you're dead. Ask Martin.'

'Martin's death was an accident. Even his caddy said that. He shouldn't have driven on those roads with a hangover.'

'Well the other thing then, given these batches are so unpredictable, is to get Anne to give you the new formula and you find a reliable producer.'

Jake reminded him this was Anne they were talking about. If there was a more stubborn woman he wouldn't like to meet her. And finding a producer with sufficient skills and who could be relied on to keep his trap shut wasn't easy. 'The mark 2 stuff, if it does half what Anne says it will do, will be worth a fortune. And speaking of fortunes, do you know how much Anne will make if you win tomorrow? Just from bookmakers?'

Samson knew his odds. 'Twelve times what she's staked, if she backed me ante post. What did she put on me?'

'Not far short of £500,000. So, £6,000,000 if you win. You think she's going to turn her back on that money? Or that Jason and Ian will? They're not like you Samson. This is the only way for them.'

Samson shook his head. 'Crazy woman. You make sure you tell those other guys everything Jake. Everything. About the mark 2 version as well. Let's all put some pressure on her.'

'Well, I know Mitchell's been trying as well. Like I said, she tells him it doesn't exist, but he says he knows it does because Selwyn told him. And I shouldn't be telling you that either.'

'She really doesn't like Mitchell.'

'Well,' said Jake, 'it's a shame she didn't realise that before she got him to do this for her. I didn't know for ages it wasn't Selwyn's stuff we were using. I thought she had an unlimited supply of the bloody stuff. Now we're all in hock to Mitchell as well. Anyone of us could put the rest in prison for years. It scares me silly Samson. I can't go on and I can't stop. And what are we doing to the game? Killing that, too?'

'Okay, okay Jake. This thing is just the pits. Come on drink the beer and let's try to get some sleep. Biggish day for me tomorrow. I've got to earn £6 million pounds for Anne. Will she share it if she wins, do you think?'

'Is she sharing the risk of losing?'

Samson stood up and Cristina with him. 'Depends which risk you're talking about,' he said.

49 *A winner at Wentworth*

Samson, sober and relaxed, was reading a book when Cristina slipped under the covers, as always without a stitch on. 'What are you reading?'

'Something I found in the library here. A golfing novel 'The Trophy Wife'. Never heard of the guy who wrote it, but it's great. Can't put it down. A bit like you!'

'Not the last few days. Is everything all right. You still want me? Or shall I call Stefan?'

'Everything is fine. Maybe I'm just growing up. I promise tomorrow night, win or lose, I'll make sure you never think of Stefan and his huge nose again.'

'Can you make me forget his huge yacht?'

'Yes, that, too. But I need to get some sleep. Is that okay with you?'

She snuggled up to him and for a moment he regretted his decision to stay chaste until the tournament was over. But his resolve, unlike other things, stayed firm and he fell asleep at last, to dream of glory and triumph at Wentworth.

His dream was still with him as he shook hands with the South African giant on the first tee. He had two shots to make up and initially it wasn't easy. He concentrated and tried everything he knew, but the South African matched him blow for blow and at the turn, was still two shots to the good. At the tenth, Samson's ball found the trees. *Bollocks. Why did I do that? Too much bloody shoulder turn. I'm not concentrating. Too much else going on up there. Poor Martin. I'm bloody well going to do this for him.* He called for a referee who trundled out in his buggy. 'What do you want to do?'

'Well I can't play it and if I drop it one club length away, I still can't play it. I'll need to go two drops away.'

'Okay,' said Hamish, the referee, knowing full well it wasn't, 'but that'll be two shots the course will have back from you.'

Samson resigned himself to taking his medicine and with the fearsome Boer standing close by, took two drops and hit the ball onto the green.

Four shots behind, now in joint second place with Jason, and only 8 holes to play, Samson could have been forgiven for giving it up as a lost cause and settling for a good high finish. But not with Cristina watching and not with what he knew her expectations were of him. Or Anne's bet. Christ, what a weight that was to carry round eighteen holes. On the next, though, he felt something like the old certainty return. He chanted his mantra and the ball started to fly just as he commanded it to. For three holes he was invincible, before the old stager halted his progress with a birdie or two of his own. On the seventeenth, Samson cracked a delightful shot to within four feet and holed the putt for another birdie and to draw level again.

On the last, a difficult par five, the age of the Cape Town warrior finally told. He tried too hard for birdie and found the water to the left of the green with his second shot. He dropped out and chipped onto the green for four. When his putt dropped for a good scrambling par, Samson had two putts to win. He ran his first right up to the hole and he tapped in for birdie. Grinning from ear to ear, the South African was the first to congratulate him. He hugged him and whispered into his ear: 'Don't know what it is, but can you put some in my tea?' Samson was careful not to react in front of the cameras. He covered his mouth with his hand and said: 'You got that all wrong mate. Say it anywhere else and I'll see you in court. Pal.'

Madelaine did the post victory interview. Samson warned her not to follow up her story about the inspectors or he'd walk off. But she was having none of it. 'I lost my bloody virginity again to get that story, so you can bugger off,' she told him. 'The inspectors want blood now, and so do I.'

50 *Love is on the air*

J ason had come third. He'd had two top ten finishes and a win in as many
weeks and no-one could quite believe he'd done it fairly. He left the course
and the interviewers were waiting. Jake was there too, and steered him away.
'The inspectors want to test you again and they're doing blood tests now.
Media pressure. When did you take your last dose?'

'I had a quick sip as a steadier on the seventeenth. Just a nip really. About
half a bottle. I made sure it wasn't on camera.'

'Jesus. I remember Selwyn saying it took about an hour to disappear from
the blood. Look. Take a long time checking your card. Think of some sort of
rigmarole, get it checked and rechecked. Then get to the medical tent and
complain of a headache, a stomach-ache and back pain. Make sure they give
you a full examination. Then come back to me and I'll have at least another
three media interviews lined up as well as the biggie with the satellite folk.
After that, there is the presentation and that takes precedence over everything.
We can use all that to spin it out way beyond the hour and the inspectors can
do nothing about it.'

Jason nodded his agreement. He signed more autographs on his way to
the scorer's tent than in his entire life before. He found some fans from his
home town and spent a quarter of an hour chatting and posing for
photographs with them. They clearly thought he was a great guy. 'A people's
nearly champion,' as one of them put it. Two hours later, all interviewed out
and with his third place medal in his hand, he entered the doping enclosure
and waved his favourite club at the chaperone. 'You aim it, I'll fire it,' he said.

Phil had been given instructions to stop the interviewers asking questions
relating to the dope tests. But when Madelaine effectively told him to get lost,
he tried another tack with her. 'Look,' he said, 'have you considered the fact
that if these guys are using something to improve their game it might be
technology not dope?'

'What? You mean range finders and stuff, or special clubs? What
technology?' Phil promised a world exclusive to the TV company on illegal
new technologies in golf, if they backed off the drugs thing.

Madelaine had her own instructions, though. She wasn't going to budge.
'We've got to push this drugs thing. I've invested a lot of very personal capital
in this story. If it turns out to have no legs, then I'll come back to you on the
other thing.'

'And if it does have legs, which it won't, there won't be a Phil to come
back to.'

'No, I suppose not. Not a CEO Phil at any rate.'

They shook hands and Madelaine went off to interview the winner, Samson Gregory. On the platform she congratulated him and they talked briefly about his fantastic comeback from four down. Then she sprang it. 'Most folks can't believe someone with your track record could do that unaided, Samson. Will you be taking a test after this interview?'

'Winners are always tested when the inspectors are on site. But I'd appreciate it if you'd clarify your earlier remarks.'

'Well, after a fairly undistinguished career, you've now won two tournaments back to back, in spectacular fashion and your stablemates have had two wins and a series of top ten finishes off the back of even less successful track-records than yours. Surely someone has some explaining to do?'

'That's a pretty uncharitable stance to take in the face of all the hard work we've put in, the changes we've made and the fact that one of our colleagues has just died in pursuit of his golfing ambitions.'

He could see he'd rattled her. 'Died? Who? Of an overdose?' Samson pounced on the slip.

'Overdose? One track mind, Madelaine. In a car accident, actually. In Austria. Martin Pascal and no suspicious circumstances. That might have been a more worthy target for your investigatory instincts don't you think?'

'Of course, we are very sorry to hear that and will follow the story up right away. It doesn't mean we have stop discussing what we were discussing.'

'<u>We</u> weren't discussing it. You were.'

'Fine, and I don't mean to be offensive at this clearly difficult time, but we do deserve a response. Is there any truth in the rumours, and I didn't start them, that you are being aided by maybe legal performance-enhancing substances?'

'Yes,' said Samson, 'there is.'

Madelaine nearly dropped the microphone. 'It's true?' she croaked, 'well what sort of enhancement?'

'Well, in my case,' said Samson, 'It's called love. It gets under your skin and into your blood, makes you feel like a million dollars and ready to take on the world. I have the woman of my dreams behind me (sadly not you, Madelaine) and I felt like a million dollars out there, so I took on the world and I beat them. In addition, we all loved Martin and we were all out there today trying to win for him. Love, Madelaine. Remember that? But you know what this is don't you, Madelaine? This interview? This is the uproar of the butterflies.'

'What? What on earth is that?'

'P.G. Wodehouse, Madelaine. About distractions in golf. Some people can't concentrate on what's real, what matters, on what they need to do to win because of imaginary noises off stage. And that's what all this crap is. Just an uproar of the butterflies, Madelaine, an uproar of the butterflies. Get yourselves on track and stay real.'

★

Anne watched the interview, in disbelief and shock when Samson appeared to confess and finally with yelps of delight as he bested Madelaine comprehensively. Anne had heard what Madelaine did to get the story and she could hardly have wished for a more satisfying outcome. She hoped desperately that Samson would prove clean and that the interview wouldn't be evaluated later as the bravado of a man about to be hanged. She would be six million pounds poorer if that happened. She explained it to a rather baffled-looking Cristina, too, and made sure she understood well enough what Samson had said and how effectively he'd said it. Anne wanted Cristina on side. She could see herself, even before the confirmation she'd just heard from the horse's mouth, what this woman meant to Samson. So she meant a lot to her, Anne, too. And Anne, having cultivated Cristina's friendship, knew she was being pursued by the big-nosed billionaire. It wasn't hard for her to see how tempting that would be for a poor young woman like Cristina.

She found Jake still down on the course and discovered he'd seen the interview in the flesh. He told her not to celebrate too early. The blood and urine samples had to be analysed first.

Samson arrived back at the hotel, exhausted, triumphant, confident of a clean test, and desperately in need of a drink. Cristina was waiting with the largest gin and tonic he had seen for some time and he downed it in one. She hung her arms round his neck, pressed herself close and thanked him for what he'd said, live on TV.

He thanked her for making it possible for him to say it. 'What about the blood tests? Will they show any results?'

'Impossible.'

'Why is it impossible? This is blood and urine. There may be things; small things.'

'Impossible because I haven't taken any of the bloody stuff since we came back from Portugal, six weeks ago. I am the cleanest man outside the municipal baths.'

He had to explain what municipal baths were and the joke lost some of its punch as he did so, but he made sure she understood the message. Samson had won clean. He had won fair and square. Cristina's delight was obvious and far more powerful than he anticipated. He had clearly underestimated how worried she'd been by the stuff he'd been taking. He hoped it would be enough to make her stay.

51 *The results come in*

T he German invasion of Phil's office took him by surprise. 'Bloody hell, Blitzkrieg,' he thought as Stefan barged in unannounced followed by a flustered and apologetic Marilyn and an amused-looking Bradley. 'You must be anxious for the results,' Phil said and confirmed what Stefan already knew. The blood test results for Samson were perfectly clear, whereas Jason had slightly raised levels of naturally occurring body chemicals. 'Mainly proteins and hormones. The testers said he could easily have got them from a big beef sandwich. So they are both clear and Samson shiningly so. The testers said he was ultra normal. Whatever that means. He says it is to do with being in love with Cristina,' Phil said.

Stefan grunted. Like most people, Phil had picked up the rumours of Stefan's passion. But he knew more. Bradley, in a rare moment of normality in his dealings with Phil, had let slip exactly how obsessed his boss was with the young Portuguese woman. 'He will have her at any price and he always gets his way. He'll have her, chew her up and spit her back out into the gutter she came from. And I quote!' Bradley had told him.

Stefan's tone was sarcastic: 'It is not to do with love or drug. It is the laws of the universe that are being abused,' Stefan said, proud to have uttered this sentence in English. 'That South African, a German in his middle I think, was yesterday beaten by Einstein, not Samson Gregory. Is that what I am expected to believe?'

Phil made sure his face betrayed nothing. 'Steady, Stefan,' he said, 'however unlikely that may look, we can't rule it out. But if you ask me, this whole cheating business is just about to go away and that's in all our interests as we move to the Open. We can go to St Andrews without having to hold our breath. I don't think Jason was on anything, because I don't believe there is anything he can be on.' Bradley looked at the ground and rubbed the back of his hand. Phil could see he was trying to appear uninterested while listening intently. 'And if he is on something, it is stuff clever enough to beat the best analysts you can provide, Stefan.'

Stefan acknowledged that they may be right but said he would not stop watching and testing. Something, he said, was not quite right in the state of golf and he did not want to be caught out because he had let his guard down.

The telephone rang. The secretary said the TV lot was on the line for Phil. It was Madelaine: 'We hear the results are negative.'

'Double negative,' said Phil, 'do you want to follow up my offer?'

'Shove your offer back where it came from. It stinks. You really think we can switch straight from accusations of doping to a different cause and have any credibility at all? You saw a way of discrediting us and tried it on.'

Phil denied it vehemently. He said it was a strong suspicion and he wasn't clever enough to be that Machiavellian. Besides, TV was the sport's biggest sponsor. Anything that damaged them, would hurt golf, too. Why would he do that? But the phone went dead before he'd finished. 'The TV mob's off the case,' he said.

Phil suggested that everything had reached a satisfactory conclusion and that they could look forward to St Andrews with a spring in their step.

'Careful you don't stumble on that step.' Stefan said in German. Bradley translated with a wink at Phil.

52 Marilyn is hacked

On the Tuesday after Samson's victory, Phil was flat out on the sofa in his office. It was late and the building was deserted. His head was on Marilyn's lap and her fingers stroked his head and hair. It was as relaxed as he'd felt for weeks. This was as intimate as they'd been and Phil wondered when he would ever feel good enough, relaxed enough, to take it further.

Marilyn's revelation that her husband was a tour pro had stopped Phil in his amorous tracks. Shagging a tour professional's wife would amount to gross immorality in office and bring instant dismissal. He'd checked, discreetly.

He tried to enjoy the moment and clear his head. Marilyn's fingers helped. He tried to imagine them somewhere else but nothing stirred inside him. It was a dead zone in that area. Try as he might, he could find no peace. In his mind he turned over how things were standing. His position was still hopeless. He was trapped and at the mercy of Mitchell. Pictures of his family were arriving daily. He spoke to his kids on the phone but their happy teenage insouciance and ignorance of any danger, just made things worse for him. And there was Matt. There had been no word from him or about him. Matt would have been someone to talk to, to turn to. Without him there was no-one, except Marilyn and that wasn't the same.

If Matt was dead would that make Phil an accessory to murder for not reporting him missing? Given the potential good the Jake Godwin drug, as he called it and insofar as he understood it, could do, was he being a traitor to the whole of mankind by keeping it secret?

Phil, restless and unable to stay still for long, sat up. He went to the drinks table and poured himself a large scotch and another gin and tonic for Marilyn, who was beginning to look and sound a little worse for wear. He offered her the drink and she tipped it back. In two swallows it was gone and she went over to the table by the big picture window, a little unsteadily, for another. Phil watched her but said nothing. If she was trying to find some Dutch courage to mount an attack on his modesty, she would be disappointed. It wasn't the last thing on his mind, but it was a long way down the list.

'I have to tell you something Phil. Something bad.' He was back on the sofa next to her. He felt her take his hand. 'Here we go,' he thought and downed the rest of his scotch in a single gulp, too.

'What about?'

'My husband. He has been going through my emails.'

'One of the consequences of staying in the marital home, even if you are both away most of the time. Change your password.'

'He is the rich one, not me. That's what this battle with him is all about. I can't afford to move out.'

'I could help. I will help, in time.'

He got one of the smiles he was addicted to and kissed her, briefly.

'There is a big problem, though. I did change my password. I wrote it down in my little notebook and put it away in a safe place.'

'That's okay then, isn't it?' She shook her head.

'It wasn't a safe enough place and he found it.' Phil was about to say something and she stopped him. 'It wasn't the only password in the book. He found yours too.'

'Mine. Why did you have mine?

'I'm your PA. I write half your emails.'

'Okay. He found my password. So?'

'He hacked your emails. Simple when you have the password and know the email provider. He read them all.'

Phil's mind raced through all the stuff in his email box, trying to work out if there was anything incriminating.

'Well, that should be okay. I keep private and work stuff very separate, so there's absolutely nothing about you and me. He has absolutely nothing on us. Where is he now, by the way?'

'In the States. Florida, working on the PGA tour for a Canadian broadcaster. It isn't a personal thing he found. He knows, Phil. He knows about the whole business. He found your file marked 'Godwin' and read the lot. He knows everything.'

Phil ran through what might be in the file. Oh God yes. There were messages to Matt about it all. Instructions about keeping an eye on them. Questions to the Home Office about Millican, probably and then, oh! Yes. A long email with details of his suspicions and thoughts about performance enhancers to the inspectors. Still, a suspicion was one thing. Knowledge was another. His email had never claimed actual knowledge. He said as much to Marilyn.

'I agree,' she said. But Andre is clever. He knows the Godwin team and he knows the weak ones. He paid a girl to be very interested in Martin. Martin apparently got so drunk he should not have been able to do anything. But the girl says he cleared his head at will, 'on command' she put it, and then went at her like a stallion for half the night. Of course, she asked him how he did it and when he told her, she didn't believe him. But she still told Andre and he did believe it. So, armed with this information, he wormed his way into Martin's company, this is all weeks ago in France, by the way and don't forget how popular Andre is with his colleagues. And the idiot Martin not only told him everything, but let him try some of the stuff, too.'

'So he does know. More than I do, too. It's all true. Bloody hell Marilyn, this is a disaster. What's he going to do about it?'

'Nothing. He just wants in.'

'What?'

'He wants some of the stuff for himself and he wants your protection.'

'What sort of protection can I give him?'

'Martin told him they were getting support and assistance from the very highest levels. Andre thinks that means you.'

'Martin was lying. What made him say that? How pissed was he when he said it?'

'We're talking Martin, don't forget. Anyway, whatever made him say it, Andre knows and wants a part of it. I'm his messenger and I hate it. But if you don't play ball …?'

'I can't play ball. I don't know anything about it, other than that it exists and half the powerful world wants it for one reason and the other half wants it for another. And they both want exclusive rights, or something. I don't really understand what's going on and I certainly don't have any access to the stuff itself. It appears to be very tightly controlled. Shit Marilyn, I hope you're as innocent in this as you say you are and that you didn't put him up to it.'

'I hate the man,' she said, 'and I love you. I wouldn't ever do something like this to you on purpose, I promise.'

'I can't handle this. I can't think straight. Marilyn, don't take this the wrong way, but I'm going to have to ask you to leave, love. I need to sort this out in my own head.'

He called her a cab, brought her coat from the cupboard and, when the cab arrived, kissed her goodbye on the cheek.

He went to a drawer in his desk and took out a mobile phone. He hit the only number in contacts and when Bradley answered he said: 'I need to see you. (pause) Of course it's urgent. (pause) I'm just doing what you said and what we agreed. I think there's a serious risk that someone's got hold of information that will be very damaging. (pause) It's not in my interests for anybody to know about the enhancers either. You've pointed that out enough times. (pause) No, I'll be here. Just tell the night officers. They'll be expecting you.'

He put the phone back in the drawer and poured a very large scotch. Only then did it hit him what Marilyn had said.

53 Bradley in action

B radley wasn't surprised to get the call from Phil. He knew this job would be a loose one when he took it on, but it had chimed with his ongoing overarching mission: keeping an eye on big pharma. Dangerous work, never dull and richly rewarded. He was currently pulling down three salaries from different employers. They all had generous pension schemes. The trick in his line of work was to live long enough to draw them.

But this mission, chasing promone, this little detour mission from his mainstream work, was just crazy. Half the people involved were idiots and the other half were clueless. Let something with the potential of promone loose on this gang and it was only a matter of time before the world knew about it and the genie was well and truly out of the bottle. 'Identify and infiltrate, control and contain'. Those had been the key words on his mission protocol. Easy enough for some desk agent to write. Murder to operate though, even with his experience. 'Identify': easy enough; who was who and who knew what, who were the baddies, who would be useful and who needed removing from the scene. Keep careful records and send them in regularly. Job done. 'Infiltrate': not so easy. Get so under the skin of relevant organisations that they never doubt for a second that you are one of them. Do it so well that sometimes you have to remind yourself who you really work for and where your loyalties lie. It was like that with his new boss Stefan, sometimes. It was really hard not to like the big guy, especially in German, where he was much funnier and more human than in English. Less comic-book. More intellectual. But he had caught Stefan looking oddly at him. So care would be needed. Perhaps if he could get him the little Portuguese he so fancied, it would help the trust issues?

But 'control and contain': that was the lulu, especially with these spoiled creatures, earning millions for hitting little white balls or, like Phil, organising shows where others could do it. He sometimes wished he'd never come across bloody promone. But since he had, he could see it had to be tested in real world conditions and he'd had no say in how that was being done. And once he'd passed on the message about mark 2, the balloon had gone sky high and they'd made it his number one priority. But control and contain? Keep it within bounds and under wraps? With these shallow hedonists? No chance, in the long term. So he was in short term mode. See a risk and eliminate it. Quickly. The infection would inevitably spread, but you could slow its pace.

And then there was Mitchell. A real operator. He was being extremely useful and once Bradley knew where Mitchell's final loyalties lay (apart from with Mitchell himself, of course), he would know how to deal with him. *That's not going to end well, I suspect.*

Anyway. At least he had full operational bandwidth. Control, identify, infiltrate: use any means necessary. He looked at the code number on his mission protocol. Nine digits ending 007. He laughed. Somebody at base had a sense of humour, at least.

*

Miami airport was a vast, sprawling semi-civilised cauldron of corruption and criminality. The surface order and regulation was a sham. Bradley arrived at the immigration queues and felt sorry for the ordinary Joes. 10 hours in a cattle truck across the Atlantic and now this. Stuck in a line forever, waiting to face a surly immigration officer with problems of his own. Bradley looked down the row of booths. There was one with an officer inside and no queues. The stewards were directing people away from it. On a board above the booth was the single word: Diplomat. Bradley, with papers announcing him as Maurice Cholain, a perfumier from Rouen, walked through that booth, flashed his immunity pass and walked out past baggage reclaim to a small private waiting area, where his sealed bags were brought to him. He knew the Yanks would have cameras all over the room and did his best to appear pleasant.

Bradley felt at home in this environment where, he knew, everything was for sale and life was lived by laws that weren't the ones published in statute books. A sub-culture of mutual suspicion, greed and the search for basic satisfactions operated below the polished surface. He could operate here, too. There was no hypocrisy and the strong survived, prospered. And he knew he was strong.

He took the transfer shuttle to the car hire terminus, picked up a pre-ordered hire car and set out for the safe house where he would spend the night. He opened the door of the apartment with less than his usual caution. This house had been provided by the one employer he could rely on. In the bedroom was a robust-looking safe which he opened with his personal code. Inside were new papers in a different name for the flight out and a gun of the make he preferred. He blessed the efficiency of the organisation that had provided them and went straight to bed, to get as much rest as his jet lag would allow him before the longish drive down towards the Keys and the golf course where his office had told him Andre was doing his bit for French Canadians.

Next morning, before 6 a.m., he swung his car onto the Turnpike and a few miles later onto the US 1. The sat nav in the car did most of the work. He'd had no time to prepare for this, but his briefing signals from base had been excellent and the travel organisation, including a first class flat bed, smooth and flawless. The bed in the safe house had been comfortable o even at this time on a US morning, when he should have been soft-headed with jet lag, he was sharp as a pin, focused on his mission and how he would interpret it. The sunrise over the Florida Keys was wasting its effort on him. He barely saw it as he ran through the moves he would use when he finally found Andre. With any luck, he realised, if this light traffic (for the Keys road) continued, he'd be able to surprise Andre in his bed. He wondered if he'd find him alone.

One hundred and twenty miles south of Miami airport he turned his car into a hotel car park. He knew the room number and a 50-dollar bill got him a key card from the reception desk. He didn't knock. He opened the door of room 233 swiftly and walked in, gun held expertly in his hand. He saw Andre Duclos sitting on the edge of his bed in a towelling robe, fresh from the shower. He looked suitably startled, satisfyingly so. *This is going to be easy.* It was.

He introduced himself as Maurice Cholain and addressed Duclos in perfectly serviceable French; people were usually more scared in their own language he had found. There was a research project in it, he was sure. Perhaps when he retired he would indulge himself. For now, Duclos had to be convinced that it was not in his interests to pursue the line of enquiry he had started into the uses of a certain performance enhancer. As an act of solidarity with Phil Henshaw, whom Bradley saw as one of the more reasonable of the muppets he was currently supervising, he added a few pointers on how Andre should behave towards his wife in the matter of their divorce.

By way of persuasion, in case his own threatening and inexplicable presence, gun in hand, hadn't quite done the trick, he ran Andre through a few of the documents and photographs provided by the wonderful people Bradley worked for and which would be so welcome to the world's press if they should happen to find their way to the editors' desks. Bradley/Maurice hoped that would not be necessary. As the cherry on the cake, Bradley/Maurice produced a website history. 'I guess you thought you were in private mode? Yeh, I believed the browser messages too, for years. How can we be so gullible? Well, if anybody were to see the sites you've been visiting Andre, I guess you would find it would put a dent in that legendary charm of yours, wouldn't it?'

He stepped nearer to the cowering Duclos and with the snout of his silenced automatic pushed back the flaps of his robe. He put the end of the barrel on the end of Andre's member. 'And if that isn't enough, remember how easy it was for me to find you and how little fight you're feeling now. You know what happens when you shoot a man through the prick and balls? Well, as you would expect, it is very painful. Very, very painful. There is a lot of blood. You'd expect that, too wouldn't you. Perhaps what you wouldn't expect is that the man lives, slowly losing everything that makes him a man, until he gets to the point where he wishes he'd been shot straight through the heart. And the pain never goes away. The physical pain, as well as the mental anguish I mean. Now I have only done this 12 times so far, so it is hardly a scientific sample. It could be that I have got it quite wrong and the next time it will turn out differently. I am curious to see; I would like to continue my research. How keen are you to help me, Andre?

Bradley was confident that Andre would be a good boy. There were a few documents to be signed, some incriminating, some simply renunciatory before Bradley/Maurice left. He killed a few hours in Miami, dropped off his car, enjoyed a snack and a glass of champagne in the first class lounge and sent an email to Phil Henshaw. He was sure it would be the first of many Phil and his PA would receive from Florida that day; and they would all be good news. He could imagine that Phil would be in need of some good news. It felt good to be able to end at least some of the misery he was causing Phil, as a positive side-effect of his little jolly to Florida. He would put an end to the rest, if he could, as soon as he could. It depended a bit on Anne and where she'd hidden it. He put Phil out of his mind and concentrated on the bigger picture.

He was back at Heathrow by 06:20, ready for a new day at the office.

54 *Mitchell and Bradley*

B radley held his mobile close to his ear trying to compensate for the poor signal. He looked out of the villa window across a long steep alpine valley to an almost three thousand metre peak, still snow-capped in late June. He could see why Hitler had picked this place, or one close by, all those years ago. It shouted Germany at you. It was strong but beautiful countryside, with a freshly laundered feel to it.

'Sorry, Mitchell, missed that, could you repeat it? Line went a bit funny.'

'What I said was I'm having no luck with Anne. I can't keep bringing it up in polite conversation with her. It's going to take some direct action, I think. She still absolutely insists there is no such thing as a mark 2 version. But everyone else knows there is and is screaming for it because they don't trust the stuff I'm churning out.'

'Can't blame them. It's been getting dodgier and dodgier. Must be downright lethal by now.'

'Well, that's down to you, pal. It was your idea to experiment with the formulation, not mine. Let's make the bastards dance a bit, you said. Anne still thinks it's because I'm a rotten chemist. Maybe that's why she won't release mark 2 to me. If she saw the place we make it she wouldn't think so. I thought she would have coughed the secret up by now, just to save her precious boys, but she just tells me to get my act together and get it right. And you're wrong. It isn't lethal. "No animal has been harmed in the making of this product", not so far at least, though it does have some unusual side-effects, apart from the ones we already know about. You ought to see what it does to the chimps.'

'That single side-effect alone, if we could isolate it, should be enough to make our fortune if we struck out as independents. God it was fantastic. I tried it once,' Bradley lied, 'I went from one chick to the other and each time was better than the one before. I was the talk of the orgy. In Berlin this was.'

'Careless talk costs lives. No more talk like that, even on these phones. But you may be right. It could be the way to go. Let's get mark 2 before we consider our options. For just a little while longer we need the big pharma back-up. Speaking of which, how's Stefan?'

'In love.'

'Yeah, I know. I mean how much does he know about anything else?'

'Hard to say, Mitchell. He's a clever sod. You think you have him fooled and the next minute he can astonish you. He is resourceful, ruthless and very, very street-wise. Well, boulevard-wise, I suppose you'd have to say in his case, given his circles. Can't be sure how much he knows and can't be sure he believes what he tries to get me to think he believes. He's bloody hard work. But I still have his ear and as much trust as he ever gives anyone.

What about Matt Prosser?' Bradley sometimes forgot the bigger picture as his conscience got the upper hand.

'What about Matt Prosser?' Mitchell was a little defensive.

'How's he taking to his unexpected break from duties. You've had him for weeks. Phil Henshaw is finding it hard to cover his absence. The press will get wind of something soon, I think. Is Matt comfortable, wherever he is?' Bradley asked.

'If you don't need to know, it's best you don't. He's as happy as you might expect given the circumstances. I imagine he's in the same frame of mind as a certain Monsieur Duclos you told me about. How is the happy Mr Henshaw these days? Still concerned about his family?'

Bradley smiled: 'Very much so and with good reason. Gloucestershire can be such a dangerous place for teenagers. He still thinks it's all real enough. Now, of course, unlike Matt, he does at least have a comforting pair of arms around him. And legs, too, by now I should think.'

'Right. Not my taste, but there you go. Anyway. I'll look after Matt Prosser. You have complete deniability. Can I rely on you to keep the Hartmann end happy? Do their bloody paperwork? And say nothing to them about mark 2 and some of the riskier stuff we've been up to?'

'Riskier stuff?'

'Well, like the Millican impersonation. Not my finest hour, especially when I had to do it in front of Stefan Greiff. Not sure that was my best idea ever. He saw straight through me. Anyway, the paperwork is your job. Keep us straight with the chemists at home.'

Bradley said there was nothing he enjoyed more than Hartmann paperwork.

'One last big thing,' Mitchell said. 'What do you make of Samson? He says he's clean, he looks like he's clean and from what I can see on the camera, he screws like he's clean. Cristina's looking a lot less haggard these days.'

'You got cameras I don't know about?'

'No. I mean the ones you put in his room at Wentworth. We could do with the same again for the Open Championship.'

'okay, I'll fix some up for when they get there.'

'When's that?'

'Late next week.'

'So what do you make of him?' asked Mitchell. 'Samson?'

'Well,' Bradley said, 'if it walks like a duck, quacks like a duck and looks like a duck, it's usually a fox in disguise.'

'Exactly. I think he's on something still, but intermittently perhaps. Maybe he has an old supply from when I wasn't fooling around with it. These batches last a lot longer than I tell them they do. Or perhaps, just perhaps, he's got some of the mark 2 new improved stuff?'

Bradley thought for a moment. 'Who could make that? Isn't it supposed to be a much more complex formula?'

'Well, we only have Selwyn's word for that and he is, as we know, a dead parrot. He could have been lying when he told me that. He had nothing to gain from telling me the truth. So she could have another manufacturer, somebody in Albania who doesn't give a toss, or something. Or, if Selwyn was lying, she could be making the stuff in her own kitchen, just for Samson. She only needs one of 'em to be on it. Much easier to keep tabs on just one. And one more thing. I did suggest to Anne that an explanation for Samson's saying he was clean but still winning was that he was on something different from the others, and she agreed it was possible.'

Bradley thought for a moment: 'But she might have been thinking what you said earlier. That he was using an early mark 1 batch, good stuff, made by Selwyn even, before we started messing with it.'

'And then again she might not. She doesn't know his sex habits have changed too. It was her way of keeping us off the true scent. If we think it's early stuff, so much the better from her point of view. Think about it, Bradley. What else could explain how Samson keeps winning and staying fit, if it isn't mark 2. We need to hear what he says in private to Cristina. Maybe we could get away with just audio at St Andrews? Cheaper and safer?'

'But videos are more fun. Have you seen that Cristina?' Mitchell acknowledged he had and was suitably impressed. Bradley went on: 'She is spectacular. Stefan's seen highlights and he can't wait to have a slice. She'd have monks in a monastery queuing up to buy a one-way ticket to hell. I think I'll stick with video. Has it occurred to you by the way, that she could unlock this for us?'

'You mean, she's the key to Samson's heart?' Mitchell said.

'I mean she's the key to his tongue. If he doesn't squeal to save her lovely skin, I'm a Dutchman.'

Mitchell hung up and Bradley thought it through a little more. The more he pondered, the more he thought it might suit him to agree with Mitchell. It was just possible that Samson had the new stuff, though he would need some convincing. But he could see that if Mitchell believed it, it might cause him to do something very rash indeed, especially since he'd just planted the idea. And something rash was just what Bradley was hoping Mitchell would do. This was going to be tricky for Bradley. He had to fool not just Mitchell but Hartmann and Stefan. And each of the last two thought he was their loyal employee spying on the other. But Bradley's real employer was a little old lady in a very large house in London, keen to retire but not sure there was anyone she could trust with the job she'd done for so long.

Bradley looked at the Hartmann protocols on his desk. The ones he should have been filling in to keep Mitchell honest with Hartmann. They were still blank and an idea was forming in his mind.

55 *Rhine Gold*

S amson, with Cristina by his side, flew into Frankfurt's splendid airport, was whisked through VIP exits and installed in Stefan's chauffeured Mercedes in minutes. Their bags were collected by Stefan's staff and placed in an accompanying van. Stefan opened and poured the champagne in the roomy rear cabin of the executive land-cruiser that was his version of a car as it slid silently away from the parking bay and into the late evening traffic towards Frankfurt. *How the hell am I supposed to compete with this? The man's as ugly as sin but I bet all this makes him handsome enough for a poor girl from Portugal. I've done my best to give her stuff and a good time, but this? This is way beyond that.* How could she fail to be dazzled by this display of conspicuous wealth and power? He was too. It was the power even more than the wealth, he decided on reflection, that had made such an impact. Who would not want to feel that important? Who would not want airport rules and security to melt away at their approach? Who would not want a man rumoured to be a strong contender for the EC Commission presidency to open bottles of ludicrously expensive champagne for them, in the back of his custom-built Mercedes? Cristina was not just human; Samson knew she was ambitious. He had seen her poor background and knew from his own experience how that affected you. If you suddenly discovered you had an asset that people wanted, you made sure they paid for it. Samson was busy trading on his assets before they faded. He could hardly blame Cristina for doing the same.

An hour later, tipsy from the champagne and without lifting a finger or exerting a second's mental energy, they were sitting on board a large river cruiser, their home for the next few days, as the sole passengers alongside Stefan and, of course, always in the shadows, Bradley. Samson had no real idea where they were. 'We're on the Rhine, near Koblenz,' Cristina told him, 'just about at the point where two rivers meet. That's the Mosel over there; and this is the Rhine. And that,' she said, pointing to a huge statue of Kaiser Wilhelm on horseback towering over 'German Corner' at the great confluence, 'is Kaiser Stefan.' The significance of her error, it that's what it was, was not lost on Samson.

★

On deck, smoking cigars in the warm evening and watching the lights come on in the hillside and riverside villages along the Rhine, Samson knew he was being groomed. Bradley sat slightly away from the two men, his face hidden in the shadows. Cristina was asleep in bed. Samson was tormented by the dreams she might be having.

'I have great plans for golf in Germany, Samson. Great plans. We have wonderful cities and a few great courses but there is much untapped here. Koln, Hamburg, Berlin, Stuttgart, Munchen, Freiburg, especially Freiburg. Freiburg, I love. And I need you as a figurehead, to promote it. We have a famous German golfer or two, but they are not so handsome like you, Samson, and would not get the women excited, like you. Like I said, you are cool, Germans are not. I need you. I will make you very rich. You see I am already like Croesus. I could lose a pile and not notice. You could have that pile Samson, and then help me make it back.'

Samson wondered what he would have to do for it. Or give up for it. 'Is Cristina any part of this deal?' he asked. Stefan gestured to Bradley, who withdrew further into the gloom, still in sight but not able to overhear what was said.

'For her to decide, my friend, I should think. She is aware of my interest, of course, and I can see you are. But that is all a side bet. It should not interfere with a good business deal. I won't blame you for trying to hold on to her in the face of all I can offer, even if you succeed. But I will keep trying. But whatever the outcome of that little contest I will expect you to work hard for me as the ambassador of German golf here and abroad. And for that you will get 50 million over 5 years, plus whatever you can win. But that comes with the condition I told you before. I have changed it a little now you have won Wentworth. I need to see that you can make the top 5 at the Open next month. Without that you have much less currency. I need the top man. A top 5 finish will make you number one in Europe and three in the world, I believe. The second condition is that you need to do it with no tricks.'

'There are no tricks. I am straighter than a Roman road. We've been through all that.'

'But not all your colleagues are and the suspicion is still there with you, too. I need a clean Open Championship success. Then I pay the big bucks. And I do a bigger deal. Win the Open and I will stop chasing Cristina. Yes? I see that interests you.

Now. You say you are a no tricks player but sadly, in this world, I am no longer able to operate on trust. There will still be close scrutiny and inspectors. I need to get you properly tested Samson. You personally and all your equipment. You agree? It could be an invasion. I need access to your body, Samson, as well as your golf bag.'

'I understand. I don't like it but I can see where you're coming from. You want me to sign something? And you can poke anything you like anywhere you like, on <u>my</u> body.'

Stefan roared. 'You will do well working with me, Samson. Very well.'

Samson picked up his glass. It was empty and so was the bottle. Before he could ask, another appeared and his glass was full. He leaned on the rail and watched the last cars drive along the Koblenz riverside. Kaiser Wilhelm's giant statue, illuminated and stern, stared back at him across the water. Samson felt sleep creeping over him, but the lights, the reflections on the water, the warmth of the evening, the prospect of limitless wine and the thrill of his exotic surroundings made him fight against it. Eventually, disorientated, elated and feeling like a king of the world, he staggered towards his room. A young housemaid intercepted him and suggested he might not want to wake Cristina. He let himself be shown into a single cabin and spent the night alone, more unconscious than asleep.

★

They breakfasted together, alone, on the fore-deck. The town across the river was wide awake and well into its day. Traffic noise, bird cries and the sounds of the crew making ready for sailing made conversation both difficult and in an odd way unnecessary. They learned that Stefan and Bradley had flown out that morning and were not expected back. The cruiser was at their disposal. More silence followed that announcement.

Samson felt he had to break the impasse. 'I didn't want to leave you alone last night,' he said. 'They told me you asked not to be disturbed and were asleep. If I'm honest, I think they put something in my drink. They were trying to clear the decks so Stefan could have a crack at you. That would be my guess.' Long pause. 'Did he?'

Cristina shook her head: 'Just as I was falling asleep, there was a knock at my door. I knew it was not you. You would just come in and I thought it would be the maid. But it wasn't. It was that Bradley man with flowers, champagne and a note. I took the basket in and read the note. It was written in Portuguese. Bradley speaks it. He said something to me when he gave me the flowers. So first I thought it was from him, but it looks like he was just translator.' She passed the note to Samson, who looked at it and shrugged. 'I'm not as good as Bradley at this stuff.'

'It says: I think you know that I want you as my Rhine maiden. You know what I can do for you and how much you are in my head. You can see what I offer, but many women have seen that. To you I offer my heart as well. Samson will not come to you tonight. He has his own suite. I need no answer. If you accept, leave your door unlocked after midnight.'

'I cried when I read it. I thought how cruel it was. And I was worried at you. How had they stopped you coming to me? But I admit I let myself have some fantasy. I thought of my father and my mother. He would make them wealthy too. That was why it was so cruel.'

'So what did you do? Did he come at midnight?' There was a long pause. Samson wondered whether she didn't dare tell him, or whether she was making him sweat.

'I locked the door. At two minutes after twelve, the handles turned, twice, but nothing more. The same thing at one o'clock.'

Samson leaned across the breakfast table and kissed her. 'Are you surprised?' she asked.

'No. Not surprised. Grateful. Thank you.' She was amazing. He had to wonder why she would want to stay with him. So he asked her if she would, no matter how much she was offered?

'Of course I will stay with you. I am not a prostitute. But will he still offer you job without me in the deal? That was the only question for me.' Samson, sceptic and cynic, chose to believe her, because the alternative would be unbearable.

'Yes, he will and did. You aren't a condition and never were. I just have to perform out of my skin at the Open. I have to win it.'

Graham Jones

Part 4 Endgame

56 *Centre of attraction*

S amson was reading the sports section of 'The Scotsman'. He was smiling at a piece on golf, not just because he knew the man who wrote it, but because he was the man they'd interviewed and the views were his, more or less. He showed it to Cristina and tried not to let his pride show too much. He couldn't work out why his sudden celebrity had made his opinions more valuable all of a sudden, but it seems they had. Even Madelaine, who had turned away whenever she'd seen him after he humiliated her at Villamoura, was keen to show her forgiveness if he'd come and give his views on air. 'What about?' he asked.

'On anything. Life, the universe and anything. Things must have changed for you. You're a two times winner. You're famous now. A household name, not just well-known.'

'Doesn't change what I think or what I have to say though, does it.'

'No, but it changes what's happening to you and what you're going through doesn't it? Look, winning any tournament makes you a bit special. You know, I mean only really good golfers, really exceptional golfers get anywhere near it.'

'Yes, so what? The world's full of exceptional people.' Samson didn't really get the fame thing, not when he was the famous one, because he knew he was the same old idiot as before. And fame was bad for Cristina. He didn't like sharing her with the world and she resented the loss of privacy.

'But you've won two big ones, beaten big names and now you're favourite to win the Open. Don't pretend you don't get it.'

'I get it but I don't particularly want it or want to encourage it. I just don't have a lot to say. This is not where I do my talking.'

'I have good reason to know that's not true,' said Madelaine. 'And you know what I mean.'

'Well, what will you want to know? I can't get into private things and there are some areas which are taboo. And <u>you</u> know what <u>I</u> mean!' She laughed and they both relaxed a little.

'Listen, Samson. You're in the entertainment business and the people who pay your wages, the public, want to see you and get to know you a bit better. Your image isn't the best and this is a chance to put it right, isn't it? And as for what we'll talk about, well, it's pretty obvious. If winning any tournament marks you out as special, what on earth does winning two and playing in a major do? It makes you superhuman. So we'll ask you how that feels, if it changes you and if so how and what's different about your life now. And that's your chance to be gracious.'

'Gracious? How do you mean?'

'God, Samson. You're making me earn my corn today. Look, fame may be mostly a steaming pile of dung, but people don't know that. They all want a piece and the money that goes with it. So you have something everybody wants and they have given it to you, in a way. So show them you are grateful. You can bang on a bit about how difficult it is sometimes, but look as if you are enjoying it as well, for God's sake.'

'Okay. Anything else?'

'Of course. Look this is a major and you are favourite. Every name on the board is a top golfer but the camera will be on you. The crowds will follow you. You will be the headline story, win or lose, in the sports pages, and elsewhere probably. What the hell is that like? How the hell do you play golf with all that going on? How do you prepare for it? And so on. It isn't rocket science.'

'A man I once knew briefly said it was, but that's a different story. Okay, I'll do it.'

'Great. We'll look forward to seeing you both, tomorrow at four okay?'

'Both?'

'Yeah. Both. You and Cristina. You're not the only famous one.'

'I don't think she'll want to be involved. She's not so confident in English. If you could do it in Portuguese, though ...'

'I haven't finished the course yet. It's both of you we're after, sorry. That's the real story, or the human angle, at least.'

'So it's both or none?'

'Yes. But it will be great.'

'Sorry Madelaine. I've just remembered. Four o'clock is no good. I'm washing my hair.'

They must think I was born stupid and have got dumber since. Bloody Madelaine.

★

This chance to have a crack at his first ever major and to beat a group of world-class professionals had been earned by his two victories at Villamoura and then Wentworth. He still had the letter of invitation in his pocket. There was something just so other planetary about it. The words were humble:

'The Royal and Ancient Golf Club of St Andrews has reserved a starting tee time for your consideration on day 1 of the Open Championship, which this year is to take place at the Old Course, St Andrews. Should you be in a position and of a mind to accept this invitation, the committee would be obliged if you would inform the secretary of your intentions on or before the 1st June. The committee hopes you will honour the championship with your acceptance and we look forward to being of further assistance in any particular.'

So no pressure then. He was doing them a favour. *It's like Miss World writing to ask if I'd mind giving her one. Or car makers Bugatti writing to ask if I felt inclined to take a Vieron off their hands.* The letter included a list of invitees. Half an hour after he received it, Samson could recite every name on the list in alphabetical order, and every time he did so a shock of excitement turned his stomach, followed by a mild panic attack as he realised what he'd taken on. The names on this list were his heroes, role models and, in one or two cases, gods. And he, a major tournament rookie, was supposed to beat them? *Just how was that supposed to work?*

And he had Stefan's offer pressure on top of that. On the Rhine he'd been sure the offer would be withdrawn at some point when it dawned on Stefan that Cristina wasn't just playing hard to get. But nothing of the sort happened. They just got off the cruiser three fantastic days later and heard nothing more. And then, about a week later, a package arrived in Jake's office addressed to Cristina. It was a DVD of a film 'Indecent Proposal'. No message and no sender information. Cristina took it straight to Samson and they agreed it was a hardly subtle nudge from Stefan. Samson put it straight in the bin with not a bat's squeak of protest from Cristina.

'Why did he choose that film? It has a bad ending for the old rich man. He loses.'

'I know,' Samson said, 'but he does get his end away a few times first.' There was a pause. 'Maybe that's all he wants,' he added.

Cristina was silent, puzzled by 'getting his end away'. Her phone translator was not much help. She asked Samson, and he said he would demonstrate later. His wide grin told her all she needed to know.

★

On the Sunday before the championship, at 7.05 a.m., Samson's buggy drew up on a remote part of the course. He got out warily, his golfing cap pulled down over his eyes. He looked round the course over towards the beach. Not a soul as far the eye could see. The odd dog walker and bird watcher perhaps. But no press and no cameras. It was a calm, quiet morning. A flat, grey sea stretched out to meet a faintly yellow sky. On the horizon, beyond the massive solitary Bass rock, a few tankers waited for a berth along the coast in Aberdeen. The chill of the night still lingered. The air coming in from the shoreline trembled with the excitement of the contest to come and Samson breathed it in and felt it run through him, quickening his senses and bringing him to life. He shivered a little. It was the chill of the air and the prospect of the fight. He pulled a large blanket off the rear bench, revealing Cristina lying across the seat, out of sight of prying eyes. 'You're okay,' he said, ' there are no press dogs, or TV cameras or anything. We can have a stroll and a shot or two in peace.'

Cristina got out. Like Samson, she was wearing a golf cap. Her dark hair was curled and tucked beneath it. Like him, too, she was dressed in a caddy boiler suit. Samson thought they were as nondescript as he was ever going to make them. The boot opened and he took out a small carry bag with half a dozen clubs, slung it across his shoulders, took hold of her hand and they walked away from the buggy towards the shore and the most distant greens he could find.

'I'm sorry you have to do this. I just hate them. I never be in the movies. I hate it. I hate the camera, the picture. I hate what they say about me. I hate what they say about you more.'

'Yup. Goes with the territory, though. I'm getting used to it. I don't enjoy it, but I can live with it.'

'Not me. I cannot live with it. Perhaps later. Not now. It piss me off.'

'Pisses. It pisses. But that's not the best way to say it. It's not me they're after. I mean they're not interested in you because of me. It's you they want. They think you're a star. They would be after you wherever you went. Whoever you were with.'

'No need to say that Samson. I don't want big nose.'

'No. I don't suppose you do.' They were about 100 yards from a green. Samson dropped a few golf balls on the ground, took the bag from his shoulders and propped it upright on its stand. He took a club and punched a ball onto the green. 'Now you.'

Cristina chipped a ball cleanly to the front of the green.

'Hey, that's not bad. You are improving. You been taking anything?' He ducked as a club flew past his ear. 'Careful. I'm a hot property.'

'Samson,' after sending a few balls with mild success towards the green, 'how can you keep calm so much when you get pressure? How, when world number 1 is playing with you. And so much money. How your eyes not cross with fear. Your hands don't shake. How?'

'They do, sometimes. It doesn't show on the outside, but everything drains to your shoes and you go weak. Weak at the knees as they say. As I said when we met. Then it's down to training, all the practice you've done. Somehow you hold your nerve and let the muscles take over. That's where the drug was good, when I used it. Now it's just me. How much I believe in myself. Confidence is the key.'

'It is impressing. I am very impressioned. I think you are great. All of you. But you are best.' She threw her arms round him and kissed him.'

Three hundred yards away, standing on the Swilken bridge with a telephoto lens, a photographer got a strange picture of two caddies kissing on a remote fairway. It made the front page of the Sun next day with the headline 'playing around!' But hard though the photographer had hunted, he hadn't been able to track the couple down and though the picture went viral the kissers remained nameless.

57 *Anne's severance costs*

A nne saw no reason to hold back the raw tears as she wandered through the house she had shared with Selwyn, for the final time. It's bareness, now that all the furniture had gone, left her feeling empty and cold, too. She tried to explain it to Jake. 'It's just a space,' Jake said. 'Nothing but air and not even the same air you breathed together. The memories are inside <u>you</u> and you'll move to your new house and take them with you. They won't stay behind here.'

She bit his head off. 'Where did you study philosophy? You can't have much soul to think like that. It's very human to have a feeling about a place, good or bad. We live in spaces, not in our heads. Sometimes they define us. A prisoner isn't a prisoner just in his head. He is actually in a prison. This felt a bit like one for me at times as well, and I know I have to move on. But if you can't see why I'm sad, too, then there must be something fundamentally different between men and women.'

'Of course I can see it, and feel it. I was just trying to offer a bit of comfort, get you to re-frame it all a bit. You did win a packet at Wentworth; you have bought a great new house and we will be living in it together. So a bit of regret is in order, but not too much, eh?'

'No. I'm sorry. I'm not hankering after Selwyn. No need to be jealous. But I started married life here, learned to cope with it here and saw properly into the heart and mind of another person for the first time. I knew what it was to have a partner, to have rights over another person and to accept that they had rights over you. I learned to make all the little accommodations you have to make, to put up with the endless negotiations about big and little things. I suppose I learned to be a grown-up, a married grown-up, here. Leaving it does feel like a big change. As if there are some of those things I'll have to learn again, because they applied between these four walls in a way they won't elsewhere. You and me will operate by different rules, Jake, I expect.'

Anne thought Jake had no hope of understanding what she felt. He had never been married and lived only by his own rules. He was going to find it hard to live by hers, if he wasn't already. Poor Selwyn, she thought. He had been a kind old stick. Kind, brilliant and emotionally blind. She should have taken more care of him, helped him through it all with a bit more understanding. Instead, she had seen him as an opportunity to be exploited and that didn't just leave her feeling bad about herself: it had probably got Selwyn killed. That was still all a mystery, but she felt a little guilty that

Selwyn's needs hadn't been met at home. If she'd met them, he might well be still alive.

She couldn't work out whether she was sad for him or herself. For him, she decided. There was little point feeling sorry for herself. Jake had just listed the blessings she was meant to count. But for the moment, she wanted a moment alone to dwell on the past. The present was hard, emotionally; the future could well be harder and she was finding the past didn't have too many compensations either. She looked round and said her goodbyes to Selwyn. And she thanked him. 'What are you thanking me for?' she heard him ask in her head, 'making you a millionaire?'

'No, for loving me like you did. Just for that and I'm sorry for not responding like a proper wife.' Selwyn didn't respond so she thought he'd heard her and been content.

Jake went over to her and held her, kissing her hair and forehead. She leaned against him, needing his strength, anyone's strength, just for now. She felt tired, exhausted almost. The road ahead looked too steep for her wavering legs. The strain of keeping all this stuff together was becoming too great. How much longer would they need to do this thing for, she wondered? How much longer could she carry the burden? Three dead, Larry gone AWOL, Mitchell unreliable and spies everywhere, she suspected. The press suspicious and intrusive, doping inspections getting tougher. She'd had her share of press interest and the slapping incident had been a nightmare. It was all just dying down again, partly because the story had no real legs. Now she was going to give it some by moving in with Jake. Right to the centre of the trouble. The press would be back with greater vengeance. She would become 'The Slapper' again.

'Jake. I've been thinking.' Her head was still against his chest. 'If we move in together, it puts me firmly in your camp. The press will be all over us and they'll start digging into my background, again. The slapping thing is still recent. If they have another dig, they'll get to Selwyn and work out what he did, how he died and, bingo, they have a link to chemicals. At the moment, I'm a nobody again. But because of Samson, and the others, you're big news. I know this is out of the blue, but can I stay in the background for a bit longer, until we get to the end of this? I won't even be able to have a little flutter on it if I'm officially your partner. I'm not saying anything but that. I'm not saying let's cool it. We can still do all the bedroom stuff and I do want to because you do it nicely; just not live together, just yet.'

'Is that one of your rules?'

'No. One of my gut reactions. I'm not being sentimental because of this place and Selwyn and all that. I'm just being sensible. This is not a good time to go public. I want to make a huge amount of money. A huge amount. We've made a pile already, but not enough. I want to make it so that we can spend some time developing mark 2. And then do you know what we're going to do?'

'What?'

'Make even huger amounts of money. But without the risk.'

58 Practice at St Andrews

The old lady had put on a new frock, done her hair, got out the family jewellery and was doing her best to dazzle. And she was succeeding. The tour circus moved in and St Andrews, the old lady in question, accommodated them among its many courses as if they were not there. Tents, caravans, coaches, temporary offices, hospitality tents, huge trailers for physiotherapists, medics, inspectors and equipment makers, rolled in and were allocated the places they had always had. This was Golf's home, the beating heart of all its traditions and history. The Old Course at St Andrews, and there was no course like it in the world.

Phil's admin team, that spirited band of women, had travelled the world and seen lovely courses in exotic locations. They had been chatted up, wooed and won (and more often than not, won bets with their friends that they would be) by some of the world's stars in some of the most romantic places. Here, though, they went about the business of setting up their office quietly and with a respect they couldn't quite explain. It was like entering a church. You moderate your behaviour. You sit more demurely. You whisper if you speak at all and you wander slowly round, taking in the things the guide books point out for you. And the mood persisted for the whole championship. There were rules, standards of conduct and language, that didn't quite apply elsewhere. Here they did and the women frowned on any golfer, or humbler creature, who showed too little respect for the very special atmosphere of the Old Course. It was indeed a grand old lady, stern, old school, unassailable, commanding huge respect and everyone fell under its spell.

Phil and Bradley were standing on the thirteenth fairway, by small, deadly bunkers known as the coffins (because once in, you didn't get out, Phil explained) looking across at the view of the town; its spires and roofs almost a part of the course. Each man had a small carry bag of clubs and they were playing a gentle friendly round, off the forward tees. Phil had come to accept Bradley as someone with privileged access. He was Stefan's man and that bought him all sorts of credit. Besides, getting Marilyn's husband Andre off his back and her back in his arms, if not yet his bed, had been a huge relief to Phil and given Bradley unquestioned bona fides. He didn't enquire how it had been achieved. But he acknowledged Bradley's contribution and this round was designed to say thanks.

'I'm astonished this is a public course. Anyone can roll up and play it? ' Bradley asked.

'Well, that's the theory, but you want to try it. It's closed now anyway, for the Open, but otherwise it's booked solid.'

'And why all the hype about this course? What's so good about it as opposed to say Augusta?'

'Okay. I have played Augusta, just the once, and it wasn't in the Masters. I never quite qualified. I played at the special invitation of the Committee, after the Villamoura win and before they found out what an animal I was alleged to be. By the press.'

'And?' Bradley asked.

'This is in a different class, environmentally, sociologically and in the demands it makes on golfers. It's a hard test but fundamentally a fair one and there's something primal about it. You feel pitted against nature as she really is, rather than the manicured version Augusta offers. That's a different sort of beauty.'

They pottered on and reached the most famous hole of all, the seventeenth, with its infamous road bunker and back wall. For a few minutes, since there was no-one behind them, they stood on the back tee, the championship tee and looked at the shot the professionals would face. Phil explained that the target was the rear yard of the hotel. You aimed at the wall and hoped to carry it with a slight draw onto the fairway. If you missed the fairway the grass was long and clinging. And beyond the grass, the heather and gorse were unforgiving. And from the fairway, you needed a good five iron to reach the green, or if you were unlucky, the monstrously steep-sided bunker known as the road bunker. This giant sand-filled hole dwarfed the golfer who stepped inside it. It had been the scene of countless humiliations as legends of the game had been reduced to near tears in their attempts to escape, realising as the ball returned to their feet for the second time, that the championship they had thought to win had just slipped from their grasp. It was a dasher of hopes, a ruiner of fortunes and a breaker of hearts.

'You're just trying to scare me,' said Bradley. 'And it's working. Jesus, that is some hole.'

Phil watched him hit a perfectly respectable drive and then, unable to resist showing off, demonstrated how it could be done.

He tried to do the same with his second shot, but played too much club, overshot the green and came to rest on the 'road', a path behind the green and very much still in play. Behind the road was a narrow strip of grass and then a low stone wall. Phil had been here for real in the past. This time, he was glad it didn't matter. 'What's so hard about that?' Bradley asked. 'Well, most times when you get right up against an obstacle like a road or a path you can drop the ball with no penalty. Not here. Here you play it wherever it lands.'

Bradley's third shot rolled inexorably into the great bunker. He grabbed a sand iron, jumped into the giant trap, swung instinctively and fearlessly, and watched the ball clear the lip of the bunker to fall nicely onto the green beyond. 'Shot!' said Phil. He marked Bradley's ball, picked it up and dropped it back in the sand. 'Now do it again!'

★

Later, with a large beer in front of them, they sat in the room assigned to Phil as an office. Photographs of every Open winner for a century and a half adorned the wall. There was a huge ancient desk and large office chairs with green leather bottoms. Studded leather armchairs and a large brown Chesterfield filled the remaining space. 'This room,' Phil said, 'is where the rules of golf were agreed and signed off. Every subsequent revision has been confirmed in this room.'

'I feel the weight of history on my shoulder.' Bradley said. *Irreverent sod.*

'I'm sorry we won't be seeing Stefan at this tournament, Bradley. He'll be missed.' He could be irreverent too.

'Don't be too sorry too soon. His office rang this morning to reserve accommodation and VIP access for two people. And, of course, the girls fitted him in. He's not coming to make trouble though. I think he's checking on an investment.'

There was silence for a moment or two too long.

'I really haven't thanked you properly for sorting out the business with Andre.'

'I think you did, but what you haven't done is asked me how I did it.'

'No. I'm not sure I want to know.'

'Yes you are. You just aren't sure about the etiquette. But it's not an issue. I went to see him. It was all very informal. I found him very open to negotiation and extremely flexible. He very quickly realised that there were things more important to him than his wife and bank balance.'

'What were they?'

'Things very close to his heart. Quite close anyway. I take it there hasn't been any further negative development on that front?'

'It's remarkable. He has agreed to a divorce, will pay for Marilyn to live elsewhere until it's completed and will agree to splitting the finances as her solicitor as suggested. She should be free of him in weeks. She is over the moon and I am getting the credit for it.'

'Just as it should be. You made the right call, when all's said and done.' Bradley paused, as if looking for the right words to say what he wanted to say. 'Phil, forgive me, but given the splendid outcome of my frank discussions with Andre and the fact that it has all gone a little quieter on the cheating scene, I would expect you to be a jolly little soul, full of the joys of spring. Instead, there is something about you that says the opposite. I'd say you are a very troubled soul, in fact. I'd like to be wrong. Tell me I am.'

It was Phil's turn to pause. How much could he trust Bradley? He was desperate for someone to share his burden, beyond Marilyn. 'I can't say anything. It isn't something it would be wise to share.'

Bradley went over to the wall with the photographs and examined one or two of them closely before he spoke again. 'I don't believe you. It's your business entirely, of course. I got it wrong. I thought we might have moved on a bit. After Andre and our very pleasant round today. I thought we were sort of presenting our mutual bona fides to each other. Your call, of course. If you tell me to mind my own business, then of course I will, and we will go on as before. Without moving to the next stage, like good friends do.'

Phil could feel himself being 'played'. He'd been around too long to miss the clear smell of bullshit. 'And if there were a few background problems for me, why would you want to know them?'

'What's wrong with normal human sympathy as a reason? Jesus, I wonder sometimes what these jobs do to us. We end up trusting nothing and no-one. I like you for God's sake and I'm concerned on a normal human level. You look like a man searching for a cliff to leap off when you should be heading for the nearest party. But all right. I am concerned for the same reason as before. I have interests to protect. Very important ones. But that doesn't change the fact that we seemed to be getting on. I don't make many friends in my line of work.'

'Which is?'

'You know what it is. I work for Stefan. Amongst others, as I said.'

'I can see Stefan thinks you work for him and when I asked my government contacts about you, it went very quiet. I couldn't get a straight answer from them.'

'Phil. You can hardly be surprised at that. Look, whatever I'm up to, I'm not doing anything that's not in the interests of your organisation. I thought I'd demonstrated that.'

'Equally, you can't expect me to pour out all my secrets to a spook.'

'Okay. Let's just stay at the human level. What the hell is eating you up? What 'background problems?' asked Bradley, examining the photograph of a golfing legend with his back to Phil.

Phil was suddenly tired of it all. *I have to tell somebody. I have to take the risk.* 'What do you know about Mitchell Walker?'

Bradley turned round. 'Mitchell Walker? Nothing. I mean I don't know anyone called Mitchell Walker. I remember you talked about spotting Millican as someone you called Mitchell, but that's all I know.'

'That's the man. Mitchell Walker. And he has certainly heard of you. I don't know what he is or who he represents but he has me by the short and curlies.'

'How?'

'He is threatening my wife, my ex-wife that is, and children at home in Gloucestershire. He has them under surveillance. I get pictures every day. They clearly haven't a clue what's happening. I'm not sleeping much, as you can imagine. He has Matt, too. Matt Prosser. God knows what he's done with him. I haven't heard from him for ages. Not since the meeting when you said he was too ill to attend.'

'He was ill but I remember you got a cryptic message to meet him somewhere. You rang me about it and I said you should go. Was he not there? You never said.'

'And you never asked. I did wonder a bit about that. Why you never asked, I mean.' Bradley shrugged and Phil continued. 'Anyway, Matt wasn't there but Mitchell was and he threatened to kill Matt and harm my family if I didn't do as he wanted. He said he'd already sorted Larry out. Killed him, I mean.'

'He was lying. Larry is safe, like I told you. He's been texting all and sundry.'

'His phone has. Odd he never rings anyone.'

'You may have a point,' Bradley said. 'Do as he wanted', you said. What did he want you to do?'

'Keep quiet about anything I knew about cheating. Say nothing, put people off the scent. And tell no-one about him, either.'

'Well that's more or less what I asked you to do, and you agreed without any pressure from me. So there must be something else.'

'Hang on, Bradley. You did put pressure on too. It was much more subtle, but it was pressure. You in effect said keep my trap shut or lose my job and go down as the man who wrecked the tour. And you could afford to be more reasonable because I wasn't threatening to expose you, was I?'

'Because there's nothing to expose. But you were threatening Mitchell Walker?'

'Well I know he's in with the Jake Godwin group because that's where I saw him, and recognised him as 'Millican'. He must have guessed I recognised him. I never made any explicit threat of exposure, because, like with you, I had nothing to expose, really. Just suspicion, which he confirmed by what he did. But now I have to keep my trap shut about it.'

'And have you kept it shut?'

'Of course. And I hate myself for it.'

'You've just told me.'

'Should I be worried?'

Bradley shook his head. 'No. Not at all. Just the opposite. But you're afraid he's going to ask for something else, something really awkward at some point?'

'Of course. What if the inspectors find something he doesn't like? Who's he going to get to suppress it? And how would I manage that? And I don't know what the hell's happening to Matt. I feel I have abandoned him by not going to the police. That's probably the worst of all.'

'For God's sake don't change your mind on that or you will have a dead Matt on your hands.'

'You think he's still alive?'

'I imagine he is likely to be.'

'So what do I do?'

'What did you do last time there was trouble?'

'Call you?'

'And that's what you done again now. I'm sorry you think your family is in any danger and I can't do much straightaway on that front. I think I know what Mitchell Walker's game is if he's thick with the Godwin group and I'll sort him. I might need your help.'

'Anything.'

'Exactly,' said Bradley. 'Anything he asks you to do. Do it. But tell me first. Anything odd you see, especially from Godwin's group call me. Anything, anytime. And meanwhile, do as Mitchell asked and keep silent. For Matt's sake.'

'And my family's.'

'Yes, of course. For them too.'

59 A long spoon

Anne had never liked the look in Mitchell's eyes and as she looked into them now, contemplating the nature of the offer she had just received from him, she understood fully why. There was something hard and cold at the heart of them, something uncomprehending and unconnected. They would never show compassion or remorse. They were pitiless. They were the eyes of a man capable of anything, she thought, and she was more than a little frightened.

An hour or so earlier he had rung up and invited himself over, ostensibly to bring the latest batch and talk about his production problems. He had been pleasant enough when he arrived and had admired the new house. At the sight of him Anne had immediately regretted delaying Jake's moving in.

The minute he arrived Mitchell started talking aggressively about the product. He was hampered, he claimed, by supply issues. The proteins and hormones were expensive (Anne reminded him he was well funded for those) and under restricted supply. He risked detection with every order and had had to smuggle the last lot out, because he had exceeded his quota. Anne, regretting the distance she had always maintained from this process, had no way of knowing whether this was true. Who, for example, was he smuggling them away from? Merricole? Why?

He pointed out that he was taking all the risks. He was in effect, defrauding Merricole and could expect no mercy if he was caught. Anne thought of Stefan, Merricole's admittedly distant owner. She suspected <u>that</u> part of Mitchell's story was true. He would be ruthlessly prosecuted through the courts. And she would be dragged into it.

'Not quite all the risk,' she said. 'If you were prosecuted, the trail would soon lead to me.'

'But you would still get away alive.'

'And you wouldn't?' Anne was disbelieving.

'Nobody would be at any sort of risk if we could get the mark 2 product. That, according to your husband, would be safe, undetectable and secret. Everyone knows about this one. They have no proof, but they all know. That's why getting the raw materials is so hard. The suppliers know they have us over a barrel. They can smell how desperate we are. Selwyn would have made sure the mark 2 ingredients were synthetic. No human or chimp matter.'

He's lying. He has no idea whether mark 2 is different or not. He can't possibly know and if he's lying about that he's lying about everything. He gets nothing from me, whatever he says. Or does. If anyone gets it, it won't be this animal. 'I'm sorry. There's nothing I can do to help.'

Mitchell's whole demeanour changed in a flash. The charm had gone. Mitchell's thug was on view. 'I don't believe you and I'm not prepared any longer to put my life on the line for a lying bitch like you.' The words stung Anne, but she didn't flinch. This was a Mitchell she hadn't seen before.

Slowly and deliberately, Mitchell gave her a version of what had happened to Selwyn. He told her all about Julie and what had been going on between her and Selwyn. He said he could give her pictures if she wanted but she would be better off without them. He told her Selwyn had exploited Julie and then she had died, been killed, by the same forces, he didn't know yet exactly who they were, that had done for Selwyn. And these ruthless forces were on her trail now. The risks he was taking would lead them to her eventually and they would get the truth out of her in minutes. He knew how they worked.

Anne believed him even less than he believed her. The man he described didn't sound like her Selwyn at all. If all that had been going on and the deaths had been linked murders, why had the police not done more? Mitchell had laughed at that point and said simply: 'The police were overruled.'

Finally, he showed her the letter he got from Christopher Stamp, and its contents. Anne took the letter from him and read it with shaking hands and tears in her eyes. 'He asks you to help Julie. But you didn't.'

Mitchell said he had gone to her house too late to help her, and that what happened to her could easily happen to Anne. Anne's resolve, softened by the letter, didn't break.

'So,' he said, 'there is a mark 2. It's there in black and white in Selwyn's letter. And you are lying when you deny it. Something else I know: Samson Gregory is using mark 2. How else can he be winning big tournaments without the ill effects the others were suffering if he wasn't? The stuff you get from me is cut with laxatives and Samson hasn't been suffering any stomach cramps like the others. How come, unless he's on mark 2 and getting a supply from someone other than me? Namely you, Mrs Smalling.'

Anne said he could not possibly be on mark 2 because he couldn't be taking something which didn't exist. 'And by what right are you adulterating the promone?'

'Force majeure. And you are lying again to protect your interest. There is more than enough evidence that it does exist and I will not be deterred from getting it by lies from a selfish bitch like you. If I have to cut Samson open and rip it from his entrails, I will do it.'

And that was the point when he made Anne the offer and she looked into his eyes, cold and diabolical. That's when she got really scared.

He spoke more calmly, but his eyes were wild still: 'Come into partnership with me and we can do this right. We can look after each other, make the stuff under proper conditions and keep the profits for ourselves. We can leave the golf scene and go to something even more lucrative. And I will make sure the vicious people who got to Selwyn leave us alone. They know about mark 1 but they think its weaknesses make it useless in the long term. Mark 2 is what they're waiting for. But they'll never get it. For you and me, mark 2 will be worth huge amounts more than mark 1 because, just as Selwyn told me, it will be absolutely safe and completely undetectable. It just rearranges what happens naturally in the body. And its uses are virtually limitless.'

'He said something similar about this version, too,' said Anne, thinking she would sooner do a deal with a caged and hungry tiger asking her to step inside the cage and stroke it, than go into any sort of partnership with this man. Let alone the sort of partnership she assumed he was asking for: 'There is no version 2. It seems Selwyn told you more than he told me. And if he told you the truth, its whereabouts went to the grave with him. His killers did themselves a bad turn.'

Anne hoped Mitchell's rage was an act, but she wasn't sure and was wide-eyed with fear. Whether he noticed it and thought he'd overdone it, or whether the adrenaline left him she didn't know. But he was calmer, apologising for his anger and telling her to consider his offer carefully and get in touch. The rage had turned to ice. 'Meanwhile there will be no further supply of mark 1 promone. The material stock has dried up and if I even suspect you're trying to find an alternative source, I will drop you and your outfit so deeply in it you will never remove the stink. Think hard. Do the wise thing. We could make beautiful promone together.' With a movement too fast for her to avoid, he grabbed her jaw with one hand and held it tightly as he kissed her roughly, full on her tightly closed lips. 'We'll return to that, too, when you've had a think.' And then he was gone.

Anne collapsed in a chair, weak and shaking from the strain of maintaining her calm and steadfast manner in the face of the onslaught. It was half an hour and two brandies later before she rang Jake, told him a version of events and he promised to come straight over. She told him to bring a suitcase and stay the night. She asked him to stay the next day too. And then the next. Pretty soon, there was no point staying anywhere else.

60 *Professional practice*

S amson, grinning like a schoolboy, shook hands with his practice-round
partners: two Americans and a young man from Northern Ireland with a
legendary swing that had been compared to Samson's. Samson, watching him
for the first time in real life, could see the similarity but felt it was unfair on
the younger man. There was an effortless balance and speed in the swing that
Samson felt he couldn't match. He looked at this opponent and experienced
something unusual. A sense of inferiority. The boy was much better than him.
On a good day he would beat the pants off Samson and Samson was sure he
would have some of those good days in this tournament. *Boy that's some swing.*
What I wouldn't give... He told himself he was the form horse, coming off
back-to-back wins and the bookies' favourite for this one. But that fast, fluid,
balanced swing haunted his dreams and turned them into nightmares. The
confidence he felt on the course with Cristina evaporated. He knew he
couldn't win. The best he could hope for was to avoid a very public
humiliation.

He found the two Americans, both highly fancied for the championship,
companionable and helpful. One of them had a highly unusual swing. He
simply stood over the ball and belted it. Sometimes, he would lose his balance
in the follow-through, but the ball would still fly improbable distances.
Samson warmed to him. He was a guy who would always give you a chance.
He was beatable. He wasn't a perfect swing machine.

Samson wondered if they noticed he wasn't quite as sharp as he'd been in
recent weeks. They didn't seem to. They congratulated him on Wentworth
and set about mapping the course with their caddies. Samson would normally
have enjoyed the two practice rounds in their company and made use of all
the stuff they were happy to share about the course as they saw it. But he was
more aware than they seemed to be that his form was not quite as it had been
at Wentworth and the more he dwelt on it, the looser his game got. He
prayed it would come more into focus when the tournament proper started.
At one point he saw the three of them in a huddle on the course. *They're*
talking about me, saying how crap I am.

He spent the last practice day on the range, hoping to find an elusive
something to take with him on the course. He tried the old promone mantra
and while the charts he had made under the influence of the drug were still
useful, the chanting of the code had no effect. He didn't get the wonderful
feeling of automatic pilot from his muscles when he said it. So he stopped the
chants and charts and went back to his older sense of measure and feel. And
he knew it wasn't really working. This was going to be bad. Failing was one

thing. Failing in front of a world-wide audience, under the pitiless and omnipresent gaze of the cameras was a horrifying prospect. Samson considered feigning a wrist injury, or a back injury and withdrawing. He had to summon more guts and fight than he had for years, just to get himself to the starting block.

Samson had kitted Cristina out against the cameras in an Australian outback hat and a long coat with wellington boots. On the last day of practice he let her watch him from a few yards away but her words of support whenever she judged a shot to have been particularly well struck were not helping. She was merely underscoring his inconsistency. They went home and Samson was loving, but not interested in anything more. He could see Cristina was trying to boost his confidence and in a strange way that made it worse. Whatever he read or watched convinced him of his inferiority and the inevitability of failure. His win at Wentworth obviously hadn't been clean. *I must have had some still in my system. Who knows how long it lasts? And that's why I won. That's where the game came from. It's gone now and the old Samson just isn't up to it. Shit. I can't afford to fail.*

Winning would give him the European number one spot, millions of pounds in prize money and sponsorship and, of course, the contract with Stefan, which would set him up as a rich man for the rest of his days, and he wasn't getting any younger, was he? That was too much to lose. Cristina was still trying: 'You will still have me. I will still love you. And we will still have more money than we need.'

He smiled at her. 'That's true,' he said, 'I nearly forgot that for a while.'

61 Open: Day 1

T he starter, the same immaculate, terse Scot as ever, saw them approach the tee box from his sheltered position behind the small lectern and curved plinth and didn't envy them. He searched their faces for clues to their emotions and saw nothing on the face of the Australian and the Frenchman. On the Englishman's face, he could see the clear indications of anxiety and strain. As a Scot, that should have pleased him, but his emotions were as subtle and sophisticated as his announcements were brief. He wished Samson luck, sincerely, and told them the order of play.

It was a brute of a day for golf. Early rain had cleared, but the biting wind, blowing straight off the sea, had caused the spectators to don more layers than a July day should need. And now, just before three o'clock, the wind appeared to be strengthening and on this first hole, just as Samson's group was about to start, it veered round from the north to blow straight into the golfers' faces.

Samson, rigid with tension and wracked with self doubt, was last to go. He watched as his two playing partners hit their first shots with three woods into the wind and straight down the middle. It was his turn. He tried to relax his shoulders and take the tension from his legs. He told himself he had done this a million times and a million and one would be easy. The fairway shrank as he looked at it. He seemed to have no more than a two metre strip as a target. He took his stance and a bright flash behind him caused his caddy to remonstrate with a spectator. 'Read the Effing Manual', his caddy said pointing to the sign banning cameras. Samson smiled and relaxed a little. The fairway widened a touch for him and he swung, just a little hesitantly, through the ball and watched as it joined the others down the middle.

It was a false dawn. Samson could not get going and his touch around the greens, normally the thing that saved him when other things weren't going well, deserted him temporarily too. Only excellent play on the seventeenth, of all holes, and the eighteenth, both of which he birdied, averted disaster and he finished with a seventy-four, two over par and six behind the leader. The wind had helped by ensuring that no-one had run away with the tournament in the first round.

His mood at dinner was black and he was almost as sorry for Cristina as for himself. He knew she just wanted to be sympathetic but in wanting to give the impression that all was not lost or that he'd not played badly she did just the opposite. She concentrated on the birdies on the last two holes and how well he'd used the wind on earlier ones. She said she was surprised at the control he'd shown and was sure his short game would come back. He heard just the opposite: how badly he'd played on the first sixteen and how he'd let the wind blow his game to pieces.

He opened a bottle of wine and noted her amazement. They shared it over a morose dinner. He was aware that she had never seen him drink on the night before a significant round. So he could only imagine what she was feeling when he opened a second bottle.

62 *Open: day 2*

W ith not a trace of a hangover to show for his modest excess of the previous night, Samson squinted up at the sky as he approached the starter's plinth. The wind of yesterday had moderated to a stiffish breeze, gusty, but not unplayable. The sky, a hazy blue, was studded with white clouds. No rain was forecast and Samson told himself a morning start, like today, was best in the unpredictable Scottish climate. What was forecast wasn't always what you got.

He felt good. He had a plan. He was going to win the tournament at all costs, by fair means or foul. He shook hands with the starter, who complimented Samson on his more confident bearing and the round began. Samson began in fearless style. He thumped a huge driver, instead of the safer three wood, straight down the first fairway, pitched on for two and holed a putt for birdie. He lost that shot to a bogey on the second, but bold play and brilliance out of bunkers kept him at level par for the front nine.

His form continued through the first seven holes of the back nine and the leader board told him he was only four off the new leader as he stood on the tee of the Road Hole. With yesterday's birdie as his goal, Samson whacked a tee shot out of the middle of the club. As the ball began to draw, a gust of wind pushed it further left than Samson intended and the ball skipped across the fairway and into deep grass beyond. Samson cursed and followed the ball. His heart sank as he saw it, sitting right at the foot of stalks of tough grass. Samson tried to muscle it out but succeeded only partially and the ball, intended for the green, fell short and into the face of the road bunker. Four shots later, Samson was back to six behind. A visit to the valley of sin and a strange three putt meant he was seven behind. By the end of the day, as the weather and the scoring continued to improve, Samson was ten behind the young Irishman he'd practised with on Monday and Tuesday. The one with the swing to die for.

He knew what he had to do. He had wrestled much of the previous night with the decision and, when he finally made it, fell into a sound sleep. Now, after the second round, he went in search of Anne and Jake and found them on the balcony of the hotel alongside the course, talking to Phil, just about the last person Samson expected, or wanted, to see there. He asked to speak to Anne alone and they agreed to meet at five in the cottage she had rented on the outskirts of town.

★

Bradley got a call from Phil. 'There's something going on with Samson. He looked pretty anxious and more or less demanded to meet Anne at her place later.' Bradley told him not to worry and went back to his van to make sure that the bug in Samson's hotel room was active. It was.

★

Samson's demeanour and demand for a meeting had alarmed Anne. It didn't take much these days. On their way to the rented cottage, Anne had briefed Jake to say nothing, whatever he heard. He wasn't a brilliant actor and she couldn't trust him not to betray the truth, so she told him that he was to keep his trap shut, whatever Samson said or how she responded. Anne felt her depression take a firmer grip. Samson was the star of the team. Everything depended on him. Not just her usual enormous bet on tomorrow's outcome, but the morale and continuing co-operation of the rest of them. Samson was the undisputed leader. They followed his lead unthinkingly. They were already in embryonic revolt. Stomach cramps, diarrhoea, and bladder complaints had weakened their enthusiasm for the programme more than somewhat. A losing and demoralised Samson could be the death blow. 'The end of the road, if we're not careful,' she told Jake, 'and don't look so bloody happy about it.' She felt beaten, weary at carrying the full load, surrounded by men who, she sometimes felt, were not fit to lick her boots. She was sure of only one thing. It would take more than a good slap to get Samson going again this time.

Samson walked in a few minutes after their arrival. They gave him a cup of tea, talked about the round, then switched the TV on to watch his post round interview. As always, he gave a good account of himself, was amusing and informative. They tried to catch him out by asking who he tipped as winner and he told them he was far too modest to answer that. They pressed him on his strategy for overcoming a 10 shot disadvantage and he said it was his swing change that was the problem and he was going back to the way he'd been doing it in his win at Villamoura. They asked him why he'd changed it in the first place. 'To make life interesting,' he told them, 'and to give the others a chance.'

Anne turned the TV off and told Samson he was a cheeky devil, but she loved him anyway.

'Do you know why my game is off, these days? Anne shook her head. 'Because I'm clean. I have been since Villamoura. I won Wentworth clean, or at least I'd been off it for a while. I think there were some after effects, some residual benefits, I don't know. But it is gone completely now. I haven't got a shred of confidence left. I don't know what happened to the old Samson. Maybe the stuff did that too.'

Anne, who had staked two million of her new fortune on a Samson top four finish, was not entirely pleased to hear this. 'So you want some more? To get you through the next two days? Why didn't you ask Jake? He's your boss, not me.'

Anne saw Jake out of the corner of her eye. He looked as if he was about to say something. She silenced him with a look. Whatever he was going to say, it wouldn't have had a positive effect. *Why can men never do as they're told? Idiots.*

'Because I don't want the old stuff. I want the new stuff,' Samson said.

This surprised Anne who had been ready to give him the last of her supply, enough for a week. 'What new stuff?' she said looking at Jake and thinking him the likely source of this information.

'I don't know what you call it, but the stuff that doesn't have the side-effects. The reliable stuff that doesn't give you the runs like Jason gets whenever he takes it.'

Anne was thinking fast. 'I might have a little bit left of the old stuff. And it is from a while back, so it is from a good batch. You won't get the runs.'

'No good. Cristina wouldn't wear what it does to me, and what I do to her. I'm practically a rapist when I'm on that stuff. I'd sooner lose.'

Anne inwardly sympathised with him, up to a point. And that point was her two million. And then the solution came to her. *Worth a try. You never know.*

'okay,' she said. 'You're right. It's still at a trial stage, but I have a small batch of it in the kitchen. She saw Jake's eyes pop and shot him another of her looks. 'It's safe. Jake's tried it and it's great.' Samson looked at Jake, who nodded unconvincingly. 'You sure you want to try some of that?' Anne asked.

Samson said he had no choice. It was kill or cure. 'That, Samson, is an unhappy choice of phrase. The worst thing it will do is fail to work, but I have every confidence that it will do the trick, because Jake has performed miracles with it. Real miracles. On the range I mean. There are no bedroom effects. In fact it isn't dangerous in any way and there are absolutely no side effects. I'd give it to my baby, if I had one. Stay where you are. I'll be right back.' She went into the kitchen, where she dissolved two tablets of glycosomate in a small bottle of water, added a few drops of lemon, vanilla essence and some sweetener, shook it together and took it back into the living room. 'You only take this once a day. One tablespoon in the morning, or at least two hours before you want it to work. And then you do exactly like before. The only extra thing you need to do is run through your charts again before you play and with the liquid inside you. And no peeing for four hours after you've swallowed it.' Anne's invention stalled at that point. *And you can stand on your head as you take it if you think it will help.* She handed the bottle to a delighted-looking Samson, who kissed her, said 'I won't let you down, I promise,' shook Jake's hand, thanked them both and left, beaming.

63 *Necessary evil*

S amson returned to the hotel in the same high spirits. That had gone better than he could ever have hoped. He had mark 2 and the blessing of Anne to use it. He knew beyond doubt that Anne must have her own reasons for letting this precious stuff out her sight, and he wondered just how big her bet was. His ante-post odds had been twelve to one again, extremely generous he thought at first, but then he saw that statistically his chances of winning three big ones in a row were slim. So perhaps not that generous. When he found out from Jake that bookies all over England were busy laying off Anne's bet and that she would be worth another £24 million if he won, he was no longer surprised at how easily he got it. For that money, she would give him anything to keep him playing. *I should have asked for that hand job again.* He thought of the length of the jail sentence she was risking and winced. This had better stay in-house.

He knew what his next problem would be. He hadn't seen Cristina angry often, just once in fact, but it was the full Portuguese. How was he going to handle it? Lie? Dissemble? She was too good an interrogator. Even in a foreign language, and English was her third, she was too skilful for him. Are all women like that? The truth was the only way. Get it out and get it over with. It would make tomorrow on the tee seem easy. There was just a chance she wouldn't ask. If he could act as if nothing had happened, like he'd just come from a team talk or something.

His changed demeanour couldn't be hidden. No matter how he tried. She was on to him straightaway. *Here we go; strap yourself in.* 'Samson. Look at me. What have you been doing?'

'Well, tomorrow's going to be tough and we need a win. And from where I am on the scoreboard the only way is get some help again.'

'And have you?'

'Yes, I have.'

'And are you going to take it?'

'Yes, I am.'

If she was faking the tantrum that came next, Sampson would have given her an Oscar on the spot. It came out in two, possible three languages and contained a lot of important words, like honour, self-respect, decency. Angry or not, she was right.

'However,' he said, when the storm had blown itself out, 'this is not the old stuff. This is the new improved stuff. Mark 2. Jake's tried it extensively and there are no effects. None at all. This is mark 2 and it is, apparently, the answer to a maiden's prayer, if you get my drift, which you probably don't.' Silence; hostile stares, but silence. *I'm winning.*

'Cristina. This is our shot at a wonderful future. For however long we can make it last, forever I hope, we can be rich, comfortable, the envy of the world and powerful too. We can change things, make things better, for your mum and dad and thousands like them.'

'You remind me of Stefan.'

'How come?'

'Because he wants me to do a bad thing for a better life, too. The problem is that the two things don't mix. Not for human people who are built properly. But okay. Go ahead. Just this one last time. I am no saint.'

★

Bradley, in the back of his van, had heard enough. He picked up the phone to Mitchell and let him know he had been right. Samson has got mark 2. It does exist. Mitchell said nothing for a while and then: 'Okay. Crunch time. Leave it to me and I'll be in touch. How is Phil Henshaw holding up?'

'Rock solid and scared shitless would be my estimate. He's grown quite fond of me, but he's terrified of you. An ideal combination, I'd say. Good cop, bad cop.' Mitchell hung up.

Bradley sat for a while thinking. When he was sure there was nothing else to do but wait, he turned his equipment back on, made sure the rest of Samson's evening was immortalised on video and went off to wait for Stefan's arrival at Edinburgh airport.

★

An hour later Bradley's special phone rang. He could see it was Phil and he was impressed. Mitchell clearly hadn't wasted any time. Phil had got his new instructions. Bradley was surprised to hear what they were. Phil was an amateur and Mitchell was sending him to do a professional job. Snatching people was not easy. Any number of things could go wrong. Witnesses not least; passers-by with have-a-go tendencies as well, not to mention the odd lucky blow struck by the kidnappees themselves. Bradley winced at the memory of his own disasters in the field.

'Why has he chosen you? Or rather, what exactly has he asked you to do?' Pause. 'Ah, that's different. That makes sense. She will go with you, of course she will. No questions asked and nothing for any witnesses to get excited about. Are you going to do it?'

Bradley listened to the wretched man on the other end, explaining how he had no option. Bradley wondered when the best time would be to tell him. To put him out of his misery and tell him his family was in no danger. Then Phil said something which brought him up short.

'Are you sure Phil? He wants you to take her all the way there? Cristina will start to wonder where you're heading at some point. Are you going to restrain her in any way?' Pause. 'No I agree. A step too far.' Pause. 'Yes, if you tell her that, she'll sit there good as gold, I should think. So you are going to do it? Good. When? I see, final day when it's over. Get round here first thing tomorrow and I'll give you some stuff that will help us. Trackers and things.' Pause. 'Okay, that's fine. See you then. By the way, you know what he wants? Yeah, that's it. But do you know why he thinks Cristina can help him get it at this precise time?' Pause. 'Quite. Well guessed. I'll fill you in on that, too, when we meet. See you in the morning. Sleep well!'

Bradley had the picture. Mitchell had gone all independent on him and was using Phil to get Cristina into a car as soon as the tournament was over. So much easier than using force. Then Phil was to take Cristina to her temporary little prison, where she would be kept in absolute comfort, of course, until Mitchell got what he wanted from Anne and Samson. The only niggling little question in Bradley's mind was what role Mitchell had in mind for Phil when he'd delivered his passenger to the secret holding venue? He was sure Mitchell would have a conclusive answer, but since Bradley didn't know anything about the plan at all so far as Mitchell was concerned, he couldn't call him to ask. He liked Phil. If he died, he died, of course. There was a bigger picture. But it would be helpful to keep him alive. The decent thing to do. The British thing to do, perhaps. He resolved to do it. At whatever cost to Mitchell. He dialled a number and a phone rang on the top floor of a Hartmann building.

64 Open: day three

S amson could sense that something had changed, inside and out. Outside, the world looked sharper, fresher, cleaner as if a heavy shower had washed away the dust from a long dry spell. But inside, too, he felt a new purity of purpose, a new desire to show something to the world, to prove himself a champion on the greatest stage of all. A ten shot deficit was not irretrievable. If he played well and the leaders began to go backwards, the pressure might start to tell on them this time.

And with the new wonder drug inside him, he felt no pressure at all. He had taken the liquid late the previous night, watching for symptoms of the old drug, but nothing happened except he slept like a baby and woke with this feeling of having been cleansed. The doubt, the niggling sense of inferiority that often made him underperform, the awareness of limitations and the ever-present feeling of vulnerability had been washed away, by the liquid he presumed, and he knew he was ready. Whatever Anne had given him was powerful stuff.

On the range, during practice, it was all there again, but different. As instructed he reviewed his charts, now second nature in any case, and was thrilled by the way his body reacted to the stimulus of the codes again. He felt the pulse of his brain's command surge through his arms and legs and that old feeling of control was back. He was centred in his own athleticism and the ball sang as it left his club head. Later, broadcasters showed footage of this practice session and described what they saw as Samson reborn, a man so comfortable with his swing and so immaculate in his execution, that it was a profoundly aesthetic experience for anyone with a receptive eye.

One veteran commentator, no mean golfer in his day, said watching Samson swing was like a sinner looking at a picture of a saint. You knew that was how life should be lived, but knew you could never live it that way yourself. There was comfort and grace though, he said, in knowing the world had such immaculate people in it. Samson as a saint was not an image much used before, but something struck a chord with viewers and that's what Samson was called for the rest of his illustrious career: Immaculate Sam.

For now, Samson was a believer. He blessed whatever the liquid had in it and offered up prayers for the soul of its inventor. He shook hands with the starter on the first tee and started the round that was to make history. No-one on the European Tour had ever shot a round below sixty. Ever. Anywhere. There were some who said it was beyond human ability. There had to be a limit below which no human golfer could shoot and some thought that was sixty. Several, including Samson himself, had done it in practice, so it was clearly not the absolute low that these people claimed. But while not everyone agreed that there was a physical barrier as well as a psychological one, there would have been world-wide unanimity that if it was going to be done, the Old Course at St Andrews was not the place it would happen. Too difficult, too intimidating, too sacred. It would be like raping a nun, the same commentator said when, on the fifteenth hole, another birdie, his twelfth, brought the prospect of a sub sixty round ever nearer for Samson.

And then, after a birdie on the last, the picture that went round the world: Samson on the green, arms raised to the heavens, mouth wide open, finger pointing skyward, wide-eyed with delight and relief, every emotion etched clearly on his face and his whole body straining to contain the flood of passion he had released in himself. The Sun printed the picture across the whole front page with nothing else but the number: 59! The TV men devoted a whole programme just to the one round and the one golfer, each shot analysed and argued over. Was that the best bunker shot ever played on the seventeenth? Was this the most exquisite putt, the longest drive, the sweetest chip?

Everyone wanted a piece of Samson, and Jake, supported by Phil, worked late into the night trying to protect their new star asset and to satisfy demands. Sponsorship offers were already pouring in and Samson could just about name his price.

★

On a TV nearby, the event was viewed differently. Stefan was calculating how this would affect his chances of securing the contract with Samson that his foresight had told him would be a brilliant deal. He had already worked out how badly it was going to affect his chances with Cristina and what he might need to do about that.

65 Open: day four

Everyone in the media talked about the inevitable sense of anti-climax the final round would bring. They were wrong. The party atmosphere, the feeling of a golf festival rather than a serious competition lingered only to the point where the two golfers in the final pairing of the day confronted each other on the tee: the young Irishman who'd seen his 10 shot lead wiped out despite a perfectly respectable round himself, and Samson, the immaculate, the saint. From the moment they looked each other in the eye, unsmiling, and shook hands, firmly and with obvious mutual respect, the scene was set for an intensely human drama and it was clear to every observer that the eventual winner just had to come from this pairing.

Samson had not quite recaptured the sense of invincibility that had carried him through his epoch-making round of yesterday. A late night, though a sober one, constant demands for his time and his endorsement and the reluctant retreat of the high of exhilaration he had understandably experienced, had taken their toll, and he was glad of the later starting time. He felt good enough, though, and ready for the challenge he knew he would face. Whichever one of them won this would be Europe's number one golfer and for both of them, already rich beyond their recent expectations, status was now as important as money. To be number one and then to stay at number one had been motivating the young Irishman for weeks and had kept him away, for the most part, from all the temptations, so injurious to form and performance levels, that follow a handsome, rich, young man on tour. Whenever such a one falls from grace, don't look for complicated explanations. It isn't a change of swing, or grip, or coach. It's too many visits to too many bedrooms and too many mini-bar clearances, or powder sniffing sessions in all-night celebrations of lust and the need to party.

Any sense of the anti-climatic was dispelled by the opening drives. The two balls finished within a foot of each other, both perfectly placed for the second shot. Two opening birdies confirmed the growing feeling that the final day would offer something special, too, in a different way. Yesterday had been about the excellence of one individual, putting all other performances into the shade. Today would be about competition, rivalry, steadiness under the most intense pressure and scrutiny; grit as much as talent would count today and there was enough of it on show to melt an iceberg.

First the Irishman had the lead, then he lost it to a brilliant eagle from Samson, who hit a startling second shot to the green of a par five when the wind in his face dropped suddenly, for a minute or two, and allowed him to change clubs and risk all on a shot to the green. Improbably, the ball skipped over a bunker, ran around the lip of another and finished in the centre of the green. Samson's finger went skyward again, in thanks to the Great Chemist in the Sky, he told himself, and another picture went instantly around the world.

Samson lost the lead once more and almost regained it at the sixteenth when his putt seemed about to drop, only to rise from the dead, circle the hole and stop on the very edge. But then the Irishman made the only bogey of the match and the scores were level at the Road Hole. The two were, by now, mentally exhausted. Both were feeling the sort of pressure that makes steam engines work, and sometimes explode. Their bodies were on autopilot and they struggled to control the potentially disastrous effects of adrenaline on their sense of distance.

Samson's systems let him down on the seventeenth, the Road Hole, when his second shot went over the green across the eponymous road and stopped two feet short of the stone wall that bounded the hole. The Irishman had two putts for a par. Samson seemed to have no shot at all. Standing over the ball with the wall behind him left no room to swing the club. All he thought he could do was nudge it forward, then play a shot over the road and on to the green for four, with a single putt for a five. That would leave him one down at best going to the last: a hole he knew the Irishman had birdied twice in the three previous rounds. It was looking bleak for Samson.

He summoned everything within him in the search for courage and control. His caddy whispered something to him and Samson's eyes widened. He looked carefully at the wall. The caddy was right. Most of it was rough and uneven, but there in the ideal spot for Samson, was a flat, square stone with a polished even surface. Samson had a sudden vision of what to do. He saw the shot as clearly as if watching a film of it. He stood over the ball, facing the wall, with his back to the green. The TV commentators were incredulous. Surely he wasn't going to try a rebound off the wall? An impossible shot. Not at this stage of the competition. Not even in the monthly members' medal, let alone a major championship. Samson heard them in his head and banished them. The film returned and this time he ran it to the end. Then he chose his spot on the wall, struck the ball and saw it rebound off the chosen stone and fly back inches from his knee. He turned and watched it clear the road and find the green. He held his breath and the great gallery and the commentary box and the millions watching live around the world joined him. The ball sped past the hole and on to the slope at the back of the road bunker. There its forward motion was halted and it seemed to pause for a second before it began the inexorable downward slide back towards the hole, bang on line and at a perfect pace.

The shout from the crowd when the ball dropped in the hole echoed around the world. The TV commentators were speechless and then disbelieving of what they had seen. The most incredible birdie in the history of golf. The shot was replayed over and over before everyone remembered there was another golfer on the green. The young Irishman had watched the shot with a feeling of resigned expectation. Sensing he was going to be part of something the planet would always remember and conscious that at least one camera would be on him, he smiled ruefully and offered Samson a very dignified handshake by way of congratulation. Then, still smiling, he walked back to his ball and holed his putt from twenty-five feet. Level! The gallery erupted again and the TV pundits sent out for a fresh supply of superlatives.

66 Anyone seen Cristina?

T he two golfers had nothing left. If there <u>was</u> anything anti-climactic about the final day, it was this hole. It was won by an unspectacular, by recent standards, birdie from Samson and, in the absence of Cristina, who'd had enough of the press the day before, the two men hugged each other, convinced that the day had put them into a bond that would stay firm for the rest of their lives. And they both knew there was money to be made from it.

When the hug was over, amid scenes that grew wilder by the second, Jake hurried the new Open Champion from the green, where stewards were having great difficulty holding the gallery back and people were clambering in hordes, dangerously, over the steeply banked tiered seating behind the green, to get to their heroes. The atmosphere was frenzied. The outrageous spectacle the two had provided had infected the watchers, and if they couldn't <u>be</u> the golfers, they wanted to touch them. It was pagan. The golfers had become healers, spiritual guides, leaders, and their followers wanted to demonstrate their loyalty.

Jake guided Samson into the scorer's hut where Anne embraced him, in a manner not entirely maternal and got him into a small side room where she had something important to impart, she told him.

'I guess you want to tell me how much you've won on me today.'

'Twenty-four million pounds. There are weeping bookies all over the country. But no, that isn't what I wanted to say.'

'Twenty-four million! So now you give up, retire. Drag Jake off to some honeyed matrimonial home and fester forever?'

'On that amount? You are kidding me. That barely buys you a decent yacht, these days. A home and a boat will take care of that little pot. And then how I am I going to pay the crew and the servants? No, that's just the start.'

'Well you are on a winner with this mark 2 stuff. It's a lulu. Works like a dream and feels completely natural. Not a side-effect in sight. Some would say that's a pity, but I know you and Cristina won't.'

'Well, that's what I wanted to talk to you about. There is no mark 2.'

'You mean there's none left. I've had it all?'

'No. There is no mark 2. It has never existed. You had sugar water. What you've done in the last two days, and congratulations again on two magnificent rounds of golf, but what you did was entirely on your own. You must have learned something, or your body did, from the earlier potion, perhaps. But you are driving with a clean licence now. What we had the pleasure of witnessing was raw Samson, pure and undiluted. And Samson, it was a privilege to be here to see it. You are a bloody genius.'

When she finally convinced Samson, his relief and sense of liberation, allied to the sheer bliss of his victory, overwhelmed him and she had to hold him for minutes as he wept, unable to comprehend the significance of what he'd done in the light of what he now knew. He was, he tried to comprehend, the greatest golfer in the world, and not just a bloody good cheat.

Cristina, back at the hotel in Edinburgh, was watching it all unfold on TV. She was in a dilemma; she wanted to be there with Samson and bask in his reflected glory as well as support him, but she loathed and feared the intrusiveness of the press, their determination to get revealing pictures, up her dress, down her dress, sitting, standing, bending, their endless questions about her background, her sex-life, Samson's habits, what he liked in bed, any sex 'romps' they'd had, any threesomes and much worse. And then they invented the answers and she couldn't respond.

So when Phil knocked at the door and said he had a secure car downstairs and could get her to Samson without any fuss, she caved in and agreed to go. She'd met Phil many times on the tour in recent months and liked and trusted him. Today she could see he was tense. 'Just what's going on at the course,' he explained. 'It's mad. I've never seen anything like it. But you'll be fine with me, don't worry.'

Phil hadn't been told where to take her. He had been told to drive to a nearby car park and await further instructions by telephone. That seemed a sensible precautionary measure on behalf of the kidnappers. What had occurred to Bradley the night before, had also occurred to Phil. If he got Cristina to the hostage venue, he was a dead man. So his plan, agreed with Bradley, was to go as far as the car park, get the directions, tell Cristina what was going on but not to worry and drive her somewhere safe. Anne's rented house was his first choice. There was no way he was going to deliver her into the hands of whoever was behind all this, and he wasn't convinced it was just Mitchell. Then, with Cristina safe, he'd go to the place he been asked to deliver her and tackle whatever he found there, with Bradley's help if possible. As a final act of insurance, and defiance, he let Bradley tape a tracker device to his chest. Belt and braces, he thought. Just in case they're a step ahead of me.

The car Phil had been given, parked in a lane behind the hotel, had heavily tinted windows, which let the occupant look out from a private interior. So, after she climbed in the rear seat and the door was closed, Cristina had a perfect view of the two hooded men who grabbed Phil and clubbed him to the ground with a short baseball bat. For good measure they kicked him in the ribs and chest and hit him once more over the head. Phil became very, very still. With absolute clarity and a rising sense of panic she saw them open the boot and toss Phil unceremoniously into it. The front door of the car opened and a third man got into the driving seat. The two assailants got in the back with her. One put his hand up her skirt and grabbed her roughly, the other man put tape across her mouth, told her to be a good girl and she wouldn't be hurt and barked something in a language she didn't recognise to the driver. The car sped away towards a remote part of the country where Mitchell had some days ago found and hired a cottage for himself, though not in his name. It made one brief stop on a deserted road to unload Phil and continued its journey. Phil was dumped behind roadside shrubbery, on the edge of a wood. His bleeding, battered body was unnaturally still.

An hour later, dirty, bruised, sore, very uncomfortable and terrified that the men would carry out the unspeakable threats they had issued if she did anything untoward, Cristina, strapped to an upright wooden chair, wept quietly beneath her hood. The contrast between where she found herself and where she should have been added a raw frustration to the physical and mental pain. For the moment the men had gone and she wondered what would happen to her when they came back.

She shook her head backwards and forwards and found she could get the hood to a point where one shake would release it. She thought for a while. If the men returned expecting a hooded woman and realised she had seen them and could identify them, they would surely never release her. She let the hood slip back on her head and gave in to the absolute nature of her despair.

67 *Helpless*

The crowd outside the scorer's hut was threateningly large. Fans, desperate to be part of the greatest tournament ever, as the TV men were billing it, had breached security, trampled down the flimsy barriers and stormed the hut. Samson was taken somewhere safe by security, who took two hours to contain the mob and secure the area, while Samson sat, incommunicado and missing Cristina. Eventually, around five o'clock he was released into the arms of the inspectors, to whom he happily gave a sample before he could enter to the players' hospitality area, where a huge welcome awaited him. He caught sight of Bradley and Stefan pushing their way towards him.

Stefan shook him warmly by the hand. 'Congratulations, champ. What a show. All Europe is talking about it. You will not forget our deal now that you are a world superstar? That would not be very British.'

'How could I possibly forget an offer as generous as that, Stefan? It's the deal I'm struggling to recall. But, I don't know, I can't seem to move for offers, just now. Perhaps if you were to put yours in writing, so that my lawyers can run their eyes over it? And, of course, there is Cristina to consider.' Samson looked around as he said it, hoping to catch a glimpse of her somewhere. He was sure she'd get here and she was the one thing he needed now to make his world perfect. He was sure he would weep when she hugged him. And more when he told her he'd done it clean.

'Ah yes, Cristina, of course. I hope there are no bad feelings there, Samson. I behaved well, but Cristina behaved better, perhaps. I just offered her a choice.'

'You offered, not very subtly, the biggest bribe the world's ever seen, Stefan. Why it didn't work is a mystery. You're right. We have to give Cristina the credit for it.'

'Ah well, let gone byes be gone byes. My offer is flexible and better than the others you will receive. And it has no strings!'

From that point Samson was swept up in a whirl of interviews, offers, congratulatory celebrities, more interviews, groups of players, official receptions, prize givings, autograph signings and all the things associated with winning a huge event. His head swam. He felt giddy with success and attention, overwhelmed by the slowly dawning realisation of not just what he had done, but the manner of his doing it. It would be the way he played on the last two days, as much as the fact of winning that would ensure he was an enduring legend of the game. A shock of sheer delight hit him at the thought. In his head he saw what the future held for him and he liked it. Very much.

And the icing was that it would be a future shared with Cristina. *Where was she?*

Hours later, around seven, as the crowds dwindled and the day seemed to be ending, he escaped the official duties, missing Cristina and desperate to see her and share the day with her. He rang her hotel room and got no answer. Reception recalled seeing her leave with a gentleman some time earlier, but could not be sure when. No, they were sorry, they couldn't say which gentleman and no, she had left no message. Samson was immediately worried. He was about to set off for the hotel when a rather grubby-looking Phil came into the hospitality area, somewhat unsteadily. He spotted Samson and waved him to a quiet area off to the side.

'You been drinking?'

Phil took a huge glass of champagne from a passing waiter and gave Samson a version of events, saying he had answered personally a request for secure transport from Cristina, and the next thing he remembered was coming to in a ditch outside town, with this note pinned to his chest. He'd started to walk back to town when he'd been picked up, to his amazement given the way he looked, by a passing truck. He had washed up in the toilets as best he could so that security staff would not ask too many questions. 'So where is Cristina?' Samson felt something hot, thick and unpleasant rise in his throat.

Phil said he didn't know and handed the note that had been pinned to his chest to an increasingly frantic Samson who was now having to cope with a complete reversal of his emotional state. Samson tore open the envelope and read:

YOU HAVE SOMETHING WE WANT. YOU KNOW WHAT IT IS. WHEN WE GET IT AND ARE SURE WE HAVE IT, YOU WILL GET BACK WHAT YOU WANT. UNTIL THEN, WE WILL AMUSE OURSELVES WITH IT. THE POLICE WILL NOT HELP YOU, BUT THEY WILL BE VERY INTERESTED IN WHAT IT IS WE WANT AND JUST HOW YOU WON THIS GREAT VICTORY. ALL WILL BE ASHES FOR YOU. WAIT TO BE CONTACTED. KEEP ALL MOBILES (overleaf) CHARGED AND ON.

On the back were the numbers of three mobiles, Samson's, Jake's and Anne's.

Samson's first instincts were to tear the paper to shreds. Instead, he howled with anguish and frustration, picked up a chair from a table and hurled it to the ground. If the first reporter to reach him thought he'd got a scoop, he soon had a different view. Samson's push sent him sprawling and the air was foul with his expletives. He found Jake and Anne, dragged them to one side, now a little more aware that the world's media were still around and must have seen the commotion. They moved into a private area and Samson told them the story. In turmoil though he was, Samson picked up on Anne's steely response. 'These bastards are not going to take what's rightly mine,' she said.

'So the stuff does exist?' said Samson. 'Then for Christ's sake give me some and let's get this thing done.'

'I didn't mean the stuff. What I told you earlier is true. It doesn't exist. I mean they are not going to wreck this whole operation.'

'Well,' said Samson, understanding for the first time what it meant to be at your wit's end, 'let's give them mark 1'

'We are not giving them anything. Whoever they are they've probably got that anyway. The sooner they realise we won't play ball, the sooner they'll release Cristina.'

'Or kill her!' Samson had finally let this thought penetrate his skull and he felt all the breath in his body punched out in a spasm of terror that left him in a need of a seat. He sat down, his head in his hands. 'What the hell are we going to do?'

'We have to wait until they contact us. Then the talking starts.' This was Phil.

Samson looked up. *How the hell can I wait till then?*

★

An hour or so earlier and fifty miles to the north, Cristina had the hood snatched off and the gag removed. She took deep gasps of air and swallowed hard several times. She freed her tongue from the roof of her mouth and found herself looking at a man she recognised. She thought quickly. It wouldn't be good to show she recognised him. 'Who are you?'

'You know very well who I am,' said Mitchell. 'And I suspect you know what I want. When I get it I'll let you go.'

'Even though I've seen your face?'

'Well, let's see. You'll have the choice between justice in the abstract and a life of luxury. Turn me in and I tell the world how your little friend got so almighty good and almighty rich. Keep your trap shut and your life goes on as before. And I become almighty rich, too. Sound about right to you?'

'It is right. I won't make any troubles. We could even work together to get what you want. It is no skin off my cheek. I can help you.'

'How.'

'Put me on a phone and I can tell them how badly I am being treated, which is true, and beg them to give you what you want, assuming they have it. I am a good actress.'

'I know they have it and so do you.' He took out his phone and played Bradley's recording of her and Samson in the hotel room.

'So that's what you want. I know where you can get buckets of it.'

'If only that were true. We could have a happy life together. But it isn't and you must hope your friends value you more than money.'

'Samson will. He'll persuade them.'

'That's what I'm counting on.'

'Don't let those men back in. The ones who bring me here. They are animals.'

'Don't worry. If all goes well you won't see them again. And if it doesn't, you'll only see them once more. And how pleasant that meeting will be, and how long it lasts, is rather up to them.'

Cristina shuddered.

68 *Who to turn to?*

While Anne and Jake sought to calm a frantic Samson, Bradley took Phil aside. 'What the hell's happened? You didn't show up at the car park rendezvous and then your chest tracker device stopped moving.'

'You know what's going on. You must do. You've got to be in on it.'

'No. I don't. How do you work that out? Mitchell Walker's your enemy. Not me. Come on. See sense.'

'They jumped me as soon as I got to the car and ditched me out of town somewhere. Was it your lot picked me up?'

Bradley said it was. 'Your chest tracker survived the beating and when it stopped moving I sent one of Stefan's guys to find you. It was a risk, but I paid him well. I couldn't get away from Stefan myself.'

'Well, what's going to happen to my kids now? If Mitchell thinks I've screwed up?'

'Well, first you haven't. You did exactly what Mitchell wanted and got Cristina through the hard part of any snatch. Thumping and dumping you early was a clever part of his plan. My bad. I should have seen it coming. And second, that trick with the photographs is simple if you have the contacts. There's nobody watching your ex-wife and kids. The photos are all grabs from security cameras. They could pick any from dozens every day. It just needs a bit of money, a good piece of face recognition software and Bob's your uncle.'

'Are you sure?'

Bradley was very sure because he'd been operating the trick. 'I've used it myself. Believe me, there's no threat to your wife. No-one has the resources to do that level of sustained surveillance.'

Phil, mightily relieved but even more furious, rounded on him. 'Why didn't you tell me that before, you bastard. You've been keeping me dangling too. You've used me as well.'

'But for very different reasons and but for a bit of bad luck, we would have had Mitchell locked up and poor old Matt safe in his bed. Probably.'

'So if you're not part of Mitchell's plan that means you have no more idea than I do where Cristina is being held, assuming she is.'

'Correct.' Bradley said. 'That was the point of the tracker. But there is hope.' He took a postcard of a small cottage out of his pocket. 'This was let only last week. Don't ask me how I know, because you wouldn't understand the answer and it would cause confusion. It just came my way. I don't know for sure that it is where she is, but it is about twenty miles further along the road from where you were picked up.' Phil looked at the picture of a crofter's cottage, smartened up for the tourist trade. There was a name, Leekie Cottage, an address and postcode with some helpful instructions on how to find it.

'Don't say I never give you anything,' Bradley said. 'Anyway, she's no good to him dead. So long as she does as she's told she'll be okay. Thing is, this is one of those jobs where none of those involved, even the people in the middle like you, can go to the police. So it needs sorting unofficially and while it's being sorted, he'll have no reason to harm her. He's not the sort to top her for a bit of fun. She should be okay. If I were you I'd leave it to them, the Godwin crew, to sort out. Mitchell will be in touch with them before long I should think. Keep mum. Stay out of it. Mitchell won't want to use you again, I would guess. So keep it shut and you'll walk away as clean as a whistle. By the way, assume your office is bugged and Mitchell can hear every word. Under the desk top would be my bet.' Bradley patted him on the shoulder and went back inside to look for Stefan.

★

Stefan saw him approach and signalled him to stay away. He was in conversation with a very distraught-looking Samson, who'd started by accusing him of kidnapping Cristina. Stefan's outrage, heard across entire room, had told Samson that he was wrong and forced him to change tack. Now he was pleading with Stefan to help him find her.

'Me? I'm a foreign national. I can't get involved in things like this. This is kidnapping. You have to go to the police. They know how to deal with these things. They have trained specialists. I can't help, whether I don't want to or not.'

Samson, frantic but trying to seem reasonable and controlled, said the kidnappers had said no police or she would be killed.

'And not because the police would be very inconvenient for a new winner of the Open?'

Samson nodded. There was little point in dissembling now. Only one thing mattered. Cristina. 'For both reasons,' Samson said.

Stefan was triumphant. The truth, at last. 'So I suppose the kidnapper wants your technology secrets, hey? He wants to know how you propel and guide the ball? You see I know more than you think.'

Samson hadn't a clue what he was talking about and said so.

'It's no good lying to me Samson. I know there have been technology wins and some wins without. That wall shot of yours. Humanly impossible. The ball had to be guided into the hole, of course. Is it a tractor beam?'

'Look,' said Samson, 'I don't know what you're talking about. I have played nothing but straight golf in any tournament for months and months. I don't know anything about the technology stuff, but I am telling you that this can't go to the cops because half the people in this room would get arrested and there's more money at stake than any of us, except possibly you, can imagine. Now, will you help me or not. This is Cristina we are talking about.'

Stefan said his assistant, Bradley might know some people who could do something, but he wasn't very hopeful. He turned to where he had last seen Bradley. Someone looked back, but it wasn't Bradley. Stefan scanned the room, but Bradley appeared to have vanished. He shrugged, turned back to Samson, wished him luck and told him to stay in touch. 'Business keeps going, you know, through all the crap and bullshit. Business keeps going. We still have a deal. And Samson. I'm sorry about this. Of course I understand about police. And I tell you. If anything comes out where I can help, I will. Most certainly. And if anything happens to Cristina someone will answer to me, as well as you no doubt. But I think she was on the point of choosing me. This might help make up her mind.'

Samson's fury was almost an independent creature. Stefan rose to his full height in anticipation of an assault, but none came. Samson crumpled as the emotional supercharges that had surged through his system ever since the victory finally took their toll. He felt utterly defeated. For appearances' sake, he pulled himself as together as he could manage and went back inside to wait for the phone call that could ruin the rest of his life, so soon after it had begun.

69 *Phil takes over*

W hen Bradley left him, Phil limped across to his office to make himself more presentable and to make some quick decisions about how to schedule the rest of the tournament events: presentations, dinner and so on, without the availability of the champion himself. He was on his knees under the desk top when Marilyn came in. He emerged holding a tiny transmitter which he held up to her in triumph.

'You said you wouldn't be surprised if Andre had us bugged. Well you were half right, but it wasn't Andre.'

'God Phil. You look like shit. Are you all right?'

'Concussed. My ribs are cracked, I've got a three-inch gash in my scalp, but in some ways I feel better than I have for weeks.'

'Because?'

'Because I was about to do the right thing. Just didn't have the experience.'

He ran quickly through the events of the last few hours for her. She grabbed him and hugged him hard. 'Ouch,' he yelled, but when she let go he pulled her back. 'What's a few cracked ribs between friends.'

'You could have been killed. Thank God somebody found you.'

'Bradley again. I just don't know what to make of him.' He told her about his family too. Now there was just Matt to worry about. 'And Cristina,' she said.

'Of course, Cristina.'

Phil didn't need long to work out the implications if any of this got out to the police or other authorities. Bloody Samson winning everything would just make it worse. A huge scandal in the home of the game would be a killer. And as for him? He would be the man who killed the game. That wasn't going to happen.

'We have to get Cristina back and I think I know where she is. What I still don't know, exactly, is what they want in exchange for her. How much of the mess here do you think you can handle? There's a lot of PR needs doing and a lot of stuff needs finessing.'

'If I have your authority I can deal with all of it. And there is one other tournament director here today. He can fill your upfront role.'

'Great. Can you start by getting Samson and Jake up here? As soon as. And Marilyn, which two of your ladies do you trust most? And would they be up for helping with a delicate and perhaps slightly risky scouting job?' Marilyn left and returned minutes later with two excited young women, eager to do anything that would help their new hero, Samson. The overtime pay offer helped, too.

He called Bradley. There was no reply. Then he went to his desk and opened the locked drawer. Inside were four pistols and ammunition. There was a drawer with these contents in every room he used as a tour office. He took out three of the four guns and checked them. Using them had been part of his training. Golf was played in some volatile countries.

70 *A plan of sorts*

P hil looked at the faces before him. Samson, drawn and anxious. Jake, inscrutable for once. Clearly composing himself for some awful exposure. Anne, the only one sitting, phone in hand, looked lost, beaten. He could tell without asking that there had been no contact with the kidnapper. Samson was on to him as soon as he appeared.

'So you know who the bastards are who've got her. You know where she is?' Samson was all for leaving immediately but the others calmed him down.

They all now knew the version of the truth he'd told Samson. Cristina was about forty minutes away by car. He said he believed Cristina might be frightened and uncomfortable, but her life wasn't in danger.

'Bollocks to that.' Samson, of course. 'How the hell can you know whether she's in danger or not. We haven't heard from the bastard yet. He could be doing anything to her.'

'If we haven't heard, then she's definitely still alive. They'll have to prove that to you when they plan the exchange. And once they have the stuff they want, whatever that is, why bother killing her? We all know who's behind it and we all know it has to stay in-house, as it were. It's a simple business deal. Killing would complicate things for him.'

'And you are sure it's Mitchell?' This was Anne. Her face was a picture. Phil had never seen guilt so clearly etched on a countenance before. He wondered quite why. He nodded.

'Well, if it's him, he's after some special stuff we call mark 2. He's sure I know all about it,' she said

'But the point is, there is no stuff to give them. It's all a sham. Tell him, Anne.' Samson gripped her arm.

Phil interrupted. 'Samson. This is a terrible time to tell you this. Did you know Mitchell had a listening device in your bedroom? He had one in here, too.' Phil held up the de-activated device he'd got from under his desk. 'So he heard every word you said to Cristina last night.'

'Tell him, Anne. Tell the idiot what you did,' Samson said.

Anne looked guilty. 'I let Samson think he was getting the new stuff. It was a placebo. What you saw him do was done clean. That was the real Samson deal. He's been clean for months. And, he's right. There is no new stuff, either made, in process of being made or,' and here she crossed her fingers behind her back, an old schoolgirl habit, 'in any sort of research papers or blueprint or what have you.'

Jake confirmed it: 'I haven't a clue what she's on about half the time. But there is no mark 2. I know that. So when he makes his demands, what are we going to do?'

Phil answered. 'When he makes contact, we'll ask to see or speak to Cristina. She's a smart girl and she might give us some sort of idea where she is. If she does, great. If she doesn't we'll have to trust the information I have. and then we'll go in to get her back. If there's no demand by ten tonight we go in anyway.'

'And why don't we just go in and get her now.' Samson pleaded.

'Well, we could. But we don't know how many of them there are and what the security is like. Waiting will give us time to plan and observe. I will have people discreetly observing things at the likely holding place within a couple of hours. I can't do it any quicker. Their reports will help what little planning we have time for. It's seven-thirty now. I'm only proposing to wait an hour or two and to make good use of the time. Besides, there may be a better way to do all this when we hear from our snatcher.'

Samson remained a dissenting voice. Phil advised Samson to act as normally as possible. Samson looked at him as if he were mad. 'The kidnapper could be watching, or having us watched and the sight of a calm Samson going about his business might calm his jitters, too. If they see police arrive or us dashing off on a rescue mission, what'll that do for his nerves?' Phil said. Even Samson saw some sense in that and went off to meet the press and others after making them promise they would not do anything without telling him, or leave him behind when they went to get her.

Phil looked at the distraught Anne. He wondered if she didn't have the answer to all this. *What if she could solve it all at a stroke? What would it take not to do it? What would it take to let someone die to protect your own interests? Would it make her an iron lady or an evil witch? And is that what Anne is doing?*

'Anne,' he said. 'It would be useful to have a contact at base. Marilyn will be too busy with the tournament stuff. Could you bear to be inactive and keep this end of things tied down. It would be really helpful.' She agreed quickly. 'Thanks Phil. I'm not sure I'd be much use to you out there in any case.'

Phil looked at her. He hardly knew her and had no idea what her role in all this had been. But he sensed that she was a woman who might be capable of anything. And he didn't want one of those standing behind him with a gun on her hand.

71 By the back door

P hil checked his watch: ten-thirty p.m. The adrenaline of the last few hours had turned to acid and the pain in his stomach was bad. It competed for his attention with the ache of his cracked and bruised ribcage. Overall he was feeling lousy. The gun was heavy in his hand and he holstered it. He was lying flat on his stomach in longish grass near the top of a hill. Above him the stars were beginning to appear in a darkening sky. He should have checked whether the moon would arrive at some point. The ground was damp and the moisture seeping through his clothes added to the discomfort. Phil should have been at the point where he was regretting his recklessness in organising this venture. But he wasn't. Somewhere in the cottage fifty or so yards away was the man who'd given him the most difficult days and weeks of his life. And all for greed, he assumed. Phil was going to get the bastard or perish in the attempt. He knew Samson felt the same. More so, probably. He looked at Jake on his left. Jake didn't look like a hero in the making. He looked for all the world like a man wishing himself anywhere else on the planet but this remote, damp and chilly part of Scotland.

Phil's watch told him they had been in position for half an hour. Reports from the two brave young women who'd driven slowly past the building at ten minute intervals earlier in the evening, had indicated no unusual activity. Phil checked his phone again. The signal was good even at this level. He got the text he was waiting for. The young women had arrived back safely in civilisation, a hamlet some miles back down the road and were drinking gin and tonic in a small bar they had spotted on the way up.

There had been no movement from the cottage in the 30 minutes he had been watching. There was nothing to indicate that it was sheltering a number of people. And no real evidence that it wasn't. A single light burned somewhere at the rear of the building. As the women had reported, there were no security lights. What would be the point out here? He could see the window on the left hand side of the house was not fully closed. The women had spotted that too. Between Phil and the cottage was a small road. One van had travelled along it in the time they'd been there. The approach to the cottage to the left and right was over a small whitewashed wall and into a narrow unkempt garden, no more than 10 yards wide at any point. Phil could see that the chances of getting to the wall of the cottage undetected were high.

He was ready to deploy. He had told Samson to go to the rear of the cottage first. A ground plan they'd found on the holiday cottage website had shown a second exit there. Samson had been told to cover it, using whatever he could find to remain undetected. Jake would go left to the unfixed window and Phil would cover the front. When he judged it right, he would go in the front door, Phil told them. They were to wait in position for Phil's instructions, or to use their initiative if none came, for whatever reason. It was barely a plan. It was all they had.

To his left, he noticed the thin curved rim of an enormous yellow moon starting its irregular night-shift over the top of a nearby hill. It had to be now. He gave Samson the signal to go and watched as he crossed the road, leapt easily over the wall and disappeared around the side of the cottage. He was about to nudge Jake and was on his knees ready to go when a light went on in the house, and then another and another. Soon, the cottage was ablaze with light. Phil had been stopped in his tracks and watched with dreadful anticipation as the front door opened. He gasped when he saw a man emerge, wielding a huge knife and carrying a revolver. Another man appeared behind him, silhouetted against the light of the cottage hallway. Phil fell to the ground and raised his gun, ready to fire. Jake fell beside him, gun still holstered. The man in the doorway turned towards the window and presented a perfect target. The safety catch on Phil's gun was off and his finger was on the trigger. A voice shattered the still air of the highlands. It was Samson's. He was the man in the doorway and Phil had almost fired at him. 'We're too late. She's not here.' The second figure came up behind Samson. Phil levelled his gun again and then saw that the man wasn't attacking Samson, he was punching the air, and now jumping with apparent delight. 'Christ,' said Phil. 'It's Matt.'

★

Inside the cottage, Phil gave Matt a quick man hug and then set off on a cautious inspection of the other rooms, ignoring Samson's view that there was no-one else here. Mat was in no state to give a coherent account of what had happened to him. That would come later. But it was clear he hadn't been treated well and his thin frame had shrunk within his clothes. Matt had heard the girl, not always in a good way, but they'd been kept in separate rooms and he hadn't seen her and had little idea what had happened. 'They were still here a couple of hours ago. Then I heard a car drive off. Strange though, because then there was another car, diesel this time and that came and went in minutes. Then the first one came back, I assume it was the first one again, and that left pretty quickly too. None of them bothered to look in and see how I was. They just left me taped up and tied to the radiator. I could have starved to death.'

'That wouldn't have happened. We'd have got to you before then.'

'But they didn't know that,' said Matt, reasonably enough.

Samson was by this time inconsolable. He had found a pair of grubby red pants next to a single chair in a small bare room at the back of the house. He knew whose they were.

72 *Desperately Seeking Cristina*

When Samson, back at St Andrews, heard Matt talk about Mitchell and his unpleasant pair of helpers, he feared the worst and pounded the walls of Phil's office so hard that Marilyn came running in to see what was what. He swore at anyone offering comfort. He wanted none of it. He wanted Cristina. Over the next few days Samson tried everything. He rang Cristina's home but without worrying her parents he couldn't push too hard. He managed to find out that they hadn't heard from her since the final day of the Open. He thanked them, through an interpreter, for their congratulations, promised to visit soon and hung up.

He hunted for Mitchell, of course, whom Matt had confirmed as the perpetrator, but there was not a trace at Merricole or anywhere. He interrogated Phil about the kidnap and suspected he knew more than he was saying, but there was no proof and no budging Phil on that point.

Samson was a hollow ball of misery. If Cristina was alive, why hadn't she telephoned? His frustration was intense. There was simply no trail. He could not, however, bring himself to call in the police. That would mean whatever had happened to Cristina would be compounded and make it all seem completely wasted. He tortured himself over that decision, but was bolstered by Anne, as well as by Phil, who pointed out that the police would be more interested in prosecuting him and them than finding Cristina. So, feeling powerless and weak, he carried on his fruitless investigations as best he could.

And then it happened. He got a telephone call. He heard Cristina's voice. 'Samson. Ask me no questions. I am well. I am fine. No questions. We will speak again.' And then she was gone and Stefan was on the line.

'Good morning Samson. I thought you had suffered enough. Cristina is well and in good hands.'

'Not true. She's in your hands, you Teutonic bastard. Put her back on the line.' Samson's relief had turned rapidly to anger.

'All in good time. After all, she is aware that she is with a man who can protect her; a man who saved her. And she knows you were not man enough to do that. It means much to a woman like Cristina. And, of course, she is afraid it will happen again. That the men who took her will come back for her. They did very unpleasant things with her. And she is very afraid. So she is happy to hide for a while.'

'You bastard. What have you told her?'

'Only that you put your interests before her. That you did not call the police. That you risked her safety to protect your reputation, the name of golf and, of course, your prize money. And maybe something else?'

'But that's a pack of lies!'

'Is it?'

'You know it is. I risked my life to rescue her.'

'No. You risked hers by not rescuing her. Even though you knew where she was. I was the one who rescued her and she is now safe with me. And very, very grateful.'

Samson was eaten up with rage, frustration and jealousy. Stefan was still talking: 'Of course, there are deals we can do. I have not actually said any of those things to her yet. I am not a whole bastard. She just thinks we are keeping her safe and that you have agreed to it and is best to tell no-one where she is. But, of course, she is safe because those trying to harm her have been dealt with, I hear. I know this but you don't and nor does she. She might well be thinking the things I said, but from her own thoughts. I haven't said them yet. And maybe I won't have to. We have a deal remember? Sadly, I don't think I can make it as lucrative as it was going to be. You will have to take a big cut in wages, Samson. But if you honour the deal, who knows what the benefits will be? So, it seems to me that whether you get Cristina back depends on three things.'

'What are they? What's the first thing it depends on?'

'You.'

'And the second?'

'Her.'

'The third?'

'Ah, yes the third. For that you will need to speak to Bradley. He knows all the details. And it will need the help of all your team, I think. Especially the Anne lady. Especially her, I think.'

73 Debrief

P hil chose to believe that the worst was over. On his computer were hundreds of emails of congratulation from all over the world. His favourite was from his counterpart in the States:

Hi Phil. Great Job! What a show. A star is born. How come I never met Samson? How come he wasn't in the Cup (he meant the Ryder Cup) last September. You limeys don't usually miss a trick but you sure missed one there! But all my congratulations. If we put on a show like that at the Masters I'll be the happiest man alive. Great for European golf and a great string to your bow, Phil.

'Feather in my cap', you lamebrain, not 'string to my bow'. Great sentiments, though. Not a single email mentioned anything but golf and 90% raved about the reverse wall shot as if Phil had played it himself or at least coached Samson into playing it. Of kidnapping, cheating, dope tests there was not a mention, so far as Phil could see, anywhere in the media either. There were some good people to thank for that. He planned to see them later today.

There were others who perhaps deserved rather less applause, but who had at least kept their nerve intact and their traps shut. They were waiting in his Wentworth office antechamber at that very moment. Before he saw them he did what he had done several times a day since the Open Championship ended. He checked for emails or texts from Bradley. And the result was the same. Nothing. Bradley, like Mitchell, had disappeared from the face of the planet.

He buzzed Marilyn and she brought in his first three appointments. Anne, Jake and Samson sat before him and he was pleased to see they were suitably apprehensive. Phil couldn't quite make his mind up whether they'd been an ultimate force for good or evil. All he could be sure of was they'd given him some of the worst moments of his life. As well as some of the best.

Uncertain how to begin (and even more unsure how it might end) he handed it over to them: 'Why do you think you are here today?'

'For a bollocking.' - Jake

'To tell you what we're planning next?' - Anne

'To collect a medal for services to European Golf?' - Samson

'Okay. That's a start. Tell me more.'

Jake went first: 'No real need to say much more is there? You know now what was going on. It isn't going on any more. Some of my team have suffered permanent changes, in poor old Martin's case very permanent. What's happened to Ian lately is every red-blooded man's nightmare and Jason can't forget a word he reads, which is a lot worse than it sounds. Larry is still missing, gone for good we assume. Only Samson is relatively normal, though hardly unscarred from it all. So a bollocking would be in order but anything more would be pointless and destructive. We've learned a lesson and I can't see that putting all this before the public would help anyone's cause. And if that's your plan, Phil, you'll find me a harder opponent than you ever did on a golf course.' Anne squeezed his hand.

It was her turn: 'What we're planning next? That would be telling. But not anything that will need your attention Phil. Rest assured.' Not too much contrition there, either, Phil thought.

Jake again: 'And Mrs Smalling has asked for my hand in marriage and I have consented. Meet the Mrs Godwin-to-be.'

'Congratulations.' Phil said. 'I hope you'll both be very upright and moral together and enjoy a long and peaceful break from criminal activities.'

Anne: 'Bit harsh, Phil. We only fed 'em hormones and proteins. There's worse stuff in a slab of steak.'

'And you, Samson. That 'assisted' win at Villamoura sticks in my craw, for obvious reasons, but okay, I'll have the medal commissioned. Shot of the century without a doubt. And all down to raw talent, guts and a slice of fortune. I reckon you just about redeemed yourself. Forgive me for asking this if it is too painful. Cristina?'

Samson: 'Still punishing me I think. I hope that's all it is. We have a meeting arranged next week in Munich. Jake has agreed terms with Stefan for a long term loan agreement, and I'm the property being loaned out, and we'll all be going out to celebrate that. Cristina is still up in the air and still enjoying Stefan's patronage and protection, by all accounts. Her parents are out there with her. We talk a little, but she isn't the same. I think what she went through ... Well, she won't speak about that, so we can only guess.'

'I'm sorry. I hope it all turns out for the best.' He saw a twinkle in Anne's eye and wondered what he wasn't being told.

Phil hadn't quite finished. 'What you all did, you too Samson, could have finished everything. God knows how you got away with it. Without a shadow of doubt I have things to thank you for, not least your courage at the end, but there are many more things I have to condemn unreservedly. So I want you to know this. In that safe behind me is enough evidence, documents, letters, emails, photographs and sound recordings, to implicate you all very squarely in an unprincipled attempt to cheat your way to the top. In doing so, you did things that led to murder, kidnap and extortion. By association, you are as guilty as anybody of those crimes. That evidence will stay with me and be used if ever there is the merest suspicion of wrongdoing from any single one of you in relation to golf. I include you, too, Samson, even though you had the sense to see the right path well before it was too late. So, Jake, if that's a bollocking, you were right. I see it as a piece of fatherly advice. I'm far from sure you deserve a second chance but I am giving you one in any case.'

Anne: 'Fair enough, captain. We know, now, what you went through and are genuinely sorry for that. For the rest, I don't think the badness came from us. What's golf in the grand scheme of things? It's just a stupid sport, a spectacle like the games in ancient Rome. We added to the spectacle and gave you a world-beater. The evil came from others and I don't see them in this little kangaroo court.

So too much moralising doesn't sit well with you Phil. You wouldn't survive the sort of exposure you are threatening us with. Why would you ever want to open that safe? Why not just drop it overboard somewhere? We'll still behave ourselves. We have learned our lessons, though not perhaps the ones you think or hope. We were never bad, really. Just a little more imaginative and daring than most. We still are, I'd say. Watch this space, Phil.'

'I suspect we all know what would happen if this all got out.' Phil said. 'I think I know how I'd be judged, but I can at least live with my conscience. I just tried to protect some people I love and the game I'm paid to protect. What were your motives and how well are you sleeping at night? Look, let's end it like this: when the proverbial hit the fan, we all did the right thing, wouldn't you say?' He held out his hand and, slightly to his surprise, everyone shook it. Samson said 'well played' as if they were finishing a round together.

The next group was altogether different. Bonuses, certificates and genuine words of praise and thanks were showered on Marilyn's team and Matt. The unsung heroes trooped out of their private ceremony, arms around each other's shoulders, grinning broadly, pleased and proud. There were tears of pride in Marilyn's eyes.

74 *Phil's reward*

M y heavens, Phillip Henshaw,' said Marilyn when she first saw Phil's house, a small urban semi somewhere in Surrey, 'You're the only man I know whose office is bigger than his house.'

'And how many men do you know?' he retaliated.

'One and a backup.'

'Welcome to the backup's pad. Nice of Andre to let go of the leash.' Phil turned the key and pushed the door open.

'I never did find out how that was done.'

'And you never will. Now, do we go inside, or are we going to stand here so the neighbours can get an even better look at you?'

'Let them get a good eyeful. They'll know me next time.' Phil was delighted to hear her intentions so casually confirmed.

★

A month or so later, Phil's quiet crossword moment on the sofa in the small but comfortably modern sitting room of his house was interrupted by a yell from the kitchen. The serving hatch between the two rooms flew open and Marilyn's head appeared. That smile again. He would never get tired of that. 'This is the umpteenth time I've used this kitchen and I can never remember where you keep your blasted thingy.'

'What thingy?'

She saw what he was doing. 'Six letters: takes the skin off an early Constable.'

'What?'

'Six letters. It's a crossword clue for the thingy. Six letters: takes the skin off an early Constable.'

'Peeler.' He said.

'Exactly. Now where do you keep it?'

'I don't keep it anywhere. It has an independent existence and makes its own decisions. Sometimes it's in the dishwasher, sometimes the drawer under the hob. It took up residence in the fridge once and remained comfortably incognito for months. Days, anyway.'

'Got it. Mash okay this time?'

'Fine'

An hour or so later she said. 'This is a really comfortable settee.' She was lying with her head at one end and her legs across his lap. 'Yes, it is.' The TV was on, the volume low, and neither of them watching.

'You know that little ceremony you performed for the unsung heroes last month, as part of the debrief?'

'Yes.'

'Well. I never got a debrief. And this sofa seems just about perfect for it. You fancy de-briefing me?'

'You serious? Just like that? After all this time?'

'No. Not just like that. First you have to tell me how you shut Andre up.'

'So you want to be briefed and then de-briefed.'

'Is that unreasonable?'

'I think we have a deal,' he said, reaching for the remote control.

75 *Mitchell's eyes are opened*

In the room at the top of the Hartmann building Mitchell Walker, complete with new identity, was trying to project a confidence he didn't really feel. It was some time since he'd been here, but it was not an experience you ever forgot. He was here now for an appraisal meeting. They were reviewing his year as head of security operations (field) with particular reference, the calling papers had said, to his work at Merricole and his field operations in relation to the European Golf tour. He shifted almost imperceptibly but constantly in his chair. In preparation he had gone over his performance as a whole and thought he had done pretty well, despite some patchy parts. He had, after all, infiltrated the biggest rival, Merricole, installed cameras and patched them into Hartmann's systems, and fed across information on new developments regularly and with occasionally sensational results. He had also turned Bradley, the Merricole boss's most trusted adviser, and made him an invaluable Hartmann asset. An absolute triumph. Of course, he had his secrets even from this lot. He hadn't let them in on everything he knew about Selwyn Smalling's wonder drug or his own plans for it. Just as well considering how that had all turned out. He still didn't know for sure what had happened to Cristina.

But that was history and this lot knew nothing of it, or of the hunt for mark 2. He had much to be proud of and was expecting to be awarded code gold status and a very substantial salary rise, or perhaps even to be made up to partner. The whole sorry business with Cristina, were it ever to get out, would be a big stain on his record, but he comforted himself with the thought that Bradley had his back on that one. That was an independent operation and even Bradley had been in the dark at first. It could have all ended badly when Cristina escaped. He wished now, of course, that he'd involved Bradley in the whole scheme from the start, but while there was a chance he could pull it off alone and keep all the glory, it had been a risk worth taking.

Anyway, he had involved him after it all went wrong. Bradley had called him all sorts of idiot and said he'd take care of it. He told Mitchell to stay clear of it all. He would do the necessary Hartmann paperwork and tidy up any fallout, which might get very messy, depending on who had taken Cristina and what they'd done to her. Bradley was the safest pair of hands he knew, so Mitchell came back to base and waited to hear from his colleague.

And two days later he had this summons. The room, as usual, was unlit, with blinds drawn fully or partially. There were shadows everywhere and the two other men round the table were not consistently visible to Mitchell. At the back of the room, in deep shadow, Mitchell thought he could make out another man, but he wasn't sure. It was, and was designed to be, disconcerting.

'Good morning. I trust you are well?' The old man, whose age and appearance belied his acuity, smiled at Mitchell. Mitchell smiled back and said he was very well and looking forward to the interview. 'Good,' said the ancient chairman, 'do you know my colleague Dr. Grayson?' Grayson said nothing. He leaned forward and scrutinised Mitchell with ice-cold eyes. Then he sat back in the shadows.

'Is there another gentleman at the back of the room?' Mitchell asked. They would understand why he asked, he was sure. They would expect it of their top field agent.

'Not someone to concern you, Mitchell. We are all observed. Even our processes are open to scrutiny. That should reassure you.'

Mitchell wasn't reassured. He wasn't sure why he should need to be. But he was already no longer quite as comfortable as earlier. The shifting in the chair became more obvious.

'I am not entirely reassured,' he said. 'It's against recommended procedures, as you must be aware. I should know who is witnessing this appraisal.'

Grayson leaned forward again and said. 'Recommended procedures do not apply in this room. Don't tell us how to do our job. We will proceed.'

Mitchell felt twitchy. This was asking a bit much of him. They were asking him to ignore procedure and that was most unHartmann-like. *Should I insist? They seem pretty sure of themselves and I have asked twice. Leave it.*

'Now. Your work at Merricole.' The older man picked up the appraisal thread. 'Outstanding in many respects. Your position there is high profile, but yet you remain undetected. A remarkable achievement. I believe you know Stefan Greiff, the proprietor?' He spat the last word out, as if it sullied his mouth. Hartmann had partners, not an owner. Its humanitarian mission went far beyond grubby commercialism. Greiff was scum. Rich scum, but scum, nonetheless.

Mitchell said he had met Greiff on occasions, undercover. 'And you were not recognised as an employee of Merricole by him?'

Mitchell assured them that Greiff would not know him as an employee and there were no signs that he had done so. 'It was a risk, nevertheless, was it not Mitchell. If he had seen through your disguise as Millican, a little obvious we felt, by the way, or come across you at Merricole ...'

Shit. They know about Millican. And they haven't authorised it. Think fast. Think fast.

'You pay me to take risks.'

'Wrong.' This from the man in shadow, who leaned forward again. 'We pay you to get results. Risks are for the stupid who can think of no better way forward.'

'Forgive my colleague's abruptness.' The old man was clearly not reprimanding his neighbour. 'It is sometimes necessary when we are confronting folly.'

'You think I have been foolish?'

The old man smiled again. 'Mitchell. We think you have been both unwise and incompetent. Whether we also think you foolish is irrelevant. There is enough in the first two judgements.'

Mitchell was angry. 'But I have done everything you asked and produced results. You know about Merricole. You now have complete access to all their management decisions and product development. I gave you that.'

The old man's face was impassive, but he nodded.

Mitchell resumed: 'Someone issued two, three if we include Don Rawson, Code Red orders. Selwyn Smalling and Julie Maidstone died as a result. It would have been helpful to have let me in on it. Or given me the contract. I had to pick up the pieces after that particular piece of institutional ineptitude.'

'There were good operational reasons for keeping that task out of your hands. Perhaps if you had told us what you and Smalling had discussed at your Merricole meeting it would have been different. But you didn't and that's where our concerns began.

And now you have also betrayed us to the person at the rear of the room, who could be anybody. Why did you not insist on having his identity revealed before proceeding with this. Before you accuse us of issuing, what do you call it, Code Red orders, in front of a potential witness? Is all that not an indication of the incompetence of which you stand accused? As it is, the observer is accredited. But you could not know that.'

Mitchell was silenced. They were right. He should have insisted. It had been a test and a trap. He had let the atmosphere get to him.

Ice-eyes moved into the light again: 'all could be excused if you are able to put onto the table the formula for the Selwyn Smalling 'mark 2' performance enhancer.'

Mitchell tried not to look shocked. *Who had told Hartmann about mark 2?*

'I am not able to do that.'

'Then the incompetence charge must stand.'

'The third charge is disloyalty,' said the chairman.

Mitchell's blood ran cold and his face turned white.

'That visit to Merricole by Selwyn Smalling. Why were we not informed of that?'

Think fast! Fast for God's sake. Mitchell heard himself pause a heartbeat too long. 'It was a social visit. He saw me as an old friend. He had things on his mind and he also wanted to pick my brains.'

'He wanted to pick your brains, Mr Walker? The brilliant chemist sought the help of a, an … whatever you would call yourself?'

'I know about receptors in the Endocannabinoid system. More than he did. It was an innocent enquiry, so far as I was concerned. He didn't mention anything about his work or security status at Hartmann.'

'Ah, yes, innocence. That's what we were trying to establish. But you see, that visit by Mr Smalling was just the start. That's when you first saw the possibility of independent action and a little personal profit isn't it?'

'No,' said Mitchell, 'and why do you say 'the start'. I have never given you any reason to doubt my loyalty.'

'We are referring to your kidnap of a certain person and attempts to obtain the mark 2 serum by extortion for your own gain.'

'Not true,' Mitchell's voice was thin and uncertain. 'I was working with the turned agent, Bradley. I recruited him, you investigated him and I was told he was reliable. We worked together. He knows we were doing it for Hartmann.'

'If that is true,' said the chairman, 'then the bungled fiasco of a kidnapping risked dragging Hartmann's name into an abominable scandal. You failed in your task and there are loose ends that we are taking steps to tie up for you. None of this activity or the existence of mark 2 was reported to us. We knew consequently nothing of it until reports emerged from elsewhere. If you do things in our name there are procedures to follow and you did not do so. We can only conclude that you were acting independently and in a disloyal manner.'

'But Bradley was acting with me. He knew all about it. He was supposed to keep the office informed. He was meant to see to the protocols.'

'A desperate accusation from an understandably desperate man. We have of course checked all this with agent Bradley and it appears he is unable to confirm your story. There are no operational protocols on file to demonstrate the truth of your assertion. Therefore it is a lie. Are you able to describe to us how the kidnap ended?'

'I returned to the place the hostages were being held and found the door open and the main hostage gone.'

'Do you know where she is now?'

'No.'

'Who knew of your plans and the hostages' location?'

'No-one. Maybe Phil Henshaw could have worked it out. But he was turned, too, and under pressure.'

'And none of this was known to our home unit. You were acting independently, for your own purposes.'

'Not true.'

'Then why did we not know?'

Mitchell saw it now. He had been suckered by Bradley and he must have been the one who rescued Cristina. And now Bradley was skewering him. Hartmann would have to ask Bradley some straight questions.

'Ask Bradley about it all.'

'We already have. As we told you.'

'Ask him again. Forcefully.'

'We intend to. But now, Dr Grayson, do we find the charge of disloyalty proven?'

Grayson leaned forward and looked directly at Mitchell. He nodded.

'And the penalty, Dr Grayson?'

'Code Red.' He pressed a button on the desk surface. Mitchell, ashen-faced, turned to the door. Two armed and very large security men entered and put their arms under his shoulders. They lifted him and dragged him, inert with fear, out of the door and into the security lift.

When he had gone, the man from the deep shadows got up from his chair and sat in the one Mitchell had just vacated. From the chair, Bradley looked at the other two and smiled. The lights in the room came on and the two Hartmann men relaxed and smiled back.

'I believe there is a job vacancy?' said Bradley. 'Are we in a position to discuss salary? And terms?'

The Hartmann men nodded. 'Salary yes. Terms are for us to decide. What terms do you mean?'

'Just the one: I work without supervision or I don't work at all. I need your total trust.'

'You can name your own salary, within reason. Get the results we want and ever greater material rewards will follow if that's what you want. Bring us mark 2.'

Ice-eyes spoke. 'But no-one works in Hartmann without supervision. Not even me. It will be discreet. But it will be there. But first, you heard what Mitchell Walker had to say. He accuses you of lying and failing to report to us what he asked you to report.'

Bradley nodded. 'We have been through all that. Mitchell told me nothing of his plan. He was working alone. I was working with him on the mainstream plan. It's true he recruited me, because I could see that Hartmann was a better bet than Stefan Greiff's outfit. I suppose I was a little flattered.'

Ice-eyes wanted to know what the mainstream plan had been.

'Well,' said Bradley, 'we wanted a perfect product, no side effects and with a range of controllable outcomes, as an exclusive for Hartmann. So the plan was first to keep the knowledge of any sort of performance product away from the media and others. That meant obfuscating if necessary and throwing everyone off the scent and on to the track of a technology scam; second, we needed to eliminate 'loose elements' who were busy shooting their mouths off and threatening to give the game away; third, we wanted to run a guinea pig experiment on the Godwin team to find out just what different formulations of mark 1 would do, and while all this was going on we were putting pressure on the woman, Anne, to reveal whether there really was a mark 2. And it was all working. Interest in any illegal reasons for the golfers' success was waning and the woman would have cracked eventually without any dramatics. The unpredictable effects of the variable samples on the golfers were very worrying for her. On top of all that we had learned a lot more about the enormous potential of mark 1. So there must have been strong reasons to make Mitchell abandon that plan and act independently.'

'What might they be?'

'Perhaps he had another employer and was following instructions from them.'

'Who might they be?'

'The same people who provided him with the Millican cover and excellent references and who are also interested in the product we were investigating.'

Ice-eyes nodded again: 'You mean he was a government agent.'

Bradley noted the past tense: 'For at least one government!' he said.

Later, considerably richer in prospect and more than a little relieved, Bradley stood at a window looking out towards the incinerator. He saw the chimney start to belch white smoke. As he watched, the smoke turn black. 'Must be burning something nasty,' he muttered. He felt a twinge of sympathy for Mitchell before he remembered the bigger picture.

How long would he have before two of his employers, Hartmann and Stefan, realised that the description he'd given of Mitchell's employment position was in fact nearer to a description of his own. And how long before they realised that he was loyal only to himself, firstly, and then to the little old lady, sitting in her palace, wondering like him how long she could continue. He gave himself six months. But he was sure of one thing. These bastards would never get their hands on mark 2, or a controlled mark 1, for that matter. He would be the one who decided where it did end up and maybe he could please everyone, except Hartmann.

76 End Product

The French maison de maitre was beautifully restored. Upstairs, large bedrooms with high ceilings, elaborate cornices, grand windows and solid doors opened onto wide corridors. Downstairs a huge and well furnished kitchen led to a dining room of presidential proportions and on into elegant drawing rooms and a gallery. But it was the garden and grounds which really impressed. Immediately outside the front door was a spacious patio and courtyard, with shady areas under large plane trees, roomy outbuildings and comfortable social areas. Beyond the courtyard, with views across to the Pyrenees, the grounds opened up. Vegetable gardens, orchards, flower beds, banks of lavender and flowering shrubs at one level, lawns, croquet green, boules area and tennis courts at another. Round to the left, a serene pond, fully a hundred metres by eighty, languished under a warm sun; frogs climbed on the floating lilies and croaked their satisfaction; snakes slept in the shade along its banks.

In the centre of the grounds was a 30 metre swimming pool, in which a solitary figure ploughed slow length after slow length. Wealth, ease and luxury were housed here in perfect harmony.

In dappled light under a cane roof, Cristina looked up from her book. She smiled fondly at her eighteenth month old son as he tottered around, collecting wooden bricks to add to the tower he was trying to build on a low table. 'Stefan,' she said and blew him a kiss. Stefan had no time for that nonsense. He had towers to build. Cristina laughed, delighted by the show of masculine instrumentalism in her young son. She sank back on her lounger and drank in the wonderful atmosphere and surroundings. How lucky could one simple Portuguese girl get? Whatever the price she'd paid.

She watched as the figure in the swimming pool got out, dried herself a little and came towards her. The woman stopped by little Stefan and tickled him under the chin. 'When's daddy coming home, Stefan?'

'Not tomorrow I hope,' said Cristina. 'Daddy's playing in Munich and Big Stefan is expecting him to win, isn't he,' she said to the baby. 'So he'd better not come back early or he'll have some explaining to do.'

Anne laughed. 'He won't miss the cut. The crowd won't let him. It's not often they get the world number 1 at the German Open.'

'But you know what Samson can be like. He doesn't do what people expect.' At the sound of his father's name, little Stefan looked up. 'We know what Daddy can do, don't we Stefan?' And little Stefan stood up and imitated the swing of his adored daddy, Samson.

Anne watched little Stefan, smiling and applauding. She turned back to Cristina: 'It's so good that Stefan and Samson buried the hatchet. And even better that you made the right choice. So big of Stefan to make no fuss about it all.'

Cristina looked at Anne with a question in her eyes. 'Samson says that was your doing. He says you were key and you played your cards well.'

Anne said nothing at first. 'Stefan wanted something I had. I let him have it with strings attached. But Bradley was the real key to it all.'

A relaxed silence between the two was broken by babble from little Stefan. Cristina could see that Anne was looking hard at Stefan. She knew what question was coming.

'Can I ask you something woman to woman?'

Cristina smiled her assent.

'In all that time with Stefan, did you ever give in to his advances? He must have made them.'

Cristina took a sip of her drink before responding. 'If I told you no, would you believe me? And if I said yes would you think I was a faithless woman?'

'I think you are a smart and beautiful woman who would have done what she had to in everyone's interests. I'm a pragmatic materialist. Morality for me is anything that works. I think it is for you, too.'

'In that case, when little Stefan is in bed, and after a little wine, you can ask your question again. It might work better then.'

Later that evening, after dark, wrapped in the soft balm of a starlit French night, Cristina poured them both a second glass of wine and thanked Anne again for her hospitality. 'No need to thank me. It was Jake's idea really. He wanted to be with Samson and Stefan in Munich to celebrate the new management plans. He thought we might like to renew an old friendship that had lapsed a bit.' A pause. 'Are you ready for my question now?'

'Where do you want me to start?' Cristina asked.

'Well, if you can bear it, what about the kidnap and the aftermath? No police, no press, no gossip. I got to know nothing. You seem to be the only one who knows what happened, two years ago was it?'

'It was. And no-one knows the whole truth, just the bit they were involved with. I never told Samson everything. It would hurt him too much. I am sure you know all about Mitchell Walker and what he wanted. Your mark 2 stuff. And at the time I thought we had some. I thought it existed. I thought Samson had used it to win the Open. And the men who took me thought Samson would hand it over. I will not tell you what his two men did to me in those terrible few hours. I have locked it away and forgotten it. And I will not open the box. But you can imagine, and what you imagine will not be bad enough. But we have had our revenge.'

'How?'

'You know the man who took me from the kidnap house? Bradley? He made sure Mitchell Walker was punished and then he brought the two men to Stefan. They are still alive, but I know that every day they wish they were dead. Stefan is merciless and when he told me what he was doing to them, I knew then that I could not stay with him. Of course I was his lover for a while, out of gratitude if nothing else, but he was the one who suddenly lost interest. Something happened and he told me I could make my own choice. So I did. I chose Samson.'

'And the baby is Samson's, without doubt?'

Cristina nodded. 'We called him Stefan to honour what the big man did for us and the fact he let me go without complaint.'

'You have Bradley to thank for that, really.' Anne said. 'And Jake. Bradley knew, from Jake, all about the second version of the performance enhancer, mark 2. He arranged everything for me in complete confidence. I got the patent and the sole rights to it went to the government. The British government. Stefan's company got the licence to produce and develop. At Jake's suggestion, Bradley made letting you go without fuss the price Stefan paid for that privilege.

'So there really was such a thing as mark 2? Samson was never certain. He still isn't.'

Anne put her glass down and spread her arms wide. 'We have two more places better than this, one in Florida and one in Surrey, near Wentworth. Where do you think that sort of money comes from? And Sir Phil Henshaw and Matt Prosser, CBE? You don't get gongs like that for nothing.

So yes, there was such a thing and it now has a nice long unpronounceable name. And it's all down to our dear friend Bradley. Think back. Just about everyone of us has a reason to be grateful to Bradley. He rescued you, saved Phil Henshaw's bacon, sorted Marilyn's husband issues, found Matt, kept Stefan and the inspectors at bay and though I didn't know it at the time, was a good friend to Selwyn. As for me and Jake, well, Mitchell was pretty close to losing patience with us before he disappeared from the scene. I always assumed Mitchell's disappearance was Bradley's doing, too, and you have just confirmed it. At the time, Mitchell was trying hard to scare me into handing over the secret. He said he'd lost control of the manufacturing process and there was a real danger to our golfers. Bradley told me that was a lie and helped keep me going. Without him, I'd have lost my nerve.' Anne giggled: 'Probably.

Anyway, Bradley called in his debts and guaranteed us freedom from prosecution, gongs for Phil and Matt and a decent share of any profits for me if we turned it all over to him. Given his credentials it was a no-brainer. And encouraged by Jake, Bradley made sure Stefan knew you had to be a free woman, if he wanted in on the deal.

So now it's licensed by the UK government, being developed and tested under strictly controlled conditions by Stefan's outfit and will eventually be very, very profitable. We won't do anything naughty with it because we don't need to. You'll be pleased to know it promises to be a really effective and legitimate medicine now. And doing some fantastic work in trials. You know all those muscle-wasting conditions, muscular dystrophy and the like? They can be helped enormously by one prototype version of what we used to call mark 2, and some cerebral palsy patients will soon be able to live an almost normal life as a result of taking another variety. So, basically, it's all down to our man Bradley. He told us to look at the bigger picture and then he fixed it all for us.

And it's just as much fun making money legitimately as it was doing it the hard way, and boy do we make money. And there's more to come. The stuff does incredible things already and they're still discovering more properties and potential. Memory improvement, that sort of thing. It appears that Selwyn, bless him, was a rare genius. A Nobel prize would have been the least he got. Now, Stefan might get it.'

'So all that dangerous nonsense with muscle memory and golfers is a thing of the past?'

There was a long pause. 'It's Wimbledon next week,' Anne said, 'if I were you I'd have a little flutter on a young Scot. He's not seeded and not much rated. He's 100 to 1, but I just have a feeling about him. Know what I mean?'

'How much of a feeling?' asked Cristina.

'Well, a couple or so million's worth!'

★★★★